Beast Mode

A Novel By
Keisha Ervin

D1521239

Color Me Pynk Publications is accepting manuscripts from aspiring or experienced fiction, romance, interracial, urban, black woman/white man, alpha male, erotic, supernatural and fantasy authors. The review process can take up to three weeks. We will contact you once a decision has been reached. NO PREVIOUSLY PUBLISHED MANUSCRIPTS WILL BE ACCEPTED.

WHAT WILL SET YOU APART FROM THE REST:

The ultimate alpha male. He's drool worthy, confident, arrogant, strong, great in bed, complicated and flawed. He messes up but is willing to change to better his life and his woman's.

Female leads that are sassy, sweet, loving, ambitious, funny yet beautifully imperfect. She puts up with drama to a certain extent but learns to stick up for herself and what she believes in.

A story that is dramatic, shocking, action packed, sexy, hilarious, romantic and tear jerking.

If you'd like to join the Color Me Pynk fam, dare to be different! There is no story that hasn't already been written so make it fresh and new by adding a new twist to it. We want stories that our readers will read twenty years from now. To be considered please email the first five chapters of your manuscript, synopsis and contact information to colormepynksubmission@gmail.com

Follow us:

IG: ColorMePynkPublications

Other Titles by Keisha Ervin

The Untold Stories by Chyna Black

Cashmere Mafia (Material Girl Spin-off)

Material Girl 3: Secrets & Betrayals

Paper Heart

Pure Heroine (Sequel to Me and My Boyfriend)

Emotionally Unavailable (Chyna Black 2)

Heartless (Chyna Black 3)

Radio Silence (Chyna Black 4)

Smells Like Teen Spirit Vol 1: Heiress

Mina's Joint 2: The Perfect Illusion

Cranes in the Sky (Messiah & Shyhiem Book 1)

Postcards from the Edge (Messiah & Shyhiem Book 2)

Such A Fuckin' Lady (Chyna Black 5)

First Wives Club Vol. Melanin Magic (Chyna, Mo & Gray)

Beast Mode Playlist

Bri Steves "Regret"

Bow Wow "Outta System"

Kiana Lede "Wicked Games"

Summer Walker "CPR"

H.E.R. "2"

Phora "Everybody Knows"

Joey Purp "Karl Malone"

Trey Songz "Me 4 U Infidelity 2"

Summer Walker "Girls Need Love"

Alex Isley "Smoke and Mirrors"

H.E.R. "Can't Help Me"

Jay Rock "WIN"

Alex Isley "My Theme"

Alessia Cara "A Little More"

Trap Beckham "Birthday Bitch"

Usher & Zaytoven "Birthday"

Jay-Z "Allure"

H.E.R. "Jungle"

Rowdy Rebel feat Bobby Shmurda "Computers"

Dawn Richard "Jealousy"

Brandy "I Tried"

Summer Walker "Session 32"

Pussycat Dolls "Don't Cha"

Victoria Monet feat Bia "Freak Remix"

Meek Mill "Almost Slipped"

Phora "Her"

The Carter's "Summer"

Juicy J feat 2 Chainz & Lil Wayne "Bandz A Make Her Dance"

Too Short feat Lil Jon and The Eastside Boyz "Shake That Monkey"

Juvenile & Soulja Slim "Slow Motion"

Fat Joe & Lil Wayne "Make It Rain"

Mell Mill "We Ball"

Meek Mill "Trauma"

Loren Allred "Never Enough"

J. Cole "Kevin's Heart"

Meek Mill "Almost Slipped"

Brain McKnight "Never Felt This Way"

Russ "Ain't Nobody Takin' My Baby"

Alessia Cara "Out of Love"

Previously in First Wives Club Vol.1 Melanin Magic

Gray stared down at the ten carat, oval-shaped, rose gold ring on her ring finger in awe. She was officially a married woman. After a 48-hour, required wait, she and Cam really went to the courthouse and tied the knot. It was crazy fast and totally out of her character, but she didn't regret her decision one bit. Cam had shown her more love in the past two months than Gunz had in ten years. They barely knew each other but Gray was confident they'd transition from friends, to lovers, to husband and wife without missing a beat.

The first order of business was telling Gunz. A week had gone by since she said 'I do'. Before she revealed her news, she had to put some things into place. That Wednesday afternoon, she sat on the windowsill, awaiting his arrival. She'd called him and said they needed to talk. The girls were in their room playing. Nervous energy raced through her veins. Gunz was sure to flip when she told him what she'd done. She didn't feel like arguing, but because of their kids, she owed him the right to know the status of her relationship.

Gray sat up straight and took a deep breath as the elevator door opened. He was home. There was no turning back now.

"Gray!"

"I'm in the living room."

"You going on a trip or something? What's up with the bags by the door?"

"That's what I wanted to talk to you about."

Gunz sat down on the couch and waited for her to continue.

"We're leaving," she said, matter-of-factly.

"Where y'all going? The kids got school tomor, don't they?"

Gray hung her head and scoffed. Gunz was a sorry piece of shit. He didn't even know if his girls had school or not.

"They have school tomor but we're not going on a trip. We're moving out."

"Moving where?" Gunz frowned, furiously.

"I got my own place."

Gunz stared into her bright blue eyes, flabbergasted. Silence gnawed at Gray's insides. Silence hung in the air like the suspended moment before a falling glass shattered on the ground. The silence was like a gaping void, needing to be filled with sounds, words, anything. The silence was venomous in its nothingness, cruelly highlighting how lifeless their relationship had become.

"You can leave but my kids ain't going nowhere."

"Gunz, the girls are going with me," Gray said, calmly.

"Where is this coming from?"

"Are you serious? Do you not remember gettin' a girl pregnant? This shit been coming."

"I know what I did, but that don't mean you get the right to take my kids away from me."

"You know I would never keep the girls away from you. You can see them whenever you want."

"I don't wanna be on no visitation shit. I want you and the girls here wit' me!"

"Well, I'm sorry to inform you but my life doesn't revolve around you anymore. I told you a long time ago I was done, and I mean it. You wouldn't give me the apartment, so I got my own. You will no longer hold this place over my head. I don't need it or you."

"I know this Tia shit got you upset, but you don't need to be making no rash decisions 'cause you're emotional." Gunz reasoned.

"Actually, I'm numb. The things you do no longer affect me. I have moved on with my life but you're too self-absorbed to notice that. This whole time we've been talkin' you haven't even noticed the ring on my finger."

Gunz glared at her hand. A diamond ring shined from her ring finger that wasn't the one he'd given her.

"Me and Cam got married last Wednesday."

This time, silence seeped into every pore of Gunz and Gray, like a poison slowly paralyzing them from either speech or movement. The silence stretched thinner and thinner, like a balloon blown big, until the temptation to pop it was too great to resist.

"Fuck you mean you married him? You belong to me!" He roared.

"Gunz, I haven't belonged to you in years. You and your dick is for everybody," she said, unfazed by his fury.

"You know I fuckin' love you!"

"Gunz, you don't love me. You don't even come home. I haven't seen you in days."

"You want me here, but you don't even fuck wit' me. You still angry over some shit I did last year!"

"Because . . . how do you say to me, Gray, I want to be with you and I want my family back and then you don't show up? You don't come home. You say one thing and then do another. I'm over it! I don't wanna do this no more!"

"The reason I don't come around is because you didn't wanna have anything to do with me."

"I DON'T WANNA FUCK WIT' YOU 'CAUSE YOU STAY FUCKIN' OTHER BITCHES!" Gray screamed at the top of her lungs.

"That don't mean you run off and marry that nigga!" Gunz got in her face. "I gave up my old life for you!"

"No, you gave up a life of crime, nigga! You did that for yourself! I motivated you to do it, so you wouldn't wind up dead or in jail! Yo' ass wanted to be a 60-year-old thug? You sound stupid as fuck right now!"

"If it wasn't for my drug-dealing past, you wouldn't have shit! I invested in that punk-ass magazine! I took you back after that nigga raped you! I helped you get your life back on track after you killed that nigga and had blood on your hands! I helped you sleep at night! I helped you get back on your feet! After all that, you got your li'l magazine and gave me your ass to kiss! And you wonder why I cheat!"

"Shut up! Shut the fuck up!" She forcefully pushed him in the chest. "You ain't gon' blame this shit on me!

You sit here and you tell me you want me back, and then you go runnin' to her! You must live with the bitch! Don't you? Y'all live together? 'Cause you ain't never here wit' me."

"Yeah, we live together, but she pay her own fuckin' bills." Gunz shrugged.

"So, you don't pay for the spot you rest yo' head at?"

"I mean . . . I bought the place, yeah."

"You mad 'cause I got married but you ran and bought your baby whore a place to live?"

"It was an investment."

"In what, y'all relationship? 'Cause if so, that's exactly where yo' ass need to be, instead of in my fuckin' face!"

"Fuck all that, Gray! You already know this is what I want! Me fuckin' other bitches is just for fun—"

"Oh my god, you are so fuckin' stupid! Do you really think you tellin' me you fuck other bitches for fun is gon' make me want you back?"

"You wanted the truth, so I'm giving it to you. I love you. I fuck other bitches 'cause you be holding out on that pussy. I wanna put all of this behind us. I want my family. You give me another chance, I'll leave that bitch where she's at. She only carrying my seed. This shit wit' her is business. Me and you is personal. What we got is a partnership. I would never put none of these hoes before you and you know that."

"Do I? I don't know shit 'cause at that basketball game yo' ass acted like you barely knew me. And you let that illiterate, ratchet, walking AIDS virus talk about my fuckin' daughter! You full of shit, Gunz! You keep sayin', Gray, I want you back! And, Gray, I love you! And, Gray, I wanna family, but I call your phone and you layin' up in the bed with another bitch! Who tells me y'all are in love and the only reason why you still deal with me is because we share a light bill together. I got my tubes tied because of you. Now, I can't have no more kids, but you get to go on with life and have as many kids as you want. ALL YOU DO IS FUCKIN' HURT ME! WHEN YOU WERE GETTIN' YOUR BUSINESSES OFF THE GROUND, I WAS THERE FOR YOU! WHEN YOUR FATHER DIED, I WAS THERE! WHEN UNCLE CYLDE DIED, I PUT MY FEELINGS ASIDE AND STOOD BY YOU, BUT YOU AIN'T NEVER DID SHIT BUT TURN YOUR BACK ON ME, DISAPPOINT ME AND LIE!"

"I love you, Gray. You are the person I love. You are the person I wanna be wit'."

"You don't love me," she repeated.

"As a man, I'm admitting my faults."

"You're not admitting faults 'cause you're blaming me."

"All you see is Gunz can provide. Gunz is that dude. Gunz got this. What about me? What about my heart, Gray? You don't provide that! And now you gettin' mad because I'm fuckin' with the next bitch? You walked away from me, Gray! You put that punk-ass magazine and your career ahead of me!"

Gray stepped back, as hot tears scorched her face.

"As much as I stood by you . . . ten years . . . and you couldn't even fuckin' marry me." Her heart broke with each word.

"But guess what, I's married now." She wiggled her fingers. "And I love him. He makes me feel stupid for even wasting ten years of my life on you. I ain't never in my life experienced a love like this. Just the thought of the taste of his dick in my mouth make me cum. He ain't nothin' like you. You will never measure up to the man he is. You ain't nothin' but a 42-year-old li'l boy. Me and my kids gon' be fine without you. I can't wait for them to meet Cam. I'm sure he'll be a better partner than you, a better provider than you, a better lover than you and I know for a fact he gon' be a better father than you!"

Gray knew she'd gone too far but didn't care. She meant every, single word. She loved Cam wholeheartedly and couldn't wait to start her new life with him. Protecting Gunz's feelings was no longer a priority for her. Finally, she was able to get everything she'd been harboring off her chest. It felt good to see him hurt. He deserved it and much more.

Heated that she had the nerve to speak to him that way, Gunz squeezed her shoulders, then slapped her with so much force she torpedoed into a glass vase. She and the vase fell onto the floor. Shattered pieces of glass pricked her skin, as he dragged her kicking and screaming across the marble floor. Gray couldn't believe what was happening. Gunz had yoked her up and pushed her, but he'd never actually hit her. She could hear the girls crying hysterically for him to let her go, but he wouldn't. Gunz was no longer there. There was no life in his eyes. He'd completely blacked out. Hovering over her, he reared his closed fist back and punched her in the face.

He'd told her if she ever tried to leave him, he'd kill her, and he meant it. Letting Gray go was too much for his brain to handle. He couldn't—no, wouldn't—lose her. She was his and a marriage certificate and a ring weren't going to change that. When and if he decided they no longer had to be together, it would be his decision, not hers.

Gray tried covering her face from his ruthless attack, but he removed her hand and punched her again. Her eye instantly swelled up. Gunz beat her so savagely that all she could do was burst into tears and beg him to stop.

"Get off my mama!" Aoki tugged on his arm.

Hearing the distress in his daughter's voice snapped him back to reality. Gunz stood back and eyed his handy work. Gray lay curled up in a ball on the floor, wailing, as if someone had died.

"You got me fucked up if you think you gon' have another nigga around my kids. You ain't gon' never see them again! C'mon, Aoki and Press! Y'all coming wit' me!"

"No, Daddy! I want my mommy!" Press cried.

"Don't make me tell you again," he warned.

Scared that he'd hit them too, Press and Aoki, reluctantly, followed their father.

"Gunz, please! Don't take my kids!" Gray tried to rise to her feet but was so weak she fell back down.

"Fuck you, bitch! You're dead to me!" Gunz slammed the door behind him.

After laying there for what seemed like hours, Gray pulled herself off the floor. In front of the mirror, she examined the damage that had been done. Gunz had given her a black eye and a busted lip. Shards of glass from the vase were stuck in her hair and clothes. Cuts and scrapes covered her back, arms and legs. Using a wet piece of toilet tissue, she wiped the dried-up blood from her lip and stared into her own empty eyes. She barely recognized herself. Gray gazed around the now deserted apartment. She was alone and hated it. Since Gunz couldn't break her sanity, he took the one thing that she loved the most—her kids. He knew it would break her and it had. Stifling a sob with the scuffed palm of her hand, she sunk to the floor and cried until she couldn't cry no more.

And now…

"I said some shit that I do regret."- Bri Steves, "Regret"

#1

When I'm with somebody, all I think 'bout is you.
When I'm alone, that's all I wanna do. Outta Control by
Bow Wow played for the tenth time in a row. It was Cam's
personalized ringtone. Sitting on the floor against the
elevator door, Gray ran her trembling, blood ridden hands
down her face and inhaled deep. The sound of her phone
ringing was driving her insane. She desperately wanted to
answer, but if she did, the hell she was in would only get
worse. She thought about answering and pretending that
everything was okay, but she couldn't get shit past Cam.
He'd pick up on her hoarse and shaky voice instantly. Then
she'd be forced to tell him what Gunz had done. Telling her
new husband that she'd been beaten by her ex would be
like releasing a Pitbull from its leash. Gray didn't have the
strength to reel in Cam's crazy. She had her own emotions
to sort through. She would deal with him later. Her focus
was solely on getting her girls away from their abusive-ass
father. She didn't think Gunz would put his hands on Aoki
and Press but before he'd slap fire from her mouth, she
didn't think he'd hit her either. Sadly, it had become
abundantly clear that she didn't know the man she'd given
her heart to for ten years at all.

Like all the other men in her life, Gunz was nothing
but a beautiful liar and a perfect stranger. The love they
once shared had morphed into hate. Bitterness and blood
from his slap to her face soaked her tongue. Visions of him
striking her repeatedly with a grim look of satisfaction on
his face caused her eyes to well with tears.

"I can't believe that muthafucka put his hands on
me." Gray wiped the lone tear that slipped from her eye
away.

She hoped and prayed that she didn't get glass anywhere on her face. Shards of glass from the vase that fell when he slapped her were still on the floor. Gray knew she needed to sweep the mess up but simply didn't have the strength. Her main focus was on Aoki and Press. Her baby girls had to be scared out of their minds. They'd never seen their father behave the way he had. Hell, Gray had never seen him act that way either. He'd punched her several times like she was a nigga off the street.

Gunz was a monster. There wasn't an ounce of remorse on his face after he'd beaten her. It was almost like he took pleasure in her misery. He was dead set on making her life utterly miserable. The nigga was straight on some *'if I can't have you, no one else can either'* type shit. Gray didn't even know why he was still holding onto her. He had a whole other woman and a baby on the way. Once Gray learned about his side family, any and all feelings she had for him went out the window. He'd moved on and so had she. She'd promised her love, heart and fidelity to Cam. He'd shown her more love and respect in two and a half months than Gunz ever had. Dealing with him made her see that Gunz was nothing but an oversized boy dressed up like a man. Only a coward-ass nigga would put his hands on a woman. Come hell or highwater, Gunz was going to pay for every foul thing he'd ever done to Gray.

Palming her iPhone, she dialed his number for the hundredth time, but just like she wouldn't answer Cam's phone calls, he wouldn't answer hers. *What the fuck am I gon' do,* she willed herself not to cry again. Gray's entire body was on fire with pain. She couldn't stop shaking. Planting her face in the palm of her hands, she tried to figure out her next step but the eerie silence of being in the penthouse alone fucked with her head. Instead of focusing on a way to get her girls back, all she could concentrate on was the sound of her screams that echoed in her brain.

The last time she'd screamed that loud and high pitched was when Aoki's father tried to kill her. She'd never been so terrified in her life, but she refused to die. Gray had herself and baby to live for, so she did what she had to do to survive. In the end, she lived to see another day and Aoki's father didn't. After the horrific incident, Gunz was her savior. He witnessed firsthand all the trauma she went through. It was crazy how ten years later he'd add another layer to her emotional and physical scars. For this, she'd hate him forever.

When I'm with somebody, all I think 'bout is you. When I'm alone, that's all I wanna do. Removing her hands from her face, she looked down at her phone. For the first time, since she'd fallen in love with Cam she needed him to leave her alone. She couldn't think with him constantly calling her. Refusing to answer, she focused on the screen until it stopped ringing. Once it did she felt a sense of relief. That went away quickly. Without warning the elevator doors opened, causing Gray to dip backwards. Quickly, she placed her hands on the floor to break her fall.

"Why the fuck you ain't been answering the phone?" Cam stepped off the elevator.

Confused, delirious and shocked that he was there, Gray looked up at his angry face. He towered over her like a god. Tears welled in the brim of her eyes. Cam was the most beautiful man she'd ever seen. Even when he was mad he was still gorgeous. He possessed the kind of beauty that stopped you dead in your tracks. His 6'4 muscular frame, sweet butterscotch skin, freckled cheeks, pointy nose, pink, full lips and a well-groomed beard took her breath away. The black Champion sweatshirt hoodie, matching jogging pants and Pine Green Air Jordan 1's gave him that sexy thug appeal she liked.

Gazing up into his eyes, she wanted to hide her face, so he wouldn't see all the damage Gunz had caused but there was no use. He'd already seen it. Besides, Gray couldn't take her eyes off of him. At first she thought she didn't need him, but now that he was there, she realized he was her main source of comfort. She needed him like she needed air to breathe. Seeing the expression of shock and horror on his face caused Gray to cry as if her brain was being gutted from the inside. An emotional outpour of pain flowed from every pore of her body. Out of her mouth came a cry so raw that even Cam's eyes became misty.

Gray usually didn't like to cry in front of other people. She always felt it made her look weak but now she gave away to the enormity of her grief. With her head held low, she cried into her hands. Tears dripped between her fingers like rain pouring from the sky. Her breathing was labored and short. Cam stooped down and gently removed her trembling hands. Softly, he caressed her blotchy tear-stained face. His usual playful smirk had drawn into a hard line. Enraged, he examined her closely. Gray's eye was swollen shut. Bloody spit drooled from the side of her busted lip. Cuts and scrapes covered her once blemish free face, neck and arms. Nothing needed to be said. It was obvious what had occurred. Gray swallowed hard. Cam's rage was like wildfire. She could literally see the flames roaring from his eyes.

"How did you get in here? The concierge didn't even notify me." She spoke barely above a whisper.

"Fuck all that. That nigga did this to you?" Cam turned her face from side-to-side and examined the damage.

"He got mad when I told him I was leaving him for you." She winced in pain.

"Where the girls?" He let go and clenched his jaw.

Gray's bottom lip began to shake.

"He took them." Her chest heaved as she sobbed. "And he won't give'em back. I've been callin' but he won't pick up. What if he don't give me back my babies? Cam, I can't live without my girls. I can't." She wept hysterically.

Closing his eyes, Cam took a deep breath in hopes of calming himself down, but it didn't work. His face was red with suppressed rage.

"C'mon." He stood to his full height and helped her up.

"Where we going?" Gray rose to her feet.

"To get your fuckin' kids back." Cam pressed the down button and waited for the elevator to open.

"How we gon' do that? I don't know where he is." Gray asked once they were inside.

"I do."

Minutes later they were in his red Mercedes Benz G-Wagon speeding down the highway. Cam had his phone pressed up to his ear while Gray sat nervously beside him in the passenger seat. She could hear the phone ring as he white knuckle gripped the steering wheel.

"Hey babe." LaLa answered.

Curling her upper lip, Gray looked at Cam like he was crazy.

"I know the fuck you didn't. Have you lost your fuckin'—"

"Shhhhhhh." He cut her off.

"Don't fuckin' shhhhhh me." She pushed him hard." Why the fuck are you callin' that bitch?"

"Unless you want another black eye, I would suggest you keep your hands to yourself."

"Oh word? You gon' go there?" Gray's heart constricted.

"Do you want your fuckin' girls back or nah?" He glared at her.

"Of course, I do."

"Then sit back, shut the fuck up and let me do me."

"Let you do you?" She screwed up her face. "Boy you got me fucked up. All y'all niggas are foul as fuck. Let me out this fuckin' car!" She yanked on the handle like he wasn't going 70 mph down the highway.

Once again, Gray felt like a dummy. Cam was just as disrespectful as Gunz. He was just as big of a hoe as he was too. Both of them were no good. She should've known better than to trust that he'd have her best interest at heart. Marrying him on a whim had to be the dumbest decision she'd ever made. She had no business falling for a man like him. He was a notorious playboy. He switched women like he switched cars. How gullible was she to believe that he'd be the man to take all of her pain away? The nigga went from not wanting to be in a relationship to proposing marriage. The shit was doomed from the start.

"Pull over!"

"I ain't pullin' over shit! You better calm yo' half black ass down."

"Cam!" LaLa yelled.

"I ain't calming shit down!" Gray snapped back as he put the call on mute. "Here I am thinkin' you came to save the fuckin' day, be my knight and shining armor and shit, and you done called this big forehead having ass bitch like I ain't sittin' right here. You disrespectful as shit! *And the bitch callin' you babe like we ain't fuckin' married!* You know what? I ain't got time for this shit. Let me out this bitch!"

"Man, sit back."

"Pull over!"

"No."

"No?" She drew her head back. "Let me out, Cameron. I'm not gon' ask you no more." Gray said as calmly as she could.

"The fuck I'm supposed to be scared? Don't nobody give a damn about you callin' me by my name like that's supposed to be effective."

"Bitch! Let me out this muthafucka for I kill both of us!" She screamed so loud it pierced his ears.

"Then you really ain't gon' get your girls back." Cam shot sarcastically.

"You think this a fuckin' game, you ole freckle face bitch! Let me out!" She kicked the dashboard leaving her footprints everywhere. "I fuckin' hate you! You don't care about me! You just like him!" She tried to open the door again to no avail.

"Yo, you real live crazy." Cam eyed her in disbelief.

"I'm not playin' Cam! Turn the car around and take me home! I'll get my daughters back by my damn self." She shot with an attitude.

It took everything in Cam not to pull the car over and ring her fuckin' neck. Gray had him beyond fucked up. Glaring at her, he attempted to burn a hole through her forehead with his eyes.

"CAM!" LaLa screamed.

Her heart was racing so fast it felt like it was going to explode. No way was Gray in the background while he was on the phone with her.

"I know you hear me talkin' you!"

Instead of responding, Cam continued to stare at his wife. Gray tried to ignore him but the anger radiating off him wouldn't allow her to.

"What the fuck are you lookin' at, stupid-ass?" She finally gave him the attention he wanted. "You heard what I said. Take me home."

"Chill the fuck out, wit' all that bullshit. I'm tryin' to help yo' simple ass."

"Fuck yo—"

"Say it and I swear to god I'll snatch yo' fuckin' esophagus out yo' throat." He leaned over the center console and got in her face.

"But—"

"You heard what the fuck I said."

"Ooh, you get on my—"

"SHUT THE FUCK UP!" He cut her off again, causing her to jump.

Cam instantly felt like shit. Furrowing her brows, Gray held her breath. When the tears in her eyes hit the back of her throat she couldn't hold it in any longer. A weight of sorrow clouded her brain. Her heart grew cold and numb with pent up emotion. She felt congested with agony, fury, hurt and dread. Taking out her frustrations on Cam wasn't helping anything. All she could do was cry so she let it out in one loud wail that reached the heavens. With every fiber of her being, she prayed her cries for help reached God's ears.

"I ain't tryin' to beef wit' you ma. If you would calm the fuck down, you would see I'm tryin' to help you. Ain't nobody on no funny shit." He assured by taking her hand in his.

Inhaling deep, she gazed into his warm brown eyes. There was nothing but sincerity there. Gray was tripping. She was letting her anger towards Gunz cloud her judgement. Cam had never done anything to purposely hurt her. In all honesty, he'd been her one stable force throughout all the madness Gunz put her through. She had to trust that whatever he was doing wasn't meant to be malicious. That didn't stop her from being mad tho. She still didn't like him talking to his ex, especially not in her face.

"I'm sorry." She sniveled, feeling lost.

With their fingers intertwined, Cam remained silent and kissed the back of her hand as he took the call off mute.

"This nigga done lost his damn mind. I know damn well you ain't call me while you wit' that fat bitch!" LaLa shouted.

"Bitch, what's your location cause I'm about tired of y—" Gray yelled before Cam covered her mouth.

"Shut your fat-ass up! That's why you ain't got neck!" LaLa quipped.

Cam wanted to laugh, but knew if he did, Gray would fuck him up.

"Aye! Aye! That's enough!" He interjected instead.

"Don't check me! You need to check that fat, sloppy, supersize, McFlurry with extra Oreos, Big Mac eating ass bitch!"

"Shut your dumb-ass up for I come put two in your chest." Cam warned her. "Now give me Tia's address."

"Why? You wanna fuck her too."

"Keep on talkin' shit and I just might. Now give me the fuckin' address."

"5698 Lafayette. What you need it for?" LaLa asked but didn't get a reply because Cam had already hung up.

After a quiet car ride, they pulled up in front of Tia's house. Gray gazed up in awe. When Gunz admitted to buying his side chick a place, she assumed it was a little apartment. Boy was she wrong. He'd copped Tia a three-story, row house right in the center of Lafayette square. Homes in Lafayette Square started out at $100,000. This muthafucka had spent bread on her. Gray couldn't believe how blinded she'd been by his lies. Seeing Tia's home made her see how much she meant to Gunz. A pain like no other surged through her chest.

Gray hated that it affected her so much, but it did. Gunz always succeeded at making her look and feel dumb.

She was so happy that she was getting the fuck away from him. He'd caused her enough pain to last a lifetime. Cam cut the engine off and grabbed his 9mm Pistol. Methodically, he attached the silencer to the gun.

"What are you gon' do with that?" Gray's eyes damn near bulged out of their sockets.

"What you think I'ma do wit' it? C'mon." He hopped out the truck.

"Baby wait!" Gray panicked, running behind him despite the pain she was in.

"Don't try and talk me out of this Gray. You saw what that nigga did to your face. It's only right I push his wig back." He banged on the door then covered the peephole with his thumb.

Tia waddled down the steps. She was six and a half months pregnant, tired and her feet were swollen. When Gunz popped up at her crib with his daughters in tow she was stunned. On numerous occasions, he said he wasn't ready for her to meet his daughters. Without asking, he told her the girls would be there indefinitely. Tia wanted to meet his girls, but she didn't want them staying with her. She was young, twenty-one to be exact and had her own baby to worry about. She wasn't trying to play mama to some other bitches' kids. It didn't make it any better that the li'l heffas wouldn't stop crying and begging for their mama. There was only but so much sobbing she could take. She tried telling Gunz to take them home, but he refused. He went on a whole tangent about Gray being an unfit mother, how she ran off and married Cam after only knowing him five seconds, her trying to take his daughters away from him and refusing to let her move on with another nigga and have him be around his kids.

Tia tuned his ass out after that. She couldn't care less about Gray being with Cam. What she did care about was Gunz being pressed over her being with someone else. It sounded like he still cared about Gray, even though he repeatedly said he didn't. Only a nigga that still had feelings for his baby mama would feel some type of way about her moving on. That was something Tia couldn't tolerate or take. She'd played the role of girlfriend #2 for long enough. They had a baby on the way now. A son as a matter of fact. The same son that Gunz had always secretly wanted. She would be damned if she sat back and allowed him to play her like he'd played Gray for ten years. Him and his oriental kids could kiss her ass, as far as she was concerned.

"Who the fuck is banging on my goddamn door?" Tia yelled, bypassing Aoki and Press who sat on the couch cuddled together.

Aoki hadn't let her li'l sister leave her side since they got there. They both were scared, hungry and ready to go home. Gunz had made Tia cook but Aoki refused to eat; therefore, Press did too. She was sick to her stomach to learn her father had a baby on the way with another girl.

"UPS. You got a package." Cam disguised his voice.

"Next time ring the damn doorbell." Tia unlocked the door and opened it.

Before her brain could calculate that it wasn't a UPS driver but Cam on her doorstep, he'd already barged past her.

"What the fuck are you doing here?" She asked, rubbing her large pregnant belly.

"He's here to help me get my fuckin' kids." Gray spat pushing her out the way.

"Mommy!" Aoki and Press ran towards her at full speed.

They were so happy to see their mother. A joy like no other filled their heart. Gray bent to her knees and scooped them up into her arms. She'd never been so happy in her life. Finally, it felt like she could breathe again. Hugging the girls tight, she savored the smell of their long, curly hair as Cam rushed over to Gunz. He was sitting at the kitchen island eating dinner. Like Tia, he too was shocked by Cam's sudden appearance. Completely caught off guard, he watched as Cam swiftly picked up a barstool and slammed it across his face. Gunz fell to the floor with a thud. He'd fallen so hard it felt like his spine had snapped in half. Cam didn't give him any time to react, before he repeatedly beat him with the stool. The only thing Gunz could do to protect himself was cover his face with his arms.

"Fuckin' pussy!" Cam used the seat to bang him upside the head.

The blows were so explosive that the legs on the stool broke. Furious, he threw the destroyed barstool across the room and grabbed Gunz by the collar of his shirt. Cam had lost it. He allowed the darkness he bottled-up on a daily to swallow him whole. Completely blacked out, he released the boiling anger he harbored inside and swung his hard fist into Gunz defined jaw. The impact was like a car crash to his face. A sudden rush of pain surged throughout Gunz's body. Blood soaked his tongue. Repeatedly, Cam swung his fist into his face. A deathly blow to his nose cracked it in half. A gush of blood rushed down his chin. There was so much blood that he began to choke. Gunz felt like he was going to die. He would be lucky if he even remembered his own name, once everything was said and done. Breathing heavily, Cam stood up and wiped the sweat from his brow.

"Get yo' bitch-ass up. You wanna fight a girl. Fight me nigga."

"I'ma call the police, Cam! Get the fuck out my house!" Tia tried to scare him in order to get him to leave.

She'd clearly forgotten that Cam wasn't scared of the police. He didn't fear a muthafuckin' thing. Death didn't even scare him.

"Cam, c'mon that's enough." Gray pleaded.

"Nah, he wanna put his hands on you in front of your kids. What kind of nigga are you? Fuckin' pussy." He kicked Gunz in the stomach.

Disoriented, Gunz held his abdomen and coughed up a glob of blood. He could barely breath. It hurt his ribcage to even inhale. His head was also pounding but that wasn't gonna stop him from fuckin' Cam up. He wasn't gonna let him get the best of him. Cam may have had a few inches on him in height but Gunz was bigger in size. Bruised and winded, he rose to his feet and weakly squared up. Quick on his feet, Cam punched him twice in the face. The jabs caused Gunz to step back and steady himself. Batting his lashes, he tried to blink away the stars that clouded his vision.

With his dukes up, Cam two-pieced him again but was surprised when Gunz came back with an uppercut to his chin. Like a defensive lineman he tackled Cam with a spear to his midsection. Both men fell to the floor. Finally, the one in the power position, Gunz rained down blows. Cam absorbed the trauma, accepting the pain like a G. He'd been through far worse. The sound of rapid gunfire rang in his ears, taking him back to when he was on the frontline during the Afghanistan War.

A switch in his brain clicked on and he went into military mode. Cam was no longer in Tia's home. He was back in the warzone made of dust and dirt. The unrelenting sun baked his skin as he lay on the ground dressed in fatigues. A rifle and bayonets were slung over his shoulder. Explosives were being detonated simultaneously all around him. Screams and cries from wounded soldiers filled the air. Cam had to survive. He couldn't die. It was either kill or be killed. In beast mode, he elbowed Gunz in the eye which caused him to place his hand over the bruised area. Cam took the opportunity to flip him over and place him in a chokehold. In his mind, he was still in Afghanistan, so his natural instinct was to grab his pocket knife.

"CAM!!!"

A thunderous scream ripped through him like multiple gunshots to the chest, but Cam was no longer present. Killa Cam had entered the building. Flicking the pocket knife open, he placed the cold blade up to Gunz's neck. The knife was so sharp that simple contact caused his neck to bleed. A fever-pitched scream came again from a frantic, petrified . . . female.

"CAM!!!!" Gray shrieked as he reared his hand back to slice Gunz throat.

Coming back to reality, Cam's eyes landed on her grief-stricken face. Gray, Aoki, Press and Tia were all in a heap of tears. Cam's eyes widened as his pulse quickened.

"Please don't kill my daddy." Aoki begged.

The blood in Cam's face drained away as he realized where he was and what he was about to do. He wanted Gunz dead, but he wouldn't be able to live with himself if he did it in front of Gray's kids. Stepping back, he released Gunz from his grasp. Damn near on his death bed, Gunz fell to the ground. Tia quickly rushed over to his aide.

"Baby, are you okay?" She held him in her arms.

Badly bruised, Gunz groaned in distress. Cam looked at his face. He looked far worse than Gray. Gunz was hardly recognizable. He was a bloody mess. His nose was no longer centered. It was now pointed to the right and both his eyes were swollen shut. He lay with his arms wrapped around his guts like he was holding them in. Black and blue marks would be all over his body the next day.

"I bet you won't put your hands on her again." Cam mean-mugged him as he pocketed the knife.

"Get the fuck out!" Tia yelled, rocking Gunz like a baby.

"Shut the fuck up. He gon' put his hands on yo' dumb-ass next." Cam mushed her in the head on the way out the door.

Gray and the girls followed behind him. The entire car ride home Aoki and Press cried in their mother's arms. They wouldn't stop shaking. Gray didn't know what to say or do. She knew Cam was only trying to protect her, but he'd gone too far. She and the girls would never be able to get the visual of him about to slice Gunz's throat out of their minds. It was a gruesome sight to see. Gunz deserved to get his ass kicked but he didn't deserve to die. Although she hated him, he was still the father of her kids. Gray would've never forgiven Cam if he'd actually killed him.

The whole situation had her doubting everything. She'd already been privy to Cam's crazy, but this was a whole other side of him she'd never seen. Cam had

~ 33 ~

morphed into a human killing machine. When she gazed into his eyes, Gray was shocked to find nothing there. It was like she was looking into a never-ending pool of darkness. She loved him dearly, but she couldn't be married to someone like that. She most definitely couldn't expose her girls to that kind of vicious behavior. By the time they pulled up to her new house, Gray realized that marrying Cam was a huge mistake. Now she had to figure out how she was going to tell him it was over.

After unlocking the front door, she let the girls in and told them she'd be in shortly. Closing the door behind them, Gray turned and faced Cam. The sun was starting to set. Pink and orange hues filled the winter sky.

"Why we standing out here? It's cold as fuck. Let's go inside. I'm tired. I need to lay down and take a nap."

Gray bit the inside of her cheek and shuffled her feet.

"I don't think I can do this."

"Do what?"

"Us . . . this marriage." She tried to explain.

"Excuse me." A young white guy approached them.

He was dressed in a plaid, button-up shirt, khaki pants and brown loafers with The Book of Mormon in his hand. "Would you like to accept god as your savior?"

"Are you fuckin' serious?" Cam ignored the man.

"Dead ass." Gray responded. "What just happened back there was crazy. That type of behavior might be normal for you but it's not for me. I can't have that kind of energy in my life."

"So 'cause a nigga got a li'l crazy you don't love me no more?" Cam stepped into her personal space.

Gray swallowed the lump in her throat as she gazed up into his angry eyes. A cold November wind blew through her hair and kissed her cheeks as she willed herself not to cry. Breaking up with Cam was harder than she thought it would be.

"Do you know that Jesus died, was buried and rose again on the third day?" The guy tried to get their attention.

"Me loving you ain't got nothing to do with my decision." Gray's voice croaked.

"It got everything to do wit' your decision." Cam barked.

"Jehovah said I am the first and the last; I am he who liveth, I am he who was slain; I am your advocate with the Father." The man read from the bible.

"You and I both know we rushed into this. I barely know you. My girls just saw you almost kill their father. It's too much." Gray confessed.

"If you gon' be my wife, you gotta understand, ain't no leavin'. We in this till you stop breathing."

"Cam—"

"Nah, I'm waiting. Say you ain't never leavin' me."

"I can't."

"In the beginning God created the heaven and the earth." The white guy continued on.

"Well, I ain't never leavin' you." Cam focused on Gray.

"You know Solomon had several wives." The guy interjected once more.

Whap!!!

Cam smacked him upside the back of his head so hard the man cowered down to the ground.

"Get the fuck off my porch!" He kicked him in the back, causing him to tumble down the steps. "Don't bring yo' weird-ass back around here no more with that sister fucker bullshit!"

"See, that's what I'm talkin' about. That was totally unnecessary." Gray reasoned. "It's obvious we rushed into this. We're completely mismatched and I don't know anything about you."

"My mama died when I was 13. My daddy basically died the same day cause he emotionally shut down, so I practically raised myself. I like basketball, fast cars, good weed, tight pussy and you. What else you need to know?"

Gray ran her hands down her face.

"I just need a minute to think. I can't think right now." She paced back-and-forth.

Cam stopped her.

"You ain't gotta think. That's what I'm here for. Let me take care of you." He kissed her forehead.

"Maybe we should just get the marriage annulled." She looked down.

"Don't put yo' head down when you say that shit." He placed his index finger under her chin and lifted her head. "Woman the fuck up and look a nigga in the eye when you tell'em you don't wanna be wit' him no more. Now say that shit again to my face."

Unable to verbalize her feelings, she pulled her face away from his grasp. Gray didn't know what she was doing or what she was feelings. The only thing she knew for sure was that she needed to separate herself from Cam. Like Gunz, he was doing nothing but wreaking havoc in her life.

"Yeah, that's what I thought. You can't say that shit 'cause you don't mean it."

"I do." Gray blurted out.

This bitch can't be fuckin' serious, Cam thought. He couldn't believe that Gray now looked at him like he was the enemy. She acted like he was the one that knocked her in her shit. Maybe one of the punches to her head had caused her brain damage. She couldn't even look him in the eye when she said she wanted out. How had they gone from basking in the promise of their forever to parting ways? He never sought to hurt her. There had to be more to it than this. She'd just been ecstatic about their life together. It was like all the love she had for him morphed into pain; pain became fear and fear sowed into her ending things before they had even begun. Maybe she was just erecting walls to protect herself. Either way, Cam wasn't gonna beg her ass to be with him. There were plenty of other bitches that would die to be in her position. If she wanted to throw everything away then so be it. He would never be pressed over no bitch.

"So that nigga can cheat on you, have a baby and beat yo' ass and you stayed with him for ten years, but I fuck a nigga up behind some shit he did to you and you wanna throw in the towel after two weeks of being married? What I need to do? You need me to bring in a side chick? Will that make you feel more comfortable? LaLa available. She stay down for a nigga."

"Fuck you." Gray pointed her finger in his face.

"Oh, you big mad now. What is this really the fuck about, huh?" He stepped forward which made her step back in fear.

Cam had that crazy look in his eye again.

"You so concerned about me affecting your kids but how you think they felt when they saw your face? You think it's okay for them to witness they lousy-ass daddy treatin' you any kind of way? He the one you should be mad at. I ain't did shit to you. You just lookin' for a fuckin' excuse to go back to that nigga. You like to get treated bad. You like sharing dick don't you? You like chasing antibiotics."

"And you wonder why I want a fuckin' divorce. You think you're so much better than Gunz but yo' ass ain't shit either." She shot back to hurt him.

"Keep lyin' to ya'self but you know what? You doing me a favor. If I would've known you was this damn dumb, I wouldn't have ever married you. Matter of fact, let me see what LaLa doing. Maybe she wanna take a nap wit' me." He smirked before walking away.

If he'd wanted to hurt her, he'd succeeded. Gray watched him leave as her heart broke into a million pieces. Her legs wanted to run after him, but her feet stayed planted in place. Ending things now was for the best. Cam was a fuckin' asshole. The heartache she felt now would only intensify if they stayed together longer. Determined not to break down, she entered the house and went straight into mommy mode. She bathed herself and the girls, cooked dinner and put them to bed. She lay in the bed with both girls until they fell asleep. Even after that, she stayed with them for an additional hour. The fear of never seeing her girls again consumed her.

Alone in her bedroom, Gray held her phone in her hand. She'd been checking it all night to see if Cam had called. Of course, he hadn't. He wasn't the kind of man that chased a woman. Women chased after him and here she was pushing him away. Cam had some fucked-up ways, but at the end of the day, he was a good man.

"What the fuck have I done?" She said out loud.

Her finger hovered over his name. All she had to do was press down but her ego wouldn't allow it. She knew how Cam was. He wasn't going to answer, and if he did, he was going to go off on her and make her feel stupid. Her heart couldn't take another beating so instead of calling she laid down and went to bed. For hours she tossed and turned. Nightmares of never seeing him again and her dying alone filled her head. Salty tears strolled down the plains of her face as she cried in her sleep. Then a warm heat and a strong set of arms comforted her body. She turned on her back, and when she opened her eyes, she saw Cam embracing her.

She and Cam shared a silent conversation as they stared into each other eyes. Tears burned her irises, but she couldn't look away. Gently, he used a wet wash cloth to wipe her teardrops and the left-over blood from her lip away. Burying his face in her neck, he kissed her and inhaled her scent. Gray had bathed in the Chanel body gel he loved. Cam's lips brushed her ear as he whispered, "I missed you."

"I missed you too." Gray blinked back her tears.

Studying her face, Cam grimaced. It pained him to see her black swollen eye. Why anyone would want to mess up a face so beautiful baffled him. Her ocean blue eyes were so tranquil he felt held prisoner by them. A galaxy of freckles were sprinkled across her button nose and rosy cheeks. Her brown, honey blonde wavy hair lay gently over her shoulders, kissing her skin softly. She was stunning with cuts and scrapes and all.

After her little performance on the porch, Cam rode around the city smoking trees and drinking his misery away. His callous mind wanted to say fuck Gray but somehow she'd hogtied his heart. Cam hated the hold she had on him. After how she'd done him, he should've walked away for good but here he was tending to her cuts like the wounded bird she was. Cam wasn't good with emotions, but he was going to do everything he could to fix what was broken inside of her.

"How do you keep gettin' in my house?" She died to know.

"Earlier, I threatened to kill the concierge if he didn't let me up and I got in this muthafucka by pickin' the lock. We gon' have to get you a better security system ma."

"You crazy as shit but I always wanted somebody to love me enough to pick my locks." She chuckled, shaking her head.

"Nah, you the crazy one. Out here tryin' to leave a nigga 'cause I beat yo' weak-ass baby daddy up. You hurt my feelings with that bullshit."

"I'm sorry. I didn't mean it but today was just too much. Gunz made me eat the cake like Anna Mae. I realized I'm married to a real live Huck that's in B6-13. LaLa said I ain't got no neck." Gray cut her eyes at Cam. "And I know you wanted to fuckin' laugh you bitch."

"On my mama I swear to god I did. That shit was funny as fuck." He chuckled.

"It was but fuck her." Gray laughed too. "Just know it ain't gon' be funny when I put my foot up her ass. It's on sight when I see that bitch. But for real, I ain't mean none of that shit. I just got scared."

"I know yo' goofy-ass didn't. That's why I came back. Despite what you think, I ain't that nigga. I would never put my hands on you. And when you get scared, ain't gon' be no pushing me away." He ran his thumb across her lower lip. "Gray, I'm crazy as shit and I'm crazy about you so ain't no way I'm lettin' you get away from me that easily."

"I'm just scared." She admitted.

"You don't think I'm scared? I done married a Chinese woman with two kids. I'm scared as fuck."

"I'm Korean and black jack-ass."

"Korean, Polynesian . . . they all the same. Straight up, I know I ain't the best nigga and I know we got married hella quick but trust when I say a nigga all in. All I see is you babe. We in this forever so know that I ain't never lettin' you go."

Gray didn't think it was possible, but at that moment, she fell deeper in love with him. The fractured pieces of her heart were instantly glued back together.

"I don't want you to." She admitted.

"Yo ain't have no fuckin' choice."

"Leave me now then fuck me later. It's always later, later, later, later. And I let you comeback 'cause stickin' 'round is in my nature."- Kiana Ledé, "Wicked Games"

#2

Cam stared at the blunt in his hand. It was almost short enough to burn his fingertips. Taking another quick pull, he leaned forward then smashed it in the ashtray. After dealing with Gray and her Lifetime drama movie bullshit, he needed to get high. Even though they'd made up, he couldn't get over the fact that she had the audacity to try and leave him. The notion still pissed him off. Gray was out of her goddamn mind. The only way she was leaving him was in a body bag. She wasn't some bitch off the street he was fuckin' or just a woman he called his girl. He'd made her his wife. There wasn't no breaking up. Unless Cam decided he wanted to end this shit they were in it for life.

He didn't want to admit it during their argument because he wasn't trying to hear what Gray was saying but she was right. They didn't know each other. He really didn't know shit about her except she was fine as fuck, had kids, used to own a successful magazine, was cool as fuck, had some bomb-ass pussy and was sweet. He knew he couldn't base a marriage off just that but letting Gray go wasn't an option. Lord knows he didn't know how to properly love a woman but for her he was willing to try. He wasn't dumb enough to let some other nigga come and swoop her up. Plus, there was something about her that he felt he desperately needed in his life.

Maybe it was because she called him out on his bullshit or because she challenged him to be a better man. It also could've been because she was drop dead gorgeous and her pussy always sucked in his dick like a vice grip. It didn't even matter that she could no longer have kids. He liked her so much that he was willing to figure something out. Maybe he'd hire a bitch to carry their kid or adopt. One way or another they were gon' have a child. It was imperative that he have a little person that looked just like him.

And no, he wasn't in love with Gray, but he cared about her a lot. Love for her was in his heart but it didn't run river deep. Cam knew the feeling was there, but he didn't feel truly connected to the emotion. The fear of losing Gray didn't keep him awake at night. He wanted things to work out, but if they didn't, he'd gladly let her go. He was sure she wasn't head over heels in love with him either. If she was he'd be truly surprised. Cam figured they'd fall in love, eventually, but that would take time. They would never get there tho, if she tried to run every time some bad shit popped up. Dealing with a hood, gun-toting, nut-ass nigga like him, crazy shit was bound to go down.

Cam and his pot'nahs, Stacy and Diggy, sat in his office talkin' shit and getting high. Business at his luxury auto shop was booming. He had three locations around St. Louis, as well as several liquor stores. Gray didn't even know about his stores or that his main source of income was transporting drugs. Cam didn't have any intentions on telling her either. Somethings were better off left unsaid. He'd just been promoted to Lieutenant after his predecessor Dame retired. Being Lieutenant was the second highest position in the Gonzalez cartel organization. He was responsible for supervising the hitmen and falcons within their own territory. Cam was also allowed to carry out low-profile murders without permission from his boss. Jefe Victor Gonzalez expected tremendous things from him. The less Gray knew about his criminal life the better. He planned on keeping her far away from that part of his life. He didn't want to taint her like he'd done with LaLa.

Cleaning his money through her salon was one of the worst decisions he'd ever made.

"Roll up a fatty." He told Diggy.

"I already got another one on deck." He pulled out a freshly rolled blunt.

Cam eyed his friends. Stacy was a big stocky nigga with a potbelly and a mean right hook. Diggy literally looked like Diggy Simmons. He was years younger than him and the sanest out the click. They both were dripped in diamonds and designer furs. Cam was dressed in a dark blue dad hat, oversized denim jacket, gray t-shirt, blue and white fitted track pants and canvas Off-White sneakers. A gold Cuban link and a chain with a gold dog tag decorated his neck. He couldn't have been prouder at how far they'd come. They'd been riding with each other for years. Cam, Stacy and their other boy Quan had known each other since middle school. Diggy was Quan's little brother. They all ran the streets and got money together. They were more than friends. Quan, Stacy and Diggy were like family to Cam. He was closer to them than he was his own blood brothers.

"Yo, I think I'ma propose to Tara." Diggy said out of nowhere.

"Shit, bout time. You been wit' her for damn year thirty years." Stacy joked.

"That's what's up li'l bruh. I'm proud of you. You told Quan yet?" Cam questioned.

"Yeah, he gon' go ring shoppin' wit' me."

"Aww ain't that sweet." Stacy made fun of him.

"Fuck you nigga. Yo' ass need to be tryin' to find somebody to take care of you. In a minute you gon' be 500 pounds and countin'."

"Nigga, I'm thick. These ho's love me." Stacy popped his collar.

"But for real. On some serious shit. I ain't tryin' to go into 2018 on the same shit I been on. I'm almost thirty-two. We got two kids and a baby on the way. A nigga gotta step up and get my shit together. Tara loved my black-ass even when I was unlovable. I done took her through some shit man. Fuckin' these ho's, going to jail, playin' wit' her heart and she still stuck around. If I could take it all back I would. But I can't so at this point I just wanna marry her, be a good father to my kids and take my ass back to school and get a fuckin' degree. This street shit ain't even for me no more, dawg. I just wanna be wit' her and my kids 'cause at the end of the day, if I ain't got them, I ain't got shit."

"Fuck you been watchin', Fix My Life?"

"Nah," Diggy chuckled. "I just been thinkin'. I can't call myself a man if I keep disrespectin' the person I say mean the most to me. And this shit just don't faze me no more. It's the same bullshit over and over again. I done fucked every bitch there is to fuck. I got the money, I got the cars, the jewels, the house but don't none of that shit make me happy. You know what does? When I walk in the crib and my shorty yell out daddy. That shit get me every time. I ain't tryin' to lose that for no bitch or no street shit."

"I feel you." Cam rocked back-and-forth in his chair. "I'm tryin' to get on yo' level wit' Gray."

"Speakin' of Gray, so you straight ran-up in Tia shit and beat that nigga ass?" Stacy bugged up laughing.

"Beat the brakes off that nigga. I was about to slice his shit, but Gray scary-ass stopped me." Cam shook his head.

"Yo, you wildin'." Diggy chuckled, sparking up the blunt. "You can't go around slicing niggas up. You ain't in the army no more."

"Yeah, you right. Her shorties were there. I couldn't pull that shit off without my mama's ghost haunting me for life."

"It's crazy cause I used to have respect for the boy. Gunz was an OG out here in the streets. He put in mad work. He got hella bodies."

"Man, that pussy-ass nigga soft as baby shit." Cam waved him off.

"I don't know fam." Stacy massaged his jaw. "This shit ain't over. That muthafucka gon' do something. He ain't gon' just let that shit ride. You fucked him up in front of both his girls."

"Gray ain't his fuckin' girl. She's my fuckin' wife. Don't make me have to fuck yo' fat ass up."

"You always got a fat joke. I ain't Gunz nigga. You ain't gon' just beat my ass wit' a barstool. I'ma shoot yo' tall lanky-ass." Stacy bugged up.

"Yeah, if yo' fat ass can catch me first."

"Ya'll niggas gon' chill wit' all them fat jokes. When a nigga slim down don't say shit when I take all y'all bitches."

"Who bitches?" Cam and Diggy said in unison.

"Y'all bitches." Stacy pointed at them both. "Gray, LaLa, Tia, Kema, Mo 'cause I like 'em dark chocolate and yo' baby mama Diggy. I see the way she be lookin' at the kid and she fine as fuck. I know she gotta have good pussy 'cause you stay nuttin' up in her."

"You high off Twinkies and Ho-Ho's if you think my baby mama want yo' fat ass. She don't even like fat people."

"And neither do Gray." Cam chimed in.

"The fuck?" Stacy drew his head back. "She fat too."

"Yo, don't call my bitch fat. She pleasantly plump. There's a difference." Cam cracked up laughing. "You got my baby fucked up. She bad as fuck."

"She is, and she got a fat ass." Stacy licked his lips, imagining Gray's voluptuous backside.

"Gray can get it. You wifed up a baddie bro." Diggy agreed.

"Aye yo. Watch your fuckin' mouth." Cam ice grilled them both.

"Oh, my bad. I forgot she wifey now." Stacy chuckled.

"I still can't believe this nigga married." Diggy said in disbelief.

"Shit me either." Cam looked down at his ring.

"Aye! You can't go back there!" He heard his manager say as his office door swung open and forcefully hit the wall.

Next thing he knew, LaLa came storming into his office looking fine and furious. He hated that despite the foul shit she'd done, he still found her attractive. Every time he came in contact with her, she made his dick hard. LaLa was a beautiful girl. She looked just like the Instagram baddie Jasmin Jaye. Before she got with Cam, LaLa was considered pretty. Once he bought her a set of veneers and 34 D breast implants, she went from pretty to bad as fuck. She had butter colored skin, almond shaped brown eyes, a small mole by her nose and big, full, juicy lips that he used to love to kiss. Being a hairstylist, she kept a fresh weave. That day she wore her hair parted down the middle with two feed-in braids going down the sides. The black smoky eye and nude pink lip gloss she wore went perfect with her blush pink and black Louis Vuitton letterman jacket, skintight white tank top, black patent leather skirt, six-inch pink and black ankle strap heels and Louie V crossbody bag.

"Yo what the fuck is wrong wit' you?" LaLa snapped.

"Aww shit. This gon' be good." Stacy leaned back and placed his hands behind his head. "I wish I had a snack for this."

"You put your hands on my pregnant fuckin' niece!"

"What?" Cam screwed up his face.

"Don't play stupid nigga! You heard me! You punched my niece in the fuckin' face to impress that Jenny Craig, Slim Fast, drinkin' ass bitch!"

"Here she go with the fat jokes too." Stacy frowned. "That's why I'm team Gray now. Big people gotta stick together."

"Shut the fuck up, Stacy! Ain't nobody talkin' to you! Matter of fact get the fuck out!" She pointed her finger in his face.

"Bitch, I got stock in this shop. I ain't going no fuckin' where."

"I bet you would leave this if I told you it was a food truck outside."

"Sure in the fuck would but it ain't so I ain't going nowhere."

"What can I help you wit'? Why are you here?" Cam spoke in an even tone.

"I'm here because you're foul as fuck! Tia is like family to you, but I guess now that you wit' that wide body bitch, you think it's okay to put your hands on her."

"Man, get the fuck outta here. All I did was mush her dumb-ass in the head."

"That ain't what I heard. She told me you came in there like you was high off bath salt punching everybody. She said you damn near killed Gunz, tore up her shit, stole off on her twice and the whole time Baby Bop fat-ass stood there laughing with her bad-ass kids."

"Yo, I'm up. I'm tired of you muthafuckas." Diggy rose to his feet. "Ya'll niggas been arguing for years. Just do the world a favor and break up."

"What the fuck is you sayin'? We been broke up." Cam interjected.

"I can't tell."

"For us to be broke up you stay dippin' that dick in this pussy!" LaLa tapped her clit.

"Aww nah! I really gotta go yo. She done grabbed her pussy and shit. I'ma get up wit' you later fam." Diggy gave Cam a pound.

"Nigga yo' life suck. Good luck with that." Stacy stood up to leave too.

"That's why your fat-ass lonely now." LaLa quipped, rolling her eyes.

"And that's why Cam don't want you cause your titties lopsided."

"My titties look better than big-bone Brenda."

Pausing, Stacy looked at her in disbelief.

"Damn, you really threatened by shorty. You need to tightin' up your tracks, ma. Jealously not a good look on you."

"Bye nigga!" She pushed him out and slammed the door in his face. "Now back to you." She turned and looked at Cam. "I thought me, and you was better than that."

"I don't know why you thought that. We are what we are."

"And what's that?" LaLa folded her arms across her chest.

"We friends. Better yet coworkers." Cam smirked.

Glaring at him, LaLa tried to hide the cracks that were breaking in her heart. She would rather he took a knife to her face than treat her this way. He spoke to her as if she was a stranger and not the love of his life, but this was what Cam did. He tore her down to build himself up. Without an ounce of remorse, he'd looked dead in her eyes and say whatever he could that would hurt her the most. Since their break up, he'd somehow made himself into the martyr and her the villain. Yes, cheating and getting pregnant by another man was the ultimate sin. She regretted her decision every day, but Cam couldn't act like he hadn't pushed her into the arms of another man.

"That's fucked up and you know it." Her throat filled with tears. "I can't believe you would say some shit like that. I don't care what we go through, you ain't have to punch my niece."

"I told ya' dumb-ass I didn't touch her."

"Well, what you go over there for?"

"Not that it's any of your business but I pulled up on her weak-ass baby daddy 'cause he laid hands on Gray."

The air in LaLa's lungs evaporated. She'd tried telling herself that his erratic behavior had nothing to do with Gray but his hidden demons. Now that she knew the truth, she felt like the wind had been knocked out of her. She wanted Gray out of their lives. Things weren't great before she'd entered but at least she had some of Cam's time. Now she barely ever saw him.

"Why you involving yourself in their business? That's between her and that man."

"I got my reasons." He replied.

"Well, you need to let me know something 'cause the way this shit lookin' don't sit right wit' me. You ain't never even went this hard for me. Since when you been captain save a fat hoe?"

"Chill wit' all that fat shit."

Cam understood she was hurt and jealous, but he'd be damned if he allowed her to talk cash shit about Gray.

"No! Why do you care so much?" LaLa lost her shit. "Is this more than a fuck? It gotta be 'cause you ain't been fuckin' me. You claim to keep it real wit' bitches, you so big and bad. Let a bitch know what's up. You really riding for this hoe? What's good wit' you and Fat Albert?"

"I'ma tell you what's up since you wanna know so bad." Cam took his feet off the desk and sat up. "Gray . . . that's me. That's my baby, my heart . . . my wife." Cam stated coldly.

LaLa swore she'd died.

"Your wife?" She screwed up her face.

"Yeah, my wife." Cam showed off the gold band on his ring finger.

An expression of devastation washed over LaLa's face. Any color she had drained away. Cam wanted not to give a shit. He was supposed to hate her, but he honestly felt bad. He hadn't planned on telling her this way. He never intended for things to play out like this, but she'd forced his hand. Now she sat across from him in a heap of tears. He wanted to ease her pain but there was nothing he could do but wait it out till she stopped crying. Under different circumstances he would've comforted her but now that he was with Gray that wouldn't be appropriate. Cam licked his bottom lip and gazed off to the side. It was tearing him up to see LaLa cry. At one point and time he was madly, dangerously in love with this girl. He would've given the world to see her smile.

Why did she have to go and fuck things up, he thought. LaLa ripped his heart out of his chest when she'd opened her legs to another man and had a baby. Cam hadn't felt a hurt like that since his mother died. He would describe his heartache like the music from the Philharmonic Orchestra. Sometimes it was low and allowed him to function. Other times the cello would play, and he'd be blue. Then out of nowhere his despair would rise to a crescendo and fury would gust from his chest in a vicious rage. At that very moment he felt regret. What they could've been was no more. He'd crucified her for her transgressions. He'd yelled, he'd screamed, he'd smoked until his chest was sore but deep down he knew it was his fault why they weren't together anymore.

LaLa was a good girl before he broke her down to nothing. With her hand clutching her chest, a torrent of tears raced down her face. After seven years of holding him down, four of which she was his girl, this was the thanks she got? She'd poured herself into Cam for so long that it was all she knew how to do. She'd been the one by his side during his darkest times. They'd been broken up for three years, and no matter how cold he was or how many times he shut her attempts of reconciliation down, she remained steadfast. But this new wound that he'd added to the collection of scars from over the years cut deeper than all the rest. This one was life threatening.

She felt like she was on cardiac arrest. LaLa always thought she would be the one he'd marry. She assumed that since they still messed around there was a chance they'd get back together. Never did she think he'd run off and marry some chick he'd only known a few months. He had to know how much the news would hurt her. Maybe he didn't care, but when she looked at him and saw the sorrow in his eyes, she knew he did. Cam still cared about her. The bond they shared was too strong for him not to. Their history was too long. Their lives were too intertwined. Gray and a marriage certificate wouldn't stop him from loving her.

"Ay yo, wipe your face." He handed her a Kleenex.

LaLa snatched it from his tattooed hand and blew her nose.

"You barely even know this girl. For all you know she could be the op."

"I know her enough."

"This is some straight bullshit." She continued to cry.

Cam ignored her sobbing and pretended like her tears didn't affect him when each one pounded on his conscious like a bass drum.

"Business between us will continue on as usual." He said nonchalantly.

"Oh really?" LaLa cocked her head to the side. "Does your wife," she made quotation marks with her fingers. "Know you wash your money through my shop?"

"Nope and she won't either."

"Hmm . . . maybe I should tell her." She threatened with a smirk on her face.

"Maybe you'll die. It's up to you."

"Fuck off. I'm not gon' tell yo' bitch nothin'. You know I'm not a snitch." She got up and threw her snot filled tissue at him.

"Yo! What the fuck? Don't be throwing that nasty shit at me." Cam dodged the throw.

"You better be glad that's all I did." LaLa pulled herself together.

Crying wasn't going to change the fact that he'd ripped her heart from her chest.

"Tell me the truth." She placed her hands on his desk and leaned forward.

Cam couldn't help but take a look at her sumptuous breasts. She'd planted them dead in his face. Visions of how he used to suck and bite on her nipples while she screamed out his name filled his head.

Snap! Snap!

LaLa snapped her fingers to get his attention.

"My eyes are up here nigga."

"Shit, you put them big muthafucka's in my face. Plus, I paid for 'em so I'ma look at 'em whenever I want."

"Whatever. You love this girl?"

"I wouldn't have married her if I didn't."

"Are you in love with her?"

Cam avoided eye contact with her and licked his bottom lip.

"That's what I thought." LaLa stood up straight with a devious smile on her face. "Y'all marriage built on a lie. It's doomed to fail. It ain't gon' last."

"You talkin' all that bullshit but what you fail to realize is whether I'm in love with Gray or not doesn't negate the fact that I'm still not in love with you."

LaLa tried not to stumble back. His confession was like a karate kick to the chest.

"I chose her. I don't want you. My baby got what you want and that's me. So, check this out, don't call me, don't text me, don't pop up here tryin' to throw that pussy at me. I don't want none of it. It's done. This shit is over." He tried to convince her and himself.

Securing the strap of her purse onto her shoulder, LaLa looked him straight in the eye and said, "It'll never be over between us. You know it and so do I."

"Baby where would I be without your love beside me?"- Summer Walker, "CPR"

#3

Cameron Parthens Jr. wasn't afraid of shit. He'd survived his mother dying in a plane crash, being the only surviving member of his squad in the Afghanistan war, a stint in jail, being on probation, numerous shoot outs and a broken heart but being someone's husband had him shook. After his conversation with LaLa, he was starting to question whether or not he could be everything Gray needed him to be. Maybe Gray was right. Maybe they had jumped into things too quickly. Hell, he wasn't even in love with her. He just knew he wanted her in his life. For three years, he'd been walking dead. He'd been running from himself and his demons. His insides felt rotten. He didn't laugh or smile. All he did was drink, smoke, fuck mad bitches, and go upside niggas' heads. Cam went through life existing and not living. With Gray by his side he felt alive and renewed.

She was love and beauty personified. When he looked into her sapphire eyes he saw visions of his future kids. With her he felt at home. The only problem was he'd only been faithful once in his life and that had gotten him nowhere. After LaLa, he swore he would never give his heart to another woman. Then Gray came along and shook up his whole world. From the moment she walked into Principal Glanville's office, she had his heart. Unknowingly, she'd snatched it out of his chest and pocketed it for safe keeping. He'd tried to fight his obsession but the harder he tried the more obsessed he became.

She was everything he wanted in a wife; strong, funny, confident, feisty and smart. The only problem was he had no idea how to be anyone's husband. He knew even less about being a stepdad. He'd never witnessed a successful marriage or been a part of a blended family. People thought his parents had the perfect marriage. Everyone in the neighborhood thought they were the second coming of Ruby Dee and Ossie Davis, but Cam knew the truth. His parents' marriage was just as fucked up as everyone else. Marriage was supposed to be based off love, trust, compromise, respect and fidelity but every man he knew cheated. The last thing he wanted to do was hurt Gray. She'd been through enough trauma to last her a lifetime and beyond the grave.

His run-in with LaLa didn't make the situation any better. She'd really fucked his head up with her parting words. *It'll never be over between us. You know it and so do I.* He wished that he was confident enough in his convictions to say that her words didn't hold any weight but he and LaLa had a complicated history. No one but Quan understood how deep their bond went.

All in his head over their conversation, Cam felt like he needed to do something for Gray to show how much she meant to him. He couldn't let LaLa be right. Come hell or high water he was going to be the man Gray desired. He had to be. Being a loving, committed husband was now his mission. Cam had failed once at love. He wasn't gonna come out on the losing end of the stick again. He was determined to prove LaLa, himself and all the naysayers wrong. He and Gray were gonna kill this marriage shit.

A man on a mission, he hit up Plaza Frontenac in search of gifts for his baby. He even copped a few things for her li'l mamas. By the time he made it to her crib, the sun had gone down. With the gifts and a Louis Vuitton overnight bag in tow, he unlocked her door and walked inside. Tired of him constantly breaking into her shit, Gray gave him a key to the crib. Gray's new place was fly as fuck. She'd purchased a four-bedroom, five-bathroom, brick home in DeBaliviere Place. It had oak floors, stained glass windows, crystal chandeliers and pocket doors. Every room had a floral theme. Big portraits of roses covered each wall. The esthetic of the home was rustic and modern with a hint of glam. Cam didn't know if he'd be able to spend a lot of time there. Gray's home was way too girly for him. He was used to his bachelor pad in the city. Figuring out their living situation was one of the first things they'd have to map out, after he fucked the color out of her eyes.

Laughter rang through the air as he placed his bag down, causing his heart to skip a beat. Cam eagerly walked towards the angelic sound. Now he understood what Diggy meant. This was what he wanted to come home to every night after dealing with niggas all day. He'd always longed for a family and now he had one.

Quietly, he walked into the kitchen and found Gray and the girls finishing up making dinner. Despite everything she'd gone through 24 hours earlier, she wasn't letting any of it keep her down. Only one of her eyes was functioning and all of her movements were slow to alleviate pain, but she refused be laid up in bed. She had a household and a family to take care of. Moments like this reminded Cam why he married her. It made him confident in their union. Gray was the one for him. She possessed the same strength and resilience of his mother.

There she was in all her splendor and grace. She had the refinement of Lena Horne and classic elegance of Phylicia Rashad. Her long curly hair was pulled away from her face in a messy ponytail. Tendrils of curls framed her heart-shaped face and kissed the nape of her long neck. Her face was bare. Not a stich of makeup graced her butterscotch skin and she was still as beautiful as any model on the cover of a magazine. Even though she hadn't left the house, Gray still made sure she looked presentable for her new husband. She wore a white spaghetti strap, floral detailed sundress that crisscrossed in the back. Despite not wearing a bra, her 30 D breasts sat up firm with no support. Her hard nipples rubbed against the delicate fabric of the dress, making his dick thump against the crotch of his pants.

Cam often wondered if she knew how stunning she was. He was almost sure she didn't. The saying was beauty is in the eye of the beholder but for Gray that was true for everyone she came in contact with. Everyone fawned over just how pretty she was. Strangers gawked at her when she wasn't looking. She was unlike anything the world had ever seen. Her African and Korean features, paired with her caerulean slanted eyes and thick curvaceous frame, was of a different breed. She didn't have to do much to be seen. She was all about simplicity and made things uncomplicated for herself and everyone around her. Maybe that was why she walked the earth with an angelic glow. An inner light shined from the inside out. Whenever she smiled and laughed, Cam couldn't help but smile too. To be in her presence was a true blessing from god. She was much too good for him. He knew it and eventually she would too.

"Break yo' self fool!" His loud voice echoed, scaring the crap out of Gray and the girls.

Aoki and Press shrieked while Gray held her chest.

"Boy, don't be scaring me like that." She quickly turned to hide her face.

Even though Cam said he didn't care about her wounds, Gray still felt self-conscious. No woman wanted her man to see her in such an ugly state. Every time she looked in the mirror she saw a hideous monster staring back at her.

"Shut up and give me a hug." He pulled her into his strong hold.

Gray hesitantly wrapped her arms around his waist. She wanted to fall into his embrace and kiss him all over his handsome face, but the girls were standing right there. They still didn't know that they were together, let alone the fact that he was her husband. Looking up into his eyes, she made sure she relayed her true feelings. She missed him like crazy. All day she'd been craving his presence and touch. When Cam was around she felt whole. The weight of the world didn't rest on her shoulders. She felt as light as a feather.

"I can't tell you how good it is to see you."

"Try." He held himself back from kissing her.

The sound of his raspy voice made the hairs on the back of Gray's neck stand up. She had to press her thighs together to constrict the pulsating in her clit. It had to be a crime to want a man so much. Every time she came in contact with Cam, she wanted to jump his bones. The fire between them was so intense she wanted to peel out of her dress. Gray couldn't remember feeling this way with another man.

"I missed you incredibly."

"I missed you too, Star."

"You been drinkin'?" Gray could smell the liquor on his breath.

"Diggy and Stacy came by the shop and we tossed back a few," he lied.

He'd really had a few cups of Ciroc after LaLa left.

"Here." He handed her a bouquet of pink roses to take her mind off the fact he'd been day drinking.

A smile a mile wide sprouted on her face.

"Oh my god. These are so beautiful." Gray inhaled the potent scent. "Thank you." She blushed.

Scrunching up her face, Aoki looked at her mom like she had lost her mind. She couldn't believe that her mother was hugged up with the op, the same op that was Makiah and Ryan's rude-ass uncle and the man who had decimated her father and nearly killed him. She already had issues with Gray. All this did was add another layer to her disdain for her mother.

"Umm . . . what the hell is he doing here?" Aoki rolled her neck and placed her hand on her imaginary hip.

"There you go being grown again. You ain't gon' learn until you get yo' ass beat Karrueche Tran." Cam responded.

"Cam." Gray hit his chest. "Hush and you." She turned to Aoki. "You betta watch your mouth before I hit you in it."

Aoki stood silent with an embarrassed look on her face.

"You're tall." Press craned her neck back to look at Cam. "Are you a giraffe?"

Cam looked down at the miniature curly-haired beauty. She was a replica of her mother. The only thing she was missing was Gray's signature blue eyes. Press' eyes were brown like her fathers.

"Nah, shawty. I'ma real-ass nigga."

"Oh lord." Gray hid her face with her hand.

"I wanna be a real-ass nigga. Mama, can I be a real-ass nigga too!" Press jumped up and down while tugging on her mother's dress.

"No, you may not."

"Aww man." She poked out her bottom lip.

"Don't pout li'l mama. You can't be a real-ass nigga, but you can be a real-ass bitch."

"Cam!" Gray shrieked. "You cannot talk to a six-year-old like that."

"What?" He looked at her confused.

"You the man that beat up my daddy. Are you our daddy too?" Press' little mind tried to comprehend what was going on.

"Hell—I mean nah he ain't our daddy." Aoki quickly clarified.

"To answer your question." Gray eyed Aoki with disdain. "This is my friend, Cam."

"Friend?" He screwed up his face and bent down. "What's up pretty girl?" He shook Press's hand. "Don't mind yo' lyin' ass mama. I ain't her fuckin' friend. Friends don't do what we do. I'm her man."

"Cam! You cannot curse in front of my kids." Gray damn near had a heart attack.

"Chill out. They cool. You know not to say curse words, right?"

"Yeah. Aoki told me just to do it when mama ain't around."

"Damn right." Cam agreed, giving her a high-five.

"Let me catch either one of you cursing and I'ma beat both y'all ass." Gray warned.

"Yo' ass talk too much." Aoki said to Press under her breath.

"Shut up booty-head." Press stuck out her tongue.

"Here, I got you this too." Cam handed Gray more gifts.

"What is all of this for?"

"I just wanted to let you know you were on my mind." He told a half truth.

He'd really bought her the gifts to ease his conscious and to put a smile on her face. But what does a man buy a woman after she got her ass beat? Cam lacked the emotional intellect to know that Gray didn't need his gifts. His strong masculine presence and warm smile was enough.

Excited, she placed the bags on the kitchen island and ripped each box open. She didn't need or want any of what he'd gotten her, but she accepted the presents because they were from Cam. He'd bought her several pairs of shoes. The first was a pair of $950 Prada, patent and neoprene booties. In the second box were a pair of $1,290 Fendi, embroidered knit booties. Gray lost her shit when she opened the box that held the blue and red, zip-tie, PVC, mule pumps by Off-White. Last but not least was the Fendi Mania, logo pumps that everyone was going crazy for. He even went as far as to get her the Fendi Mania, striped, shoulder bag.

"Cam, these gifts are wonderful. I love them, but I don't need this. It's too much."

"Who don't want designer shoes?"

"Me. Things like this don't move me. I can buy all of this myself. I would much rather you buy me a bouquet of flowers and a nice card than a bunch of materialistic crap. I don't want a man to buy my affection. Gunz did that and you see where that got us."

"You know how much money I spent on that shit?"

"Exactly. No way should you have spent damn near five racks on a bunch of stuff I don't need."

It became abundantly clear that she required more than material things from him. Things Cam didn't know if he'd be capable of giving.

"Well shit, I got them something too. Should I take it back?" He handed Aoki and Press their gifts, bewildered.

He'd gotten Aoki a $3,795 Dolce & Gabbana embellished crossbody bag and Press a rose gold, metallic, Miu Miu crossbody purse.

"You only got us one thing and got my mama all that?" Aoki curled her upper lip. "Uh ah, here I don't want it. Take it back." She handed him the gift.

"Yeah, Cam, that ain't cool. Mama, he need to level-up like daddy but I'ma keep my li'l purse anyway. My American Doll can wear it." Press pursed her lips together.

"Both of y'all can give me my shit back." Cam spat heated. "Makiah and Ryan will love that shit."

He wanted to call them some ungrateful bitches but even Cam knew that was going too far.

"That was very nice of you to do that for them, but Aoki and Press don't need designer purses. Please return them and get your money. Girls, tell Cam thank you anyway."

"Thanks." Press hugged his legs.

"Yeah thanks." Aoki replied begrudgingly.

"Yeah, whatever. That's why the boogeyman gon' come get you tonight." Cam taunted her.

"If you don't leave her alone. Everybody go sit down. It's time to eat." Gray inhaled deep and prayed that her first family dinner with Cam went well.

So far things weren't looking so good. Cam took his seat at the head of the table, awkwardly. Sitting down for family dinner was new to him. He was the kind of nigga that grabbed fast food or takeout and ate alone in his car or in front of the TV. The only time he sat down for dinner was when he visited his father's house which was a rarity. It was also uncomfortable because he could tell by the scowl on Aoki's face that she didn't want him there. He could already tell it was going to be a problem between them. He hoped and prayed he didn't have to put his foot up Gray's daughter's ass. He would hate to have to fuck up a ten-year-old kid.

"Here we go." Gray sat the dishes of food onto the table family style.

She'd prepared a smorgasbord of Korean dishes. After everything that had gone down, she needed some good ole comfort food to make her feel better. There was Kimchi (fermented vegetables), Bimimbap (rice, seasoned/sautéed vegetables and a fried egg), Seolleongtang (ox bone soup) and Haemul Pajeon (seafood vegetable pancake). Cam was hungry as fuck until he saw what she'd made. None of the things she prepared looked appetizing. Holding his breath, he held his stomach and tried not to throw up. There were so many different foreign smells permeating the air. Where was the fried chicken and macaroni and cheese? Gray was on that bullshit. They'd just gotten married and she was already trying to kill a nigga.

"Looks good don't it?" She beamed, sitting down beside her man.

"It look like something." Cam swallowed the vomit in his mouth. "What's that?" He pointed towards a bowl filled with meat that looked like it had been boiled in seaman.

"Oh, that's Seolleongtang. It's ox bones, ox meat, brisket, green onions and minced garlic in a milky white broth. It's delicious, trust me."

"What I tell you bout lyin' all the time?"

"I swear to god, it's good." She laughed. "Now bow your head. It's time to say grace." She placed her hand in his and reached across the table to hold Press' hand as well.

Cam held out his left hand for Aoki to take it, but instead of taking his hand, she looked at him and mouthed the words, "Li'l nigga, please." It took everything in him not to thump her mean-ass in the forehead. Unaware that any of this was going on Gray closed her eyes and prayed over the food.

"God is good, god is great, thank you for this food, amen."

"Amen." Aoki and Press said in unison.

Cam opened his eyes and gazed around the table in disbelief.

"What kind of ghetto-ass prayer was that?"

"That's the only one I know." Gray began to fix everyone's plate.

"You gon' have to do better, ma. That was pitiful."

"Well, you gon' have to teach me a new one."

"It's a lot of shit I'ma have to teach you, I see." He smirked, watching the curve of her hip as she bent over the table.

"Nasty-ass." Gray placed his plate and bowl before him. "How was school today, girls?"

"Me and King played Catch a Girl, Get a Girl during recess." Press replied happily.

"My nephew a G." Cam clapped his hands.

"I'ma have to watch you and King." Gray said genuinely worried.

For Press to be six and King seven, they acted like two long-lost-lovers.

"How was your day, Aoki?"

"It was terrible. I hate my school, I hate my teacher, I hate my classmates, I hate my life. I just wanna go on antidepressants like all the other kids at my school?"

"Aoki, if you don't hush. For the last time you are not depressed." Gray handed the girls their food.

"But mom, I am. I have all the symptoms. I stay aggressive and violent. I always feel agitated, restless, irritable, tired, lost and nervous. I have trouble sleeping and I don't enjoy the things that I once loved."

"Where are you getting this from?"

"The Zoloft commercial . . . duh." Press rolled her eyes to the sky.

"Y'all weird as fuck. I knew I shouldn't have got wit' no foreigner." Cam pulled out his phone and placed the call on speaker.

"No phone at the table. We about to eat." Gray reprimanded him.

"I ain't eatin' that shit."

"What?" Gray exclaimed.

"That shit look like ass."

"Cam!"

"Imo's pizza. Can I take your order?"

 "Aye yo, I wanna place an order for delivery."

"Cam!"

"Shhhhhhh."

"I told you about shhhhhhh me." She popped him on the arm.

"Let me get a medium sausage and pepperoni pizza and an order of hot wings. You want something Pretty Girl?" He asked Press.

"Ooooh, I want some mozzarella sticks."

"Don't you get her no damn mozzarella sticks and I just made all this food."

"Don't nobody want this freaky shit but you. This some muthafuckin' Korean slave food."

"But I want some mozzarella sticks mama." Press whined, poking out her bottom lip.

"I got you li'l mama." Cam ignored Gray and winked his eye.

"Yay!" She danced in her seat.

"I want some too." Aoki added.

"I ain't gettin' you shit. Nah, you depressed remember. Plus, you wouldn't even hold my hand during grace. You betta eat that jizz yo' mama made."

"I swear to god, I'ma slap you." Gray warned.

"That's why my daddy gon' fuck you up." Aoki scowled, placing her napkin onto her lap.

"Fuck yo' punk-ass daddy!" Cam yelled.

"My daddy ain't no punk. Yo' daddy probably a crackhead anyway."

"And yo' daddy got dropped in one punch just like my nieces dropped yo' ass. Now what?" Cam sat back in his chair like he'd won the argument.

"They ain't do shit! It took both of them to jump me! They ain't want no smoke one on one."

"Oh word? I bet I call them over here right now to fuck you up!" He dialed his sister's number.

"Call 'em! I don't care!"

Mo was at home laid up in the bed with Boss. He rubbed her pregnant belly as they lay watching MTV's The Challenge.

"Nigga, what you want?" She answered the phone on the first ring.

"Get the car runnin' and bring the strap!"

~ 72 ~

"What?" Mo and Boss said at the same time.

"This li'l girl over here talkin' big shit. Bring my nieces over here right now. I got five hunnid each."

"Five hunnid each for what?"

"To beat Gray's daughter's ass. She want round two."

"Cam, are you serious? Is everything alright?" Mo sat up.

She knew her brother had more than just a few screws loose. Sometimes, Cam went over the deep end and she feared this might be one of those times.

"Nigga, I'm straight! She the one that's over here talkin' heavy! She think shit sweet! I got time today!"

"How old is she?" Boss quizzed, cracking up.

"I don't know. Like 8 or 9 but that's beside the point. I don't give a fuck. She talk too much shit but today she gon' have to back that shit up."

"Are you really arguing with a child?" Mo sighed at her brother's childish behavior.

"Hell yeah. I don't give a fuck how old she is. She started the shit."

"Cam, leave that li'l girl alone."

"Nah, man, uh ah. I can't let that shit rock." He shook his head angrily.

"Hang up the fuckin' phone now." Gray spoke through a clenched jaw.

"Awwww shit. You in troooouble!" Mo laughed hysterically.

"Maaaaaan," Cam sucked his teeth. "Gray on some bullshit." He spoke low into the phone. "She sayin' I can't get her daughter beat up but be on standby. Shit still might pop-off." He hung up.

"Are you fuckin' insane? Did you really just try to get your nieces to jump my daughter?" Gray seethed with anger.

"What? She started wit' me?"

"How old are you? She's ten! You're 38, stupid-ass. Grow up!" Gray smacked him upside the back of his head.

"Fuck that. When it's on, it's on and when they see you it's on sight." Cam warned Aoki. "Wit' yo' bad-ass."

"I ain't scared of them! I'll be at school tomorrow bright and early! I'm always TTG!"

"TTG?" Gray repeated perplexed.

"Train-to-muthafuckin'-go!" Aoki rocked back-and-forth like a real live hood bitch.

"Keep talkin' shit." Cam pulled his gun out and placed it on the table. "I dare you. Say something. Say one more muthafuckin' thing and I swear to god I'ma light yo' shit up."

"Put that damn gun up!" Gray ordered on ten.

"Nah, she need her ass beat. She too damn grown."

"Oooooooh, can I hold your gun? Will that make me a real-ass bitch?" Press said eagerly.

"EVERYBODY SHUT UP!" Gray slammed her fist down, causing the dinnerware to rattle. "I HAVE HAD ENOUGH! Have y'all forgotten what happened to me? Look at my face! I can only see out of one eye. I cooked all this food, even though I should've been on bedrest, but I did it 'cause I wanted to make my family happy."

"No, you wanted to make him happy." Aoki spat with an attitude.

Gray used what little energy she had left and leaned across the table. Once Aoki was in her grasp, she gripped the collar of her shirt and yanked her tiny body forward.

"Let me tell you one thing, don't let this swollen eye fool you. I will still beat yo' ass. You will not disrespect me or anyone else in this house, period. If I hear one more curse word come out your mouth, I'ma stick my foot so far up your ass even the doctor won't be able to get out. You hear me?"

"And she got some big-ass feet." Cam chimed in.

"Geuneun geugeos-eul sijaghaessda. (He started it.)" Aoki shot back in Korean.

"Geuga dalieseo ttwieo naelindamyeon neodo geuleohge halgeoya? (If he jumped off a bridge would you do it too?)"

"Uh ah, ya'll ain't gon' start that shit. Speak English or I'm shooting everybody!" Cam waved the gun around.

"Ani, geuneunhaji anh-assda. Geulaessji. (No, he didn't. You did.)" Gray disregarded his command. "Neo munjega mwoya, jeolm-eun agassi? (What is your problem, young lady?)"

"Naneun geuui beoteuwa eoniga eongdeong-ileulbogo sipji anh-a. (I don't like his Big Bird, Bert and Ernie lookin' ass.)"

"Naneun neoege dasineun malhaji anh-eul geos-ida. (I'm not going to tell you again!)"

"Jib-e gago sip-eo. naneun uli appaga pil-yohae. Wae yeogi issni? Naneun geuleul joh-ahaji anh-a. (I wanna go home. I want my daddy. Why is he here? I don't like him.)"

"Waenyahamyeon nan geu nampyeon-iya. Geuge iyuya. (Cause I'm her husband, that's why." Cam replied in Korean to everyone's surprise.

"HUSBAND?" Aoki slammed her tiny hands down onto the table.

"Oh my god, Cam." Gray massaged her temples.

It felt like she was about to have an aneurism.

"I wasn't ready to tell them yet."

"Shit my bad, babe." He genuinely felt bad.

He hadn't meant to out their secret. It was an honest slip of the tongue.

"I knew you were our new dad." Press dug into her food.

"Mama, tell me you didn't marry him." Aoki pleaded with tears in her eyes.

"It was a spur of the moment thing. I was going to tell you girls after things had calmed down a bit." Gray reasoned, feeling like a horrible mother.

"How could you do this? What about daddy? You were supposed to marry him."

"Aoki, you saw what your dad did to me. That wasn't okay. A man is never supposed to put his hands on a woman. I've told you that. I couldn't marry him or stay with him after what he did."

"But what about us? What about what we want, or did you not think about that? Maybe I don't wanna live here. I wanna go home." Salty tears dropped like atom bombs from Aoki's stormy blue eyes.

"This is our new home, baby."

"This ain't my fuckin' home!" Aoki shot up from her seat.

Her entire body was shaking; she was so distraught. She held onto the edge of the table in hopes that her violent shaking wouldn't cause her to fall. Her blue eyes were so thick with tears that she could barely see.

"Aoki, I understand that you're upset but—"

"No! I don't wanna hear what you have to say! I wanna go home! I want my daddy! I don't wanna stay here with you and you can't make me!" She raced out of the dining room and into her bedroom.

The force of her slamming the door rattled the artwork on the walls.

"Now I feel bad. I can't even have my nieces fuck her up no more." Cam stared out into space.

"I'll be back. Let me go check on her." Gray got up from the table and walked into Aoki's room.

"Get out my room!"

Gray took two big steps and grabbed Aoki by the arm. Her grip was so tight that the blood circulation in Aoki's arm slowed. Using the back of her hand, Gray popped her dead in the mouth twice. The hit was so hard it caused Aoki's teeth to clank together.

"I don't know what the hell has gotten into you, but you have lost your damn mind. You don't run shit around here. This is my house. You ain't got no room. You have a space I let you reside in. All this shit can be taken away. Yo' ass will be sleeping on the floor if you keep fuckin' wit' me. You may go to a school wit' a bunch of white kids but you ain't white. I will tear yo' spoiled, bratty-ass up. Do you hear me?" Gray forcefully shook her.

"Yes." Aoki cried.

"Yes what?"

"Yes ma'am." She began to wail.

"Now, what is wrong wit' you? You have been showing your ass for months now. Is somebody at school bothering you? Ain't nobody touched you sexually have they?"

"No." Aoki sat down on her bed with her head down.

"Well, what is it 'cause you haven't been yourself lately." Gray sat beside her and brushed her hair back.

A stream of tears poured from Aoki's eyes, causing Gray's heart to constrict.

"It's everything." Her chest heaved up and down. "You and daddy broke up. I was scared when he hit you then you moved us here. I miss my old room and I don't like Cam. How could you marry him, mom? I know what dad did was wrong, but we were supposed to be a family."

"I understand you're upset but you can't go around acting like that. You can't curse, and you can't disrespect your elders. I didn't raise you to be disobedient and disrespectful."

"I know." Aoki hiccupped.

"Listen to me." Gray raised her chin. "I know this is a lot, but mama is going to figure everything out. Just know that I love you."

"I know you love me but why don't you love daddy anymore?"

"Daddy hasn't been very nice to me, so mommy had to make mommy happy by putting herself first. No matter how much you love a person, you can't let them treat you bad."

"So, you do still love daddy?" Aoki asked hopeful.

"I'll always love daddy 'cause he gave me you and Press." Gray placed a soft kiss on her forehead. "I just can't be with him anymore. I love Cam. He's who I want to be with."

"Well, I don't want him around. I don't like him, and I never will." Aoki pushed her mother's hand away and laid down in the bed with her back facing her.

Gray's bottom lip quivered. Her eyes became glacier blue under the gleam of water. A sadness like no other flowed through her veins and numbed her mind. It poisoned her spirit, killing any emotion she'd ever endured. It was as if a black mist settled upon her soul and refused to shift.

Seeing her first born child in such distress made her feel like she was failing as a mother. Aoki was too young to understand that love sometimes made you act crazy and that you'd find yourself doing things you never thought you would. Even she didn't know why she'd married Cam. Outside of him making her feel special, being fine, laying down the pipe and sparking a flame inside her chest, she had no good reason. None of the ones she'd listed warranted marriage. What was Gray to do?

Everything in her life had changed, so of course, it changed for her kids as well. They'd gone through a major transition. Their whole life had been turned upside down. They'd gone from a four-family household, to seeing their father physically abuse their mother, to moving into a new home and finding out their mom had run-off and gotten married. She was mentally scarred, so she knew they had to be as well.

This was supposed to be the best time of her life. She was a newlywed, but she couldn't even enjoy it. Everything in her life was out of place. She needed a minute to get things back on track but there seemed to be no time. Life just kept pushing on and she had to struggle to keep up.

Gray had no idea how she was going to manage motherhood and being Cam's wife. Both demanded so much of her time and attention. In all honesty she was afraid. Things between her and Cam had progressed so fast. There was so much she didn't know about him, like the fact that he knew Korean. How she was going to make this marriage work was beyond her understanding. Cam was irrational, commanding, immature, brooding and maddening. Press took to him instantly, but Aoki refused to give him a chance. The question now became how could she stay with a man her daughter didn't like? What kind of mother would she be if she chose a man over her kid?

Knock, Knock

Gray looked up and found Cam at the door.

"C'mere."

Gray looked back at Aoki who was curled up in the fetal position. She wanted to stay with her child, but it was obvious Aoki didn't want anything to do with her at the moment. Maybe it was best she give her space until she could figure out how to please her daughter, her man and herself. Closing the door behind her, Gray walked into Cam's awaiting arms. He pulled her close and gently rubbed her back. The side of her face rested against his firm chest. Despite the hollowness in the pit of her stomach, butterflies fluttered. Notes of violet leaf, jasmine sambac, black leather, cardamom, patchouli and white moss from his Tom Ford Ombre Leather cologne wafted up her nose, easing the tension in her limbs. Gray sank into the warmth that his muscles provided, thankful for the simple gesture of a hug. No matter what happened, Cam was always there to comfort her when she was in need. She would never be able to find a better man than him. She felt foolish for doubting their connection. His touch made the crisis she was in feel less bleak. In that moment, his arms squeezed tighter and Gray's breathing slowed. This was what real love felt like. There was nothing fake about what she and Cam shared.

He'd caught her at the right time and resuscitated her heart. His love was like CPR, it brought her back to life. She was at the edge, ready to end it all but he came along and made her feel like life was worth living. Sometimes, she hated how good he made her feel 'cause she was sure a day would come when he'd mishandle her heart.

"Stop crying, ma. Everything gon' be okay." He assured.

"How you know?"

"Cause I said so." He held her tighter and rubbed her back.

"Promise?"

"Have I ever let you down?" Cam kissed the top of her head.

"No."

"A'ight then. We got time. We gon' figure this shit out."

"But Aoki hates you." She continued to cry.

"Li'l mama whole world been rocked. I wouldn't like me either. She'll come around eventually. If not, I'ma shoot her," he joked.

She didn't want to laugh but a soft giggle escaped Gray's lips.

"You stupid."

"I'm for real. Shorty gon' like me one way or another."

"Hold up." Gray lifted her head and gazed up at him. "How the hell you know Korean?"

"I was stationed there for a year." Cam replied nonchalantly.

"You were in the army?"

"Yeah."

"How long?"

"Six years."

"When were you gon' tell me that?"

"When it was necessary." He shrugged.

"What else don't I know about you?"

Cam looked down at Gray. There were so many questions in her innocent eyes. She was so sweet. He didn't wanna ruin her with all his shit. Thankfully, the doorbell ringing saved him from having to answer. His pizza had arrived. Gray waited for his reply but instead he took her hand and led her to the front of the house. Gray wasn't ready for the demons he harbored. If she knew a sliver of what he had to deal with, she'd run for the hills.

"Thought I was up in my room, crying myself to sleep. I was with a better you. While you were busy playin' me, I was playin' you."- H.E.R., "2"

#4

In a perfect world Gunz would be Gray's man and she'd be his girl. Once upon a time, he was supposed to be her knight in shining armor, but in reality, he was the evil prince that made her life a miserable hell. The constant cheating, lies and disrespect destroyed them before they even began. She'd never truly forgiven him for his past transgressions. Gray always walked around on pins and needles. She stayed waiting for the other shoe to drop. It always did. No matter how much she tried to have faith in Gunz, he always let her down. Maybe she'd put too much pressure on him. He was never the kind of man you brought home to meet your mom and dad. He ran the streets, living life, getting cash and spending it fast. No day in his world was promised, so he lived life doing what pleased him in the moment, regardless of how it made anyone else feel.

And no, Gray hadn't been a perfect angel. She had her faults too. She put her career before her man. She refused to ever be broke and hungry again, so she worked herself to the bone to mask the fear of being poor. There were plenty of nights that Gunz begged her to come home, and instead, she stayed at the office. After the Devin fiasco, she put her heart on reserve only giving him bits and pieces of it at a time. So now after ten years and two children together here they were officially broken up. For Gray, there was no turning back. It was over. She'd moved on. Any love she had left for Gunz evaporated into thin air the second he hit her. She'd never look at him the same way again. If it wasn't for their kids she'd hate him. Because of them she couldn't afford to. That's why after a week and a half of radio silence, she sat alone at The Tavern in Central West End awaiting his arrival.

It was a quaint, sophisticated restaurant with a vegetarian and gluten free menu. Gunz and the head chef had opened it a year before. Gray used to order lunch from the restaurant often but now she felt awkward being in his establishment. The employees who knew her saw her ring and immediately thought she and Gunz had gotten married. When she revealed that he, in fact, wasn't her husband, things got hella weird. Gray couldn't wait to leave.

Cam would have a fit if he knew she was there. She thought about filling him in on her meeting with Gunz but at the last minute decided to keep it to herself. There was too much bad blood between the two men. Cam would want to come along and that would only result in another altercation. She did not want another battle royal to ensue. Gray refused to let the shit go down. Besides, dealing with Gunz and his fucked-up attitude was enough. She didn't have the strength or patience to deal with Cam going ballistic too. He went from mellow to a fit of rage in 1.1 seconds. Things were just starting to settle down. Gray refused to kick up any mess, so she'd keep her meet-up with Gunz to herself. That was if he showed up.

A half an hour had gone by and he still hadn't arrived. Gray would've been left but he'd text and said he'd be pulling up soon. Gray looked out the window. Rain bore down from the sky, pounding onto the rooftop of the restaurant. It was a gloomy day. The sky reflected hues of silver and grey. Gray loved the rain. The comforting hum as rain plunged to the ground, the random flashes of lightning and loud thunderous claps of thunder; she loved it all. Thank god, she'd worn the neon yellow, hooded, faux fur, black, Gucci, sweatshirt, black zippered leggings and pointed-toe botties. The warm outfit shielded her from the harsh weather.

Fifteen minutes later in walked Gunz looking like the abominable snowman. It wasn't even that cold outside. Gray swiftly realized that he was so covered up because he was trying to hide his face. He donned a black leather baseball cap low over his eyes, black Ray Ban shades, a twill scarf, black puffy Polo coat, gloves, black jeans and black Timbs. The only part of his body that was visible was his bandaged nose. The scarf he wore was draped around his face and neck. A devilish grin graced the corners of Gray's lip. It was obvious that his face was still messed up from Cam's beating.

"That's what his ass get." She whispered under her breath.

After speaking to his staff, Gunz made his way over to their table which was in the back. Gray crossed her legs perturbed that he was late. Gunz was trying to assert his dominance over her but today it wasn't going to work. Refusing to acknowledge her presence, he sat down and removed his gloves and scarf. Gray's pupils dilated at the sight of him. The swelling from her black eye had gone down. There was still some discoloration underneath that she covered with makeup and cuts and scrapes on her body but Gunz was still a battered mess. His cheeks were swollen like a chipmunk, due to his broken nose, and his bottom lip was still split in half.

Gray sat there waiting on him to speak. When she realized he wasn't going to, she inhaled deep and rolled her eyes so hard she thought they were going to fall out. The nerve of him to show up forty-five minutes late and then not speak. He ought to have been happy she'd even agreed to meeting him. His mere presence made her sick to her stomach. Gray couldn't believe that, at one point in time, she was head-over-heels in love with this clown.

Gunz made himself comfortable. Gray's beauty filled the room. Damn, he missed her. The mean expression on her face revealed that she didn't feel the same. Gunz didn't understand this new Gray. Things between them was all good just a year ago. Now, she had a new man and was acting hella brand-new. She'd turned into a straight coldhearted savage. Had he done this to her or had time changed her?

"You asked me here to talk about the kids so talk." She quipped with an attitude.

"When are you coming home?"

"What?" Gray's mouth formed into a frown.

"I let you and that nigga get y'all shit off—"

"Boy please." Gray waved him off. "You need to be sayin' thank you. If it wasn't for me yo' ass would be dead right now."

"I'm done going back-and-forth wit' you. I want you and the girls home today."

"What about I'm married don't you understand?"

"You don't love that nigga for real. You just did that shit to get back at me and it worked. I can't let you be with nobody else. It's me and you or nothin'—"

"Excuse me?" Gray scoffed.

"I fucked up. I get it now, but you need to come home, Gray. A nigga been sick without you. I can't eat, I can't sleep. I ain't even been able to go back to the crib 'cause I know y'all ain't there. C'mon ma, we got too many years invested together to just end everything over a misunderstanding."

"A misunderstanding? Having a baby with another woman and beating my ass 'cause I don't wanna be with you anymore isn't a fuckin' misunderstanding, you fuckin' sociopath."

"Look." Gunz placed his well-defined arms on the table and leaned forward. "We can figure this shit out. Love just don't go away overnight. I know you still have feelings for me."

"You are so fuckin' delusional. Gunz, I stopped loving you a long time ago. The only reason I stuck around is because I didn't want Aoki and Press to grow up in a home without their father like I did but fuck that shit. I'll be damned if I spend another second of my good years on a lyin', cheatin', dick slangin', piece-of-shit like you."

Gray's malicious words rocked Gunz's brain, leaving it moving in foreign ways; ways he'd never been accustomed to. Usually, he'd be able to tear down her walls with a few sweet words but this time she wasn't budging. Her defiance was getting on his nerves. He wasn't used to it. His guilty conscious was telling him to leave her be. Gray deserved to be happy. He'd destroyed pieces of her that she'd never be able to heal. Maybe with Cam was where she needed to be. She seemed happier, but like always, the selfish part of him won out. Gunz couldn't fathom another nigga putting a smile on her face, stroking her middle or being around his kids. The thought alone was like a thousand tiny paper cuts to his heart. He was determined to get Gray back. Not having her under his thumb was something he'd never be able to adjust to or comprehend. Gunz was willing to do anything necessary to get her back whether it be begging, pleading, lying or conjuring up some fake tears. Like the ain't shit nigga he was, he was going to say whatever she needed to hear to get her ass back home.

"Well, guess what? I still love you. I always will. I ain't gon' ever stop. You're my heart. I can't see me living without you. Losing you ain't an option."

"You lost me the second you put your dick in another bitch, and the bitch after, and the bitch after that, and the bitch after that." Gray repeated sarcastically.

"And I'm sorry for that. I was being a fuck nigga. I should've focused on you and the girls, but a nigga got caught up in some shit I shouldn't have. But I see where I went wrong. I want you Gray. No, fuck that I need you. You're my family. Me, you, Press and Aoki belong together. I don't want our kids to be punished for the mistakes I've made."

All Gray could do was shake her head and roll her eyes. Gunz was so full of shit. He was talking all this sweet shit, but as soon as he couldn't get his way, the real Gunz would appear.

"Since we've been here, you haven't apologized once for what you did to me. Do you even care? Do you feel even an ounce of remorse? Better yet, do you give a fuck about any of the foul shit you've done? You cheated on me so many times I can't even keep count. You made me get my tubes tied 'cause you said you didn't want to have any more kids. Then you turn around and get another girl pregnant. And if it couldn't get any worse, you put your hands on me. Me?" Gray's lips quivered.

You bet not cry in front of this nigga, she mentally scolded herself. She hated herself for getting emotional but for half her adult life she'd loved him with everything she had to give. It hurt like hell that in the end the same love wasn't reciprocated.

"The woman that stood by you when you had no one. I was the one that held you at night when you woke up feeling like you were about to die. I was the one by your side when Bishop was murdered. I was the one that held your hand and supported you when you opened your restaurants. I was the one that gave you not one but two beautiful little girls that love and adore you despite your flaws. I was the one that gave you the family you never had. Me." She pointed at her chest.

Gunz wanted to curl up into a ball and die. He never thought the day would come but Gray was really done with him. The words of regret she spewed at him ate at his core. Everything she said was true. She'd gone above and beyond to prove her love to him and what did he do? Fuck her over every chance he got. Gunz knew he was rotten to the core. He could barely stand to look at himself in the mirror. He'd allowed a broken childhood to turn him into a man that even he couldn't stomach. The pain he never truly dealt with was used to make others feel like shit. Hurt people, hurt people. Gunz was the poster child of self-hate. He made it his mission to make everyone around him feel miserable but the pain he'd caused Gray would haunt him for the rest of his days.

"You saw what Aoki's father did to me." Gray tried to steady her breathing. "Then you turn around and assault me the same way he did. What happened to you 'cause the nigga sitting before me isn't the same man I fell in love with all those years ago. Or maybe you are. Maybe I was too young and naive to see the real you. Maybe I made you out to be the man I always hoped you'd be in my head, but in reality, all you do is hurt people. You walk around living life like the shit you do doesn't matter. And maybe it doesn't matter to you, but it matters to me. I deserve better than you—"

"Gray, I love you." He cut her off unsure of what else to say.

Usually, by now, she would've caved in, but Gray was stronger. She wasn't the same weak girl that fell for anything he said. Gunz was truly mind blown.

"I wasn't in my right head when I did what I did to you."

"You can't even say it, can you?" She mocked him in disbelief.

"No! I don't wanna think about that shit. I wasn't in my right mind and you know it. I wouldn't have ever done that shit if you wouldn't have been actin' all crazy."

"So, it's my fault you beat my ass?"

"I was scared, and you wouldn't listen. Then you come tellin' me that you married that nigga. What the fuck was I supposed to do?"

"Not put your hands on me."

"You're right. I fucked up and I gotta live with that shit for the rest of my life. Just please . . . give me another chance to make this right so we can be a family again."

"And where does your baby fit into this equation?" She cocked her head to the side.

"That's the thing." He swallowed the lump in his throat. "I was thinkin' we could talk Tia into letting us raise him."

He ain't just say that, Gray thought to herself.

"Nigga, are you sleepy? Are you drinkin' bleach? You must be high off Clorox if you think I'm gon' raise yo' side baby!" She screeched, causing the other patrons to look their way.

"Yo, stop yellin'." Gunz placed his hand on top of hers to calm her down.

"Don't touch me!" She swatted his hand away. "You are never to touch me again! Do you understand me?" She pointed her finger in his face.

Gray was so upset she was practically shaking. The fact that he thought it was okay to touch her after what he'd done infuriated her.

"Cool." Gunz placed his hand up in mock surrender. "I won't touch you. My bad."

Gray eased back into her seat and took a deep breath. Once she calmed down, Gunz continued.

"Listen, I know the shit sound crazy, but you always wanted another baby, especially a son. This could be our way of having one since you know . . . you can't have no more kids."

"And whose fault is that?" Gray shot furiously.

"Mine. All this shit is my fault. I fucked up everything. That's why I'm trying to fix it. Let me fix it for you. Let's raise the baby together."

"You are certifiably insane. Like dead-ass. Do you hear yourself right now? I don't wanna raise that ugly-ass, Benjamin Button in the face, illegitimate-ass baby."

"Yo, chill—"

"No nigga you chill! I don't like you. I don't even wanna be in the same room as you. What makes you think I wanna raise a child with you, let alone be back with you? The sight of your face makes me wanna vomit. You make my insides curl. If it's not about the girls, I don't have shit to say to you."

~ 93 ~

Butt hurt behind her words the real Gunz began to emerge.

"You know what, Gray? I didn't realize until this moment that you had me fucked up."

"Nah, nigga, you got the game fucked up. You thought while you were out runnin' the streets with that baby bitch that I was at home cryin' and worrying over you but oh no homeboy. That was the old Gray. You had no clue that I'd changed. I started doing me and in came Cam. I could've kept screaming at you to change, but before I knew it, I was too busy screaming his name. You ain't give a fuck about me so I stopped giving a fuck about you. So, let me break it down to you how this shit gon' go so I can get back to my husband. Don't contact me unless it's about the kids. I don't wanna hear from you. I don't wanna breathe the same air as you. I don't wanna smell you. I don't wanna see you. I don't fuck wit' you. I don't like you. We will be nothin' but co-parents for the rest of our lives. Got that, Ike?"

Pissed that she had the nerve to talk to him like he wasn't shit; the demonic side of Gunz he'd tried to hide in order to get her back came out in full force. His ego wouldn't allow him to let her crush him. He'd tried being the nice guy. He'd tried buying her love, dicking her down, threatening her life, hell, he'd even beat her, and she still stuck to her guns. Gray wasn't coming back to him. He'd lost her for good this time. Unable to articulate that, the center of his chest felt like it was caving in. Gunz did what he always did; lashed out.

"Gray, shut the fuck up. You talkin' all that shit like I won't take my kids from you and put one in that nigga's dome. Don't let that nigga gas you up into thinkin' I won't have you and him touched. Let me find out you got my girls around that punk-ass nigga, it's gon' be some shit. I would hate to have to take Aoki and Press away from you."

"Bitch, you wouldn't take them to school let alone take them from me. Shut up, Gunz. Ain't no judge in America gon' grant yo' criminal ass custody of my kids. Let's not forget, playboy, I know everything. Now put that in your pipe and smoke it."

"A'ight, keep fuckin' around. I ain't playin' wit' you, Gray. You heard what I said. Keep that nigga away from kids."

"Suck my dick. You ain't gon' do shit. This why I don't fuck wit' you now. Like I said, nigga, I ain't coming back. I ain't raising no baby that was created out of prostitution."

"Prostitution?" He drew his head back.

"Yeah, nigga, prostitution. You know that pussy came wit' a price." She got up to leave. "For your sake, you betta hope not a life sentence."

"Fuck you, Gray."

"In your dreams, nigga. You can come get the girls this weekend and every weekend moving forward. We'll rotate holidays. Other than that, you can kiss my ass wit' your tongue out, dickhead." She picked up her vintage, red, leather Gucci bag.

"You doing all that heeing and hawing but I give it thirty days before that nigga up and leave yo' dumb-ass for LaLa." Gunz hit her where he knew it would hurt.

As if a bullet had punctured her lungs, Gray stopped breathing. Gunz always knew how to play on her worst fears and insecurities. He always knew how to make her doubt herself and her decisions. If Cam ever cheated on her with LaLa, she'd be devastated. It would confirm that maybe there was something wrong with her that caused the men in her life to cheat. By the shocked expression on her face, Gunz could tell his words had rattled her. Victorious, he chuckled.

"You thought 'cause y'all was married that he ain't fuckin her? Oh, your dumber wit' him than you were wit' me. He a man, sweetheart. Men have needs. Needs that only women like LaLa can provide."

"What the fuck is that supposed to mean?" She stood over him.

"You a nice lookin' girl, Gray, but let's be honest. You outta shape. You let yo 'self go. Bitches with bodies like LaLa is what's in now. That's what niggas want. Why you think I started fuckin' with Tia? I don't wanna be wit' no bitch that ain't got no neck."

Unconsciously, Gray placed her hand on her neck and caressed it feeling dizzy. Gunz cut her deep before, but this stab wound to her gut was fatal. She would've preferred that he punched her in the face again, than say the shit he'd said. Gunz had always said her weight wasn't a problem. He said he liked the soft, cushiness of her stomach and thighs. Now he was throwing the shit up in her face to make her feel bad? Gray had never thought it before, but she was sure now she'd been sleeping with the devil.

"Rub on that shit all you want. It ain't gon' make it magically appear. That shit is gone so good luck keepin' that nigga, sweetheart. He gon' fuck you over, and when he do, don't come runnin' back to me cause I ain't gon' take yo' big ass back." Gunz confidently took a sip of his water.

The look of pleasure that he gained from her misery made Gray nauseous. He got off on making her miserable.

She knew, at that point, she only had two options: leave in the back of a police car or walk out with her dignity. Mustering up the little confidence she had, Gray bent down and whispered in his ear, "Let's be clear. If he did cheat on me, I will be onto the next nigga before I would ever come back to you."

With her head held high and her shoulders back, Gray sashayed out of the restaurant like the bad bitch she was. She believed in her husband and their union. She wouldn't allow Gunz to break her down. He couldn't have the same hold on her like he did before. Placing the hood of her faux fur over her head, she hit the key fob on her Range Rover and got inside. The pain she felt was like a spider web, complicated, defined and strong. In time the feeling would fade away, but in that space and time, the bliss she once harbored was gone. Gray placed her head on the steering wheel and closed her eyes. Tears stung her irises, but she refused to grieve over Gunz or their sham of a relationship. For he'd took whatever love he had for her and locked it back inside the cage he called a heart. Lifting her head, she gazed out the front windshield. Her eyes were blurry with tears, but eventually, the view came into focus.

Gunz could talk about her shape all he wanted. It didn't negate the fact that he was the same nigga begging for her fat-ass to return. He was full of shit. He knew Gray's worth just as much as she did. He knew she was stunningly beautiful on the inside and out. He would never be able to find another woman that would love him like she did. Gathering her emotions, she forced herself to push past the pain. She hadn't even put her purse down on the passenger seat before her cell phone began to ring. *When I'm with somebody all I think about is you. When I'm all alone that's all I want to do.* Immediately, Gray felt guilty. Even though she'd done nothing wrong it felt like she'd cheated. She didn't want to go into her marriage keeping secrets from her husband, but in this case, it was for the best. Gathering her emotions, she picked up the phone and played it cool.

"Hey babe."

"Where you at?" Cam's deep voice boomed.

"Umm . . ." She tried to think quick on her feet. "Leaving Heidi's house," she lied.

"What y'all was gettin' into?"

"Nothin, just catching up. I haven't seen her or my godson in a minute. I'm on my way to the grocery store and then to pick up the girls."

"A'ight." He said coolly.

"What time you gon' be home?"

"You mean your crib." Cam checked her.

"We've been over this. My crib is your crib. We're married, remember?"

"Nah, shawty, that's your place. I'm just visiting."

"Whatever, Cam." Gray huffed.

They'd been having an ongoing argument about their living situation. Cam was already tired of living out of a bag. He understood that he'd married a woman with kids, but he was a man at the end of the day, a man that wanted to share a space with his wife he'd purchased. Gray didn't feel it would be appropriate for them to move in together yet. They needed to learn more about each other before they took such a big step. When she'd married him, she hadn't put her girls' needs first. It was detrimental that she took their feelings into account this time around. Her desires would have to be put on the back burner. Aoki was still having a hard time adjusting to their new normal. Another change would probably send her over the edge.

"When will you be home?" She asked again.

"It'll be a minute. I'm taking care of some business right now."

"Okay, I'll see you in a bit."

"A'ight."

"Love you."

"Yep." He responded, ending the call.

Cam was still uncomfortable with saying the words I love you back. Hours later, Gray sat at the dining room table alone sipping a glass of Merlot. The clock on the wall read 11:00 p.m. She'd spoken to Cam twice since earlier that day. Each time he said he'd be home in a while, but he still hadn't arrived. Gray was beyond upset. He had no idea, but she'd planned a whole romantic evening just for the two of them. The lights were dimmed low. Five strategically placed candlesticks lit up the room. A fresh floral arrangement of pink peony flowers sat in the center of the table, surrounded by his favorite food. She'd cooked sweet potatoes, macaroni and cheese, greens, fried chicken, cornbread and a homemade strawberry cheesecake. On her body was a sexy black number by Agent Provocateur. It was a panty and bra set. Gray never felt sexier. The bra plunged down the center and had black PVC bindings that swept up and across her cleavage for an enticing cutaway effect. The panties were a sheer, black tulle thong with two high straps that crossed at the front and swept up around the waist to meet the thong in the back. So the girls wouldn't catch her practically naked, she wore a black silk robe to cover her lingerie.

As the clock ticked on, the angrier Gray became. The heat from the burning candlesticks were making her hot. She'd began to sweat in places she shouldn't, and the food had turned cold like her heart. Gray honestly didn't know how much more she could take. She was trying to remain optimistic but the men in her life were taking her through it. Her body had morphed into a collage of the shattered pieces of who she once was. Gunz had already drained her like a vampire, giving himself a youthful presence at her expense. Now Cam was shitting on what little love she had left to give, making her bitter. It didn't help that Gunz had planted the seed of him cheating. The thought had been in the back of her head all day, making her sick. She was a nervous wreck so much that she started following LaLa under a dummy account that she'd created on Instagram. She needed to know for sure that there was nothing going on between them. Nursing a glass of wine and an aching heart, she prayed to god that her husband wasn't up to no good. It made no sense that she had no idea where Cam was or why it was taking him so long to come home. Gray's entire body was filled with tears, but she refused to let a single tear fall. She was sick and tired of crying. At this point there was no point in feeling sad. She was used to disappointment. If anything, she felt stupid for thinking Cam would be different. A wedding band wasn't going to make a man behave. If she'd learned anything from Gunz, it was that there was no point sweating a nigga. Blowing up his phone with questions of where he was or when he was coming home wouldn't make him move any faster. Niggas like Cam moved on their own time and accord. She'd called him twice, that was enough. No, Gray was going to stich up her broken heart, put up her food, blow out the candles and take her ass to bed. Her days of running in behind a nigga were over.

"We fight then we break up. Then we fuck till we make up."- Phora, "Everybody Knows"

#5

Rolling smoking something strong
Pop a molly got me bussin'
Nigga jugging and finessing
Nigga started out with nothing
'Member I was on the Ave
Nigga used to hide a jab in my tube socks
Now it's bitches in the inner tube
Skinny dipping in the swimming pool
Same bitches wasn't fucking with you
Wanna fuck a nigga see an interview
Get to bussin', now I'm on to something
Bussin' niggas, now I'm on to something
Started out with a 28
28 turned to 56
56 turned into a 112
Poppin' wheelies, nigga fuck 12

The musical sound of Joey Purp's banger *Karl Malone* played loudly throughout the house as Gray walked inside and placed her keys down. She could hear the music all the way outside. It was apparent Cam was awake. When she'd left to take the girls to school he was still knocked out asleep. It took everything in her not to take the alarm clock and knock him upside the head with it. By the time she'd closed her eyes the night before, he still hadn't made it home. She had no idea what time he came in. Usually, when he got in bed he'd wrap her up in his arms, but Cam didn't touch her. When she woke up she found him on the other side of the bed. He'd slept as far away from her as he could. That shit tore up her heart. She'd gotten used to waking up in his warm arms. Without him finding rest was nearly impossible. All night she'd tossed and turned. She needed his comfort as much as she needed his love.

Gray didn't know what the hell his problem was. He was the one that had lied to her. She was the one that stupidly waited up for him to come home, only to be left alone in expensive lingerie that resembled dental floss. The fact that he thought it was cool to come in the house whenever he felt like it angered her to no end. If this marriage between them was going to work, she and Cam were going to have to get some things straight. One of them was she was too damn old to be playing games with anybody's son.

Determined to put him in check, she strutted down the hall to their bedroom. Fully prepared to go off, she approached the doorway of the room only to be stopped dead in her tracks. Cam stood with a freshly lit blunt hanging from his lips in nothing but a gold rope chain with a C pendant, cross chain, Nike basketball shorts and matching socks. He bobbed his head to the music as he folded his clothes. A cloud of smoke cascaded over his head. His face was stern as he rapped along to the lyrics.

> *I got dope, blow, smoke, nigga whatchu want?*
> *I got coke, blow, I got blow, nigga whatchu want?*
> *I got molly man, I got xans, I got sassafras*
> *I got trippy man, I got tabs, I got acid tab*
> *I got dope, blow, I got snow, nigga whatchu want?*

Gray was supposed to be going off, but she was stuck. It made no sense that every time she laid eyes on him he took her breath away. His low haircut, diamond brown eyes and permanent scowl always made the seat of her panties wet. She'd concluded that God was in a splendid mood the day he created the man she called her husband. The first thing she always noticed about him was his size. Cam was extremely tall and muscular but not in a body builder kind of way. His physique was more athletic. His well-developed body cast a shadow that nearly filled the room. His corded muscles rippled each time he moved his arms. The six pack of muscles in his stomach could be used to wash the clothes he stacked one on top of the other. The man was a virtual image of ancient African fantasy, a staggering figure of immense strength.

Cam was already a gorgeous specimen. The collage of tattoos all over his neck, chest, back and arms only added to his sex appeal. Gray still hadn't mapped out all his ink. The year he was born was inked into his Adam's apple. A mural of roses, his mother's name, a broken heart, flaming basketball, praying hands, a scripture, Jesus dying on the cross and names of his homies and army soldiers who'd passed all covered his chest. Each of his arms had a sleeve of tattoos. On one arm was a portrait of the city skyline, a burning basketball hoop, a lion's head, compass and more. His right arm had a pocket watch, ironically more roses, a very scary looking smoked out skull and a grim reaper. His tats and thugged-out demeanor turned Gray onto the fullest but the sprinkle of freckles on his nose and cheeks that matched hers is what she loved the most about him. It should've been illegal for a man to be so fine. As she watched him fold his clothes, she noticed his overnight bag on the bed and realized he was packing his things to leave. Ignoring the wetness in her panties, she turned the volume down on the sound system. Cam was so wrapped up in his own thoughts that he didn't even notice she'd returned home.

"Where you going?" She leaned against the doorframe.

"To the crib." Cam continued packing his bag.

"What to get some more clothes?"

"No to stay."

"You was just gon' leave and not say nothin'?" Gray's heart began to race.

"You would've figured it out eventually."

Caught off guard by his rude behavior, Gray paused and gathered herself. Her temperature had begun to rise. She didn't know what his problem was, but he had another thing coming if he thought he was going to talk to her any kind of way. Just as she was about to go off Cam's phone started to ring. She and he both looked down at his phone. Gray's upper lip rapidly curled. It was LaLa.

"Answer the phone. Yo' li'l girlfriend callin'." She quipped with an attitude.

"You love sayin' stupid shit."

"What the fuck is she doing callin' you at eight something in the morning?"

"Fuck if I know." He sent her call to voicemail.

Gray wanted to push the subject, but she had bigger fish to fry with her husband.

"So, let me get this straight. You call yo' self being mad and leaving? Even though you played me last night and didn't come home till god knows when. Matter of fact, what time did you get home last night?"

"This ain't home. This your crib, ma?"

"What the fuck ever, Cam." She waved him off. "What time did you get here?"

"Three something." He threw his clean socks and drawgz in the bag without giving her any eye contact.

"And that's okay to you?" She glared.

"Why wouldn't it be?"

Gray drew her head back, surprised.

"Umm, I don't know. I thought you were a married man. Married men don't come in the house at all times of the night, but I mean if you wanna be single, we can make that a reality."

"Is that a threat?" He glared at her with an aroused and possessive look in his eyes.

"No, it's a promise."

"You got a lot of nerve, Gray." Cam scoffed, putting his blunt in the ashtray.

"No, nigga, you got a lot of nerve." She pushed off the doorframe and pointed her finger in his face. "You come in here on some bipolar shit talking about you about to leave. What I'm supposed to cry? I'm supposed to beg you to stay? I'm supposed to get down on my knees? I think not. There go the door. Bye, if you wanna go."

"Hold the fuck up. Who you talkin' to? I don't need you to beg me for shit 'cause that ain't gon' stop me from leaving. I'm still gon' do what the fuck I wanna do. You better watch yo' fuckin' mouth, Gray. I ain't that nigga you used to fuck wit'. I ain't gon' go back-and-forth wit' you. I will leave yo' ass where you stand."

"Whatever, Cam. One minute you mad cause we don't live together, the next you throw a fuckin' tantrum and pack your shit to leave. I ain't did nothin' to you. If this how it's gon' be to be married to you then you can take that shit back to LaLa and be her husband. She'll deal wit' your bullshit. I won't. I don't have time for that shit. I just got done putting up wit' a nigga that played games, didn't wanna come home and treated me like shit. I'm not doing that with you or nobody else for that matter. If you got a problem say that shit instead of acting like a fuckin' asshole. I shouldn't even be going through this wit' you. Weren't you the same nigga tellin' me not to let a muthafucka knock me off my square but here you are the one kicking me in the back."

Gray didn't want to be yellin', cursing and arguing with Cam three and a half weeks into their marriage. This wasn't who she was. She wanted to spend every second of the day loving on him not beefing with him, but she was tired of people talking to her crazy. After Gray finished talking shit, Cam hung his head and chuckled. Gray really thought she'd done something with her li'l wack-ass speech. The only thing she'd accomplished was making him even madder.

"Now I see what Gunz was talkin' about. You always wanna play the victim when you be dead fuckin' wrong."

"Excuse me?" She folded her arms across her chest.

"You heard me. How was lunch yesterday?"

Gray's mind went blank. Her ice blue eyes stared back at him in horror. The palms of her hands instantly became a clammy wet mess. It was as if the impact of his question knocked every wisp of air from her lungs. She stood there struggling to inhale and exhale. She was caught. Like an idiot, she stood there unable to formulate words. *How the fuck does he know,* she thought. Cam's eyes desperately searched hers for answers but found none. Gray knew she had to say something. She racked her brain for something reasonable to say, but to her surprise, nothing came.

"You quiet now, huh? Cat got yo' tongue, nigga? What happened to all that mouth? Speak up, muthafucka." Cam ice-grilled her.

"You following me now stalker?" Was all she could come up with to say.

"I got too much shit on my plate to follow your dumb-ass around all day."

"Well, how you know where I was then?" She tilted her head to the right.

"Just know I got eyes on you."

"Like a fuckin' stalker. You are insane."

"Man, don't start that shit." Cam threw down a stack of shirts. "You knew I was fuckin' crazy when you started fuckin' met me. This ain't nothin' new."

"Okay, well, I ain't know you was like crazy-crazy." She shrugged.

"Stop tryin' to change the fuckin' subject. I thought you was at Heidi's house."

"I was."

"Lie again and I swear to god I'ma knock them freckles off your face." Cam charged towards her, backing her into a corner. "Now where were you?"

Although she was a li'l scared, Gray tried to play hard.

"It seems to me like you already know Sherlock Holmes. Fuck you askin' me for."

"So, you gon' sit up here and keep gettin' smart. You know what? Bye Gray." He walked away and resumed gathering his things.

Gray instantly began to panic. Cam couldn't leave her.

"You right." He nodded his head. "Maybe I should've married LaLa 'cause yo' lyin' ass ain't got no respect for me. Hell, you ain't even got no respect for yourself. How the fuck you gon' sneak and meet up with the same nigga that just two-pieced you to the dome, in front of your daughters, had you seeing stars and stripes and shit?"

"It's not what you think—"

"Fuck you mean it ain't what I think! Are you fuckin' retarded? Are you that fuckin' battered? What if that nigga would've tried to hurt you again? You just willingly walked your stupid-ass into danger! You ain't gon' get enough until that nigga put you in a body bag and I got no life insurance on you yet so I'ma be mad as fuck."

"Cam, you are overreacting—"

"Overreacting!" His rock-hard chest heaved up and down.

"See, this what I'm talkin' about. Will you calm down and let me explain?"

Cam took a deep breath and counted to ten. He didn't want to handle Gray like this, but she was testing his manhood. People just didn't go around out right lying and disrespecting him, yet here she was doing both. Gray had to learn that he wasn't the nigga to fuck with.

"Go head."

"I didn't tell you because I knew this was going to happen. I didn't want you to get upset and start going off on me. You have to realize that despite what's going on between me and Gunz, he is still Aoki and Press's father. It's fucked up what he did to me. I haven't forgot about that shit. I hate his fuckin' guts, but as parents, we still have to communicate. Yesterday, I met him to discuss our arrangement on when he'll be getting the girls. That's it. Nothing more, nothing less." She lied.

Gray made a conscious decision to omit the part where he begged her to take him back. If Cam knew that he'd surely end up on the five o'clock news for killing Gunz. The devastation Cam felt was overwhelming. His mind became a frozen wasteland. A gust of wind howled at his soul and wrapped icy branches around his heart so tight it almost stopped beating. He wanted to trust in what she was saying but the constant shifting of her eyes told him there was something missing from the story. Gray once again was lying to him.

"Keep it real, you still love that nigga."

A tsunami of emotions washed over Gray. His fear of her not loving him was mind boggling. Sometimes, she wondered if she loved him too much and too soon. Loving him had become her salvation. She loved him like he was the last of his kind. It was like they spoke the same language and no one else could. For once she didn't feel alone. When she was with Gunz she always felt like she was in a relationship by herself. It was as if she was in a windowless room with no way out and out of nowhere in walked Cam. He breathed life into her lungs. There was no way she could love another. Placing her hand on his cheek, she caressed his beard gently.

"How many times do I have to tell you that I love you and not him? What is it going to take for you to believe that?"

"You not being slick and chasing behind that nigga every time I turn my back."

"Once again, the only reason I met up with him was to talk about the girls." She wrapped her free arm around his neck.

"Yo' phone broke?" Cam scowled, looking down at her face.

"No." She replied confused.

"Exactly. That nigga could've talked to you over the phone. You ain't got no business meeting up with that nigga unless you tryin' to fuck." He pushed her back up against the wall. "You fuck that nigga, Gray? You let him have my pussy?" He brushed his lips against hers.

Dizzy with lust, Gray concentrated on the anger rising in her chest. His silly question had really offended her.

"You can honestly stand here and look me in my face and think that I had sex with that man?"

Cam didn't respond.

"You know you sound crazy. That don't even make sense and you know it. That's why you standing there lookin' like a statue."

"Nah, muthafucka's tellin' me you in your JLo fur and shit switching ya' ass. What you was tryin' to look good for that nigga?"

"Oh my god." She rolled her eyes. "No, I was tryin' to look good for myself. I had been walkin' around lookin' like a bum while my face healed. Now that I'm better, I wanted to feel pretty so I put some clothes on. Is that a crime?"

"Fuck yeah. You should've been lookin' ugly around that nigga. You shouldn't have even brushed your teeth." Cam gripped her ass.

"Now you're just being ridiculous. Move." She pushed him away.

"Answer the question, Gray." He yanked her back. "You give that nigga my shit?" He placed his hand between her legs and cupped the face of her pussy.

"Get the fuck off me askin' me that dumb shit." She pushed him again with-all her might.

This time she was successful with getting him off her. Pissed, she stormed out of the room and headed down the hallway. The fact that she wouldn't out right say she didn't fuck Gunz had Cam seeing red.

"You must've fucked him since yo' ass runnin'."

"No, I'm gettin' away from yo' stupid-ass."

"Yo' lyin' ass fucked him!"

"Fuck you, Cam!" She picked up a throw pillow and threw it at his head.

The pillow landed, hitting him in the eye. Cam really wanted to fuck her up now.

"I'm done! I can't do this shit anymore! Marrying you was a fuckin' mistake! I'm filing for divorce!" Gray turned and grabbed her keys to leave.

A volcano of anger erupted in Cam, causing his head to hurt. It was the second time in the last week and a half that she'd tried to leave him. Gray had life fucked up. No way did she think she'd get away with hitting him and threatening divorce. There was no way in hell he was letting that shit slide. The fear of losing the one thing in his life that gave him joy caused him to grip her hair and pull her back to him by her ponytail. The sting of her hair follicles being yanked went straight to the heartbeat in Gray's clit. She liked that rough shit. Cam's possessiveness should've scared her, considering what she'd just gone through, but she didn't fear him. She craved him. His brash, alpha male, behavior turned her on. With nowhere to go, Gray's back was pressed into his chest as he hooked his arm around her waist.

"Let me go!" She tried to fight him off to no avail.

His physical and mental hold was too strong.

"Shut the fuck up. You ain't going nowhere." Cam's hand was still wrapped around her ponytail as he yanked her head to the side. "You wanna a divorce, Gray?" He passionately kissed the exposed skin of her neck.

Silently, she cursed herself for relishing the feel of his lips. She needed to continue to put up a fight, but her body was betraying her. Cam's masculine scent instantly had her feeling primal and feminine. Naturally, she wanted to submit to him. He was her man. He always knew how to take control of her body. Softly, she sighed at the feel of his fingers massaging her pussy through her leggings. A pool of wetness resided between her thick thighs. Cam was only a few strokes in before her legs began to quake. Knowing he had her right where he wanted, he quickly spun her around to face him. Looking down into her lust-filled eyes, he pulled her in for a heated kiss. Gray's breath hitched. Cam was her drug. One touch from him and she was intoxicated. There was no stopping him when he wanted to have his way—not that she'd want to stop him. His scent alone sent her into a heady trance.

Her hand caressed the smooth hair on his jaw. Every single inch of Cam was all man. He had a monster ego and a monster cock. Their kisses were like a raging fire. He covered her with his massive body as he claimed every crevice of her mouth. Gripping her hair, he kissed her harder. It was crazy the power Gray had over him. He went from hating kissing to always needing to have his mouth on her.

Still stroking her middle, Cam ran his other hand up her bare arm, not fast but slow. The slight touch of his fingertips sent shivers down her spine. Each touch of his hand jumpstarted her heart. While his hands took her to another dimension where time and space didn't exist, soft kisses to her lips followed. It was funny how one second he could make her blind with rage then seconds later to be in his arms felt like a privilege and a purpose. No matter how upset she was with him, somehow Cam always found a way to revive what was lost and restore what was broken inside of her.

Gray could feel the transfer of power as she licked his tongue and sucked on his bottom lip. Cam rubbed his thick instrument against her throbbing clit. As she kissed him hungrily a guttural groan escaped his lips. The sound was lovely to her elicit ears.

"I fuckin' hate you."

"But you love this dick tho." He cockily, grinned.

Gray couldn't argue with that. She loved everything about his dick; the way it looked, the way it smelled, how hard it got and how it curved to the right. It was magnificent. Placing her hand on the top of his head, she pushed him down. It was time for him to drink from her fountain of youth. Gray thought she was in control, but Cam had her right where he wanted her. He planned on torturing her body until he drove her crazy, then he'd stop and do it all over again until she pleaded for him to stop. But he wouldn't. He was going to do all the freaky shit she loved until her body detonated.

Ripping a hole in the crotch of her leggings, he came face-to-face with her bare pussy. Gray was dripping wet. It was one of things Cam loved about her. She was always wet for him. Placing both her thighs on his shoulders, he dived in head first. Gray held onto the back of his head as she propped herself up by placing her back up against the door. The mastery of his tongue had her eyes rolling in circles. Cam's tongue extracted ecstasy from her soul. Gray's nerve ending were like butterflies sending tremors of satisfaction to her hardening clit. She could barely breath. Gazing up into her eyes, he made love to her pussy with his mouth. By the time he was done with her she wouldn't be able to walk. Gray rode his face, gyrating her hips in a circle. Swirling his head, Cam tattooed his name on her clit with his tongue.

Gray tried to take sips of air but couldn't seem to get any oxygen. Cam's tongue thrashed up and down her slit and flickered across her clit making her climax not once but twice. Moans of gratification filled the room as her legs seized up round his neck. It literally felt like she had a Charlie Horse in her thighs but the orgasm that ripped through her core made up for the discomfort.

With her still on his shoulders, Cam used his sturdy leg and lifted them off the floor while still eating her pussy. Gray couldn't believe that he was strong enough to pick her up without his legs buckling. Once they reached the couch, he laid her down. Cam didn't even waste time pulling her leggings off. The hole he'd created would be all the access he needed. Cam stroked his cock as her nails trailed down the groves of his abs. Precum dripped from his tip at the sight of her.

Goosebumps traced Gray's skin, not the kind a person gets when cold but the kind that formed when nothing else mattered except what was happening in the moment. Cam wished he had the verbal capacity to express how much he cherished this woman. In such a short time she'd grown to mean so much to him. She took him to the moon. Every time he looked at the freckles on her face he saw stars. Her beauty was blinding. The feelings he had for her scared him. It wasn't her shape, the curve of her thighs or her eyes that drew him to her. It was her soul and everything she held inside that made him feel the way he did. He prayed to god his fear of falling in love would die 'cause she deserved to be loved the way she loved everyone else in her life. Cam had already concluded that he was designed to love her. He just didn't know how.

Gray saw right through him. She saw through his signature scowl. She saw past his façade. She pushed past the wall he'd created to keep people out. When he was out rippin' and runnin' the streets all he thought about was returning home to her. She put his erratic mind at ease. The simple touch of her hand made him move in ways he'd never been taught but knew so well. With her, all thoughts of his past and future melted away. The only thing that mattered was the magic they created when in each other's arms.

Gray gazed up in her man's eyes. Her heart was beating at an unusual pace. The fast speed had nothing to do with anger or fear but her need to feel him inside of her. Hating how vulnerable he made her feel, she diverted her eyes elsewhere, but Cam could read her like a book. His eyes concentrated on the rise and fall of her breasts. Using his index finger, he redirected her face so that he held the gaze she didn't want to give him. There was no smirk on his enticing lips, only the scorching intensity of his glare that they both knew would spark the firestorm that was sure to come. Using his elbows, Cam propped his self on top of her then shoved his dick inside her like a madman. The first stroke almost ended him. The tightness of her pussy chocked his cock. Stroke after stroke, his name fell from her mouth as a plea. Cam had heard plenty other chicks moan his name during sex, but it never sounded as good as when Gray did it.

"Cam," she moaned, matching his rhythm. "Cam. Why you fuckin' me like this? Oh my god. I can't breathe."

"You still leaving?" He plunged his dick like a battering ram from hell.

"No." She thrashed her head from side-to-side.

"That's what the fuck I thought. You ain't going no fuckin' where. This pussy is mine, that mouth is mine, that ass is mine and your heart is mine. I ain't never lettin' you go."

"Never let me go, baby." She whimpered as the walls of her pussy started to constrict.

Gray was cumming again. Hearing Cam talk shit while grinding his shaft into her middle took her to another realm of ecstasy.

"I'll kill a nigga behind this pussy. You hear me?" He gripped her jaw. "You bet not ever give my pussy away."

"I won't. I swear to god, I won't."

Life became a blur as Cam pulverized her pussy by pounding harder, quicker and stronger. It took all the willpower he had to hold onto his nut. He was balls deep inside her pussy. Grunting, each breath he took burned his throat. Needing nourishment, he took ownership of her lips as she squeezed her inner walls. For over an hour he gave her everything he had. Cam and Gray's tongues dueled as they switched places and she rode his cock. His eleven-inch dick reached all the way to her esophagus. She felt suffocated and stretched wide. Each stroke of his mammoth dick hurt but she was willing to take the pain. No man had ever fucked her as good as Cam and he knew it. Placing his hands behind his head, he watched as he filled her up with every inch of him. Gray's pussy drooled as her ass cheeks smacked against his pelvis. The corners he hit inside her womb while drilling her pussy had her creaming all over his dick.

"Aww yeah." She moaned, bouncing up and down. "Oh yeah like that. Ooh this dick feel so good. Oooooooooh Cam."

"You love this dick?" He pinched her nipple.

"I love it. It's so fuckin' big, baby."

"Ride that dick like daddy taught you then." Cam toyed with her clit as the hole in her leggings spread wider.

"Yeah-yeah-yeah! I'm gonna cum! That's it, yes! Grab me! Grab me! Hold me down on that dick!"

Cam wrapped his arms around her tight, so she had no room to escape. Just when she was about erupt, he pulled her face down to him.

"You ain't never fuckin' leavin' me." He made clear before sucking on her tongue to muffle her cries.

Gray's midsection convulsed as she succumbed to his death strokes. Her fingers pressed into his chest. She'd never cum so hard in her life. She swore her pussy was destroyed. No other man could come behind Cam. Once she came down from her orgasmic high, he smacked her ass cheek to signal her to climb onto his face. The nigga loved to eat pussy, especially Gray's. She always tasted clean and fresh. Pressing his hand into the meat of her thighs, he placed wet sloppy kisses all over her clit then drove his tongue into the crease of her lips. Cam stuck his tongue so deep into her hole that he thought he found liquid gold. A waterfall of juices splashed from her clit all onto his face. Gray didn't even know she could squirt until she got with him. She'd only known him a few months and he'd discovered things about her body Gunz never had.

Needing to taste him, she spun around into the sixty-nine position. Cam's dick was so thick and long her mouth began to water. The crook in it that curved to the right made her clit ache. She got turned on just by the sight of it. The throbbing veins in his cock made her pussy pulsate. Flattening her tongue, she pushed her mouth past the tip of his dick until she was at the base and hummed. Cam closed his eyes and curled his toes. Gray was a beast at giving head. She told him that one night she wanted to fall asleep with him in her mouth. Deep throating his dick, she bobbed her head feverishly. Saliva slid down his rod as he ate her pussy. Gray sucked his dick like she had something to prove. Minutes went by before she came up for air. His entire shaft was coated with her spit. She could feel him expand in her mouth. Not ready for him to cum yet, she released him from her lips.

Cam's cock was painfully hard as she slid down and straddled him once more. In the reverse cowgirl position, she bent over so he could see her asshole and watch her pussy lips suck in his pole. Wanting to put on a show, Gray lifted up slowly, dragging his dick all the way out until only the tip was still in, then with the speed of lightening she'd sink back down. She'd established a pace and speed that made Cam bite down onto his lower lip. If she kept this shit up he was going to scream out like a bitch. Her pussy was weeping. Cam couldn't take the pressure in his cock and balls a second longer. Raising up, he held her close.

"You want me to cum?" He whispered in her ear.

"I want your fuckin' cum inside of me. Give it to me now."

"Beg for it." He strummed her nub.

"Please give it to me. Please." Gray used what little strength she had left in her thighs to ride him.

"You want it?"

"I want it so bad."

Cam placed his hand on her stomach. His dick had swelled to the size of an anaconda. Gray could feel every inch of him harden. He was about to give her what she wanted. He was about to milk her pussy with his hot cum.

"Fuck!" He growled holding onto her tight.

"Give me all your cum. I wanna feel it all in my pussy." She begged as she arched against him.

Gray could feel it coming. It was time for takeoff. Cam's toes dug into the fabric of the couch cushion. Gray's entire body trembled. A shockwave of electricity soared through each of their bodies. For a few seconds, they both visited a place where heaven and hell combined. Heavy panting filled the living area. Gray swallowed hard. Her throat was dry. Cam placed a bevy of small kisses on her neck and shoulders. Her skin was soaked with sweat, but he didn't care. Even Gray's sweat tasted sweet.

Snuggled on the couch together, he held her in his arms. Gray's breathing had returned to normal. He'd stuffed so much cum in her it had begun to seep out. She loved the feel of his warm cum. It was his way of marking his territory. Cam held her close and inhaled the fruity scent of her hair. He didn't want to fuck up a good mood. They'd just had, mind-blowing, earth shattering sex but what she'd done still didn't sit well in his spirit. Cam wasn't the kind of nigga that got in his feelings, but her deceitful ways affected him in ways she'd never understand. After LaLa, his trust issues magnified. He didn't want to punish Gray for her betrayal, but her actions were starting to mimic LaLa's. Lying about meeting up with her ex was a major no-no. The fact that he was even going to admit that she'd got to him was huge for Cam. He usually kept it pushing, but with Gray, he had to speak his mind.

"On some real shit, Star, don't ever let me hear you say you want a divorce again. I ain't like how that shit made me feel. You can't be runnin' around sneakin' seein' yo' baby daddy and threatening divorce. I don't take too well to threats. The last time a nigga threatened me they wound up dead. I don't wanna have to kill you, Gray."

"Not if I kill you first." She challenged.

Like a true sociopath, Cam's dick hardened.

"Think it's a game?"

"You would never try to kill me. You love me too much."

"That's your problem. You think shit is sweet. You think cause you fine and got some good pussy that I won't shoot some led into your pretty face, but I will if you keep fuckin' wit' me."

"I'm sorry. I didn't mean it. I was just upset."

"You can't be sayin' shit like that tho."

"I know. I'm sorry but you hurt my feelings too." She poked out her bottom lip.

"How?"

"I had a whole night planned for us and you didn't even show up. I bought sexy lingerie and cooked all your favorite foods—"

"You made me some macaroni and cheese?"

"Yep and some fried chicken too."

"That's what the fuck I'm talkin' about. I knew you loved a nigga."

"Oh really? Just a minute ago you was accusing me of fuckin' another man."

"I know you ain't fuck that nigga. You ain't crazy."

"I love you, daddy." She pecked his lips repeatedly. "I would never cheat on you."

"You're fuckin' ridiculous."

"Everyone's ridiculous, Cam. You deal with it 'cause you have to."

"Do I?" He arched his brow.

"Yeah, you do cause that's life. You're ridiculous and I'm a mess. The point of being in relationship is hoping you find someone who'll think you're okay enough to love."

"Is that what life is?"

"Yeah and it's really weird that you don't know that by now." She kissed the tattoo over his heart.

"My bad for not coming home. If I would've known—"

"You still wouldn't have showed up." Gray cut him off.

"You right. I wouldn't have." Cam chuckled.

"That ain't cool tho. You can't be gettin' in your feelings and shutting down. We grown. Tell me what I did wrong when I fuck up 'cause I'm for damn sure gon' tell you. We can't be on that tit-for-tat shit. You didn't come home on purpose to get back at me and that's fucked up."

"Yeah, it was but yo' ass lied like you always do."

"I lied to keep the peace and protect your feelings. Now I'm not saying that was okay. I was wrong. I should've told you and I apologize for that. But next time I do something that pisses you off, tell me or we're going to end up right back here. I can't do a bunch of arguing. I just left a toxic relationship. I want things between me and you to be different. They have to be or we won't last."

"I do feel bad tho. You know I never want to hurt you, Star. You gotta nigga heart for real. I ain't tryin' to beef wit' you. I'm tryin' to build wit' you." He kissed the tip of her nose. "I was mad as shit when my li'l cousin hit me sayin' you was wit' that trout mouth nigga. You can't be having me out here lookin' crazy. The streets is watching."

"Why the fuck do you care what the streets think?"

Cam quickly remembered that she thought he was strictly just a businessman. Gray had no idea that her husband supplied the whole Midwest with cocaine.

"My name ring bells out here. Niggas know what it is. They know I got a baddie on my arm. You think they ain't gon' try to test you to see if you loyal, to see if you'll bite so they can have one up on me? Niggas is dyin' to make me look stupid, especially yo' weak-ass baby daddy. You gotta realize who you fuckin' wit' Gray. It ain't a game out here. I got enough shit to be worrying about. The last thing I need is to be worrying about is what you doing when you ain't around me. You gotta keep it a hunnid. It don't need to be no secrets between me and you."

"I learned my lesson. You don't have to worry about me keepin' anything else from you."

"Good 'cause I done committed homicides for way less than that."

"Homicide?" Gray screwed up her face.

"Yeah, nigga, homicide. Now get up and fix me something to eat."

"Through the bad you saw the better man in me."-
Trey Songz, "Me 4 U Infidelity 2"

#6

When Cam woke up that morning, blue skies stretched across the horizon. The sky was clear, concise, serene and blue. Wasn't a cloud in sight. Rays of sunlight peaked through the blinds, illuminating the house and everyone's spirit. He hoped like hell the bright sun would lighten his dark mood. Holidays were always tough for him. Ever since his mother's passing he'd hated them. They were never the same after her untimely death. When Grace died, pieces of Cam died too. Out of all his brothers, he took her death the hardest. She was his first true love. Even though she had five kids, Grace had a knack of making each of her children feel special. Every Sunday dinner, she'd make Cam his favorite banana pudding dessert that no one else could have but him. While at church, she'd lay him across her lap and pat his back to keep him content. At night, she'd hold him close and read him bedtime stories. The scent of her White Diamond's perfume would always lull him to sleep.

Grace was a girly girl, but she'd learned enough about basketball to discuss the sport with him. She drove him to practice every day and attended all his games. On the ride home, they'd always stop and get a scoop of ice cream and discuss his dreams of becoming a professional basketball player. She'd often tell him he'd be the next Michael Jordan but ten times better. Cam believed her. His mother had never led him astray. She always encouraged him to be the best at everything he did. She made all her children feel like they could soar. There wasn't anything they couldn't achieve. Her favorite saying was where there is a will, there is a way.

When she passed everything fell apart. All of Cam's hopes and dreams perished. Their father retreated into himself, leaving his kids to deal with the grief of losing their mother alone. Because of this, all of the Parthens kids acted out in different ways. Kerry became a work acholic. He put all his time and energy into building his own investment banking firm. He was a loner who barely kept in contact with any of his siblings or even his twin brother. Curtis, his twin, became addicted to prescription pills. After years of battling his addiction, he finally kicked the habit. That didn't stop his wife from leaving him and taking their three kids with her. Curtis hadn't seen his kids in years and didn't try to. He was now married to a white woman who gave him two biracial boys he loved and adored. Calvin flat out refused to leave the nest and grow up. He was a hypochondriac who thought he suffered from every illness known to man. Cam's anger towards his mother dying and his father shutting down resulted in him tossing basketball aside and hitting the block. Mo, the youngest and the only girl of the family, ended up having major daddy issues and sought love from a serial cheater. Their whole family was fucked up. Eleven years later, things had gotten somewhat better but most of their family discourse still remained the same. Years of pain, unhealed hurt, secrets and betrayals lie beneath the surface brewing. Cam could feel all the corruption boiling to a scorching heat. He didn't want any parts of it but three times a year he was forced to face his family drama.

By the time he pulled in front of his father's white farmhouse, a rough sheet of mottled grey blocked the sun. The air was thick with mugginess. A storm was brewing outside and internally inside of Cam. Thanksgiving at his father's home was always a shit show. Everyone sat around laughing, eating, playing games and catching up, blissfully unaware of the truth. Only Cam and his father walked around with the deep secrets that could destroy their family.

Gray sat in the passenger seat of his red Range Rover uneasy. Cam had been in a sour mood all morning. She and the girls tiptoed around him, unsure of what to say or do. She'd never seen him like this. Cam wasn't the most pleasant person to be around, his attitude was an acquired taste but that day he was in rare form. She'd asked what was wrong. He repeatedly said nothing, so she left it alone, even though she wanted to press him to open up. It didn't feel good knowing that her husband wouldn't allow her into his mental space. She wanted to be his savior. She yearned to give him the comfort she continuously sought from him. Cam was so great at being there for her whenever she was in need, but when it was her turn to return the favor, she was constantly shut out. No matter how hard she tried, she always felt miles away from his heart. The disconnect was prevalent. She felt it internally and knowing that her husband had never uttered the words I love you hadn't gone unmissed. Gray never wanted to pressure him into saying the three words. When the time came he'd say it on his own. That's how she would know his sentiments were real. Gray wasn't in dire need to hear him announce his undying affection because when she looked into his eyes she saw love there. Even though she knew it was there, it didn't diminish the hurt she harbored. Something was wrong between them. She just hadn't pinpointed what the problem was.

She hoped he wasn't in a piss poor mood because they were about to announce their marriage to his family. None of them even knew she existed, except Mo, but even she didn't know they were married. Gray prayed they took the news well. She wasn't going anywhere. She and Cam had committed themselves to each other, not only on by exchanging vows, but with ink as well. In one of his impulsive moods Cam talked her into to getting their names tatted on one another. She got Cam inked on her hip, leading into the face of her pussy. He got Gray tatted on his right temple. Gray couldn't believe that he'd gotten her name tattooed on his face for the whole world to see but that was Cam. He always went the extra mile to solidify her place in his life. They both got their wedding date 10/25/17 tatted on their ring finger. Gray wasn't much of a tattoo girl but every time she looked down at her hand, and was reminded that he was hers, she smiled.

"C'mon." Cam opened her and the girl's door.

He barely gave Gray any eye contact when he helped her out the car. She hated when they were disconnected like this. All she wanted to do was help him, but he'd slammed the door to his heart in her face. She and the girls followed behind him up the walkway in silence. All of them were apprehensive about going inside. An invisible cloak of gloom cascaded over the beautiful home. Aoki dragged her feet slower than usual. She too had an attitude. It was the first Thanksgiving she wasn't spending with her father. Gunz would get the girls the following day but she wanted to be with him on the actual holiday, not the day after. Her ten-year-old mind couldn't comprehend why her mother didn't understand her strife. She was moving as if she hadn't spent half her life with her dad. She acted like there wasn't years of love between them. Running off and marrying Cam wouldn't erase Gunz from her life. She and Press would always be a constant reminder of her past. She didn't want to get to know Cam or his raggedy-ass family. She'd never be cool with him or their so-called marriage. Her mother could play house all she wanted but Aoki was standing firm in her refusal of liking Cam. She had one father and his name was Gavin 'Gunz' Marciano.

Holding Gray's hand, Cam led her into the house. There his family was in all their glory. His sister and Boss sat cuddled on the couch as he watched the game. Baby Zaire lay beside them sound asleep, despite all the racket. His brother, Cal, wheeled around doing donuts in his wheelchair as the kids ran after him. Cam couldn't do anything but groan. His brother was a fuckin' clown. There was no reason for him to be in a wheelchair. The nigga could walk perfectly fine.

"Well, look who decided to show up after having everyone wait for over an hour." Kerry rose from his seat.

The faster they ate dinner the quicker he could escape. Kerry had detached his self so much from his family that they no longer felt like family to him. His siblings were just a bunch of people he was related to by blood. They didn't have that familial bond that other families had. His brothers and sister didn't know shit about his life and vice versa. Everything was surface level with them. There was no depth. Sometimes, it made him sad cause their mother had to be doing backflips in her grave. She'd taught her kids to stick together. Now they were nothing but strangers.

"Unlike you, some of us do have jobs to get back to." He pushed past his little brother.

Everyone in the family knew Cam sold drugs for a living and that his businesses were nothing but a front. The fact that his brother had the audacity to say some slick shit in front of company enraged Cam.

"Shut yo' pussy-ass up. It's fuckin' Thanksgiving. Get yo' panties out yo' ass, nigga." He mushed him in the back of his head.

"Touch me again and see what'll happen." Kerry spun around furious.

"What yo' punk-ass gon' do Poindexter, press charges?" Cam stepped into his personal space. "I know you still be callin' the police on black people while they in the park."

"Kerry, no. I thought you stopped doing that?" Mo sighed disappointed.

"Even I stopped doing that." Curtis white wife Elizabeth chimed in.

"There's no reason for anybody to be in the park after 9:00 p.m." Kerry said all riled up. "It says it on the sign. The park is closed after nine. You shouldn't be listening to Jeezy, barbequing ribs, playin' spades and dominos when the park is closed. It's as simple as that."

"When one of'em knock yo' racist ass out, don't come cryin' to me like you did last time. Scary-ass nigga." Cam looked him up and down. "That master's degree ain't gon' save you from gettin' yo' ass whooped."

"You're so *thuggish, ruggish* bone, why don't you come whoop my ass, *Cameron*!" Kerry took off his Men's Wearhouse suit jacket.

"C'mon y'all don't start." Mo exhaled, rolling her eyes. "I'ma call daddy in here if y'all don't get somewhere and sit down."

"Nah, let 'em fight. I wanna see who'll win." Curtis laughed.

"I got ten on Kerry." Boss pulled out a wad of money. "He got age and experience."

"I'm wit' you, Pop." King pulled out a stack of ones.

"But Cam got speed and agility." Curtis argued.

"Don't forget he served in the army." Calvin added. "Put me in for a hunnid. Aye yo' King," he whispered. "Let me hold something? I got you when my disability check come in the mail on Tuesday."

"Nah, Unc, you said that the last time. Gon' try to pay me in M&M's." King looked at him sideways. "You still owe me five dollars."

"C'mon, man, you know I got you. You know I'm good for it."

"Anytime you askin' a seven-year-old to borrow some money, you need to reevaluate your life." Curtis screwed up his face.

"Yeah broke-ass. Get a job." Mo shot his way.

"I tried to get one, but my doctor didn't clear me." Calvin said with an attitude. "Y'all know I have mesothelioma."

"Nigga, you ain't got no fuckin' cancer!"

"Oh, shit that's what that is. Aww nah I ain't got that. I got the other one."

"The other one what?" Mo narrowed her eyes.

"Umm . . . Muscular Dystrophy. That's why I'm in a wheelchair now."

"Lyin' ass nigga. Ain't nothing wrong wit' you or your muscles. Baby, don't give him nothin'."

"You got a lot of shit to say, Mo. How is Syphilis doing?" Calvin spat back.

"Oh, don't let the pregnant belly fool you. I will get up and push yo' ass down them steps. Yo' ass will be cripple for real. Now back to the main event. Everybody got they bets in?" Mo looked around the living room.

"Y'all gon' fuck around and get this Colin Powell wanna be hemmed up." Cam sneered.

"Damn, Kerry, you do look like Colin Powell." Curtis chuckled.

"If I do you do too idiot." Kerry responded.

"Oh, that's right."

"Me and my book club always found Colin Powell to be very sexy." Elizabeth blushed. "How do you say it, Mo? He can get it, but one question. Get what? I never understood that one."

"Curtis get Becky with the good hair." Mo rolled her eyes.

"Oh, I get that one. That's Sasha Fierce. That's Beyoncé." Elizabeth pointed her finger in delight.

"All of you are a bunch of ignoramuses! I don't even know why I come to these functions! Half of you, no scratch that, none of you can complete a proper sentence. What are you hooked on Ebonics?" Kerry exclaimed.

"You got me messed up, Unc. I can complete a proper sentence." Mo's daughter Makiah rolled her neck. "See look. Uncle Cam gon' beat yo' ass. Was that clear enough?"

A roar of laughter filled the room.

"Congratulations, Mo, you're doing a great job molding the next Joseline Hernandez."

"If anything, I'ma be Cardi B." Makiah clarified.

"That's right baby. You tell'em. We team Cardi over here. Hell, I'm surprised his corny-ass even know who Joseline Hernandez is."

"You know he the type that like to jackoff to black women just not date 'em." Cam took another jab at his brother.

"Says the man with a foreigner standing right behind him." Kerry pointed out.

"She ain't no fuckin' foreigner! She black nigga . . . and some other shit!"

"Tomato-tomato same thing. I don't have time for this. I'm leaving." Kerry placed back on his suit jacket.

"Don't nobody want yo' MAGA hat wearin', Trump supportin', pompous-ass here no way." Cam shot.

"Spell pompous." Kerry folded his arms across his chest. "I'll wait."

Cam squinted his eyes in contempt. He hated when Kerry tried to insult his intelligence. Everyone knew he was just as smart, if not smarter, than him. Cam just didn't go around flaunting his intellect.

"That's what I thought. Fuckin' jailbird. If anybody should be gettin' a disability check around here it should be you GI Joe. Ain't that right Cameron . . . Archibald . . . Parthens Jr."

"Archibald?" Gray said stunned. "That's why you ain't wanna say your whole name at the—"

"Shut the fuck up, Gray!" Cam yelled.

"Now why you do that? You know damn well he go crazy when anybody say his middle name." Mo shook her head. "You know he can't stand that shit."

"Archibald?" Gray repeated again.

She'd been virtually quiet throughout the entire showdown but learning Cam's middle name was Archibald really threw her for a loop.

"I ain't take you for the Archibald type." Aoki scoffed. "Killa Cam . . . yeah right."

"Now I really gotta bust your ass. Square up nigga." Cam took off his chains. "I'm tired of talkin' to you. Here, Gray, hold my shit."

"AYE!" Cameron Parthens Senior's loud voice boomed throughout the room. "Cut out all that foolishness. What the hell is wrong wit' y'all! If Grace was here she would have a fit. Y'all know better than to carry on like this in my house. Now get ya' asses up and come eat. The food is ready."

"This shit ain't over. I'm runnin' up in yo' shit after dessert." Cam warned his older brother.

"Not if I call your probation officer. You statistic. *Clink . . . Clink.*" Kerry smirked, heading into the dining room.

This was exactly why Cam didn't fuck with his brothers. Kerry thought he was better than all of them. Curtis neglected his black kids, only to love and adore his mixed ones and Calvin was just a fuckin' idiot. Being around his father didn't help the situation. Every holiday it was a struggle to sit across from a man he didn't respect and break bread.

"Are you okay? What was that all about?" Gray asked nervously.

She had no idea that she was walking into the lion's den. She thought Gunz had a crazy family, but Cam's family took the cake.

"It's nothin. Don't worry about him."

"I'm not. I'm worried about you." She placed her hands on the sides of his face to get him to focus on her.

Once he did, she gazed deep into his brown orbs, hoping to find the answers to his inner turmoil. Cam gazed back at her and instantly calmed down. One look into her blue orbs and everything wrong in the world turned right again.

"What's going on in that head of yours? Talk to me."

Cam wanted to tell her that he hated the holidays because it made him miss his mother more than usual and that the sight of his father's face sickened him. His refusal to let her in kept his feelings at bay.

"I got somethin' to tell you." He confessed.

"What?"

"Promise you won't get mad." He held onto both of her arms.

"I promise I won't get mad." She lied.

"I got two kids."

"WHAT?" Gray shrieked, trying to break loose from his hold but Cam held her tight.

Suddenly, she felt woozy. The room had begun to spin and the muscles in her chest tightened. *So that's why he's been actin' a fool all day. This nigga got two kids and didn't tell me,* she thought.

"What the hell you mean you got two kids?" A well of tears formed in her eyes.

"Kilo! Gram!" Cam called out to the two beautiful black Rottweilers that were laying on the floor.

Like the obedient dogs they were, Kilo and Gram got up and trotted over to their owner. Cam let go of Gray and bent down to pat both canines. Gray let out a sigh of relief and wiped her face. She'd nearly had a heart attack. All she could do was hold her chest and thank god that it was all a joke.

"Aoki and Press say hi to your brothers."

"They're so pretty." Aoki quickly ran over to pat the dogs too.

"I always wanted a dog, but mommy said we couldn't have one." Press exclaimed, excited.

"Well, you do now." Cam stood up as the girls played with the dogs.

"Y'all be careful." Gray warned concerned.

Kilo and Gram were huge in size. They were like two big beasts.

"You should've seen your face when I said I had two shorties." Cam chuckled.

"That shit wasn't funny." Gray hit his chest. "You ain't tell me you had two dogs."

"My brother Cal been keeping an eye on 'em since I've been so busy but they coming home with us today."

"Oh, they are?" Gray arched her brow. "And who gon' feed and bathe them?"

"I'ma take care of all of that."

"Sure, you are."

"C'mon. I know they all waiting on us. Press and Aoki c'mon. Y'all can play with the dogs after we eat." He picked Press up and took Gray by the hand.

"I wanna play with them now." Aoki snapped back.

"Nah, we about to eat."

"So, I don't wanna eat none of yo' family's nasty food."

"Yo, who you talkin' to?" Cam let go of Gray's hand and gripped his gun.

"You. You ain't my daddy. I ain't gotta listen to you."

"You betta get her Gray before I choke her. I ain't in the mood for her shit today." Cam tried to keep his self from taking out his gun and pulling the trigger.

"Aoki Marciano, you heard what he said. Don't make me act a fool up in here." Gray glared at her.

"I don't never get to do nothin'." She mumbled, stomping her feet.

"You betta pull yourself together before I slap you." Gray spoke in a clipped tone.

Although she was still mad, Aoki knew her mother wasn't playing and reluctantly straightened up. She reminded herself that after this horrendous dinner was over, she'd be at her father's house where she wanted to be. Taking a deep breath and straightening her back, Gray gripped Cam's hand tight as they made their way to the dining room. Kilo and Gram trailed behind them, hoping to get some of the scraps from the table. As they walked, she admired a family portrait of Cam, his father and siblings. They were all dressed in white. She could tell the photo had been taken years ago. Cam already had a baby face but in the picture he looked even younger. Once they entered the formal dining room she couldn't help but take in the rustic décor that matched the farmhouse exterior of the house.

Wooden beams and a 5-light pendant, blown glass, light fixture decorated the ceiling. A large bay window with custom drapes framed the space. The entire family sat at rustic farm table with a white flower centerpiece and white China that Cam's mother collected over the years before she passed. A handwoven area rug, China cabinet and plant finished off the room. Cam Sr. sat at the head of the table. He was a tall, lean man with a bald head and skin the shade of mahogany. For him to be 75 years old, he didn't look a day over 60. The real star of the room was the food. The feast was to be served family style. Surrounding the center piece was bowls and platters of greens, sweet potatoes, dressing, macaroni and cheese, smoked turkey, roast, ham, dinner rolls, cranberry sauce and gravy. Gray's stomach embarrassingly started to growl.

"Damn bruh. You don't feed thickness?" Cal sucked his teeth and stared at Gray like she was a piece of prime rib.

"Look elsewhere bitch, before I pop ya tires." Cam scowled.

"Quit all that cussin' and introduce us to your friend?" Cam Sr. eyed Gray and the girls curiously.

"This is Gray and her daughters, Aoki and Press." He blew a raspberry on Press' cheek making her giggle.

"Gray. . . hmm so that's her name tattooed on your face." His father said more as a statement and not a question. "Nice to meet you, Gray." Cam Sr. shook her hand. "Your girls are beautiful." He smiled warmly at them.

"Thank you and you have a beautiful home by the way."

"I have my late great wife, Grace, and daughter, Mo, to thank for that. Have you all met?"

"Yes, our kids go to the same school. That's how I met Cam." Gray replied as he pulled out her seat.

"What was Cam doing at the kids' school?"

"Makiah and Ryan jumped demon seed over there." Cam nodded his head towards Aoki.

"Cam, stop." Gray hit his arm.

"Now you know better than to be fighting." Cam Sr. frowned at his granddaughters.

"She ran up and got done up." Ryan shrugged innocently.

"I thought y'all were friends again?" Mo said confused.

"We were until Uncle Cam said we needed to put the paws on her again."

"Cam!"

"Y'all ain't gon' touch me." Aoki eyed the twins with disdain.

"Nobody is touching anyone. Okay." Gray declared with authority.

"So, are King and Press in the same class too?" Cam Sr. questioned.

"Yeah, Pop-Pop. That's my lady right there." King winked his eye, causing Press to blush.

"Oh lord. Let's say grace everyone."

After praying over the food, the entire clan chowed down on the Thanksgiving feast. The sound of forks and knives scraping the plate, chewing and light banter filled the room.

"Steph Curry got the best crossover game of all time." King said adamantly.

"Yo' young-ass don't know shit. A.I. was known for breakin' niggas ankles." Boss schooled his son.

"Exactly." Cam agreed. "Steph Curry ain't nothin' but Allen Iverson with two parents."

The entire family bugged up laughing, including Gray who didn't know much about sports.

"What you think, daddy?" Mo asked her father.

Cam tried his hardest not to vomit. It truly sickened him how much Mo revered their father. If only she knew the truth, she'd hate him just as much as he did.

"You know he like that old-ass nigga they wheel out every All-Star game that look like he on his last breath." Curtis joked.

"Who, Bill Russell?" Kerry inquired.

"Yeah, nigga look like the first slave and shit." Cam chuckled.

"Don't be talkin' about my daddy's favorite basketball player." Mo scolded her brothers.

"You got something on your lip." Cam squinted his eyes.

"What?" Mo touched her lips self-consciously.

"Oh, it's just your favorite lip gloss . . . nut."

Mo grimaced and hit him with the middle finger.

"Ole Bill Russell." Cam Sr. steepled his hands together and smiled. "The best basketball player to ever play the game. The league ain't seen nothin' like him since he retired from the Celtics. You youngin's think MJ was hot stuff but ole Bill has the most championship wins of all time."

"Damn, Mo, you already on plate number two." Cal pointed out.

"I am eating for three."

Mo and Boss had just learned that they were having another set of twins. With the addition of the twins, they'd now have a total of six kids.

"What's your excuse?" She quipped.

"I got an autoimmune deficiency that causes me to over eat."

"Autoimmune deficiency my ass. Yo' ass just greedy."

"Aye, Cam. Remember when we was little and Mo used to eat grape jelly out of the jar wit' a candy bar as a fork?"

"Used to? She still do." Makiah chimed in.

"Stay in a child's place and hush." Mo pointed her butter knife at her daughter.

"Aoki, you are so pretty. What do you wanna be when you grow up?" Elizabeth asked.

"I'm gonna be a world-famous DJ and photographer." She answered confidently.

"And you li'l bit?"

"I wanna train cats to bark." Press responded as she fed Gram pieces of turkey under the table.

"I'ma be her manager." King grinned.

"Oh, okay we'll y'all go head." Elizbeth clutched an invisible set of pearls.

"Okay, let's all go around the table and say what we're thankful for, so we can get out of here." Kerry said impatiently. "I'll start. I'm thankful for my investment firm and all of my employees. Oh, and my new Ashton Martin." He grinned gleefully.

"I'm thankful for my husband and all of my beautiful children, no matter how bad they are, and these two little ones in my tummy." Mo rubbed her protruding belly. "Cam?"

Taking his napkin, he wiped the corners of his mouth and cleared his throat.

"I'm thankful for this gorgeous woman right here." He turned and looked at Gray.

That day she was nothing short of perfection. Her hair was pulled up into a sleek topknot. The eyeshadow on her lids was done in a warm light brown cut crease. Black winged eyeliner traced her long, thick lashes. Matte brown lipstick painted her sumptuous lips. Diamond studs shined from her ears. Her outfit entailed a black sheer, high neck, ruffle blouse, black lace bra, light wash, denim jeans and over-the-knee, mesh and suede, stiletto heel, Aquazzura boots. Several times throughout dinner, Cam imagined throwing her fine-ass on the table, placing her legs on his shoulders and making her eyes roll in the back of her head but that could wait till they got home.

"In the short amount of time I've known her, she's made me a better man. She's everything I ever wanted in a woman. That's why I made her my wife." Cam held up her left hand.

Mo dropped her fork, covered her mouth and screeched, "You lyin'?"

"We got married last month on the 25th."

"You've been married for a month and ain't told nobody? I could kick both of y'all ass." She got up to hug her brother and her new sister-in-law.

The rest of the family greeted them with warm hugs and congratulations, except Cam Sr. He sat quiet with an expression of discontent on his face. This was typical Cam. Ever since his mother died, he'd started acting on impulse without regard of the fallout. His erratic behavior had caused his father years of pain and suffering. Cam Sr. had watched his son morph from a burgeoning basketball star to a gang banging, street thug. He'd bailed him out of jail and sat in court too many times to count. Marrying a woman, he barely knew with two children, was just another act of defiance on Cam's behalf. He knew damn well he wasn't fit to be anyone's husband. Once the commotion settled down Cam glared at his father. It was apparent that he wasn't as happy about the news as everyone else.

"What's good, Pop? What you got to say?" He braced his self for a confrontation.

"We just met this young lady and you're tellin' me that you're married. Don't you think it's a bit too soon?"

"No. I know what I want."

"How long have you two known each other young lady?"

"Three months." Gray replied sheepishly.

"And you think that's sufficient enough time to marry someone, especially considering you have kids? Two daughters I might add."

"Trust me, I have considered everything you just said. Cam's a good man. He's helped me through some really dark times. He's stood by my side and loved me back to health literally. I've never met a man that cared about the wellbeing of me and my children more. That's why I love him with all my heart." She clutched his hand and gazed lovingly into eyes.

"Mama always said marry the one you can't live without." Mo stuffed her face.

"Or the one that suck your dick the best." Cal cracked up.

"Mama was a savage." Curtis laughed too.

"I wanna give you my blessing but—" Cam Sr. began but was rudely cut off by Cam.

"I'ma grown fuckin' man. I don't need you're fuckin' blessing."

He hated when his father got on his high horse and started judging his decisions.

"Hey-hey-hey. Don't be talkin' to my daddy like that." Mo checked him.

"Shut up, Mo, and finish eatin' your third helping of dressing, fat-ass."

"Y'all ain't gon' keep talkin' about my baby." Boss kissed his wife's cheek.

"Well, tell her to mind her fuckin' business."

"Watch your goddamn mouth." Cam Sr. scolded his son.

Cam inhaled deep and tried not to explode.

"Now, as I was saying. Marriage is not a joke, Cam. It's to be taken seriously."

"Is that right?"

"No disrespect, young lady, but I doubt my son knows you very well after only three months of dating."

"Answer me this." Cam placed his elbows on the table. "Did mommy truly know you after twenty years of marriage?"

Cam Sr. clenched his jaw and placed his head down. His son had pulled his card.

"Yeah, that's what the fuck I thought. C'mon, Gray, we gettin' ready to go." Cam threw his napkin down on the table.

He'd had enough of pretending. His father was a fraud and a fuckin' hypocrite. He had no right to judge him when they both knew the truth about his sordid past. From the time Cam was nine years old, till he was thirteen, Cam Sr. would lie to his wife and say he was spending father and son time with Cam. When really he was using the time to spend with his mistress. The first time he took Cam to her house and told him to sit on the couch and watch cartoons while they talked in her bedroom, Cam didn't think much of it. It wasn't until a few visits later when he walked down the hallway to the bathroom that he heard his father's mistress moan out his name.

For four years, he was subjected to his father's extra marital affair. Whenever he was forced to spend father and son time, the hatred for his dad grew. How could a man that loved his mother as much as his father claimed he did lay up with a woman who wasn't his wife? Why would he bring his son to bear witness to his betrayal? Did he not take into consideration how his actions would fuck Cam up? So many times, passed when he wanted to tell his mother the truth. The words were right on the tip of his tongue, but they never came out. He didn't want to cause his mother any pain. She was too good of a woman to have to hurt over his father's bullshit behavior. Most importantly, he refused to tear his family apart. Everything changed, however, the day his mother died in a plane crash. Cam Sr. was supposed to be on the flight with her but lied and said he couldn't get time off work. While his mother faced death alone, his shitty-ass father had his dick stuffed in mistress's hole. Grace Parthens died never knowing her husband was a liar and cheat, but Cam knew, and the truth haunted him.

For the sake of their family, he thought his hatred would wane, but it didn't ebb, it multiplied. Hate colored his soul. It spread like wildfire throughout his system, shutting down all other feelings. His father couldn't tell him shit about love and marriage when he didn't even respect his own. Until Cameron Parthens Sr. could fess up to his family and reveal his truth, there was nothing he could say to his son. Cam was going to do what the fuck he wanted to do.

"I just need some dick. I just need some love. Tired of fuckin' wit' these lyin' niggas. Baby, I just need a thug."- Summer Walker, "Girls Need Love"

#7

Shuffling his long feet, Cam walked sluggishly towards the master bathroom with his eyes practically closed. The urgent need to pee was the only thing that dragged him out of bed. He'd been out like a light since he walked through the door at the crack of dawn. Gray was sound asleep when he got home, so she had no idea what time he got in. After days of no sleep, Cam's body finally shut down. This was his pattern. He'd have one good night of rest and several days of sleep deprivation. It was the only way he knew how to function. He'd trained his body to survive without rest. Night terrors and sleeplessness haunted his hours of darkness. Exhaustion ruled his days. His body constantly begged for unconsciousness, but at all cost, he avoided closing his eyes. Cam wished he was one of those people that could sleep and relax but sounds of rapid gunfire, explosions that could take out small countries and cries of unbearable pain filled his mind. The smell of rotting flesh and fresh blood filled his nostrils. He could feel the dirt, sweat and grime all over his skin. It sickened him to go back to those days where his life was on the line, but when he slept, he was always transported back to the second worst time of his life.

He wished he could tell Gray about his issues, but he didn't want her trying to fix him. He was unfixable. Years of therapy hadn't helped. Therapy only put a name to his problem. He suffered from PTSD: Post-Traumatic Stress Disorder. Self-medicating with alcohol, sleeping pills and avoiding siesta was the only thing that aided his stress level. The last thing he wanted was Gray looking at him differently. The man she'd married was strong, invincible and unbreakable. He never wanted to look weak in her eyes. He was her hero. He never wanted that dynamic to change. It was bad enough he felt that weak on the inside. His night terrors had crippled him in ways he'd never imagined. It made him feel psychotic and like a freak. He'd tried masking his diagnosis with multiple women, cars, jewels and other materialistic things but nothing could block out that he was a motherless child and the only surviving member of his squad.

He'd barely gotten a good night's rest after his mother died. After the war, he was really fucked up. Whenever he dozed off he'd awake as soon as sleep came. Every night it was the same routine. He'd jump out of his slumber as if a gunshot had been sounded. His heart beat fast, causing his chest to release ragged breaths like he'd ran a marathon. Cam could never go back to sleep after that. He'd rise and start moving to avoid the traumatic thoughts that plagued his psyche. That Saturday morning nothing had changed. After he relieved his bladder, he'd begin his day after only three hours of rest.

With his head back, he slipped his hand inside his boxer/briefs and pulled out his throbbing, rigid dick. His dick was aching to pee as well as slide up in some warm wet pussy. When the dam finally broke and a long stream of urine shot into the toilet, Cam felt like a new man.

"Ahhhhhhhh." He sighed.

There was nothing better than the first piss of the day. His entire body relaxed as he relieved himself. In the zone, he planted his flat feet firm against the cool marble floor, only to feel something wet and gushy underneath the sole of his foot. Cam prayed to god it wasn't shit. If it was, there was about to be a homicide. If he looked down and Kilo or Gram had dookied on the bathroom floor, he was gonna shoot'em both and send both of their asses to doggy heaven. Snatching his tired eyes open, he looked down to find his left foot resting on top of a blood-soaked tampon.

"Ohhhhh! Ohhhhhhhhhhhhhh what the fuck!" He speedily jumped back into the door, not giving a damn that urine was still streaming from his dick.

"What the fuck is this doing on the floor?" He stopped himself from peeing and tucked his dick back inside his underwear.

"What's wrong? What are you screaming for?" Gray came rushing into the bedroom to find him crouched up against the bathroom door.

"What the fuck is wrong wit' you?" He pointed to the bloody tampon.

"That ain't mine." Gray screwed up her face.

She too was disgusted by the sight of the used tampon.

"Then who's the fuck is it? You too fuckin' old for this shit, Gray?" Cam shook his head repulsed.

"On my mama that's not mine. I'm not even on my period, I swear." She crossed her heart and hoped to die.

"C'mon, Star. You gon' leave that shit in front of the fuckin' toilet. That's nasty. What if I get AIDS?"

"Nigga, don't play wit' me!" Gray smacked his chest. "You know damn well I'm clean."

"Shiiiiiiiiiit I don't know nothin' about ya' nasty ass." Cam scooted past her while walking on his left heel, so his bloody foot wouldn't touch the floor. "This too much. It's bad enough I live in a house wit' a bunch of girls but now my wife leavin' used tampons on the floor. Nah, bruh I gotta go." He grabbed a towel and stepped out the bathroom.

Cam had never been more heated in his life. It was too much estrogen in the house. He'd grew up in a household full of testosterone then served in the army where he was around nothing but men. He wasn't used to being around a bunch of girls all the time. He'd never get use to stepping on Press's toys, her begging him to play with Barbie dolls, which he begrudgingly did with a scowl on his face, Aoki acting like a pre-menopausal ten-year-old and Gray constantly singing Beyoncé songs all day.

"Babe, I promise I didn't leave that there. On my mama I didn't."

"If you didn't, who did? C'mon Star. You can't be doing no nasty shit like that." Cam barked.

As he wiped off his foot, Gram came running into the bathroom as Gray bent down to inspect the tampon. His goal was to eat the tampon.

"Get yo' ass outta here, Gram!" Cam chased behind him on one foot while clapping his hands. "See, Gray! You almost killed my fuckin' dog!"

"I told you it ain't mine." She stood up.

Cam came back in the bathroom and placed his hand over his mouth to prevent himself from throwing up.

"We gotta dog, Gray. What if Gram would've ate that and got sick? C'mon son." He paced the room.

"Cam, calm down. You doing too much."

"So, what you just gon' leave it there? You ain't gon' pick it up. Why you just staring at? It ain't gon' clean itself."

"I'm not picking up no other bitch's tampon." Gray's brows dipped down as she continued to look at it.

"It came out of your pussy, Gray! That's your pussy pad!"

"It's a tampon not a pad, jackass."

"Whatever the fuck it is, it's yours. Yo' grown ass just embarrassed."

"Look at it?" Gray picked it up with her bare hand and held it in front of his face. "Do this look like it's mine?"

"Ahhhhhhhhhhh! STOP!" Cam jumped back again. "What the fuck is wrong wit' you?"

"Just look at it." Gray placed it closer to his face.

"No!" He instinctually squared up ready to fight.

"Just look." Gray bugged up laughing.

"Stop, Gray! I can get pink-eye from that shit!" He pushed her out the way and ran out of the bathroom.

"GOTCHA! IT'S A PRANK!" Aoki recorded him on her iPhone.

The blare from the camera light instantly took Cam back to the way the sun beamed down on his face that fateful day in Afghanistan where his life changed for the worst. Beams or flashes of light was one of his triggers. He avoided high beams of light at all cost. It always sent him in a state of panic. A fear like no other ripped through his core. Beads of sweat formed on the palms of his hand. At any second, he was going to pass out. *Breathe nigga. Breathe,* Cam reminded his self.

"I knew his dumb-ass would fall for it." Aoki cackled.

"TURN THE FUCKIN' CAMERA OFF!" He tried to swipe it out of her hand while shielding his eyes from the light.

Aoki was smaller than him and quicker, so she was able to dodge his attempt.

"Get that fuckin' camera out my face!" He lost his shit.

"Chill, nigga. It's just a prank for my YouTube channel." Aoki stopped recording.

"Where my fuckin' belt? I'm beatin' yo' bad ass today!" Cam picked up his jeans and took off his Gucci belt.

The room was spinning but he was determined to give Aoki the ass whoopin' she well deserved.

"Shut up. You ain't gon' do nothin'." Aoki challenged him.

"A'ight, think it's a game. Say goodbye to Aoki, Gray. She finna die today."

"Cam, stop." Gray calmed herself down after laughing so hard she'd begun to cry.

"Nah babe, that shit ain't funny. I got blood on my fuckin' foot!"

"It's ketchup." She continued to giggle.

"Nah, that shit is real. Ain't no muthafuckin' ketchup. That came outta somebody pussy!"

"It's not blood, I swear."

"How you know?" He eyed her quizzically.

"Cause when I picked it up, I could smell ketchup."

"Man." Cam placed his belt down. "All of y'all was about to die today. I can't take too much more of this shit. I almost had a fuckin' heart attack. A nigga too fine to die so young. On the real, you gotta get a hold of her, Gray. Your daughter got my dick all over the Gram and I don't wanna hear your mouth when bitches start blowin' my shit up sayin' they wanna fuck."

Gray didn't want that at all. Every time she turned around there was a bitch calling Cam's phone. She could hardly keep up with all the names. It was one thing to know your husband was a lady's man. It was another thing to see the physical evidence of his hoish ways. In order to survive being with a man like Cam, Gray had to block out all the women he'd bedded before her. If she focused on all his conquest then she wouldn't be able to function day to day. Every time he left the house she'd be in shambles, probably bedridden if she let all the women that craved her husband's dick enter her mind. It was a technique she'd learned after years of dealing with Gunz. She'd block out all the bullshit and focus on the good things only. Gray didn't know if that was the right way to go about things, but if she wanted her marriage to work, then she had no other choice. Despite Cam being married, women weren't going to stop pushing up on him.

Nowadays, ho's had no boundaries. They simply didn't give a fuck. A ring was like a chew toy to these hungry bitches. If they wanted your man, they weren't going to stop at nothing to get him.

"I'll tell her to take it down. Now, can you stop lookin' at me like you wanna fight?"
"Nah, Gray that shit got me hot still."

"I see. You tried to square up with me." She chuckled, wrapping her arms around his neck.

"I was gon' knock yo' big ass out." Cam joked, pulling her close.

Gray was so damn pretty to him. Her beauty was ungodly.

"You would never hit me." She kissed the side of his face.

"But I will fuck the lining out that pussy. Come get in the shower wit' me. I'm about to give you the ass whoopin' Aoki deserve."

———

As always when nightfall came, Cam avoided going home. The longer he stayed out, the less time he had to rest. Keeping his secret from Gray that he suffered from PTSD and night terrors was a must. He'd been down that road before with LaLa and it had ended them. His mother's death had already hardened him. Dealing with PTSD made what little compassion he had left for humanity worse. He was even less affectionate and more volatile. His nervous system was stuck in a state of constant alert, making him feel vulnerable and unsafe; the two things Cam hated the most. This led to him feeling angry, irritable, depressed and mistrustful.

He never admitted it, but Cam knew that he never gave Lala his all. He never gave his all to anything except sellin' dope and being in the army and it had damaged him the most. When he returned home from Afghanistan, he withdrew from his family and friends. LaLa did everything she could to love him through his pain. She'd tried being patient, listening, helping him manage his stress and not pressuring him. She stayed on guard at night and held him when he awoke in a panic. She dealt with his anger and anticipated the things that might trigger his outburst. In return, Cam showered her with gifts when all she ever really wanted was the love she gave him in return. Little did she know but Cam was unaware of what it meant to truly connect with someone. The same day his mother died was the same day he emotionally shut down. He'd all but pushed LaLa into another man's arms but his ego and pride wouldn't allow him to admit that. Instead, he blamed their downfall on her and convinced himself that no one he loved was meant to stay.

So, there he sat, in Quan's mancave, filling his lungs with the strongest grain of marijuana on the market, counting down the minutes till he was forced to return home like a kid dreading a an impending whoopin'. After taking Gray from behind in the shower, and once more on the bed, he got dressed and left the crib. He'd checked on his auto shops and liquor stores, made a money drop to Victor, grabbed something to eat and got a fresh haircut. He'd spoken to Gray a few times throughout the day. He could hear in her voice that she wanted him home but didn't push the subject. Cam wanted nothing more than to be there with her as she lay snug in his arms but lounging around would cause him to doze off. There was no way he could risk that. He couldn't let her see how much of a monster he really was. Gray had no idea that every time he came home in the wee hours of the morning, he was either drunk or high. It was the only way he could rest without taking a pill.

Not telling Gray the truth was a selfish move. She deserved to know that she was married to someone with a severe anxiety disorder, but Cam was a selfish muthafucka. He collected things that made him feel good, since he didn't know how to do it for himself. Gray was one of those things. Her optimistic take on life, fun personality, tender heart and the way she loved him made him happy, so he married her. The gag was Gray unknowingly had become one of Cam's many collectables. Like his numerous cars, real estate, jewels and clothes, Gray was nothing more than a thing that gave him satisfaction when needed.

Cam didn't want to break her heart. He hoped what he felt was love and that a time would come where he'd have the courage to allow himself to fall for her. Suffering from PTSD caused him to be emotionally detached from his feelings. He never wanted to care too much about anything. The fear of losing someone else he loved was too much for him to handle. He'd dealt with enough death and losses. Until he figured out his feelings, he planned on keeping Gray content enough to stay. Cam's way of thinking was fucked up. One day he'd pay for his selfishness. He didn't want to lose Gray. She'd been a great addition to his life. She brought peace and balance to his overall chaotic lifestyle. She was the complete opposite of LaLa. His street fame and wealth didn't faze her. She wanted him despite all of his clout which is why he planned on keeping her with him forever, but knowing Cam, he'd find a way to fuck things up. Anything good in his life never lasted long. His mother and LaLa were prime examples of that.

"Quan." Kema jogged down the steps.

"He upstairs gettin' dressed." Cam let out a cloud of weed smoke.

"Oh, I thought he was down here wit' you. Where y'all going?" Kema plopped down in the loveseat opposite of him.

"Elmo's."

"Y'all love a ole hood spot. Nigga just itching to get shot."

"If anything, we'll be doing the shootin'." Cam grinned.

"You right about that. I don't know how me and Gray put up wit' y'all crazy ass. Speaking of my best friend. Y'all good?"

"Why? She sayin' somethin' different?"

"Nah, Gray ain't the type to talk about her relationship. If something was up she would suffer in silence and not say a word. That's why I'm askin' you."

Cam wasn't the type to tell everybody his business either, so he simply responded we straight.

"You know her birthday coming up right?"

"What?" He damn near dropped the blunt.

"Judging by your reaction, I take that as a no." Kema chuckled. "I guess this is one of the drawbacks of marrying someone after only knowing them a few months."

"I'm just mad she ain't said shit to me." He replied genuinely hurt.

"She got her reason. Ask her what's up."

"When is it?" Cam felt like a fool for even having to ask.

"December 14th. She'll be 36."

"Damn, a'ight." Cam panicked.

December 14th was literally two weeks away. That left him practically no time to figure out what he'd do for her.

"You ready?" Quan's deep voice entered the room before he did.

Kema gazed over her shoulder and inhaled a sharp breath. Quan's handsome features never ceased to amaze her. He and the rapper Lloyd Banks could've been twins. When they met, people warned her to stay away or keep her guard up. They said she could never fill the shoes of his infamous ex fiancée Mo. What people failed to realize was that Kema wasn't trying. Quan was going to fuck with her the long way regardless. She was a standup chick, so he had no choice but to feel her. She wasn't the type to elbow her way into any man's heart. Her laidback, no nonsense demeanor always left men wanting more. Kema never made herself too readily available. There was an air of mystery about her that Quan constantly tried to crack the code to. She kept him panting after her like a dog thirsting for water.

"Yeah." Cam stood and pulled up his sagging pants.

"You gon' stay here wit' Li'l Quan and wait up for me?" Quan leaned down and placed both his hands on the sides of Kema's hips, caging her in.

"What I get if I do?" She stared into his dreamy brown eyes.

"This dick." He said low so only she could hear.

"I can get that from anywhere."

"Oh word?" He gripped her neck and planted a sensual kiss on her lips.

The tight hold he had on her throat had Kema's clit palpitating. As his minty tongue danced against hers, the palms of her hands worked their way around his muscular arms, feeling each crevice and vein. Kema's entire body was on fire. By the time Quan was finished, she was left spellbound.

"Be in my bed naked when I get home." He pecked her one last time before leaving.

A few miles away, Gray felt like a complete idiot for having to text her friend and ask was her husband still at her man's house but she had no other choice. She'd called Cam three times and he hadn't picked up. It was taking everything in her not to say fuck this marriage. Spending her nights alone at home had become a recurring thing. Her female intuition didn't tell her he was cheating but what else was she supposed to think? This was the same man who got his dick sucked in a packed club. It wouldn't be a far stretch to think he was giving dick to one of his ho's when he stayed away at night. This wasn't what Gray signed up for. If this was the type of time Cam was going to be on then she could've stayed with Gunz. At least she was familiar with the games he played. With Cam, she had no idea what his motives were. Had he played on her intelligence and made himself out to be a man he wasn't, or had she made him into the man she wanted him to be? With each passing day, she was starting to think marrying him was a mistake.

> **Gray: Cam still there?**
>
> **Kema: Nah, they went to Elmo's**
>
> **Gray: K**
>
> **Kema: He ain't tell u they were going**
>
> **Gray: Yeah, I forgot**

Lying to her best friend wasn't something Gray usually did but she'd be damned if she revealed that Kema's fuck buddy had more respect for her than her own husband. That was something her pride couldn't expose. A million thoughts flooded Gray's mind. She wondered was he not answering because he was with another woman. For all she knew he could be knee deep in some pussy as she lay in their bed waiting for him to come home. Gray had no proof that he was fuckin' around so she was going to keep her suspicions to herself, until further notice. What she wasn't going to do was stress herself out. Refusing to hit him up again, she turned over to go to bed, only to find herself seconds later logging on to Instagram under her dummy account.

Cam didn't have an IG page but LaLa did. Gray had secretly been checking it often. Gray scrolled down and saw a bunch of selfies, outfit of the day post, Flat Tummy Tea ads and hair pics. Gray's stomach soured. She hated that the bitch was so fuckin' pretty. The heffa exuded sex appeal. If she was Cam, she for damn sure would still be fuckin' her. There was no sign of Cam on her page or Instastory. She did have a bunch of subliminal messages under her pics like missing him, she can't love you like I do, forever his and the real Mrs. P. Gray's blood was boiling. It was apparent that she knew Gray and Cam were married. Gray wondered how she'd found out. Had he told her? Whether he had or not, the bitch had balls of steel to disrespect Gray's position in his life.

It took everything in Gray's power not to post a reply. She wasn't that girl tho. Arguing with a chick online was for birds. She was way too classy for that. Heading over to Stacy's page, she checked his post. Every pic with him and Cam in it, LaLa commented with either a heart, tongue or raindrop emoji. She even went as far as to ask Stacy to tell Cam to call her. The thirst was real. Pissed off to the highest extent, Gray closed out of Instagram, put her ego aside and called Cam again. By the fourth ring she was about to hang up when suddenly he answered. All she could hear was loud music playing in his background and a bunch of bitches calling his name.

"What's up?" He yelled so that she could hear his voice over the noise.

Gray took the phone away from her ear and looked at it like he was crazy.

"The fuck you mean what's up?" She spat heated. "You ain't see me callin' you?"

"Yo my bad, ma. I got caught up."

"Caught up doing what?"

"You know a li'l bit of this, a li'l bit of that. What's up? What you need?"

Speechless, Gray held her breath. No way was he talking to her like she was one of the ho's he used to fuck with.

"What I need? What I need is for you to answer the fuckin' phone when I call! I need you to stop being so muthafuckin' inconsiderate! And most importantly, I need for you to bring yo' black, tall, lanky-ass home at night! That's what the fuck I need!"

"You *need* to calm yo' ass down and stop rollin' yo' chubby-ass neck so hard 'cause I can feel that shit over the phone and I don't like it. You *need* to take yo' ole hyper-ass back to sleep. You *need* a midnight snack?" Cam shot back.

Click

Gray was so mad that all she could do was hang up. Cam had her whole entire life fucked up. As she closed her eyes and tried to regain her composure, he called back. *When I'm wit' somebody all I think about is you. When I'm all alone that's what I wanna do.*

"What nigga?"

"Why you hang up on me?" Cam tried to sound all sexy and sweet.

"Bye."

"You bet not fuckin' hang up on me!" He barked into the phone.

"What do you want, Archibald?" Gray tried not to laugh.

"Don't play wit' me yo."

"Well, what the fuck you want 'cause if you ain't on your way home, I ain't got shit else to say to you."

"What I want is you but you ain't fuckin' wit' me right now."

"Nigga, you ain't been fuckin' wit' me all day. That's cause you too busy in the street fuckin' wit' them bitches. Let me find out you fuckin' somebody else. You and that bitch gon' find y'all ass on The First 48."

"Oh, I know what your problem is. You miss this dick don't you, Gray? You need this python in yo' life. You ain't gotta worry, sweetheart. Ain't nobody gettin' this dick but you."

"I can't tell. I don't know what the fuck you be doing until the wee hours of the morning every night."

"I don't be doing shit, straight up. This bitch wit' a fat ass just tried to suck my dick a couple of minutes ago and I told her no. Ask Quan. Watch. I'm finna put him on the phone. Quan! Tell Gray I ain't let that bitch suck my dick!"

"What's up, sis?" Quan got on the phone.

"Hi, Quan." Gray replied, dryly.

"Stop giving my nigga a hard time. He been on his best behavior. I swear to god he ain't let her suck him off. Even if he wanted to I wouldn't let 'em."

"That's good to know. Put my husband back on the phone please."

"Before I go. Kema feelin' the kid ain't she?"

"Oh my god." Gray massaged her temples. "I hate both of you niggas. Quan, if you don't put my husband back on this phone. I ain't got time for you and Kema Love and Hip-Hop bullshit. I got my own problems to deal with. Now put that giraffe lookin' nigga back on the phone before I come up there and shut all that shit down."

"Yeah bro, she ain't in the mood. She just called you a fuckin' giraffe." Quan gave the phone back to Cam.

"Baby?"

"What?" Gray groaned.

"You miss me?"

"When are you coming home?"

"Give me a minute. Let me finish this drink and I'll be there."

"Finish that—" She started in disbelief. "If you ain't home in twenty fuckin' minutes, I'm changing the locks. Try me if you want to." She hung up on him again.

Sensing her weary spirit, Kilo and Gram climbed into bed with her. Their heavy breathing put her at ease. Laying her phone on her chest, Gray gazed up at the ceiling while patting their silky mane and wondering her fate. There were way too many variables in loving Cam. She was so tired of guessing where she stood in the lives of the men she loved. Cam was on that bullshit. She'd given him her trust and he was toying with it like it meant nothing. Something was up. He was hiding something. Sooner or later, the truth was going to come to light, and when it did, Gray wasn't going to hesitate to leave his ass in the dust. She'd be damned if Cam became Gunz 2.0. She knew her worth now. There wasn't a man on earth who would be able to run over her again.

Placing her earphones in her ear, she went to her Tidal app and turned on Alex Isley's *Smoke & Mirrors*. It was a song she often listened to when in turmoil over Cam. The lyrics were an exact replica of what she felt in that moment. Since they'd met, she'd been confused by his feelings. At some moments she was so sure of his love for her, then at other times she was almost sure she was simply just a play thing for him. She prayed he took their marriage and the love she had for him seriously. She didn't want to come out on the losing end of the stick, like she had with Gunz. For her sanity, Cam's love for her had to be true but how could it be when he hadn't even uttered the words? Caught up in the haunting melody, Gray closed her eyes while stroking Kilo's hair and sang along. Her heart bled with each word she sang. By the time the second verse hit, Gray was really into the song.

(Oh I)

See flashes of your heart

I only get so far

Felt this all before

You promised me boy

Tell me you're not like the others

(You're not like the other, yeah)

You are not the same

And I already believe you

(I believe you)

Everything you claim

Look me in my eyes

(Oh, tell me)

Tell me

Make another dream to sell me

(Tell me)

Tell me you're not like all of them

All of them

You're different (you couldn't be) or

Are you smoke and mirrors?

(Is it fun and games, for ya?)

Are you smoke and mirrors?

(Am I the same to ya)

Just smoke and mirrors

(How many times have you lied to me?)

Are you smoke and mirrors?

I don't know where your charms end

And you begin but it's all beautiful

I don't know where your charms end

And you begin but it's all beautiful

You almost have me

Gray's eyes dripped with tears. Each drop soaked the fitted sheet underneath her. The sobs cut through her soul, tearing through her muscles, bones and gut. Wiping her face, she inhaled her misery and released it with a long exhale. Gray refused to cry another tear. She'd made her bed by marrying Cam, now she was forced to lay in it. Only time would tell if she'd, once again, had a lapse in judgement and gave her heart to another undeserving man.

———

In a space between consciousness and slumber Gray's breathing increased. At some point she'd drifted off to sleep. The covers were pulled off and her legs were pried wide open. The dogs were gone. Peeling up her snug fitting nightgown, Cam slipped it up her torso till the fabric covered her eyes. The cold air caused Gray's brown nipples to sprout like buds. Cam leaned forward and plunged his Henny soaked tongue inside her wet walls. He ravished her pussy like he was kissing her mouth. Round and round his head swirled as she panted frantically and reached for his head. Soft moans escaped her mouth as she struggled to awake. Cam honed in on her early morning glory. Kissing pink with pink, his tongue sank between the folds of her glistening lips. Each flick of his tongue renewed moisture as he sucked on her pearl and slid two fingers inside her warm canal. Gray's soft voice serenaded him with soft whimpers of delight. Skillfully, Cam applied pressure by pushing . . . licking . . . sucking. A rush of redness flushed his wife's face as she gushed for him.

"Mmmmmmm Cam." She uncovered her eyes.

"You missed me baby?" He pressed his hands into her thighs.

"Yes." She looked over at the clock and saw that it was going on 5:00 a.m.

She wanted to go off about him repeatedly disrespecting her and their household but the way he was feasting on her pussy caused her head to reel back. Her eyes connected to the ceiling. Every ragged breath she took was collected and condensed between her heavenly thighs. Cam's French kisses caused her pussy to explode into a fiery burst of flames. Cam fucked her pussy with his tongue. His plan was to lap at her sweet cream until she combusted, and he did just that. Gray's stomach muscles contracted as she bounced up and down. The orgasm ripping through her core caused her to see stars. A stream of pussy juices shot from her walls, saturating his facial hair.

"Baby, I can't take anymore. It feel like I'ma die." She whined as she tried to break away from his strong hold.

Cam ignored her cries until her hole was dripping wet with her sweet nectar. She was exactly where he wanted her, relaxed and loose. Licking his way from her pearl to her tight asshole he found and explored the area with his tongue.

"Cam." Gray whispered breathlessly.

A fire burned in her soul as his tongue probed her hole. Gray was in a wonderland filled with fairies and pixie dust. She'd never ventured into ass play but with Cam she was game for anything. He was her drug of choice. One touch from his fingertips and she was intoxicated. Whatever he wanted to do she was more than willing to fulfill his desires. Cam's scent alone sent her spiraling into a deep abyss of ecstasy. Sex with him was always a new experience that left her wanting more. Wet sloppy kisses were placed back-and-forth between the lips of her pussy and asshole. Before she knew it, he'd stuck his finger in her butt. In and out he went while sucking on her clit. It didn't take long for Gray to arch her back and scream out her release. Now that he had her where he wanted her, Cam swiftly unzipped his jeans and pulled out his brick hard cock.

"Ass in the air." He smacked her butt cheek.

"Wait, Cam. I ain't never done that before." Gray lay on her side, trying to catch her breath.

"You trust me?"

"Yes."

"Then you know that I won't hurt you. Ass in the air." He stroked his rigid dick.

Doing as she was told, Gray got on all fours, wondering how she'd gone from wanting to cuss him out to preparing for anal sex. Cam held her firmly in place as his throbbing, hard dick breached her backside.

"Ohhhhhhhhh fuck!" Gray squeezed her eyes shut.

"You can't tense up, Star. You gotta relax."

"But it hurts." She whined, trying to push him out of her.

"Move your hand." He smacked her hand like she was a disobedient child.

Unsure if she wanted to continue, Gray ignored his command. Cam's dick could barely fit in her pussy. How in the hell did he think it was going to fit in her ass?

"Don't make me tell you again." He warned.

This time, she listened and placed her elbows back onto the mattress. The sight of her dewy honeysuckle skin perched before him was picture perfect. Slowly, Cam eased his mammoth cock into her small hole. The sweltering sensation caused Gray to wince in agony. It felt like he was breaking her in half. Cam continued to push his way in until he filled her all the way up. Gray was so snug. He could feel her body churning. A sheen of sweat covered her back. After a few thrusts, she adjusted to being stuffed with his meaty rod. Gray worked her clit as he fucked her tiny hole with reckless abandon. Cam's loud grunts filled the bedroom. He couldn't take too much more of her anal walls. Watching her strum her clit wasn't helping him either. A spine-tingling jolt of electricity surged through his balls and cock.

"What was all that shit you was talkin' over the phone?" He drilled in and out.

Cam was fucking her so good, she couldn't articulate a response. Harder and faster he pumped, intoxicating her mind. If a response was what he wanted, he was going have to stop stroking her ass long enough for her brain to start working again.

"Talk that shit now, Gray." He gripped the back of her neck and went deeper.

Unable to speak, Gray blinked her eyes. Cam had hit an erogenous zone that caused her to temporarily go blind.

"You was gon' change the locks?"

"No." Her sweaty palms gripped the sheets.

Her vision had literally gone black. Cam pushed her face into the mattress and pumped in and out viciously.

"You ain't never gettin' rid of me. You're mine, you hear me?"

"Yes, baby. I'm yours. You got me forever."

"Fuck yeah, you mine. This ass is really mine." He bent down and licked her left ass cheek then bit it. "You like my dick in your tight hole don't you?"

"Yes."

Electrical currents soared through every inch of her frame.

"Fuck." Cam pounded her ass like it was her pussy.

"Cam, it feel so good. I'ma wake the kids." Gray lost control of herself. "Oh my god."

"Damn, Gray, you make a nigga dick so hard."

Cam pressed down onto her lower back. Each drill of his cock caused him to groan out.

"Shit, baby, I'ma about to cum!" Gray cried as her body shook violently.

Cam's response was a forceful smack on her right cheek. The sting of his hit made Gray cum again. Ready to burst, he leaned forward, placing his hard abs on her back and bit the side of her neck. A guizer like amount of cum shot from his dick into her anal. Cam filled her up to the brim. Gray panted heavily as her body shook violently. If Cam kept fuckin' her like this, there was no way she was leaving him. Gray could talk all the shit she wanted and throw out a bunch of empty threats, but she knew the truth. Cam had her in the palm of his hand.

"I'm bitter. Sorry I just can't see you with someone that isn't me."- H.E.R., "Can't Help Me"

#8

Tresses was the hottest hair salon in St. Louis that catered to a young and poppin' clientele. LaLa worked her ass off to build her customer base and roster of beauticians and nail techs. They did it all from sew-ins, hair coloring, cut work, braids, facials, microblading, manicures and pedicures. Since its opening, LaLa had been featured in magazines such as Celebrity Hairstyles, Glamour and Essence. Celebrities like Monica, Kash Doll, Miss Nikki Baby and Taraji P Henson had all been touched by LaLa. Anytime a reality star came to town to do a club appearance, she was the one referred to do their hair. Recently, she'd launched her very own haircare system that consisted of shampoo, conditioner, edge control and hair vitamins. Business was doing so well that she and Cam were scouting locations for Tresses II.

LaLa couldn't have been more thankful that Cam believed in her dreams. When they met she was doing hair out of her apartment. Cam saw how chicks flocked to her because of her skills and dope style. She needed a building to do hair out of and he needed a new business to launder his drug money through. Since they both saw a need in each other, he invested a quarter of a mill into starting Tresses. With his money, LaLa had a state-of-the-art salon that had an industrial aesthetic to it. There were exposed beams and pipes. All of the stylists worked side-by-side at a long wooden table with multiple mirrors that had enough room for each beautician to do their thing. LaLa had her own station right up front that put her work on display for everyone to see. She was a beast at doing hair, especially sew-ins and wig installations.

That afternoon she stood on her throne in her element doing a blonde layered bob. As usual, she was feeling herself. Unlike most hair stylists, she came to work every day dressed to impress. That day was no different. She rocked a white Fendi logo t-shirt, hip-hugging Fendi logo knit leggings and Yeezy, season 7, PVC pumps that showed off her freshly painted, white polished toes. Yeah, LaLa was a bad bitch, and no one could tell her any different. At 28, she was living the life that most women her age could only dream of. Due to her 334k followers on Instagram, she had niggas from all over the world dying to be with her. Niggas went bananas over her light skin, 32-inch, jet black weave, natural plump lips, double D breast implants, snatched waist, curvy hips and Amber Rose size booty. She was the shit. Bitches wanted to be her, and niggas wanted to fuck her. LaLa could have her pick of the liter but she didn't want just any ole man. She wanted Cam. While working on her client's hair, she and her niece, Tia, her best friends Alexzandria and Lynn, as well as the other stylists and customers, discussed her rival Mina Gonzalez's salon.

"Girl, I went in there and they offered me Pinot Noir and shit. I'm like what the fuck is that Pinot Noir? Y'all ain't got no pink Moscato?" A new customer dissed Mina's Joint Salon and Spa.

"She way too bougie for me chile. She think cause she married to Victor Gonzalez that she hot shit. Can't tell that old hoe nothin'." LaLa cackled.

"You wouldn't be able to tell me nothin' either, if I was married to his fine ass." Tia popped her lips. "That nigga can get it sideways, on a handstand, in the church, in my ass—"

"Now wait a minute." LaLa cut her off.

"Girl bye. You know you like to get fucked in yo' ass. You the one that told me about it."

"Right. Who am I foolin'?" LaLa stuck out her tongue. "But back to Victor. That nigga too damn sexy to be so damn faithful. I've been tryin' to fuck that nigga for years and he don't never cheat on that fat bitch."

"What's up wit' these fat bitches takin' all the thorough niggas?" A nail tech that went by the name Belizean Mami probed.

"Y'all ho's stay sleepin'." Shamari a plus-size colorist spoke up. "I told y'all last year it was our time. Bitch, you better get you a sandwich."

"I'ma need to do something." LaLa agreed.

"Yeah 'cause that big bitch definitely stole yo' man and she big-big." Lynn teased.

"Who stole yo' man, LaLa?" One of the customers asked.

"Ain't nobody stole shit. She's temporarily borrowing him." She rolled her eyes hard.

"They talkin' about my baby daddy, BM Gray." Tia adjusted herself in her seat.

She was halfway through her pregnancy and always found herself feeling uncomfortable.

"Oh damn, he wit' her?" The customer said surprised.

"I heard they got married." Shamari added.

"He married that bitch but I ain't worried." LaLa flicked her wrist dismissively.

"Shit you betta be. He ain't never marry yo' ass." Lynn joked.

"Bitch, I will throw this flat iron at your face. Don't play wit' me."

"I meeaaaan . . . it's the truth."

"Yeah, he married her but that ain't stoppin' shit we got going on. We about to open up a new salon together. Shit, I'ma always be in Cam's life. Point, blank and the period. We got too much history together. History that Porky Pig can't compete wit'."

"Well, bitch that's what you about to be . . . history 'cause that blasian bitch don't play."

"She cute tho. I like how she dress." Shamari placed a piece of foil on her client's hair.

"Yo' fat ass would." LaLa sneered.

"I used to love her magazine. LaLa, didn't you have a subscription? I used to see'em around here all the time?" Belizean Mami queried.

"Fuck that magazine and fuck her."

"Oh, you big mad. I ain't never seen you threatened by somebody, boss lady. Let me find out she got you shook."

"It ain't a bitch in this world that can intimidate me. I mean look at me." She walked to the middle of the floor and posed. "Let's be clear. They marriage ain't gon' last. He still in his feelings over Kamryn being Kingston's son and I'm gon' give him that 'cause I fucked up. To keep it all the way real, he only married that bitch to punish me. Cam ain't going nowhere. We got seven years under our belt. We got a bond that no one can break or understand.

That nigga will never admit it, but he love the ground I walk on. He will move heaven and earth to make sure I'm good. Mark my word, he gon' come to his senses and annul that shit. I'ma tell you like I told his ass. He'll never be able to leave me alone. He know, and I know it too."

LaLa hadn't even made it back to her station when the sound of Cam's limited edition, red, Bugatti Veyron by Masory Vivere came roaring up the street. All eyes were on him as he stepped out the 3.4-million-dollar sports car. Dripping in ice, he opened the salon door. Cam sauntered in looking and smelling like a bag of money. LaLa and every other woman in the shop pussy immediately started to cream. Cam was fine as shit. There wasn't one particular feature that made him so irresistible. Everything about him was exquisite. His beauty came from the intense glimmer of his russet colored eyes, hard muscles, tattoos and the gangster stride in his walk. When Killa Cam entered a room, chicks nipples pebbled like rocks. He made women want to risk it all just for one taste. Cam knew the effect he had on the opposite sex that's why he always kept his self well groomed.

He'd let his hair grow out at the top and now donned a curly immaculately lined box. His beard was also precisely lined and trimmed. The gold Jesus piece chain, All Saints black leather biker jacket, black Supreme t-shirt, black distressed and ripped Hudson jeans and Yeezy Boost 350 zebra print sneakers heightened his sex appeal. A red rag hung from the back of his right pants pocket, signifying his allegiance with the Blood gang. The way he looked had all the ladies fantasizing about the way his tongue moved in a kiss, how deep the stroke of his cock went and how the touch of his big hands would feel against the curves of their hips.

"See." LaLa quipped arrogantly.

Cam showing up unannounced only proved her point that he was obsessed further.

"You sholl said it." Belizean Mami pursed her lips, shaking her head.

"Damn, he fine as fuck." Shamari damn near drooled on herself. "I wanna have all his babies."

Cam ignored the women salivating over him. Little did LaLa know but he'd smashed Belizean Mami, her shampoo girl and the bitch sitting in her chair.

"Let me holla at you in the back for a second." He cut right to the chase.

"I'll be right back." LaLa took off her apron so he could see her body.

Cam saw her body alright. Despite how much she irritated him, he couldn't keep his eyes off her sexy physique. LaLa was shaped like a Coke bottle. The leggings she wore cupped her round, jiggly ass perfectly. She walked before him, making sure to sway her hips extra hard. Cam tried not to get caught up but her thick frame made his dick stir in his jeans. Alone in her office, he sat behind her desk as she closed and locked the door behind them.

"Nah, leave that muthafucka open. Ain't shit going down between me and you."

"So, how is married life treating you?" She ignored his request and sat with her legs crossed.

Cam didn't respond. Instead, he unlocked a drawer and pulled out the account book to ensure she'd been depositing the dirty money he'd given her into the salon's business account correctly. LaLa was ordered to deposit small amounts of money at a time. She'd been doing it for six years. Cam should've trusted her to clean the money sufficiently, but he didn't trust anyone when it came to his business. Now that he'd become Lieutenant, he had to ensure that everything was moving properly in the streets as well as on the home front.

"It must not be going so well. You look tired." LaLa cocked her head to the side.

"Yeah, tired of you runnin' yo' fuckin' mouth. I came here to handle business so close your dick suckers before I stick something in it."

"I would love it, Poppi." LaLa ran her wet tongue across her lips and pinched her nipples.

Cam shot her a look of disgust then focused back on the books.

"Hold up." She rose swiftly from her seat. "Is that what I think it is?" She turned his head sideways.

Cam forcefully smacked her hand away.

"No, you didn't go get that bitch name tattooed on you." She said in disbelief.

"It look good don't it?" He smirked.

"When I wanted to get matching tattoos, you told me no."

"You wasn't my wife, was you?"

LaLa sat back in her seat noticeably hurt. The last time she'd seen him he'd damn near killed her with his marriage news and now this. What was next, a baby? If Gray got pregnant, she'd literally slit her wrist sideways.

"When will enough be enough? How much more punishment do I have to take for you to forgive me?"

"The fact that you think any decision I make in my life revolves around punishing you is hysterical."

"Then what is it? Why are you with her?" LaLa snapped on the verge of going insane.

"I'm not having this conversation with you. You're not important enough." Cam continued his research.

"You betta be glad that I just gave my life over to Christ 'cause I wanna slap the shit out of you right now."

"Let the devil use you so I can have a reason to put a bullet in your brain."

"You always wanna shoot some damn body. This ain't M*A*S*H. Your days in the army are over, Hawkeye."

"Good one." Cam chuckled.

LaLa knew M*A*S*H was one of his favorite shows.

"So, what's going on with the shop? Have you found anymore locations 'cause the ones we've seen so far aren't up to par."

"We gon' have to put that on hold for a second."

"Why?" LaLa defensively folded her arms.

Cam flipped the page and didn't respond.

"You have got to be fuckin' kiddin' me!" She exclaimed. "I'm not gettin' my new shop 'cause you're married to her?"

"Now isn't the right time."

"When will it be?"

"No time soon." Cam replied nonchalantly.

"I can't fuckin' believe this."

"Believe it."

"Fuck it. I ain't waitin' on you. I'll open the shop myself."

"Wit' what money? You got a quarter of a mill sittin' around to start another salon?"

LaLa rolled her eyes but remained silent.

"Yeah, that's what I thought."

"I fuckin' hate you." She tapped the heel of her pump on the floor angrily.

It was taking the will of god for her not to cry. Cam was able to do whatever the fuck he wanted without regard of her feelings but kept her on a leash. It seemed like he wanted her to stay stagnant and dependent on him, even though he claimed not to want her. Lala hated the position he had her in. She wanted to give him an ultimatum that either he opened her second salon, or she was going to expose his Lieutenant status to the police, but she knew her threats held no weight in his world. The only thing that would happen was she'd wind up with a bullet in her head for real. There was no point in throwing out idle threats. She'd always lose in the end. Until she could figure out her next move, LaLa would swallow her anger and focus on the problem at hand. Cam's eyes were blood shot red but not from smoking weed. The bags under his eyes said everything.

"You haven't been sleepin have you?" She asked concerned.

Cam clenched his jaw and sighed.

"You haven't." LaLa examined his face.

Up close she could see that he was stressed. Cam hadn't been to sleep in days. His PTSD was in full effect and rearing its ugly head. Suddenly, a light bulb went off in her head.

"She doesn't know does she?" Her expression of worry turned to shock and glee.

"Leave it alone." Cam warned.

"She doesn't know. Damn . . . you can't tell your wife that you have—"

"What the fuck I say?" He looked up and glared at her.

"Don't get mad at me 'cause you keepin' secrets. Things ain't so great in Whoville is it?"

"On god I will fuckin' shoot you in your fuckin' throat. Stop talkin'. I'm tired and I don't feel like shootin' you today."

"Somebody's cranky. She must not be fuckin' you right. You can always come home to mama when you get tired of fuckin' Rebel Wilson." LaLa giggled.

"I'm done 'cause this shit about to make me commit a homicide and you don't even know it." Cam slammed the account book close and stood up.

"Truth hurts don't it?"

"Eat a dick, LaLa." He unlocked the door.

"Gladly, if it's yours. Gon' head and pull that big muthafucka out. I miss the fuck out that one eyed monster." She followed behind him.

"Mommy!" Her son Kamryn came barreling towards her at full speed.

LaLa side stepped Cam and held out her arms to pick him up. Her two-and-a-half-year-old son was the apple of her eye. She wished like hell he would've been Cam's. Unfortunately, he wasn't. He was Kingston, the popular club owner's son. Like Cam, Kingston was a hot commodity in the streets. Ho's were dying to get a piece of him. He was a six-feet, mocha, dread headed, beard rockin', tattooed god. He and Cam weren't the best of friends, but they knew of each other. Cam found him to be a snake-ass nigga. Everybody in Saint Louis knew LaLa was his girl when they were together. The fact that Kingston thought it was okay to stick his dick in his bitch was the ultimate sign of disrespect. The only reason he wasn't six-feet deep was because Cam wasn't the nigga to fight or kill over no bitch. Kingston was just being a typical nigga. LaLa was the muthafucka who was in the wrong. Whenever Cam laid eyes on him or Kamryn, he was immediately transported back to that horrible time in his life. Kingston reminded him of LaLa's betrayal and Kamryn reminded him of the child he never got to have.

"Hey, Kingston." Tia wiggled her fingers flirtatiously.

Kingston wasn't only her aunt's baby daddy but Gunz's fine-ass homeboy.

"What's good, ma?" He rubbed her stomach while eyeing LaLa and Cam suspiciously.

The first thought that ran through his mind was that they'd just finished smashing in her office.

"How the baby doing?"

"He fine. Just waitin' to meet his daddy." She replied as everybody peeped their conversation.

"How long y'all been here?" LaLa held her son in her arms.

"We just walked in. Nice ride fam." Kingston said as Cam walked past.

"Suck my dick." He shot him the screw face as he walked out the door.

Cam was never the one to be fake.

"Ole dick ridin' ass nigga." He quipped, chirping his car alarm.

"I ain't chasing after no bitch. You either wit' me or against me ho."- Jay Rock, "WIN"

#9

    Fifteen, sixteen, seventeen . . . Cam was supposed to be watching The Godfather. The movie had been on for an hour but all he could focus on was the freckles sprinkled across Gray's nose and cheeks like confetti. He'd become obsessed with them. It amazed him how they both had the same feature on their face in the same area. It was as if she was born to be an extension of him. The essence of Gray's beauty was never lost on him. Even with her hair pulled up in a high ponytail and pink, polka dot, long john pajamas and thick socks she was exquisite. God didn't waste not one bit of his splendor on her. There was something about Gray that hit him like a fresh shot of Hennessey whenever he looked at her. She was perfect, and he didn't deserve her. At least that's what he kept telling his self. Gray was cookies and cream sugary sweet. She should've been with a cooperate nigga or a government official, not a gangbanging, drug dealing, army vet with an infinity for murder who questioned his ability to love. He wanted like hell to be in love with her. She'd more than earned it but in the end it didn't matter if he was in love with her or not. He had a part of her soul now.

    She lay in-between his legs with her back pressed against his chest, reading a book on her iPad completely oblivious to his internal struggle. Cam had been battling his emotions for Gray since the moment they said, 'I do'. She deserved to be with a man that could stand firm in his love for her without questioning if it was real. Could he and her weather the storm? Would she stick by his side if she knew all the demons he battled on a daily basis? Would she think he was weird or a freak because he couldn't sleep without smelling rotting flesh and seeing the bloody faces of his battle buddies. How would she feel when she learned he used alcohol to suppress his anxiety? His disorder and constant drinking had pushed LaLa into the arms of another man. The same was bound to happen with Gray. He couldn't blind her with expensive shoes, money and jewels to keep her satisfied. The only thing her heart required was his love.

Gray was reading *First Wives Club Vol.1 Melanin Magic* by Chyna Black. When she envisioned what married life would look like, this was the picture she'd painted in her mind. Amber light from the Christmas tree lit the room. The heat from the furnace had the house at a cozy 68 degrees. The electric fireplace in the living room gave her and Cam the extra amount of warmth they needed. Gray loved winter. Wearing comfy pajamas, fuzzy socks, drinking hot chocolate and reading a book always put her in a good mood. It felt so good to have her man all to herself. For once, he wasn't out rippin' and runnin' the streets doing god knows what. She had him all to herself. After telling Cam that she didn't like him coming home at all times of the night he swore to change. So, there she lay snuggled on the couch in her man's arms enjoying life. Gray couldn't have been happier. The girls were sleeping soundly in their beds. Kilo and Gram were asleep as well. They lay on the floor snoring softly.

Twenty-eight, twenty-nine, thirty. Cam completed his count of her freckles and thanked god for each tiny dot on her gorgeous face. He was so enamored with her that The Godfather had become nothing more than background nose. Michael Corleone's descent into Hell didn't capture his attention at all like it used to. He couldn't concentrate on the classic film if he wanted. Gray wouldn't stop fidgeting. Every time she moved his dick twitched. It was already hard being so close to her without being intimate. Cam was trying to be a gentleman. He wanted to show his wife that he could spend time with her without bending her over the back of the couch and making the tip of his dick touch her spine, but she wasn't making it easy by rubbing against his dick every other second.

"What is wrong wit' you? Why you keep movin' around and shit?"

"Babe, this book is so good." Gray focused on her iPad.

"What book?"

"Chyna new book, First Wives Club."

"You still reading them porno books? Fuckin' pervert." He frowned, taking a sip of his Hennessy and Coke.

The potent drink slid down his throat with ease and warmed his stomach.

"On everything, I think this bitch wrote about us. I talked to that ho on the phone one time about you and she done put our whole relationship in this damn book."

"Star, you're overreacting. It's probably just a coincidence." He put the glass down.

"Coincidence my ass." She sat up and faced him. "The heffa gave her character's our names. We can sue. She even talkin' about Mo too."

"Let me see."

"Look." She pointed to the screen.

"That don't mean nothin'. It's plenty of Cam's out here."

"You hardheaded. Listen to this. *Don't nobody wanna fuck his dusty-ass. I'm dusty but you in here with this Ashley Stewart blazer on. Gray's mouth dropped wide open. Cam saying she rocked Ashley Stewart fashions was the equivalent of him calling her a fat ass bitch. Close your mouth, ma, before I stick something in it. He smirked.*" She recited a passage from the book.

"Oh, shit that is us. Yo' get my nigga Dame on the phone, right now. Shorty got us fucked up. We ain't got not one royalty check in this bitch. I want my money now."

"Babe, she talked about you callin' me husky—"

"Oh, that day I put you on my back." He recalled. "Yeah, you was a li'l husky that day."

"Fuck you." She hit the side of his head.

"I still wanted to fuck tho." He placed a quick kiss on her cheek.

"I just bet you did." She rolled her eyes. "She even wrote about when you told all the bloods on the block to turn my car over."

"You should'a got the fuck out when I told you to."

"Nigga, that's not the point, and she talked about when ya' nasty-ass recorded yourself jackin' off wit' my phone."

"Hold up. She wrote about that?" Cam snatched the iPad from her hand.

"Yep."

"Did she say how big my dick was?"

"Uh huh."

"No wonder mad bitches been in my face. They know your man got eleven inches of steel."

"See, I ain't tellin' that bitch nothin' else. Chyna gon' fuck around and get you and these ho's killed. You know she did the same thing with her book Gunz and Roses? That whole book was about me and Gunz."

"I'ma holla at my nigga Dame for real."

"How you know him?" Gray focused on his face.

Cam placed his blunt up to his lips and inhaled the smoke before speaking. He'd revealed information that he shouldn't have. He never wanted Gray to know that he and Dame knew each other. Being that she was Gunz's girl for years, she was well aware that when Gunz stepped down as Lieutenant, Dame took his place. Gray could never learn that he'd now taken Dame's spot in the Gonzalez Cartel. He didn't ever want his business to affect her livelihood or safety. Gray was a public figure. Her name would be sullied if it ever came out she was a married to a made man.

"We went to school together." He answered truthfully.

"Oh. . . so have you ever been to prison before?"

"Not for anything out of the ordinary."

Gray paused and looked at him.

"What the hell is that supposed to mean?"

"I been locked up for petty shit like unpaid parking tickets, driving wit' a suspended license and possession of weed. I did do a year for a weapons charge tho."

"What did you do?"

"I got caught trying to buy unregistered machine guns and silencers from an undercover federal agent." He grinned.

"What?" Gray's eyes grew wide. "So, you a real live thug, huh?"

"Nah, my bad boy days are over." Cam lied. "They got my black ass on papers. If I do anything, I'm automatically going back to jail for three to five years."

"So, your brother wasn't joking when he said he'll call your probation officer?"

"Nah, that bitch wasn't."

"How long you on probation for?"

"They gave a nigga twelve years. Can you believe that? The system hella fucked up."

"Wow." Gray lay back in total shock.

This was yet another drawback from marrying a man she'd only known two months prior to saying 'I do'. After dealing with Gunz being a street nigga, she swore never to go through that again. Loving a street dude came with nothing but heartache. Gray didn't want any parts of that lifestyle. Thank god Cam was completely legit or else she would have no choice but to call it quits.

"You ain't in the streets no more, are you 'cause I refuse to be married to a street nigga."

"Nah," he lied.

"You sure? There ain't nothin' else you've failed to mention?" She stared up at his face.

Cam shook his head no without giving her any eye contact. He could never look Gray in the eye and blatantly lie. Eventually, it would come to a point where he'd have to choose his drug empire or his wife. Right now, Cam had no plans on stopping hustling. It was the one thing outside of murking niggas that he was good at.

"Good. I don't think I could take any more bad news." Gray let out a sigh of relief.

"Speakin' of keepin' secrets. Why the fuck you ain't tell me your birthday was coming up."

Gray sank down and rested the back of her head on his hard chest. Cam peeped the anxiety on her face and wrapped her up in his arms.

"What's good? Talk to your man."

Absently, she traced his forearm with the tip of her index finger. She'd been avoiding this conversation on purpose. The security Cam gave made it a little bit easier for her to open up.

"My mother died a few days before my birthday."

"Damn . . . that's fucked up. I'm sorry, babe." He tenderly kissed her temple.

"Ever since she died, I haven't really liked to celebrate my birthday. It don't seem right. All it does is remind me that I'm in this world alone."

Cam never tripped off that Gray was parentless. Her mother was gone, and her pops was off somewhere being a deadbeat. Grace might've gone onto heaven and he might not fuck with his father but at least he still had him and his siblings. Gray literally had no familial ties to fall back on in time of need and comfort. He wanted to be her person. The one she relied on no matter the circumstance. For a woman as phenomenal as Gray should never feel alone.

"What I tell you about lyin' all the time?"

"Huh?" Gray turned her face to look at him.

"You ain't alone. You got me, Ren and Stimpy," he joked.

"Thank you, baby." She smiled gratified.

Cam always had a way of making her worries go away. During moments like this, she thanked god extra hard for making her his. Not only was he jaw-droppin' fine and strong with a big crooked dick, he was caring.

"Shut up." Gray giggled as Press stumbled into the living room.

"Mommy, I can't sleep." She rubbed her sleepy eyes.

"What's wrong baby?" Gray sat up and placed her feet on the heated floor.

"Cam, I want Teddy." Press bypassed her mom and reached out for him.

"Ain't this about a bitch." Gray frowned as Cam picked her up.

Press wrapped her tiny arms around his him and nestled her face in the crook of his neck. Cam lovingly kissed her forehead. In the short amount of time that Press had been in his life, he'd grown to adore her. From the outside looking in you'd think she was his child. Press had him wrapped around her little finger. She had Cam doing shit he never thought he'd do like letting her paint his nails, playing dolls and having tea time.

"The monsters came back because I forgot Teddy." She pouted.

Like him, Press suffered from nightmares. It was something that she had developed since they'd moved into the new house. Gray figured she too was having a hard time adjusting to their new normal. To ease her troubled sleep, Cam went out and purchased her a $9,000 Louis Vuitton teddy bear. The bear was meant to serve as her protector during the night. Having Teddy by her side seemed to be working. Whenever she slept with him she had a full nights rest.

"Okay, let's go find him so you can go back to sleep." Cam held her small frame close and headed back to her room.

Gently, he sat Press down onto her bed and searched for Teddy. It took him a few minutes, but he found him buried underneath a pile of toys. Cam put him right beside Press and pulled up the covers.

"Cam, are the monsters gonna stay away now?"

"Yeah. You a bad bitch right?"

"Yes." She nodded her head.

"If not, I'll fuck one of these monsters the fuck up!" Cam pulled out his pistol ready to shoot one in the air. "They don't want no smoke!"

"Cam, stop! That's enough!" Gray yelled from the living room.

"My bad, babe!"

"Mommy don't want me to be a bad bitch." Press poked out her bottom lip.

"That's cause yo' mama a fuckin' hater."

"I heard that!" Gray shouted.

"Shut up and continue to read that soft porn Chyna wrote!"

"What's soft porn?" Press wrinkled her brow. "Cam, can you read me soft porn, so I can go to sleep?"

"See what you did?" Gray snapped.

"Nah, you don't need to be a creep like your mom." He snuggled Press in tight.

After kissing her cheek goodnight, he sat by her side until her eyes drifted close. Before leaving, Cam took in the way her long curly hair sprawled over the pillow like her mother's when she slept. If someone would've told him he'd be this soft over a little girl, he would've called them a liar. He now had a wife and two daughters. He had to get softer. A fuck everybody attitude was no longer natural. Press had opened up parts of his heart that he didn't even know existed. Seeing that he could love a child made him want one of his own even more. Back in the living room, he retook his spot on the couch and hugged his big girl.

"When you gon' give me a baby?"

Gray drew her head back confused. Cam knew having a baby was a touchy subject for her.

"You do remember that my tubes are tied?"

"Yeah, but that don't mean we can't pay a bitch to have a kid for us."

"I gotta figure out what I'm gonna do with my life before talks of having a kid can even be a topic. This being a stay at home mom and wife ain't cuttin' it."

Cam balled up his face. He had no idea Gray was having issues with not working. He thought she was enjoying being at home. Even though the house was technically hers, he paid all the bills and made sure that her and the girls never had to want for anything. There wasn't a day that went by where he didn't make sure she had several stacks of cash on her at all times.

"I like you being at home." He circled his strong arms around her and held her tight.

"Yeah, but you're hardly ever here. When you get up and leave I spend all day here alone until I get the girls from school. I'm used to working every day. I'm used to being on the move. Sitting at home watching Daily Pop and Wendy ain't my thing. I feel lost."

I hate you so much right now! I hate you so much right now!

Gunz's ringtone started to play distracting them. She and Cam both looked down at the phone then at the clock.

"What the fuck is this nigga doing callin' you at eleven o'clock at night?"

"I don't know. I'm sittin' here wit' you." Gray replied as she picked up the phone. "Hello?"

"Hello?" Cam repeated with his face tuned up.

Had Gray really answered her ex phone call in his face?

"Did I catch you at a bad time? You busy?" Gunz spoke low into the phone.

He was sneaking calling Gray while Tia was in the room sleep.

"Nah. What's up?"

I know she didn't say she wasn't the fuck busy, Cam thought.

"I was just callin' to see if you got the flowers I sent 'cause I ain't hear nothin' from you."

"Flowers?" Cam examined the living room until his eyes landed on a fresh floral arrangement of six multi-colored roses and ten Peruvian Lilies.

"Yeah, I got 'em. Thanks." Gray responded dryly.

"Raise up." Cam pushed her off him.

"Did you and the girls like 'em?" Gunz inquired.

"They cool. What is it that you want, Gunz?"

"You, I thought I made that clear?"

"Oh my god." She groaned.

"Look, I'm sorry about what I said. I'm sorry about what I did. What is it gon' take for you to forgive me?"

"I'm sorry doesn't change anything. I'm not gettin' back wit' you. How many times I gotta tell you that?"

"Hold up. Say that again?" Cam spun around with an evil glare on his face.

Instead of responding verbally, Gray placed up her index finger telling him to pause.

"Gray, just listen." Gunz pleaded. "I miss you. I miss our family."

"You should've thought about that before you tried to channel Chris Brown. Now, I told you don't call me unless it's about the girls. You're interrupting my household, and in the future, don't call me after eight. It's disrespectful to me and my husband."

Seeing that he wasn't getting anywhere with her, Gunz switched the topic to Aoki and Press.

"When can I get the girls again?"

"We already talked about this, every weekend. Anything else?"

"Hang up the fuckin' phone." Cam seethed with anger.

"What the fuck he say? Gray, you ain't gotta listen to that nigga. You ain't gotta get off the—" Gunz shouted as she ended the call.

Sitting the phone back on the table, Gray exhaled. Gunz was wearing on her nerves. Once she regained her composure, she focused on Cam who was glaring at her like she was a dead woman walking.

"What's your problem? Why you lookin' at me like that?"

"You stay lyin' about shit then sit there with that dumb-ass look on your face like you ain't did shit! That shit infuriates the fuck outta me, blood!"

"What I lie about now? I ain't even did shit." Gray replied perplexed.

"So, when you had lunch wit' that nigga, he tried to get back wit' you?"

Gray rolled her neck in a circle. She'd completely forgot that she'd kept Cam in the dark about Gunz trying to gain her affection when they met up to talk. Now that he knew the truth, it was only going to cause another problem in their relationship.

"Yeah, Pinocchio, keep up wit' your lies. You ain't tell me that shit and the fact that you didn't make me believe that you wanna be back wit' that nigga."

"I don't."

"You got a lousy fuckin' way of showing it. Yo' ass conveniently left that part out. The question is why?"

"I swear to god I wasn't tryin' to be on no funny shit. I was honestly tryin' to keep the peace."

"Keep the peace these nuts. You know exactly what the fuck you was doing. You was protecting that nigga like you always do."

"I don't protect him and let's not act like you're a fuckin' saint. You don't even bring your ass home at night. Lord knows what the hell you be out here doing."

"Fuck that! This ain't about me right now. We resolved that issue."

"Did we? Cause I don't think we did." Gray challenged.

"Don't try to flip this shit around on me. You foul . . . you dirty as fuck, Gray." He pointed his finger at her.

"Okay, Cam. Whatever you say." She waved him off.

"I'll paralyze your whole right arm if you wave me off again."

"Like I said, whatever, Cam." She folded her arms and legs.

"So, let me guess? You mad now. You the victim. A'ight bet. I'm the bad guy. Crazy Cam doing the most like always."

"You are."

The fact that she was acting so nonchalant over the situation really fucked his head up. Gray had no idea how much she was breaking his heart with her fuck shit.

"Are you for real fam? I'm doing the most but you on the phone cupcakin' wit' yo' baby father over some cheap-ass, grocery store flowers. And you got the nerve to have the shit posted up in the crib like it's okay. Like it's a fuckin' centerpiece for Christmas." He smacked the vase over, causing it to fall to the floor and break.

The loud clash jolted Kilo and Gram from their sleep. On high alert, the dogs rose to their feet and instantly started barking.

"See what you did. You got the dogs going crazy and shit. Kilo and Gram hush! Sit!"

Trained to be obedient they both listened to Gray's command and rested on their legs.

"For your information, he sent those flowers to me and the girls. That's the only reason why I kept them in the house. The girls were here when they were delivered. You know I wouldn't have kept them if they were for me." She grabbed the broom and dust pan to clean up his mess.

"Do I? Cause you moving kinda shifty, ma. This shit ain't sittin' well in my digestive system."

"What is that supposed to mean?" Gray stopped and looked at him.

"It means I'm gettin' the fuck up outta here."

"Cam, you leaving is not going to solve anything. We already discussed that we need to talk things out."

"Me leaving is gon' stop me from fuckin' you up." He grabbed his Timbs and started putting them on.

"You not even giving me the chance to explain my side of the story. Let me explain where I was coming from." She pleaded.

"You had your opportunity to explain weeks ago when you stood there and lied to my face."

"I didn't lie. I just omitted some of the conversation because I knew you would fly off the handle like you always do. I'm tired of fighting wit' you. I'm tired of fighting wit' Gunz too. I just want peace."

"And I'ma give you that. You gon' be peaceful as fuck by yo 'self until you can learn to set boundaries with that nigga. The same nigga I could've went to jail for fuckin' up cause I was tryin' to defend yo' ole ungrateful ass. Here I am tryin' to be everything for you and you still stuck in yo' past. I ain't tryin' to compete wit' no nigga, especially a clown-ass nigga like Gunz. You supposed to be mine but you still actin' like you his."

"That's not true." Gray's heart ached.

"Bullshit and you know it." Cam flung on his coat. "I'm doing everything your way. I'm living in your crib—"

"Our crib." She cut him off.

"Your crib. Out of a fuckin' duffel bag! I'm in yo' shit. Ain't none of this shit mine. We ain't equal. You can put me out this muthafucka whenever you feel like it, even though I'm payin' all the bills. How you think that make me feel as a man that I'm layin' my head in a spot that ain't even got my name on it? I left all my shit behind so that you and your kids could be comfortable. I put up with your daughter's disrespect. I let you slide wit' being sneaky. I deal wit' you gettin' on my head about stayin' out. I constantly assure you that I ain't out here fuckin' around even though you accuse me every fuckin' five seconds of fuckin' other bitches. I'm payin' all the bills in this muthafucka and I'm still payin' for my other crib that I don't fuckin' even live in but you don't give a fuck."

"I didn't ask you to do that. I got my own damn money. I can take care of my house and my kids myself." Gray spat in return.

"That's beside the point jackass. I take care of you cause I'm your fuckin' husband. I'm a man. That's what a man is supposed to do but at least acknowledge the fact that I'm tryin'. All you think about is you and your feelings and what you got going on. You don't know half the shit I deal wit' every day."

"Cause you don't tell me shit! I ain't no fuckin' mind reader. You deal with that shit on your own cause you want to! I been tryin' to figure you out since day one but it's you that keeps me at arm's length. I've been tryin' to get you to open up. It's you that don't wanna let nobody in so don't put that shit on me." Gray clapped back.

"And why you think that is Lyin' Linda! I don't trust you! You always fuckin' lyin'! It's like your physically here wit' me but your heart is still wit' him. You always wanna tell me what the fuck I need to be doing, but it seems to me, you the confused muthafucka. You gotta figure out what you want ma 'cause I'm not playin' these games wit' you. Matter of fact, I'ma make the decision for you." He headed towards the door.

"What does that mean?" Gray panicked feeling dizzy.

"You're a smart girl." Cam put on his red Cardinal's hat. "You'll figure it out." He slammed the door shut behind him.

"In love with what I can't obtain. Besides the butterflies I don't know what remains. Can this story ever change? Guess no matter what I say you won't feel the same or will ya?"- Alexis Isley, "My Theme"

#10

A hollowness she hadn't felt in years swallowed Gray whole as soon as Cam walked out of the door. A hole the size of the Atlantic Ocean was carved in the pit of her stomach. On edge, she listened to the harrowing sound of the phone ring until his voicemail kicked it. She'd called him so many times she'd lost count. The pads of her fingers felt numb. Her repeated calling was in vain. Cam wasn't going to answer. This she knew. Throughout their relationship, he had the propensity to shut her out. He was only giving her another dose of his stomach-churning medicine. Any other time she'd be able to handle his cold behavior. This time things felt different. There was a shift in the atmosphere. His parting words felt so final. *You gotta figure out what you want ma 'cause I'm not playin' these games wit' you. Matter of fact, I'ma make the decision for you.* Was that his way of saying it was over? Was he never going to return home? The mere thought made Gray's head swim. She wanted to lay down and never wake up again. If she lost him over a stupid mistake she'd never forgive herself.

She'd called herself trying to keep the peace, only to end up with even more turmoil. Cam accusing her of having feelings for Gunz and constantly protecting him was absurd . . . or was it? Maybe subconsciously she did like his constant groveling. Having a man like Gunz on his knees was a rarity. For ten years, he'd been the one in the driver seat of their relationship. He'd held all the power. Gray constantly found herself fighting for his affection and having to prove her love. Now the tables had turned. He was the one begging for a sliver of her time. It felt good knowing that if she snapped her fingers and said jump, he'd say how high. She secretly took pleasure in making him jealous. Throwing up her marriage to Cam in his face was a major confidence booster. She loved seeing the anger on his face. She thoroughly enjoyed hearing him grovel and plead like a bitch. Was her behavior petty and childish? Yes, but for ten years she tolerated his bullshit and disrespect. Gunz dished out spoonful's of his time and love just to keep her content while giving pieces of himself to other women. He didn't give a damn about the tears she cried or her pleading for him to change. Every chance he got, he took the opportunity to stomp on her heart. He never thought she'd find the strength to leave him, let alone for someone else. To finally have the upper hand was power like no other.

Gray had been a victim of circumstance her whole life. She was born into the world a mixed child whose daddy went missing as soon as his sperm connected to her mama's egg. She never had control when it came to the men in her life. So maybe Cam's accusations did hold weight. No, she didn't want Gunz, but she did enjoy making him suffer, not at the cost of losing her man tho. Cam had left her in the cold, sad and confused. His denial of her was killing her softly. She felt raw and tender each time he didn't answer her call. It felt like her insides had been mixed up in a meat grinder, but she only had herself to blame. Instead of admitting that she was wrong and making things right, she lashed out. Misplaced entitlement caused her to spew out passive aggressive rage. Now she sat on the couch alone shedding tears and feeling like an absolute idiot. Cam was gone. There was no telling where he went or who he was with. What if she'd pushed him in the arms of another woman? A woman like LaLa who acknowledged his feelings and kissed all his worries away?

What the hell have I done, she planted her face in her hands. She needed her husband back, so she could make amends. It didn't feel good to know she wasn't a priority on his list. Worried about where he may be, she tried contacting him again. Once more he didn't answer. Sadness and anger consumed her. She hated when he acted like this. No woman liked to be ignored but she'd dug her own grave. Now she had to lay in it.

This wasn't a proud moment for Gray. She'd turned into someone she didn't know. She wasn't behaving like a strong woman with the softness of a mother. Instead, she acted like a pubescent child who was damaged and afraid. She used her co-parenting relationship with Gunz as a crutch and an excuse not to fully give herself over to Cam.

He evoked feelings in her that were so reminiscent of Gunz that it scared her. With Cam, she feared he'd one day wake up and say marrying her was a mistake or what if she found out he still loved LaLa? Her poor heart wouldn't be able to absorb the pain, so she teeter tottered on her emotions in order to keep herself whole. If she didn't give herself to him fully, she'd never have to risk getting hurt. That was no way to behave as a wife, but self-preservation was a muthafucka. She couldn't afford another broken heart. All her life, Gray had cared for others. She poured out love without measure and never received an ounce of it in return until she met Cam. He showed her that real love could be attainable and pure. Love wasn't supposed to make you feel weak and insecure. This she now understood. She couldn't continue to disregard his concerns. In order for their marriage to work she had to take his feelings into consideration and stop being in a constant state of fight or flight. If she didn't she'd be sitting on the very same couch alone for the rest of her life.

Cam parked his car in the driveway and looked down at his phone. Gray was calling him again. He thought about answering but there was no point, considering he'd be walking in the house in a few seconds. Since he'd left, she'd been blowing him up. It truly fucked him up to ignore her, but he had to. He wasn't in a clear head space to talk to. He'd said enough before walking out the door. When it came to Gunz, they were on opposite sides of the fence. He couldn't take her indifference of her exes presence in their life anymore. Cam understood fully well that he would be around because of the girls. What he wouldn't tolerate was Gunz continuously inserting himself in-between him and Gray. He'd made it abundantly clear that he wasn't going to ease up on winning her back. Gray knowing this and keeping it away from Cam pretty much said to him that there were parts of her heart he still didn't have access to. If she truly wasn't feeling Gunz, she wouldn't entertain any of his advances. She'd keep it a hunnid with Cam regarding him at all times. There wouldn't be any secrets.

And yeah, he had secrets of his own that needed to be revealed but Cam didn't give a fuck about that right now. His heart was on the line. Feeling vulnerable wasn't something he was used to. The predicament Gray put him in had him wondering if being with her was worth all the trouble. Before he made any rash decisions, he needed to clear his head. The liquor and weed in his system, along with a few hours of sleep, would help him do just that.

Sluggishly, he took his key out of the ignition and opened the door. The street was still as the moon hovered over his head. It was going on 3:00 a.m. Cam needed warm shelter and rest. He hadn't sleep in days. His body couldn't take another sleepless night. His mind needed to shut down. He didn't want to think about Gray's inconsiderate ass anymore. For the past few hours that's all he'd done. A chick hadn't gotten him this tight since LaLa. Gray had the tendency to make him lose his shit. She was so unconcerned about everything that it made him think he was the one who was crazy. She had to have known that he would flip upon seeing the flowers. The disrespect she'd displayed by having them in their home was irreversible. He'd never be able to let go of his anger. It was like she was a glutton for punishment when it came to Gunz. Cam was just being petty when he said it but maybe she really did like a nigga to treat her bad. Whatever her problem was, it was on her. He didn't have the mental capacity to dissect Gray's issues anymore. As far as he was concerned, their so-called marriage was seconds away from being annulled.

Slowly, he walked up the steps. The brisk night air chilled his tipsy bones. He couldn't wait to get in the house. He hoped everyone was asleep once he got inside. He didn't feel like talking or arguing. Laying down and resting his weary body was all that mattered. Unlocking the door, he quickly disarmed the alarm with the hope of not waking anyone up. His wish, however, didn't come true. The kitchen light popped on and out came LaLa creeping around the corner in nothing but a silk, spaghetti strap nightgown holding a bat.

"It's me." He placed down his keys and began to unbutton his coat.

"Boy, you scared the shit outta me." She held her chest and let out a sigh of relief as he took off his hat.

She'd been in bed peacefully asleep when she heard the sound of the front door creak open. LaLa was a light sleeper so any noise would awake her. She fully expected to find a burglar in her home. Not Cam. He hadn't made an impromptu visit to her house in months. She figured, eventually, he'd pop up. Sooner or later he'd need the comfort only she could provide. She was the only person who had a firsthand account of how his PTSD effected his everyday life. Others knew of his diagnosis, but she was the one who had accompanied him to therapist sessions, took him to see a hypnotherapist, suggested he do mediation and yoga, made sure he took his meds and listened to all the gruesome stories of when he served on the front line. To the world, Cam claimed to hate her guts but LaLa knew that was a bunch of bullshit. Even after they broke up, he still found his self on her doorstep seeking her aide. With LaLa, he could fully be his self. She was one of the few people he could get a good night's sleep around. Yeah, Gray might've worn his ring, but she had his trust, which was big in a man like Cam's world.

"Your wife know you're here?" She leaned the bat up against the wall.

"Turn the light off. I'll be gone by morning." Cam kicked off his boots and lay flat on the couch.

Discussing Gray with Lala was never going to be an option. And no, he had no business being at his ex-girlfriend's house, but with the way Cam was feeling, he honestly didn't care. He didn't have any intentions on fuckin' LaLa. He was in search of quiet, rest and a familiar space. It was something he used to do from time to time before getting with Gray. He and LaLa had their issues but she understood him in ways other people didn't. She'd seen him at his worse. His plan was to get a few hours of Z's and head home. Besides, Gray didn't give a fuck about his feelings so why should he care about hers?

The ignorant part of LaLa wanted to press the subject but even she knew when to back off. She'd seen the redness in his eyes from lack of sleep the last time he'd come to the shop. Cam was having a hard time. Why he hadn't told his wife about his PTSD and night terrors was beyond her. Maybe their bond wasn't as strong as they portrayed. It couldn't have been or else he wouldn't have been there in her house on her couch. Whatever the reason she was just glad to have him there. She missed his almond shaped russet eyes. She missed smelling the cedar and sandalwood scent of his cologne. She missed him needing her. Deciding she didn't want to rock the boat, LaLa headed to the linen closet and pulled out his favorite comforter. Lovingly, she placed it over his body, making sure he was warm.

"Thanks." Cam mumbled, already dosing off.

LaLa stood silent. There was no thanks necessary. His presence was all the thanks she needed. Her needing to be near him had her wanting to find space to lay next to him but there wasn't enough room. Cam wouldn't have it anyway. It was hard to leave his side after being away from him so long, but she headed back to her room in hopes that he'd still be there when she got up in the morning.

It never failed. Cam's night terrors always started off the same. There he was laying on his back paralyzed with fear as beads of sweat seeped through his pores. Heat rays from the blaring sun burned his skin it was so hot. The sound of boots crunching against the dirt and gravel ground signaled the end was near. Cam scooted back at a snail's pace as a masked member of the Taliban inched towards him, aiming a rifle at his head. All his battle buddies had been taken out. It was just him left. From the way things were looking, Cam's time to meet his maker was next. With no gun in sight, he closed his eyes and said a silent prayer to god that he'd let him into heaven when the rifle went off. Jumping out of his sleep, he screamed and thrashed around while kicking the comforter off of him. His heart thudded against his chest. Cam shuddered. Even his breaths quaked.

He didn't know where he was. The room was pitch black. There was no light anywhere. Fragments of the nightmare still clung to his brain. Was he blind? Had the shot taken his eyes out. Cam's body washed cold as he brought his shaky fingers to his eye sockets; they were still there. He swallowed the huge lump in his throat and thanked god again. After that he once again sought out light. He still couldn't see anything, which didn't help his breathing. With each breath he took it felt like his heart was going to stop beating. Upon hearing his yells of despair, LaLa came rushing out of her bedroom. Turning the light on, she found him sitting up freaking out. He was breathing like he was about to take his last breath. His brown eyes were dilated. She hated to see him in such a state of panic. Without saying a word, she headed to the medicine cabinet and pulled out a bottle of medication he kept stashed there. LaLa poured a Xanax into the palm of her hand and grabbed a bottle of water out the fridge.

"Cam, baby, calm down. I'm here." She bent down on her knees in front of him. "Everything's okay. You're not dead. You're alive." She rubbed his back soothingly.

"Here. Take this." She handed him the pill and water.

Disoriented and frazzled, Cam popped the pill in his mouth and chugged down the entire bottle of H20. Falling backwards, he lay on his back and glared at the ceiling. His breathing was starting to regulate again. He didn't know why he kept having a recurring dream of that fateful day where he'd almost lost his life. He'd lived to see another day. Before the enemy could fire off his shot, Cam pulled out his combat knife and threw it at his eye, killing him instantly. Maybe the memory terrorized him cause he was the only one to survive. No that wasn't it. The day haunted him cause he'd wanted to die along with his battle buddies. Cam always felt guilty for living when everyone else had perished. Why did God leave him to bear the weight of seeing his friends die? There wasn't a day that went by where he didn't see visions of their dying faces. Their deaths haunted him. He always felt guilty that he hadn't been able to save any of them. The guilt was so strong that he made it a point to avoid their family members at all cost. Instead of attending their funerals, he sent cards filled with money as his condolences. This was the downside of loving him. He never wanted Gray to see him like this.

LaLa rubbed his head and watched as the pill kicked in. She wanted him so bad she could taste it on the buds of her tongue. She lived and breathed this nigga. There wasn't a thing he could ask that she wouldn't do. A line of coke, she'd sniff it. Jump off a bridge? She'd gladly plunge to her death. Whatever he needed she would provide. LaLa cursed at the way she was bound to him. His soft hair glided against her fingers with ease. His follicles were raw like silk. She loved him so. Cam was the last of his kind. He was such a good man. He didn't even know how good of a man he was. She'd taken for granted his love when she had him. Now that she was single, she saw that the grass wasn't greener on the other side. Cam had been faithful their entire relationship. Dudes nowadays were accustomed to having multiple women. It was a normal thing to have several chicks in rotation. LaLa would give her left arm to have the love and faithfulness Cam provided again. If he ever gave her a second chance, she'd love him fiercely.

Cam's eyes started to flutter as he fell back to sleep. He hated to take the meds the doctors prescribed him cause it made him groggy and sluggish. He couldn't function, and in his line of business, he always had to be alert. On nights like this he had no choice but to give in and seek assistance. Minutes later, he was knocked out. LaLa was just happy he'd have a peaceful night's sleep without interruption of terror. He desperately needed it and she was happy to be the one to give him solace.

Hours later a shove to Cam's arm jerked him awake. His eyes flickered opened and he took in the sight of Kamryn's little face staring back at him. His nose was starting to run. Cam closed his eyes and frowned. He couldn't stand the sight of his face. His coco colored skin, doe shaped eyes, long lashes and pudgy stomach were adorable. Sadly, whenever Cam looked at him he didn't see the cuteness everyone else saw. All he saw was lost and that the li'l nigga looked just like his daddy. For a minute, he and Kamryn just stared curiously at one another. Cam still couldn't get over the fact that LaLa had given him his name. Thoughts of LaLa made him wonder how he'd even ended up at her crib. It took a second, but he suddenly remembered pulling up to her spot after having a few drinks at a bar. His plan was to rest his eyes for a minute and then head home but judging by the fact that Kamryn was up and dressed, he'd slept too long. The question was how long had he been asleep? His entire body felt like it was weighed down by bricks. He did feel well rested tho.

"You wanna play?" Kamryn thrusted a toy firetruck in his face.

"Nah, li'l man. I'm about to jet." Cam pushed up off his heavy arms and sat up straight.

Grabbing his phone, he checked the time. It was after 1:00 p.m. He had over twenty missed calls from Gray. The last call had come in at 7:35 a.m. Cam ran his hand over his head. He was in deep shit. He had truly fucked up this time. Panic stricken, he tried to figure out how he was going to get himself out of this mess. There was really nothing he could say or do. He'd stayed out all night and hadn't spoken to his wife since the night before. It was now after noon. Gray was sure to flip out on him and lose her shit.

"Fuuuuuuuuuuck!" He groaned, grabbing his Timbs.

He'd just gotten Gray and now he was about to lose her over some bullshit.

"Watch your mouth around my son." LaLa came sauntering into the room fully dressed, eating a bag of Migos White Cheddar With A Dab of Ranch Popcorn.

"Mommy, me and Cam finna play fireman." Kamryn tinkered with his toy.

"No, we ain't." Cam tied up his boots.

"Kamryn, go in your room and play. I need to talk to Mr. Cam."

"Okay, Mommy." He ran past her.

LaLa licked the ranch sauce off her fingers and rolled the bag of popcorn close.

"You feeling better?"

"What you talkin' about?" Cam rose to his feet and stretched his aching back.

"You don't remember? You had a night terror last night."

"I did?" He furrowed his brows.

"Yeah, I had to give you one of your pills."

"No wonder I slept so long. Shit." His mind wandered.

Cam tried to recall what had happened. His last memory was pulling in her driveway and falling asleep on her couch. For the life of him, he couldn't remember anything about having a night terror. Sometimes it was like that. He'd wake up the following day completely oblivious to what had transpired the night before until someone told him. Thank god it hadn't happened around Gray. Sometimes, he could get violent when he had an episode. Cam pocketed his phone. He had to get out of there. Gray was going to slit his throat.

"Thanks for lettin' me crash." He slid his arms inside his coat.

"Wait!" LaLa put her hand on his chest and stopped him.

"What's up?" Cam frowned.

He wasn't in the mood for whatever she was about to say.

"I just thought that since—"

"Ain't nothin' changed."

"Then what you come over here?" LaLa quickly copped an attitude.

"I gotta go."

"No!"

"Bye LaLa." Cam grabbed his keys.

"Answer me!" She stomped her foot.

"What? What the fuck do you want to talk about?" He barked back.

"Why did you come here?"

"I don't know. I just did. Does that make you feel better?"

LaLa bit down into her lower lip in hopes that the pain would ease the one in her chest. She couldn't understand why he didn't realize that when he came around the whole world and everything in it stopped.

"That's bullshit, and you know it."

"What you want me to say?"

"I want you to say that you still love me 'cause I know you do or else you wouldn't be here."

"I'ma always have love for you but it ain't like that between us no more."

"You are so full shit." LaLa shook her head.

"A'ight, La, if that's how you feel." Cam turned to leave.

"You can't keep doing this to me."

"Doing what?!" He spun around.

"You know how I feel about you, but you treat me like some play thing."

"Fuck does that mean?"

"It means you can't just show up and disturb my life when you're feeling helpless and then disappear when the world is right side up again. Not being around you these past couple of months has made me realize that you do real harm to me. So, in order to protect myself and my peace of mind, I need you to stay away from me. Unless you can sweat to me that you won't hurt me again."

Cam inhaled deep. This was the last conversation he wanted to have. He wanted to be inside his car heading home to his wife. He should've listened to his first mind last night and gone to his apartment.

LaLa's pleading eyes welled with tears of regret. She regretted, once again, putting herself on the line only for him to let her down. She should've been used to him sending her mixed signals by now. She'd poured so much of herself into him for so long and Cam secretly loved her devotion. He'd use her for his own personal gain then turned cold and shut her out. He had no qualms about adding wounds to the collection of others he'd created. It should've but his selfish behavior never stopped LaLa from loving him, but at that moment, she knew she needed to learn how.

"You ain't gon' never fuckin' change." She sucked her teeth and wrapped her arms around her torso.

She needed to barricade herself from him. Cam wanted to care about the tears that slid down her makeup covered cheeks, but his mind was so focused on Gray that he couldn't find it in him to give LaLa the attention she so desperately craved. He was a fucked-up individual that missed his mama, despised his father and loathed a woman who'd cracked what was left of his battered heart in two. The only person who hadn't done him dirty was Gray. He couldn't risk losing the one good thing in his life because he was in his feelings over something that could easily be fixed.

"Get the fuck out." LaLa wiped her own tears away.

There were so many words that were being left unsaid as Cam turned his back to leave. Those words would have to be voiced another day, at another time.

"Don't come back here again." LaLa choked on her tears.

"I won't."

"This feeling's hard to ignore. Please say you'll never get bored. Can you blame me for wanting a little bit more? A little more of you."- Alessia Cara, "A Little More"

#11

The day his mother took her last breath was the last day Cam felt like a kid. All childish things were left behind. He morphed from boy to man within seconds that horrific day. Twenty-five years later, here he was feeling like a child all over again. He was shaken and terrified at what awaited him on the other side of the door. It felt like someone had taken a screwdriver to his brain. With each step he took, his restricted feelings grew as if he was being strangled just by air. Who would've thought a woman would have him this way. Cam didn't fear much at all, but at that moment, space and time in his life he genuinely feared seeing the look on Gray's face when she saw him. She was the one person he never wanted to disappoint. Now because he decided to act out in anger, he was probably about to lose his heartbeat.

It was funny how when he'd left, he was the one in the right. His feelings were completely justified and now none of it mattered. All of his issues with Gray were completely thrown out the window. Going M.I.A. for half the day trumped any grievances he had with her. Gray was now the one with the upper hand. A paralyzing fear spread through his body like black ice. Cam clenched his fist as he reached the door. His leg twitched as he fought the impulse to haul ass, but he couldn't leave. He had to face the shit storm he'd created.

Time stood still as Gray stood on the opposite side of the door with her back pressed up against it. Breathing raggedly, she tried not to make a sound. Each second that went by seemed to play on forever as she stood like a mannequin, listening to the sounds of the man who'd murdered her heart. Her heart bled internally as she braced herself for the showdown that was about to occur. Since early that morning, she'd prepared for this moment. She hadn't slept a wink. She was functioning off pure adrenaline and rage. For hours, Gray called Cam back-to-back and got not one response. By the time the sun came up, her index finger and thumb were sore. She figured he'd leave for a few hours, cool off and return home. Boy was she wrong. Gray said a silent prayer to god pleading that he was home by the time she came back from taking the girls to school. When she returned, and the house was still empty, any feeling of empathy left her system. She couldn't believe her so-called husband had the audacity not to answer any of her calls or come home. She didn't know what type of time that nigga was on, but he had her 100% fucked up. Gray was done with being disrespected. She'd put up with this kind of nonsense from Gunz. Never was she going to tolerate it from Cam. Muthafucka's were going to learn to stop trying her. She wasn't the same soft spoken, weak chick she used to be. She was her most valuable gift in life. If no one else was going to protect her peace, she was. Gray listened intently as Cam tried to place his key in the lock. After a few tries, it finally dawned on him that it didn't fit. Gray had changed the locks.

"The fuck." He scowled, banging his fist on the door.

Each pound vibrated against Gray's back like a bass drum.

"Gray, open the door! I know you're in there."

She closed her eyes and tried to drown out the sound of his voice. If she didn't hear him she wouldn't have to feel him.

"Baby, I'm sorry! I fucked up! Let me in so I can talk to you!"

Silence

"Gray! Don't do me like this! I'm sorry!" He knocked even harder.

Silence

"If you let me in I can explain!"

More silence

Gray jammed her fist into her mouth to muffle her cries. Her breathing hitched as her knees grew weak. She knew his begging and pleading would weaken her. She was soft and pink like that. The sound of his deep, raspy voice sent her into a state of hopelessness and despair.

Helplessly, Cam leaned his forehead against the door and clenched his fist so tight he could feel the sweat trapped inside. If he could've rewound time he would've never left. He would've thugged it out with her, but he didn't and here they were. He was now locked out of his home and her heart. All he wanted to do was hold her. He didn't have to see her to know she was there. He could feel Gray's presence through the door. That's how connected their souls were. Then he heard a harrowing sound that almost fractured his soul. Through the door, he listened as Gray cried like a small child who'd lost her mama.

"Baby, don't cry. You know I hate when you cry." He spoke softly.

"Just go, Cam." She inhaled deep and willed herself to stop crying.

Crying wasn't going to solve anything. He didn't give a fuck about her tears. If he did, he would've brought his ass home last night. Fuck Cam. His disrespectful ass didn't deserve her tears or her love.

"What you change the locks for? I know what I did was wack, but you don't get a nigga back like that."

Gray stopped, stunned.

"The fact that you're sittin' up here quoting Jay-Z lyrics proves you don't take me seriously! Get the fuck off my porch, Cam! I'm done playin' wit' you! You ain't ready for this. You ain't ready for me."

"How the fuck you gon' tell me what I'm ready for?" He kicked the door angrily.

"Cam, stop! You know these damn white folks gon' call the police! They already be lookin' at us like we crazy!"

"Fuck them crackers! Let me in and you won't have to worry about that!"

"No! We're done!"

"We ain't done! You ain't fuckin' leavin' me! I already told you that! Stop sayin' that stupid shit!" He pounded his fist against the wooden door.

"I left you the moment you decided not to come home last night!" She hit the door back with her barefoot, stubbing her toe. "Shit!" She hopped around in pain.

"What happened? Baby, you a'ight?" He tried to look through the peephole.

"You get away from that door right now!" An elderly white lady that resembled one of the Golden Girls threatened Cam from her porch.

"Who the fuck are you?" He turned around and mean-mugged her.

"I'm your fuckin' worst nightmare. Mrs. Mariam Cartwright! I got you on camera! You thief! This is an upscale neighborhood! Not the welfare office! You know you don't belong here!"

"What?"

"You heard me LL Cool Bean! If you think you're about to break into that house you have another thing coming! I got you on camera homeboy." She held up an old school camcorder. "Black lives won't matter today."

"Bitch, if you don't take yo' old wrinkle ass in the house—"

"Bitch? Well I *de-clare*! You people are such a disgrace! Take me back to the days where you weren't even allowed in this neighborhood!" She scoffed, holding her chest.

"Gray, you hear this bitch? You must really want me to go to jail 'cause I'm about to knock this ole lady the fuck out!"

"Oh, now you're gonna put your hands on me Malcolm X? You're gonna shoot me?" The white lady said sarcastically. "You people kill me. All you do is drink your 40 ounces, smoke your reefa, beat ya' baby mama's, rob, steal and kill. This is why we don't want your kind living here. Nothing but a bunch of riff raff. Thank god we have Trump in office! We gettin' you coloreds out of here! We're gonna build a wall for all of ya! By any means necessary that!"

"On my mama, Gray, you betta open this door before I put two in Betty White's chest."

"That's it! I've had it. I'm callin' the cops! I got your number dip shit." She rushed back inside to grab the phone.

~ 225 ~

"Really Gray? You got this old bitch poppin' fly at me. She all in our fuckin' business. Open the fuckin' door!"

"No! Go back to wherever the hell you came from!"

"That's your word? A'ight." Cam nodded his head furiously.

If Gray wasn't going to willingly let him in, he was going to force his way in. She might've thought she'd gotten her shit off by changing the locks, but Gray didn't think about the windows. He would bet money that she hadn't checked to make sure all the windows were locked and secure. Cam jogged around the side of the house. Just as he expected, the living room window was easy as hell to get into. Taking it back to his B&E days, he jimmied it open and climbed his big ass through the window. Still at the door, Gray heard the soft sound of footsteps traipse across the floor like a threatening whisper. Eyes wide, she turned to find Cam inside. He was still dressed in his clothes from the day before. The fitted white tee hugged his corded muscles while the grey joggers he donned showcased the print of his rod. Gray licked her bottom lip. Just the sight of it made her want a taste. She could practically feel him inside of her as she glared into his tense eyes.

"What about I don't want you here does your crazy ass not get?" She placed her hand on her hip.

"You know damn well I ain't leavin'. We gon' work this shit out one way or another."

"There ain't nothin' to be fixed. Go back to that bitch house and work shit out with her."

"See, there you go talkin' out the side of yo' thick-ass neck. I wasn't even at no bitch house. I was at Diggy's. I crashed on his couch."

Cam had come up with the lie on the drive home. He knew there was no way for Gray to confirm if his story was true or not.

"I don't give a damn if you spent the night with Jesus. You don't get to stay out all night and not answer your phone when I call. You don't get to do that to me. If you're not going to respect me as a person and as your wife then take that fuckin' ring off and end this shit right now. 'Cause I will not tolerate or accept your disrespect."

This was Cam's opportunity. He could walk away now and let her find a man that could give her everything emotionally he couldn't. Spending the night at LaLa's house would just be the beginning of his bullshit. He didn't want to take her through anymore unnecessary drama. As he gazed into her teary blue eyes, his conscious told him to sever their ties and give her a clean break. The selfish part of him won out tho. It always did. Cam didn't want to feel the void of not having her in his life. She was his, always and forever.

"I'm all in, Gray. Cards up."

"Well, I don't believe you, so you need to go. I want you gone before the girls get home." She stood firm, even though her insides felt like mush.

"Are you hard of hearin'? I told yo' ass I ain't going nowhere."

"Cam!"

"Gray!" He shot back. "Cool out wit' that bullshit." He pulled her into his embrace.

Cam bathed in her warmth and the smell of her freshly laundered clothes. Gray squeezed her eyes shut.

Whenever she was in his arms, she felt like she was caught up in the Matrix.

"Let me go." She tried to wiggle loose.

"You buggin' the fuck out, Gray. Let me hug you."

"No!"

"Stop! You gon' make me tight." He kissed her face.

"So! I don't give a fuck! Get mad! Bust a vein for all I care!" She struggled to get out of his hold.

Cam held her even tighter and continued to place sweet kisses on her cheek.

"You don't love me no more?" He whispered in her ear.

"No." Gray tried to sound convincing.

"Why you lie so much, Gray? You need to go get that shit checked out for real."

"Are you gon' leave or no?"

"Don't ask me that shit no more."

"Fine." She lifted her leg and stomped hard on his foot. "I'll leave."

"Oww!" Cam let her go and hopped around on one foot. "I'ma beat yo' ass, Gray!" He massaged his toe through his boot.

Gray didn't even bother to respond. There was nothing else to say. If he wouldn't leave then she'd make the drastic decision to remove herself from him. It was the only option that made sense. Going into her walk-in closet, she pulled out her Goyard luggage and began to pack. Once she was done with her things, she'd start working on the girls.

"What the fuck are you doing? Where you going?" He followed her inside the room.

"The fuck away from you." She tossed her belongings inside the bag.

Gray was moving so fast that she was dropping stuff as she walked back-and-forth.

"You so mad you gon' leave your own crib?"

"Yep."

"Yo, you wildin'. You look mad dumb right now babe." He chuckled.

"Fuck you."

"C'mere, Gray." He tried to take her hand.

"Don't touch me." She jerked her arm away.

"Calm yo' dumb-ass down." He picked up her suitcase and held it high over his head.

"Stop! Give me my shit!" She jumped up to try and grab it.

"Back yo' big-ass up. You not going nowhere." He tossed the suitcase in the bathroom and closed the door.

With his arms folded across his chest, Cam posted up in front of it.

"Oh my god! Will you fuckin' stop!" Gray whined, trying to get past him.

"Not until you stop trippin'."

"I fuckin' hate you."

"As long as you don't leave me."

"You can't keep me here."

"Wanna bet? You ain't leavin' me, Gray. That's a dub. You wit' me. We together. Plain and simple." Cam went inside her purse, took out her wallet and keys then stuffed them in the back pocket of his joggers. "Now I got your credit cards and your keys so what you gon' do? Hitchhike out this muthafucka?"

"Why don't you just let me go? It's obvious you don't wanna be here. Let's just get a divorce."

"What you mean I don't wanna be here? If I didn't, I wouldn't be standing here beggin' yo' ass to stay. Quit buggin'. You gon' be wit' me till the day you fuckin' die or the day I kill you."

Gray wanted to laugh but didn't.

"Whatever." She flicked her wrist.

"Look how mad you got me. Look at my hand." Cam held it out. "It's shakin' 'cause I'm about to knock yo' ass out."

"You gon' get enough of threatening me."

"C'mon, Star. I need you here wit' me. I need you here by my side. You can't leave."

"I love you, Cam." She held each of his arms. "Lord knows I do but we jumped into this shit too fast. I don't know you and you won't let me. There are parts of you that, as your wife, I should have access to and don't. You're physically here but this right here." She pointed to his heart. "Is closed off. I wanna know what keeps you out at night. Where do you go during the day? Why is it that I barely see you sleep? And when I do see you sleep, why are you always twitching, tossing and turning? How was your time in the army? Did it affect you? Who are all those names on your chest? All I want is more of you. Is that so bad?"

Cam stood silent. It was as if a ghost had come and snatched out his voice box. If the fear in his chest would reside, he would gladly tell her everything she died to know but fear of her looking at him differently held him back. His pride couldn't risk her pitying him or thinking he was mentally ill for real. Most people who suffered from PTSD were looked at as circus freaks. It was a hard diagnosis to understand. Seeing that he wasn't going to respond, Gray rolled her eyes.

"Thanks for proving my point. Look, let's just call it a wrap before we do more damage to each other."

"Get out my face, Gray. Now you pissin' me off." Cam moved her out the way. "You makin' my blood pressure high. I'm hungry. I wanna take a shit, wash my ass and eat. Ain't nobody got time for you to be talkin' crazy 'cause you on your period and shit."

"My period is over so leave my ovaries out of this. It's over, Cam. Deal with it."

"I'm warnin' you, ma. You gon' make me spazz out and choke the shit outta you."

"What the fuck ever, Cam."

"Why you always tryin' to make me pull the trigger?"

"Give me my wallet and keys so I can leave!" Gray tried to reach inside his back pocket.

"Touch me and you only gon' have four fingers." He warned, giving her the eye.

"Fuck it. I'll have Tee-Tee come get me, and when he do, I'ma have him and Bernard fuck you up. And you know they know how to fight."

"Picture that. You gon' fuck around and get them booty fuckers murked."

"Don't talk about my friend!" She pushed him out the way and grabbed her suitcase from the master bath.

"Put that shit down!" Cam snatched it from her again and tossed it across the room. "Take yo' ass outside and go for a walk. You need some fresh air."

"I don't need no fuckin' fresh air."

"You need somethin'. It's either some fresh air or a casket. You decide."

"Cam, please. Just leave." She begged, feeling like she was going to cry.

"No."

"Okay." Gray started picking her clothes off the floor.

"WHAT THE FUCK I SAY?" Cam blocked her from grabbing anything else. "GO HEAD SOMEWHERE! YOU BLOWIN' ME RIGHT NOW!"

"You not ready for marriage. Your actions show it, so I'm done." She pulled more things from her closet.

"You still touchin' shit? You want me to choke you out? Grab another fuckin' thing out that closet and I swear to god you gon' take your last breath."

"I need space, Cam. We need space. Why won't you give me that?"

"No, the real question is why every time some shit go down you wanna say it's over? You always tryin' to run. How you think that make me feel? I told you I'm wit' you. I ain't fuckin' wit' no other ho's. I gave you my fuckin' last name so you don't get to run. You gotta stick it out with me and fight. Even if it hurts, even if it makes you uncomfortable, you stick around. You just don't leave me behind to figure this shit out on my own."

Gray hated when he tried to make her the villain.

"Now you're the victim? You said you would never leave me, and you did." She pointed her finger in his face. "I fucked up one time and you bounced. You stayed your ass out all night. Now you wanna make things right and I'm just supposed to forget all the pain you caused me last night? No, it don't work that way." She turned to walk away.

Cam became lightheaded. Nausea swirled unrestrained in his empty stomach. His head swam with regret. He hated when they argued cause Gray never knew when to back down. All he knew was that he couldn't let her walk out the door. If he did, he'd never be able to get her back again.

"C'mere." He turned her around and lifted her up into a bear hug. "Stop tryin' to leave me. You can't go nowhere. If you love me, you're wit' me. For real. I don't got time for your bullshit."

"Let me go."

"I can't." He placed a trail of kisses from her forehead to the side of her neck. "Don't leave me."

Gray tried to remain indifferent. Letting a cocky nigga like Cam know his effect on her would only inflate his ego, but a few seconds in, her tense shoulders slumped in defeat. Cam knew that once he kissed her neck her resistance would crumble. The heartbeat in her clit thumped as his tender lips brushed her neck. Cam's kisses became harder and more intense with each flicker of his tongue. His fingers ran through her hair. Gray's arms found their way around his back as her head began to swim. All previous notions of leaving immediately ceased. Looking her square in the eyes, he pulled her in for a kiss. A transfer of passion soared from her mouth to his as he sucked on her tongue and lips. Hungrily, Cam squeezed her ass cheeks. He needed her body in the worst way. Gray did something for him that no drug known to man could provide. Morning, noon and night he thought about fuckin' her. Her pussy was made just for him. It was always warm and snug. Gray's pussy moistened with each grope and squeeze. His hard dick pressed against her stomach making her knees weak. Despite how much she wanted to feel him explore the deepest parts of her center, Gray wasn't going to grant him access that easily. Cam had to put in work first. Biting her bottom lip, she placed her hand on top of his head to push him down.

No chick ever had the balls to force Cam to eat her pussy. Any other woman would've gotten punched in the pussy for that shit, but Gray could get whatever she wanted from him. Just not how she wanted it. Smacking her hand away, he used his brute strength to carry her back to the bedroom. Gray wrapped her legs around his waist and French kissed him along the way. Cam tossed her on the bed and watched as her body bounced against the sheets. He was over Gray tryin' to boss up on him. It was high time he reminded her why she donned *his* last name. The jeans she wore were peeled off and thrown on the floor. Cam's mouth watered when he saw she had no panties on. Gray was a freak like that. She always liked for him to have easy access to her kitty. Fully naked, his eyes traced every inch of her physique with desire. Cam loved to look at her while she was bare. Gray's body was a work of art. Her big, heavy breasts, soft pudgy stomach, fat pussy and caramel legs let him know that god was real. Parting her succulent thighs, he eased his way down to the floor. Eye level with her clit he licked his lips and groaned, "Fuckin' perfect."

One by one he let her know how much she was adored by placing sensual kisses all over her lips and inner thighs. Using his nose, he toyed with her clit and inhaled. The scent of her arousal reverberated from her cunt. Gray's head sank into the mattress as he took his first lick. It was a slow and torturous lick. Right then and there she realized this was not lovemaking, this was punishment. Cam was going to kill her. He'd just begun, and she was already going crazy. Gripping the sheets, she held on tight as he tried to extract ecstasy from her soul. The mastery of his tongue was sinful. Up and down he went, licking the sweet cream she produced like it was vanilla soft serve. Using his fingers, he parted her lower lips and placed his feather like tongue strokes to her clit. All Gray could do was moan. Cam's eager tongue mixed with her wet juices was a recipe for destruction. The nigga's tongue kissed her pussy like it was her mouth all while groaning out his pleasure of tasting her.

Nose deep between her trembling legs, his tongue lapped at her nectar. Each sample was smooth, slick and sweet. Spellbound, Gray's fingertips traced the plains of his face as his mouth devoured each release of her pleasure. The high-pitched whimpers she released signified that the alpha woman in her had surrendered to the beast in him. Cam ate her pussy like it was his last supper. His face had damn near disappeared he was so far into it. Fucking her slit with his finger he continued to assault her clit with his tongue. He ate her pussy like she out of line. Gray's legs began to shake. Fireworks were erupting in her pussy left and right.

"Oh baby." She moaned. "Eat my li'l pussy like that please."

"Mmm." Cam savored her syrupy flavor.

"Yes. Yes. Please don't stop." She cried out as her eyes rolled to the back of her head.

The fight they were having quickly became a distant memory. It seemed like it had happened a 100 years ago. Gray couldn't even remember what it was about. Whatever it was, she was fully prepared to say she was sorry. She'd gladly take the blame if this was the kind of punishment she would receive. Cam was eating her pussy like a man on death row wolfing down his last meal. He wasn't going to stop till her juices covered his beard.

Zoning in on her clit, he sucked harder while punishing her pussy with his fingers. In and out he went until her body went into shock and she came in his mouth. Panting heavily, Gray tried to catch her breath. A kaleidoscope of stars danced in her eyes. If Cam kept this up she wouldn't be able to walk or talk. On his feet, he sprung his throbbing dick from his joggers. Gray eyed it with lust and watched as it jumped. She had to suck it. His dick was calling her name. On all fours, she crawled to the edge of the bed and got down on her knees. All 11-inches of his brown python dangled in front of her face. Gray thanked god it was all hers. His cock deserved to be worshiped. Cam stood before her with his hard, erect cock in his hand. Sex and masculinity oozed from his pores. A mountain of muscles decorated his arms, stomach and legs. Grabbing the back of her head, he placed his dick at the opening of her lips and began to fuck the back of her throat.

"Yes." He growled, rocking back-and-forth.

Spit drooled from Gray's pink pouty lips as she whimpered. Cam was going H.A.M. She could barely keep up.

"This what you like?" He lightly smacked the side of her face repeatedly.

Gray let his dick fall from her lips and gulped in a mouthful of air.

"Yes."

"Yes what?" He squeezed her jaw.

"Yes daddy."

A small but teasing smile crept upon Cam's face. She was perfect. This was why he couldn't let go. Other chicks didn't satisfy him like she did. Gray was his pretty little whore. Wet tears dripped from her eyes, causing her mascara to smear. Her hair was ruffled from the way he gripped her silky strands. After she sucked his balls, he placed his dick back in her mouth and continued his oral assault on her lungs. Cam's steel rod plunged to the back of her throat nearly suffocating her. Gray nursed his dick like a starving baby at a mother's breast. Every grievance she had with him melted away. When Cam took control of her sexually there was no staying mad. Her body willingly submitted to him. He could have her any way he wanted. Every hole on her body was his.

"Open wide."

Cam didn't have to tell her twice. Gray parted her lips. She was nowhere near done savoring his meaty cocky. Inch by inch she eased her way down. Gray didn't stop until she hit the base of his cock. Cam ran his fingers through her hair and held her there. Gray's eyesight instantly blurred. Her lungs were going to collapse but the groans of pleasure Cam released made the potential threat of death all worth it. Holding her breath, she stayed put until she began to see black dots. On the brink of passing out, she came up for air.

"Good girl." Cam rewarded her with a kiss.

"Mmm . . . I love your dick in my mouth." She groaned out.

Ready to fuck, Cam lifted her back onto the bed. Settled behind her, he eased his way into her tight hole and began to pulverize her pussy. Harder, deeper, stronger, faster he stroked. Sweat formed on his physique as he panted. Each breath he took burned his throat. For fifteen minutes he gave Gray everything he had to give, determined to teach her a lesson. All talk of leaving him would be deceased. By the time he was done, she'd be high off his backstroke. Taking hold of her wrists, he pulled them behind her back and locked them in place with his hand. The side of Gray's face was pressed onto the bed. Traces of her makeup was smeared onto the white comforter. Cam pushed her face further into the mattress as he drilled her juicy slit. Loud knocks from the headboard hitting the wall filled the room. Gray clawed the sheets desperate to hold on.

"Is this what you want?" Cam wrapped her hair around his fist.

"Yes baby. Fuck my pussy daddy."

"That's why you was actin' up."

"Yes. This dick feel so good. Never stop fuckin' me."

A thunderous growl erupted from Cam's chest. Sex this good should've been a sin. Gray's pussy was a wonderland of goodness. Flipped over into the missionary position, she spread her legs as far as they could go. Cam grabbed a belt and looped it around her neck, choking her slightly.

"You still want a divorce?"

"No baby. I ain't going nowhere."

"That's what I thought." He placed the strap between her lips so she couldn't talk.

The visual of her being gagged by his belt took him over the edge. It was the sexiest shit he'd ever seen. When he first met Gray, he would've never imagined that she liked to be fucked like this. She liked for him to do her dirty. Gray got off on being controlled. Behind closed doors, the conservative woman she presented to the world vanished. She acted like the leading star in her very own porn flick.

"This pussy is mine. Ain't it?" He grunted, drilling her hole.

Unable to speak, Gray nodded her head and moaned.

"You're mine?"

"Mmm hmm." She tightened the muscles in her pussy.

Cam bit his bottom lip. Gray wasn't playing fair. She knew what it did to him when she did that. Her pussy clenched him like an iron fist. Thrusting his hips hard, he pushed himself deeper inside her walls. Turned on to the max, Gray removed the belt strap from in-between her lips.

"Oooooooh, Cam, you're gonna make me cum." She gazed up into his lust filled eyes.

"Did I tell you to take that shit out your mouth?" He smacked her titty.

"No daddy." She shrilled in delight as a orgasm hit.

Cam looked back at her. He loved watching her come undone. Gray's entire body shook when she climaxed. Squeezing her eyes shut, she called out for god and rode the wave. Never once did Cam let up. Her titties bounced up and down as he pounded her pussy at a fever pitched pace. The next time Gray even thought about threatening divorce she'd remember this day. On his back, Cam sat her on his dick in the reverse cowgirl position. Her feet rested on his knees as he fucked her hard from below. Gray was a sweaty, disheveled mess but she didn't care. The ache in her cervix was too strong to ignore. Face-to-face, Cam took her right nipple in his mouth while massaging the face of her pussy. White frothy cream covered his brown veiny instrument. In and out his dick went. With her back pressed against his chest, Cam gripped her neck with one hand while rotating his fingers around her clit with the other. Gray was experiencing sensory overload. Cam was tapping into too many erogenous zones at once. It was absolute torture and she couldn't get enough.

"Clean my dick off. You got it all messy."

In between his legs, Gray ran her tongue all over his length until her foamy cream was no more. As she sucked his balls Cam stroked his cock anxiously. Other women had liked to suck his dick, but Gray took it to a whole new level. Flames burned in her blue eyes every time she came near it. She could cum off giving him head alone. Cam's deep breaths gradually increased. Gray had deep throated his dick again. Her small hands ran up and down his washboard abs as she went to town. As if she was praying,

Gray closed her eyes and hummed like she was speaking in tongues.

"You love my dick, don't you baby?"

"Obsessed." She wiped her mouth and got on top.

Up and down, round and round she rode his cock. Lost in the moment, their tongues dueled. Cam could feel her pussy drool with each kiss. Over and over, he plunged his dick, claiming her pussy as his. Gray's innocence was stolen with each thrust. She didn't know if she could take anymore. Cam's steel shaft pushed so deep her heart skipped several beats.

"You love me?" He asked holding onto her hips.

"Yes daddy." Gray rested her forehead against his.

"Say it."

"I love you."

"Say it again." He slapped her ass hard.

"I love you."

"Again!" He pumped harder.

"I love you . . . I love you! I love you! I love you!" Gray screamed, cumming hard and fast.

Her wetness coated his entire shaft. Cam wasn't far behind.

"Jesus fuckin' Christ." He growled palming her ass as a fit of tremors took over his body.

The nut he busted seemed to go on forever. It wasn't a small dainty cum either. He released hard into her and poured as if there was no end in sight. Cam's seed erupted in her core, glazing her inner walls. Gray felt his hot liquid squirt into her pussy like leakage of love untapped. Spent, they both lay waiting for their heartrate to get back to its regular pace. As soon as her orgasmic high disappeared, Gray remembered why they were beefin' in the first place and got mad all over again. Cam could sense her energy shift and tried to reach out for her.

"Mmm no." She pushed him back. "Your dick good but it ain't that good. I ain't forgot what you did. Don't say shit to me. I'm still not fuckin' wit' you." She got up and sashayed into the bathroom.

"Gray. . . Gray!" Cam sat up.

She ignored him and slammed the door.

"That's how it's gon' be?" He laid back down. "A'ight then . . . and it is that good! You fuckin' liar!"

"If you a bad bitch and it's your birthday, gon'
head and fuck it up in the worst way."- Trap
Beckham, "Birthday Bitch"

#12

All that could be heard inside of Cam's blood red, 2.8 million dollar, Pagani Huayra BC was the irritating sound of Gray tapping the tip of her stiletto nails against the passenger side door panel. It had taken the will of Jesus to get her to place the blindfold covering her eyes on. Since their fight, she'd wanted nothing to do with him. He couldn't blame her. He'd royally fucked up. The punishment more than fit the crime. Gray made it her business to ignore him at all cost. The bitter silence was killing him softly. He missed hearing her light, feathery voice. He missed laughing and joking with her. He missed parting her legs and sucking the life out of her clit while she begged for more. He yearned to plow inside her like he was making beats. The only time he was able to get near her was at night when they slept. She'd tried to make him sleep in the spare bedroom, but Cam wasn't having it. He'd be damned if he slept apart from his wife. His parents never slept in separate rooms, no matter how mad they were at each other so neither were they.

To show her how dedicated he was to her and their marriage, Cam made it his business to be home by dinner, so he could spend time with her and the girls, even though she acted as if he was invisible. Thank god he had his buddy Press to talk to. Aoki and Gray carried on like he wasn't even there. Not talking to Gray hurt like hell, but at night when they turned down the sheets for bed, there was no more pushing him away. The distance she enforced during the day came to a halt. Cam had to have a piece of her whether she wanted him to or not. Every night she slid to the far right of the bed, but Cam would only pull her back to him and lock her in his strong, tattooed arms, so she wouldn't move. Gray would struggle for release but after a while she'd grow tired of fighting and give in. Keeping her prisoner was drastic but Cam didn't give a fuck. He had to do what he had to do.

Cuddling with Gray was the antidote to everything that ailed him. There in the darkness of their bedroom with her back pressed against his chest felt like heaven. Cam wished there was a way to extend the night, just so he could stay close to her longer. The feel of her soft hair brushing his neck brought him a sense of peace he'd never known. He could never let another woman get close to him like this. Gray was so different. She molded into him, sharing the warmth of her body as effortlessly as she shared her heart. When they lay, Cam never slept. He stayed up all night savoring being in her embrace. With her, he had nothing to fear except the sunrise. For when the sun peaked over the horizon, and she rose to start a new day, Cam was left alone. Whenever she left, she took the best parts of him. Without Gray, he was no longer whole. He was simply a broken shell of a man who could've stayed holding her forever.

Cam gripped the steering wheel and tried to focus on the road, but the scent of her Dior JOY perfume was making his dick strain against his jeans. Gray looked delectable in the outfit he'd picked out for her. It was the night of her birthday. She fought like hell not to leave the house. Every year on her birthday she felt like she died a little more. Each year it was a reminder that her mother was no longer there. Gray had survived her death as best as she could, but it nearly consumed her daily. Gunz never pressured her to celebrate. He understood her pain and let her be, but Cam was the total opposite. He fussed over her birthday like it was his but how could she get all dolled up and party when all she really wanted to do was throw her weary body on her mother's grave? She put up a fight not to celebrate, but when Cam threatened to shoot her pinky toe off, she gave in to his demands.

It was Gunz's weekend to have the girls so all she had to do was get ready. He'd taken care of everything. Mina and Heidi came over and did her hair and makeup. Wanting her to try something different for her birthday, Mina gave her a shoulder length, ombre pink bob with a feathered side swept bang. Gray wasn't so sure about the drastic change because she'd never had a sew-in or worn colored hair but ended up loving the results. Since her hair was so bold, Heidi went with a subdued makeup look. A strong brow, black winged liner, wispy lashes and a matte nude lip brought out the exotic features of her face. Out of the corner of his eye, Cam admired her thick, gold shimmered legs. The custom-made, LaBourjoisie long sleeve, mini dress covered in pink Swarovski crystals she rocked accentuated the hourglass curves of her figure. The only accessories she wore were a simple pair of 4 carat, pink diamond, stud earrings he'd gifted her and 5-inch, silver, metallic, stardust Christian Louboutin pumps. His baby looked gorgeous. Cam couldn't have been prouder to call her his wife.

"Are we there yet?" She huffed.

"Yeah, li'l crabby-ass li'l girl." Cam pulled up to the venue and parked.

The valet service he'd hired promptly came and opened his door. Cam stepped out in a Moncler, camel colored, suede and fur, waist-length coat, white, Supreme, logo tee shirt, white Balmain jeans with zip details above the knees and fresh out of the box white retro Jordan 3's. Several diamond chains layered his neck. On his right wrist were four, small, gold, diamond Cuban link bracelets and one huge one. Diamond rings adorned each of his fingers. To say he was icy was an understatement. Cam's jewels shined brighter than the moon. Personally, unlocking Gray's door, he helped her out and escorted her inside the building. Gray held onto him tight and hoped she didn't trip and fall. If she did, she was going to beat Cam's ass. She already didn't want to be wherever they were. She missed her girls. She would've much rather been snuggled up with them watching a movie, but as soon as Cam pulled the blindfold off, her mood changed.

"SURPRISE!" All of her friends and associates yelled.

Gray's mouth dropped. Cam had gone all out and thrown her a Barbie inspired 36th birthday party. Pink helium balloons lined the ceiling. Neon pink lights flashed like police sirens but much more colorful. $100,000 worth of pink flowers, pink suede couches and chairs filled the room. In the center of the space was a dancefloor with Gray's name written in cursive. There was even a photo booth, liquor infused snow cone machine and a pink ball pit. Her cake was four tiers with a Barbie on top of it, face down drunk in the icing. Guest dined on $80 Kobe beef burgers and caviar prepared by celebrity Chef Roblé. Partygoers would also leave with $1,000 swag bags.

The entire crew was there. He'd invited Kema, Heidi, Tee-Tee, Bernard, Dylan, Angel, Candy, Mo, Boss, Quan, Stacy, Diggy, Mina, Victor, Delicious, Chyna and Dame. All of the stylists from the shop were there. Journalist, editors, stylists, makeup artists and designers she'd worked with throughout the years came through to show love. Cam even invited some of her former staff members from her magazine. Tears stung the brim of her eyes. She didn't expect to see Dylan, Angel and Candy. Since she and Gunz were no longer together, she figured they wouldn't want anything to do with her since they were technically his family. As tears slipped down her face, everyone ran over to give her a hug. Gray was overwhelmed with love and Cam was to thank. The look of elation on her face warmed his heart. This was all he ever wanted to do; make her happy. He'd fucked up along the way, and probably would continue, but nothing felt better than giving his Star the happiness she deserved.

"C'mere." He held out his arms.

Gray fell into his hug. At that moment, she knew for sure she could never live without him. No other man had ever looked out for her the way he did. In him, she saw the opportunity to have the kind of love that cynics said didn't exist. The kind that spanned far longer than a lifetime.

"Thank you." She buried her face in his chest.

"I told you, I got you." He rubbed her back and kissed the top of her head.

"When did you do all of this?" She looked around amazed.

"I've been planning it the past few weeks. Kema helped me."

"So, you did this before we got into it?"

"Yeah. I wanted to remind you that birthdays are about living not death. I know your mom's passing fucked you up, but she would want you to live, ma, not mourn."

"You're right."

"Both of our mothers would want us to be happy."

Gray became lose in his eyes. Cam never talked about his mother with her.

"I know you're always sayin' I don't open up to you. It's hard for me to talk about my OG. She was my everything. Thinkin' about her keeps me awake at night. . . amongst other things. It's not a coincidence to me that god put two motherless people together. He knew we needed each other. I need you, Gray. You're my baby. I find peace when I'm with you. When you're not around I go right back to being paranoid and shit."

"Why?"

"All I know is lost. First my mom, my relationship with my dad, then my battle buddies, LaLa and the son I thought was mine. Everyone I have ever loved is gone. That's why I can't lose you. What we share means everything to me. With you I started living again."

All the anger Gray harbored over the past few days evaporated into thin air. How could she stay mad at him after that confession?

"I got you this." He reached in his pocket and pulled out a rectangular shaped jewelry box.

Gray took it from his hand and cracked it open. Inside was a gold chain with two gold diamond encrusted dog tags attached to it. On one of the tags was her mother's name, birthday and death date. On the other was his mother's name birthday and death date.

"So, you know they're with us at all times." He said nervously.

Being soft wasn't his forte. He didn't know how she'd respond to the gift.

"How do you even know my mother's name? I never told you."

"Cause I'm crazy and crazy people know everything."

Gray giggled. The party and his confession was enough for her. The sentimental dog tags only added to her appreciation. It was by far the best gift she'd ever received. Wanting to kiss his mouth, she did. Her hands palmed the sides of his face as she pulled him into a fiery, fervent kiss. As their tongues danced the world fell away. Gray ran her fingers down the back of his neck, pulling him close until there was no space left between them. Cam could feel her heart beat against his. Each flicker of her minty tongue felt like gold at the end of a rainbow.

The celebration went on for hours. Bottles of Ace of Spades, D'Usse and Bel Air were passed around. Cam had his own bottle of Louis XIII Cognac that cost three grand itself. Everyone danced until their feet were sore. Even Chyna and Mo's pregnant asses twerked a little bit. When Usher and Zaytoven's *Birthday* started playing they really showed out. In the V.I.P section Cam stood behind her puffing on a Backwoods as she bent over and rolled her fat-ass on his dick in a circle. A cloud of smoke hovered over their heads as she did her thing. Gray was in her element. The way she grinded on his dick was reminiscent of the lap dance she gave him for his birthday. Even though he was enjoying her seductive dance moves, Cam stayed on high alert all night. Any time he was in a crowded space he watched his surroundings. Everything seemed cool, but he could never be too sure. Over two hundred people were in attendance. Half of which he didn't know. He had to keep Gray safe. She was precious cargo. When his boy Hov came out and performed *Allure* he finally let loose. He and his mans rapped along to the lyrics as if they wrote them.

> *The allure of breaking the law*
> *Was always too much for me to ever ignore*
> *I've got a thing for them big-body Benzes, it dulls*
> *my senses*
> *In love with a V-Dub engine*

Man, I'm high off life, fuck it, I'm wasted
Bathing Ape kicks, Audemars Piguet wrist
My women friend get tennis bracelets
Trips to Venice, get their winters replaced with
The sun, it ain't even fun no more, I'm jaded
Man, it's just a game, I just play it to play it

Gray watched on in awe. She loved it when Cam turned up. Killa Cam was making a rare appearance. His diamonds danced as he channeled the hood side of him that made her nipples hard. All his niggas surrounded him. Cam stood front and center like the king he was amongst a group of killers, drug dealers and thieves. The crowd below was going ape shit. All you saw was hands in the air. Nobody, not even Gray, expected to see Jay perform. She got another shock of her life when H.E.R. switched on stage, dripping from head to toe in Versace while singing her favorite song *Jungle*. Each lyric was a clear depiction of her feelings for Cam. He draped his arm around Gray's neck as she pointed her finger and sang along.

Rock me real slowly
Put a bib on me
I'm just like a baby, drooling over you
The things you do

He said you're my everything
I love you through everything, I done did everything
to him
He forgave me for everything, this a forever thing
Hate that I treat it like it's a whatever thing
Trust me, boy, this shit is everything to me
He from the jungle, he from the jungle

Gray felt every word of the song. It was her shit. After their performances, she pulled Cam over to take a few pics for the Gram with Jay and H.E.R. Caught off guard by what was happening, Cam looked directly into the lens. When the flash went off, a searing high-pitched ringing went off in his ears. Squeezing his eyes shut, he placed his head down and groaned out in distress. It was happening again. His heart began to palpitate. At any second it felt like he was going to die. The heat from the Afghanistan sun was blaring down onto his face blinding him.

"You gotta open your eyes my man." The photographer said as he looked over the camera footage.

Gray looked up at Cam and saw the look of agony on his face.

"Baby, you a'ight?" She asked nervously.

"My head just started to hurt. I'll be back." He raced off to the restroom to collect his self.

There was no way he was about to ruin her night with his bullshit. At the sink, he splashed cold water onto his face. Staring at himself in the mirror, Cam took a few deep breaths to calm himself down. He hated this shit. Post-Traumatic Stress was ruining his life. After a while his breathing started to regulate. Back at the party, Gray proceeded to make her rounds to tell everyone thank you for coming. By the time she made it to Diggy, he was off by his self, standing to the side. Clubbing wasn't really his thing anymore. Like Gray, he would've much rather be at home with his family.

"Hey, Diggy."

"What's up, ma? Happy Birthday." He gave her a quick one arm hug.

Diggy knew Cam would have a fit if he saw him touch her.

"Thank you and thanks for coming."

"C'mon. You family now. Plus, I needed to holla at ya' man anyway. It's been a minute."

Shocked by his statement, Gray jerked her head back. *I spent the night at Diggy's house,* she recalled Cam saying the night he didn't come home, which was only a few days ago. Before Gray could investigate his response, Cam tugged on her arm. When he came out the restroom and spotted her talking to Diggy, he quickly made a beeline over to stop their conversation. He hadn't told Diggy that he'd used him as an alibi. He'd be damned if he got caught up after all he'd done to get back into Gray's good graces.

Gray was no dummy tho. She knew Cam was pulling her away on purpose. She wasn't going to bring it up now, but she was most certainly going to bring it up at a later date. Hand-in-hand, Cam escorted her outside for her last surprise. Everyone followed. Gray approached the curb and found a brand new, midnight blue Mercedes-Maybach G650 Landaulet. Gray was utterly speechless. The car was worth a half a million dollars.

"No more driving that punk-ass Range your weak-ass baby daddy got you." He opened the driver side door for her to get in.

Gray hopped inside. The SUV had the new car smell she adored. Slowly she ran her hand over the butter-soft leather seats. On the headrest, Cam had gotten her name engraved.

"Baby, thank you." She pecked his lips.

"I ain't done yet." He helped her out the car. "The truck is your whip to run you and the girls around but this . . ." He pointed.

All Gray could hear was a bunch of ooh's and aww's as a chrome colored Ashton Martin Valkyrie came

~ 253 ~

rolling down the street. The car looked like something straight from the future. She'd never seen anything like it. It was a limited edition, hybrid, sportscar. The carmakers claimed it was the fastest car in the world.

"Cam." She gasped. "You already got me the earrings." She touched her earlobe. "Then the clothes, heels, party, dog tags, Mercedes and now this. It's too much."

"No, it ain't."

"What kind of car is this? I don't even know what it is." She glided her hand across the hood.

"It's an Ashton Martin Valkyrie."

"The Mercedes cost a half a mill so how much did you pay for this?"

"3.2 mill." He said coolly as if it was nothing.

"WHAT? How in the hell can you afford something like this?" She died to know.

"I'ma very wealthy man, Gray."

"I mean, I knew you had money, but I didn't know you had like money-money."

Cam grinned, shaking his head. His sweet Gray was so clueless. Blowing a few mill was nothing for a nigga like him, especially when he was sitting on a cool 50 mill. Now that he was lieutenant his net worth would only expand.

"Just know we ain't hurtin' for nothin'."

"I see."

"I can't believe you got me all this. This car is fuckin' sick. I ain't never seen nothin' like it. It's gorgeous."

"It is. Though gorgeous takes on a much different meaning once a person's met you."

Gray's cheeks burned pink like a spring rose. The budding color was adorable against her freckled cheeks. Looking away, she bit her bottom lip. Cam placed his index finger under her chin and made her look at him.

"You're gorgeous."

Smiling brightly, she replied, "I know."

Gray wanted to pinch herself. She couldn't believe her life. She was overwhelmed with joy. Even though he worked her nerves majority of the time, she thanked god for Cam. He was everything she'd prayed for and more. Not only was he the most handsome man she'd ever met, he was generous and caring. Gray could look at his golden skin, hooded brown eyes and freckled cheeks for hours on end. Cam was an angel. Sauntering over to him, she circled her arms around his neck and lifted up on her tippy toes. Right there on the busy street, cars rushed past as they kissed. Gray didn't hold anything back and neither did Cam. They both wanted to feel every inch of each other's skin. The onlookers and stream of traffic faded away. It was just the two of them. Cam ran his fingers down her spine. Nothing else had to be figured out or explained. She was his and he was hers. If Cam lost her, he'd lose pieces of himself. Gray was the half that made him whole.

Her warm breath tickled his ear as she whispered how she was going to suck him until he spilled all his sweet cream into her mouth. Cam tried not to smile but slowly his lips morphed into a shit eating grin. Gray continued to talk her nasty shit as he picked her up and sucked on the side of her neck. You couldn't tell Cam that this woman wasn't an expert at keeping his heart beating. Without her, he was most certain it would stop. As he molested the flesh of her neck with his tongue, a wave of pleasure soared through his body. Her perfume had his dick on brick. The scenery around him disappeared as he kissed his way up her neck to her ear. Cam was so lost in the moment that he didn't sense the nigga parting through the crowd with a demonic look on his face. Gray did. It seemed she was the only one who noticed him. Her and the man's eyes connected as he walked behind Cam and lifted a gun to the back of his head. Gray tried to scream but no sound came out. Her lungs felt like they were surrounded by metal bands. She was paralyzed with fear. This couldn't be happening. Someone was about to kill Cam. *Lord no,* she eternally cried. He couldn't take her mother and her man.

"Cam! Cam!" She beat on his chest frantically.

It seemed like she wasn't moving fast enough. Everything was moving in slow motion. Lifting his head, he looked at her face and saw nothing but sheer panic. Cam's pistol was on his waist, but as he pushed Gray off of him and reached down to grab it, he was too late. *POW!!!* A single bullet flew out of the chamber and into the crisp night air. The bullet aimed for its mark in a straight line. With extraordinary speed, it hit the intended target in the head. Cam's body jerked forward. Screams of horror rang out as people ran for cover. It was pure pandemonium. He could've sworn he'd been shot but he hadn't taken his last breath. Gray stood before him screaming hysterically. She'd watched as the shooter placed his finger on the trigger to kill Cam. Unbeknownst to him, Quan was right on his ass. Before he could shoot Cam, Quan shot him point blank in the back of his head. The man's brain matter and blood covered the back of Cam's coat.

All Cam could hear was the sound of his own heavy breathing as everything around him moved in slow motion. In the grip of silent panic, eyes wide, pupils dilated, heart racing and brain on fire, he turned and found a lifeless corpse laying slumped on the ground. Someone had tried to kill him. The cold winter weather suddenly became warm as the realization sunk in. Once again, he'd cheated death. Once more, god had spared his life, and for the life of Cam, he didn't understand why.

"I ain't come to talk. I came to bang it out."-
Rowdy Rebel feat Bobby Shmurda, "Computers"

#13

Gray's rage built up like water currents as she stared out the living room window searching for Gunz's car. Cam told her to let him know when he pulled up, so he could holla at him, but Gray had other plans. As soon as she spotted him, her anger would come unleashed. She'd tolerated all she could from him. She'd put up with his nonstop lying, cheating, silly side bitches, side baby, mental and physical abuse but his attempt at taking the man she loved life was it. He couldn't get away with it. Gunz was going to pay big time for what he'd did. Impatiently, she tapped her foot. Every car that came down the street she surveyed in hopes that it was him. She couldn't wait to get her girls away from him. The nigga was the devil in human form. Any man that would put the mother of his kids' life at risk wasn't shit. Since the shooting, she'd been a nervous wreck. At first, she had no idea who the shooter was until Stacy recognized him as one of Gunz's old foot soldiers. Gray couldn't believe her ears. She knew Gunz's pride wouldn't allow him to accept the ass whoopin' Cam had gave him without retaliation. She figured he'd do something but having him killed wasn't one of them.

"There his black-ass is." She hissed, unlocking the door.

It was freezing cold outside, but Gray didn't give a shit. She didn't even bother putting on a coat. The adrenaline soaring through her veins warmed her insides. Gray was ready for war. She was even dressed for it. Stepping out into the brisk air, the only thing covering her frame was a khaki colored Nike hat, matching sports bra, khaki Balmain joggers and Yeezy Military Boots. Her titties bounced with each step she took down the driveway. Gunz wasn't even parked good before she yanked the back door of his car open.

"Go in the house now!" She told the girls.

Usually, Gray would try to hide her anger around them, but that day, she had no time for pleasantries. Gunz was about to get this work. Seeing their mother so enraged had the girls shook, so instead of arguing back, they did as they were told and went in the house.

"Why you snatchin' my door open like you fuckin' crazy?" Gunz hopped out.

Gray didn't reply. She watched as the front door closed behind the girls before she furiously stomped around the car to get to him. Gunz watched as the whites of her eyes turned black. The woman approaching him wasn't the sweet, subdued Gray he once knew. This chick was a savage. The blow to his face proved it. Using all the strength she had, she drew her right arm back and jabbed him in the mouth. Gray had hit him so hard she'd busted his lip. Shocked, Gunz covered his mouth and narrowed his eyes at her. His tongue was soaked in blood.

"Yeah, nigga. What's up?" Gray blacked out and attacked him with a barrage of punches to his face. "You fuckin' pussy! You a coward! You ain't shit bitch!"

"What the fuck are you talkin' about?" Gunz covered his face to dodge her hits.

"I know you did it bitch! I know it was you! You black bitch!" Gray opened her hand and slapped him repeatedly in the side of his head.

"Did what? What the fuck are you talkin' about? I ain't did shit!" He pushed her back.

Gray almost fell but she caught herself before she hit the ground.

"You know what you did! You lousy, dirty, trifling, faggot!" She picked up a huge rock and threw it at his dome.

Gunz ducked and missed getting hit by a half an inch.

"You was gon' risk my life for revenge, all because you got yo' ass beat? You deserved that shit! You put your fuckin' hands on me and my nigga returned the favor but you too much of a pussy to take that L!" She threw another rock.

"I don't know what the fuck you talkin' about!" He played innocent.

"You know exactly what I'm talkin' about!"

"GRAY!" Cam came outside and slammed the door. "Get yo' ass in the fuckin' house! I told you to leave it alone! I got this!"

"Nah, fuck that! I'm sick of this nigga!" She tried to get at Gunz again, but Cam grabbed her from behind and held her back.

"Ohhhhhhhhh I got 'em on speed dial today!" Mrs. Mariam waved her cordless phone in the air. "You negroes are going to jail!"

"Mrs. Mariam take yo' ass in the house! I ain't got time for your shit today!" Cam warned while trying to restrain Gray.

"I am president of the neighborhood watch! You and Eddie Murphy here are number one on my shit list! Your black ass is grass!"

"Didn't I tell your old ass to mind your business?" Cam shouted.

"I don't give a shit! You can't tell me what to do! If it wasn't for those no-good Yankee's your black-ass would still be picking cotton in the hot fields of Georgia!"

"I swear to god I'ma shoot that old bitch. I can't be dealin' with her and you Gray. Now please go in the house."

"This shit ain't over." She pointed her finger at Gunz. "You come for mine, I'm comin' for yours. You can believe that."

"Oh, you a shooter now? You Cleo from Set It Off? You betta listen to your man and take yo' ass in the house wit' that ghetto-ass pink wig on." He scoffed.

"Suck my dick, bitch!" Gray flicked him off.

"I ain't gon' tell yo' ass again. GO IN THE FUCKIN' HOUSE!" Cam roared.

"You betta handle him, or I will." Gray warned, trudging back in the house.

Once Cam and Gunz were alone, he turned and stared directly in his eyes. He didn't give a fuck about Mrs. Mariam being on her porch, trying to eavesdrop on their conversation. What he was about to say he'd gladly serve penitentiary time for. Cam swiped his thumb across his nose and stepped into Gunz's personal space.

"Dig this, the next time you call yourself sending one of yo' pussy-ass errand boys to do your job, make sure they know what they doing. Cause when I come for you, I ain't gon' miss."

A wicked grin spread over Gunz's face, showing his overly-whitened teeth. He was enjoying this confrontation far more than Cam knew. He lived for this shit. He got off on verbal and physical warfare. Matching his aggression, he got so close to Cam's face their noses almost touched.

"Don't worry about it. Next time I'ma do the shit myself, and trust me, next time I won't miss."

Cam squinted his eyes. He didn't think the muthafucka would have the balls to admit it. He'd underestimated the fucker.

"Just don't get too comfortable. You won't be here much longer." Gunz clasped his hand on his shoulder.

Cam smacked it away. If the girls weren't there, he would've crushed his skull in.

"Have fun makin' your funeral arrangements. They got caskets on sale. Buy one for yourself, you'll be seein' me soon." He advised, walking up the driveway.

"Oh, by the way." Gunz placed one foot inside the car. "You might wanna be careful with them late night visits to LaLa's house. I don't think my baby mama would appreciate that too much." He smirked.

Trepidation creeped over Cam like an Antarctic chill, numbing his brain. *This muthafucka got eyes on me,* he thought. Cam was slipping. He should've known this was going on. He had his people watching Gray to ensure her safety but now it was time he hire someone to ensure his. A war was about to take place and Cam would be damned if he became a casualty.

"But ya'll have a safe evening." Gunz saluted him before pulling off.

Slightly thrown off his game but ready to kill, Cam entered the house and was met with utter chaos. Aoki and Press were both sobbing hysterically. Gray held both girls close while trying to calm them down.

"What's wrong, Pretty Girl?"

"Why was mommy tryin' to hurt my daddy?" Press ran over to Cam's open arms.

"Mommy wasn't tryin' to hurt that nigga. They were just having a misunderstanding." He cradled her in his embrace.

"What's a misunderstanding?"

"When one muthafucka try to explain somethin' and the other person's dumb-ass don't get it."

"Oh, that makes sense."

"Now stop all that cryin'. Bad bitches don't cry."

"Cam, you refer to my daughter as a bad bitch one more time and it's gon' be me and you." Gray cautioned.

"Can we watch the Greatest Showman? Daddy and Tia wouldn't let me watch it." Press wiped her eyes.

"Why not?" Cam helped her.

"Cause they said they ain't wanna hear that gay shit."

"Oh, hell nah!" Gray jumped up. "I'm gettin' ready to go over there. Cam, go get the choppa. Bring Kilo and Gram wit' you."

"Gray, if you don't sit yo' ass down up here dressed liked G.I. Jane." Cam joked.

"Mommy, I don't wanna go over there no more." Aoki admitted out of nowhere.

"Why?"

"Cause half the time daddy wasn't there, and when he was, him and Tia were in the room making loud sex noises."

"Help me Jesus." Gray covered her mouth with her hand. "I think I'ma throw up."

"Papa Cam, I'm hungry." Press played with the chains on his chest.

Gray and Cam eyed each other surprised. It was the first time Press had called him anything but Cam. Instead of acknowledging what she said, Cam carried on as if nothing out of the ordinary had happened. If he did react, he might get chocked up. After finding out Kamryn wasn't his, he never thought he'd be a dad again. He wouldn't trust a female enough to take it there with her. Having Press and even Aoki grown-ass in his life proved that he was father material. The love he had for both girls started to mend the fractured pieces of his heart.

"Yo' daddy didn't feed you before you came home?" He asked.

"No. We kept eatin' cereal."

"All y'all ate was cereal the whole weekend?"

"Yeah."

"And then they ran out of milk and told us to use water." Aoki added.

"I'm really fuckin' that nigga up." Cam scowled. "I got you, Pretty Girl." He planted a tender kiss to the side of her face.

Aoki watched on jealous. Even though Cam was her sworn enemy, she couldn't help but be envious of his relationship with Press. He'd not only taken her mother from her but now he'd corrupted Press with his sarcasm and charm. They were like two peas in a pod. Instead of Press bugging her to play all the time, she now stayed under Cam. He now was the one she went to when she wanted to play make-believe or dress up. It used to annoy Aoki, her constantly being in her face, but now she missed having her pesky little sister around.

"What about me?" She quipped with an attitude.

Cam eyed her with disdain. Aoki was gon' get enough of coming at him like he was a punk or something.

"I got yo' bad-ass too."

"Dear Ms., you will never be me."- Dawn Richard, "Jealousy"

#14

Christmas had come and gone. Gray and Cam, along with the girls ain't shit daddy, showered them with gifts. They got everything from L.O.L Surprise, iPads, new phones, American Dolls, designer clothes and shoes. Gray thought after all Cam had done for her birthday that she wouldn't get anything, but Cam wasn't done. He got her a new Celine and Birkin bag. Plus, a gold chain with a diamond C pendant that matched his. For him, she got the Nike x Off White Air Jordan 1 sneakers, Off-White slides, Versace Chain Reaction sneakers, Gucci Supreme canvas backpack, a red Gucci leather duffle bag and she blew almost a half a mill on a Bulgari Magsonic Sonnerie Tourbillion watch. Spending so much money on a watch almost made her have a nervous breakdown but Cam deserved it. The man had almost lost his life. If things had gone the way Gunz wanted, she would've spent Christmas as a widow.

She still hadn't fully grasped what happened. She'd seen stuff like that go down in movies or read about it in books but never in real life. Gray hated violence. It was funny that she'd fallen in love with two of the most violent men in the Midwest. Over the holidays, she was almost sure that Cam was going to make a move to retaliate, even though she'd asked him not to. At first she was all in for the beef; Gunz deserved a bullet to his head but enough violence had transpired. Someone had lost their life. For the sake of the girls, both men needed to let their animosity toward the other go. So far, Cam had listened. Gray prayed he'd keep that same energy.

To show her love and appreciation, she decided to get dolled up and head over to his auto shop on St. Louis Avenue to bring him lunch. It was something she'd never done, so she was sure he'd get a kick out of it. It wasn't like she had much else to do. It was New Year's Eve. The girls were at Tee-Tee's house, spending the night with his daughter Princess Gaga and Heidi's son. They wouldn't be home until the following afternoon. Gray was home all alone. If it was the last thing she did, she was going to figure out her next career move. Spending idle time on her ass twiddling her thumbs was driving her mad. She'd thought about it and thought about it but still couldn't figure out what she wanted to do. All she ever wanted was to own her own magazine. She'd done that and was quite successful for a while. Gray fiddled with the thought of starting another one but the risk of it folding was too great. She wouldn't be able to sustain the heartache twice. Thank god she was wealthy. She'd made 8 million off her magazine, but that money wouldn't last forever, especially after she'd spent a small portion of it on her house and Cam's watch.

Gray pulled her hair up in a sleek ponytail then placed on some mascara and lip-gloss. She had a naturally pretty face, so she didn't need to beat her face every day. Her outfit was sick enough. It was hella chilly out, so she sauntered into Cam's place of business with gold hoop earrings dangling from her ears. A brown waist length fur, brown spaghetti strap bodysuit, Gucci belt, skintight denim jeans, brown five-inch Christian Louboutin heels and a Gucci bag finished her rich-bitch look. The chain Cam gave her, to brand her as his, shined from her neck blinding niggas. All she heard was a bunch of cat calls as she switched by. Gray grinned and pretended like she didn't hear anything. Locating the manager, she stopped. He was an older man who'd been working for Cam for years.

"Hey, Benny." She smiled brightly.

"Hey, Mrs. Gray. How you doing?" He wiped his hands on a towel.

"I'm doing good. Is my big head husband in the back?"

"Nah, he just stepped out. He'll be right back tho. There was a problem at one of the other locations."

"Okay. I'm gonna go wait for him in his office."

"Sure thing. I'll tell him you're here as soon as he gets back."

"Thanks, Benny." She sashayed away.

"Yo, who is shawty? She bad as fuck." One of the mechanic's asked while gripping his dick.

"That's boss man's lady. You might wanna advert your eyes elsewhere youngin'. Cam find out you was checkin' out his wife he gon' fire you, fuck you up then kill you. I don't think you want them kind of problems." Benny advised.

"I sure in the fuck don't. Boss man did good tho. I would've wife'd her fine-ass up too." The guy resumed working.

Back in Cam's office, Gray took a seat behind his desk and propped up her feet. His office was a quaint little space in the back of the building. There wasn't much to it except a desk, three chairs, filing cabinet, state of the art security system and a small refrigerator. The aroma from the Chic-Fil-A she bought was making her mouth water. She was trying her hardest to wait on him and not eat a waffle fry, but with each second that passed, her stomach growled more and more. To keep herself busy, Gray pulled up Instagram and scrolled down her timeline. She wasn't even deep into the Gram five minutes before she heard Benny yell, "Didn't I tell you last time, you can't go back there?"

"Babe." LaLa barged into Cam's office.

When her eyes landed on Gray and not him, she stopped dead in her tracks. Gray looked up from her phone and glared at her with contempt. A million thoughts ran through her brain. A) What the fuck was she doing there? B) Why the hell was she calling her husband babe? And C) Where the hell was she going dressed like a whore from the 1990's? It wasn't even 2:00 p.m. and she had the audacity to have on a pair of cross earrings, a black, Puma, long sleeve, cropped hoodie, an orange spaghetti strap, latex dress, black lace-up booties and a large black purse. Her wig was half up, half down with baby hairs plastered on her forehead. Unlike Gray, LaLa opted for a full face of makeup. The shit was so caked on she looked like a corpse. It was obvious she'd come there to seduce Cam in some sexy shit.

"Where is Cam?" She spat like Gray was the one who shouldn't be there.

"Minding his married-ass business." Gray put her phone down and faced her.

"Ump . . . cute. Anyway, when his married but soon to be divorced-ass gon' be back?"

"Bitch." Gray shot up from her seat. "I will slap the shit outta you. Don't forget what happened at the game. I would hate to see you have another broken nose."

"Bitch, you snuck me." LaLa flicked her wrist. "But it's cool. I ain't gon' fight you no way. All yo' big-ass gon' do is sit on me."

Aghast, Gray sucked in a mouthful of air.

"Now, I ain't gon' ask you again. Where is Cam? I got something I need to give him." LaLa put her purse down on the desk.

"You ain't got shit to give to my husband. Don't you think it's time for you to move on sis? You ain't embarrassed yet?" Gray retook her seat.

"Embarrassed? Embarrassed for what?"

"The nigga done son'd you in front of everybody I don't know how many times. He yoked you up in front of everybody on the block for me. He publicly claimed me by making me his wife. Obviously, he don't want you boo-boo."

"Bitch, he don't want you either. He just got a big girl fetish."

Gray's shoulders bounced up and down with laughter.

"That's the only thing you can say is I'm fat. Well guess what, bitch? He love my fat ass. All of it. Face stay planted in my puss. He can't get enough. He stay licking on these thick thighs, this fat-ass stomach and these big tits. You wish it was you but it ain't, bitch."

"Wish it was me? Out of everything you said all I heard is big-big-big. Girl, don't nobody wanna be you. I don't wanna have a high BMI level. I'm surprised yo' ass ain't got diabetes. Sweetheart, it's just a matter of time before he comes to his senses and is back with me and my son Kamryn where he belongs."

Gray kept an indifferent expression on her face, but on the inside, her intestines were tying themselves into a knot. She didn't know that LaLa had named her son after

Cam. She wondered why he had never told her. Gray prayed to god there was nothing else she'd been left in the dark about.

"What makes you think he gon' come back to you? Your foundation don't even match your neck. Wit' yo' basic-ass."

"Bitch, this my winter complexion!" LaLa snapped, holding her neck.

"What the fuck that mean? You still need to get the right shade. Walkin' in here lookin' like a damn orange flavored condom. Ain't you like thirty? You too old to be making fake baby hairs all over your forehead. Forehead lookin' like a 40-inch flat screen. What's the point of owning a hair salon if you can't press your edges?" Gray bugged up laughing.

"I might be fat but you're a fuckin' joke sis. You think you the shit, but you spent thousands of dollars to make yourself pretty. This homegrown right here. You think I ain't know about them teeth, horse mouth."

Embarrassed, LaLa's hand shot up to her veneers.

"Bitch, I know you looked like Donald Duck before surgery. Why you think he left you? He got tired of that project housing system you called a grill and them stiff-ass titties. Do yourself a favor ma and fall back. Quit throwing yourself at my husband under his friend's Instagram. It's over, bitch. Get it through your big head ass, Gina. The nigga put a ring on my finger. He take care of my kids. He bought me not one but two cars for my birthday that totals almost 4 mill. He dick me down every night. I'm the reason he's flourishing, the reason he wakes up in the morning and the cookie that he eats when he's hungry. You will never be me, girlfriend. You will never have what we have. All you got is some fake teeth and some botched-ass titties out of the equation. How one of 'em by yo' chin and the other one by yo' navel?" Gray held her stomach and laughed. "And to keep it a buck, the only reason you got that is because he was embarrassed to be seen wit' yo' walrus lookin' ass."

Seeing she had her on the ropes, Gray went in for the kill.

"Then yo' ho-ass gon' have the nerve to name that baby Kamryn. What the fuck is wrong wit' you? You thought that was gon' make him forget you fucked a whole other nigga. Bitch, that pussy is for everybody. He ain't wifin' no bitch like you so you can hope, wish, pray, lie, scheme and name yo' son Kamryn. It still ain't gon' change the fact that I have his last name and you're just a bitch that keep on chasing him like you Flo Jo. Well, guess what, bitch? Flo Jo is dead."

Hate colored LaLa's soul. It spread throughout her system, cutting off all other emotions. She wanted to rip Gray's head off. No one had ever talked to her the way she did. She sat her overweight ass there with a smug expression on her face. Gray thought she'd won but little did she know LaLa had the upper hand the whole time.

"First of all, who the fuck is Flo Jo? Oh, I forgot you a old hoe. You think you know so much. You don't even know your own husband."

"Oh, I don't?" Gray cocked her head to the side.

"Yeah 'cause if you did you would know he left this." She tossed Cam's red Cardinal's hat on the desk. "At my house a few weeks ago when he spent the night with me."

All I can see is your face giving my love away at some woman's place. It was a line from Brandy's song *I Tried.* Gray never truly felt the lyrics until then, as she looked at the hat. It was the same hat he wore the night he didn't come home. Gray knew it was his 'cause Cam had his name stitched into the side of all his hats. *I needed to holla at ya' man anyway. It's been a minute,* she recalled Diggy saying. He'd lied. Cam hadn't gone to Diggy's house. He'd went to see LaLa. The same LaLa he claimed to hate. An ocean of tears flooded her chest, but Gray would be damned if she cried in front of his whore.

"Yeah, pick up your face before you step on it wit' your big-ass feet Big Pun. See you might have that Cracker Jack ring on your finger but Cam ain't never leaving me alone. We got history. Who you think paid for my salon? Who you think about to open me two more in L.A. and Miami?" LaLa smirked with delight.

The look of shock and horror on Gray's face was the best gift she'd ever received.

"Oh, you ain't know that did you? Is this new information?" She mocked. "I thought you and your husband talk about everything. Did he tell you he has PTSD? Did he tell you he almost lost his life in Afghanistan? I bet you don't even know why he don't fuck wit' his daddy. Yo' dumb-ass probably think these auto shops is his only source of income. I know you don't think that nigga got 50 mill from fuckin' changing tires and replacing bumpers. That nigga got several liquor stores, property and he's the fuckin' lieutenant in the Gonzalez cartel but you looooove throwing your li'l wife title around like it mean something." LaLa took a moment to laugh.

Gray could feel it. A fire pit of fury grew in her stomach. Her entire body was hot. She felt sick. Her heart started to beat erratically. Her adrenaline rose to an all-time high. Sweat beads sprouted on her forehead. Everything LaLa said kept coming at her like waves crashing on the shore. Sweat covered her body completely. At any second, her body was going to shut down.

"That nigga like you. He don't love you. You just something to do right now. Right after he cross big girl off his bucket list you ain't gon' never hear from him again. So how bout this." LaLa placed her palms down on the desk and leaned forward. "Do yourself a favor and give him that li'l cheap-ass ring back. I can't believe he even gave you that ugly piece of shit 'cause mine looked way better. But anyway, that's neither here nor there. Forgive me for gettin' off subject. Now where was I?" LaLa put her index on her chin.

"Oh yeah, pack up your li'l illegitimate family and catch the first flight back to Japan, Kawasaki 'cause if Cam don't want nobody it's you. It's gon' break your li'l heart when he leave you and come back to me. We both know with the way my niece took your other nigga you can't afford no more heartache. Fuck around and give yo' old ass a stroke."

Gray sat utterly speechless. LaLa had dropped a nuclear bomb on her. Everything she thought true in her world had blown up in smoke. LaLa basked in her misery. Gray needed to be brought down a peg or two. Homegirl thought her shit didn't stink. Now that she'd put her in her place, LaLa picked up her purse and turned towards the door.

"Oh, and by the way. . . don't forget to tell him I stopped by." She winked and left knowing she'd triumphantly destroyed Gray and her so-called marriage.

Once the coast was clear, Gray's stomach contracted so violently that she had no time to make it to the nearby trashcan. Chunks of food from breakfast propelled into the air and splattered all over Cam's desk.

Heaving again, she sprayed vomit all over his things. Gray held her stomach and puked until only clear liquid came up. Her throat felt like fire. The foul-smelling bile burned her nose. Looking at the mess she'd made caused Gray to dry-heave again. A few minutes later, she was done. Spit drooled from her lower lip. Gray grabbed a tissue and wiped her mouth. She was a mess. Chunks of vomit were on her chest and fur. The last time she threw up was when she learned Gunz had gotten Tia pregnant.

Why had Cam kept all these important things from her? Did he not trust her with his secrets? Apparently not. There wasn't an aspect of her life that he didn't have access to. She'd been fully transparent with him. Here Gray was thinking she was his everything when really she was just an outsider. Why had Cam done this to her? Why would he cause her even more heartache? He'd witnessed firsthand what Gunz had put her through. Why would he too use her heart as a punching bag? Who in the hell had she even married?

Gray didn't even know why she was so upset. She knew this day was coming but heartbreak was a funny son-of-a-bitch. We all know it's going to happen, yet we're never really equipped for it. People took it as a joke. Heartbreak was like running into the middle of traffic, hoping you didn't get hit. You should be prepared to get ran over but people never are. Why? Because people never believed it was going to happen to them. Gray believed if she gave a man her heart, he'd treasure it. She never went into love thinking a man would toy with her emotions. For, hearts shouldn't be mistreated. They should be valued and protected. Gray wished someone would've informed Cam of this. Maybe then he wouldn't have shattered hers.

Grabbing her purse, she rose to her wobbly feet and eased her way to the door. She had to get out of there. The walls were closing in on her. Each breath she took came in longer spurts. She couldn't risk seeing Cam's face. If she did, Gray was sure she'd be in jail. No, she needed fresh air. She needed her best friends. She needed a peace of mind. For the greatest mistake Gray had ever made was thinking that loving a nigga ever mattered. Love had reduced her to nothing.

"You say you know what love is, but I swear you've never seen it in yo' life."- Summer Walker, "Session 32"

#15

"Girl, what happened and why do you smell like sour puss?" Kema asked as Gray walked through the door.

"That muthafucka cheated on me." She threw her purse down and took off her fur.

"Ooooooooooh bitch. You need a bath." Kema held her nose and fanned the air.

"I need a drink and a casket. I'm tired of living." Gray plopped down on her couch.

"I hate to say it." Tee-Tee scooted away from her. "But your pussy must be trash. It ain't even been six months and he already cheating. Sheesh."

"I will cut what little dick you have off."

"You got me fucked up. My dick swings low sweet chariot." He snapped his fingers in her face.

"What the fuck am I going to do?" Gray sank deeper into the couch and willed herself not to cry.

"Get a fuckin' divorce and call it a day."

"We don't even know what happened. You know how Gray ass over exaggerate everything." Kema sat on the arm of the couch.

"I wish this was the case, but it isn't. Me and Cam been having problems ever since we said I do."

"Which is why yo' dumb-ass should've said I don't. I told you not to marry that nigga but nooooo yo' ass just wanted to be Carrie Bradshaw and have a courthouse

~ 280 ~

wedding. Bitch, think we in Sex and The City for real." Tee-Tee rolled his eyes.

"I married him because I love him, and I thought he loved me too."

"Where thoughting ever got you in yo' life? You know every time you think some dumb shit happen, literally."

"Fuck all that." Kema waved them both off. "What he do?"

"One night we got into it cause Gunz sent me and the girls some flowers. Cam got mad cause I kept them in the house—"

"Which he should have." Kema nodded in agreement.

"Whew, girl you so dumb. You get dumber as the conversation goes on. God bless the dead, but Ms. Rose know she raised a fool." Tee-Tee crossed his legs agitated.

"Eat a clit." Gray flicked him off.

"Now that's disgusting. You know I don't eat fish."

"Will you two shut and get back to the story." Kema snapped.

"As I was saying. We argued, and he left and didn't come home until the next afternoon."

"WHAT? The next afternoon? Oh, yous a whole fool." Tee-Tee screwed up his face.

"He told me he slept at Diggy's house."

"And you believed that?" Kema said dumbfounded. "If anything, he would've slept at Quan's house."

"Reason number 5 million, four hundred thousand why she dumb." Tee-Tee chuckled.

"Let me guess, he spent the night over LaLa's house?" Kema pursed her lips.

"Bingo." Gray shot her finger like a gun. "Me and her just got into it at the auto shop and that bitch had a whole lot to say. She told me that not only did he sleep at her house, he's the lieutenant in the Gonzalez cartel, he owns several liquor stores and property. Apparently, he has PTSD and she knows why he don't have a good relationship with his father and how he almost lost his life in the Afghanistan war. I'm the one wearing his ring and donning his last name and I didn't know none of that shit. You know how stupid I felt?" She swallowed the huge lump in her throat.

"Bitch, you threw up didn't you?" Tee-Tee inquired.

"All over his fuckin' desk. I can't believe this shit is happening to me again." Gray covered her face with her hands.

"What you mean?"

"Once again, I've fallin in love with a nigga I don't even really know. I mean, you think you know someone but in reality you only know what the hell they want you to know."

"I love you girl but you gotta take responsibility for your part too, sis." Kema interjected. "How you expect to know someone after only two months? Y'all wasn't even dating that whole time. Shit to be honest, it was only like a few weeks. I know you love him, and I like Cam, but you had no business marrying that man. It was way too soon."

"I get that, Kema, but we're here now. I can't go back and change the past."

"Well, bitch, focus on your future 'cause this marriage is 9/11. It's going up in smoke." Tee-Tee clapped his hands in the air then snapped his fingers.

"That is not funny. You going straight to gay hell." Gray couldn't help but laugh.

When I'm with somebody, all I think 'bout is you. When I'm alone, that's all I wanna do.

Gray begrudgingly sat up and grabbed her purse. She was sure Cam had found the mess she'd left behind and wanted to know what made her upset. Her thumb hovered over the answer button, but she just couldn't bring herself to have the confrontation they needed to have. If she answered, the anger she harbored inside was sure to turn her into a raving bitch. Gray wasn't sure she'd be able to control herself. Words she probably would regret later would be spewed. It was best she not answer but Cam wasn't letting up. He ended one call and quickly called right back. Not ready to deal with him and the mess he'd made, Gray blocked his number.

"So, you think he fucked her?" Kema asked rubbing her hair.

"I know he did." She threw her phone back inside her purse. "Cam ain't gon' be around no bitch and not fuck her. What other reason would he have gone over there for?"

"I don't know friend. I think y'all should just talk before you jump to conclusions."

"And, bitch, you just as dumb as she is." Tee-Tee looked at Kema like she had shit on her face.

"Says the nigga that named his daughter Princess Gaga. Trick please. You can't tell me nothin'."

"Bitch, I was going through something at the time."

"Fuck all this dumb shit. It is New Year's Eve. You coming out with us tonight friend." Kema focused on Gray.

"The hell she ain't." Tee-Tee furrowed his brows. "Her big-ass ain't gettin' in the car wit' me. I gotta Mini Cooper. I can barely fit my ass in there. Between my body and Gray's neck, it's gon' feel like a pack of sardines in there."

"You know what bitch, don't nobody wanna ride in yo' old ass Mini Cooper no way. I gotta 3-million-dollar car sitting right outside." Gray shot.

"I forgot he got you a 3-million-dollar car. And you got the nerve to be sittin' here complaining. You so damn selfish. Girl, you betta let that man cheat in peace."

———

The tears piling up in Gray's stomach were pushed down. She refused to let them spill from her cobalt eyes. No matter how much she wanted to curl up in a ball and die, she held her head high and entered the club like she was the baddest bitch on the planet. The tequila in her system had her on one. She'd pregame'd hard before hittin' the club but you wouldn't know. On the outside, she looked like a million bucks. Kema and Tee-Tee had done wonders with her ensemble. Tee-Tee parted her hair down the middle and put deep wave curls in. Gray was serving the kids old Hollywood glamour with her hairdo. She'd painted her own face and gave herself a gold glitter eye, gold winged liner and a deep burgundy lip. Since she refused to return home, Gray went to the mall and bought a white satin, Only Hearts bra top that tied in the front and a crème colored bandaged skirt. On her feet were a pair of Gianvito Rossi, crème, suede, pumps that tied up the leg. The only jewelry she rocked was the C chain Cam bought her and her wedding ring. Gray almost took them both off, but her heart wouldn't allow her to, no matter how broken it was. Yes, Gray Rose Parthens looked and smelled like a diva but on the inside she was withering away by the second.

The cry she'd been holding in the last eleven hours was begging, no demanding to be released but Gray knew if she cried she'd never be able to stop. Fuck crying. She was going to drink her misery away. Alcohol was sure to numb her pain. Heading straight to the bar she ordered three shots of Patron. Back-to-back, she took all three shots to the head and wiped the leftover residue from her mouth. Gray was good and tipsy now. Buzzed, she and her crew headed to the dancefloor. The whole time she moved through the crowd, Gray had no idea she was being watched. She'd completely forgotten that Cam had eyes on her. Priest stood across the room in the shadows watching her like a hawk. He'd been shadowing Gray for months now. Usually, he had nothing to report back to Cam. He'd only caught her on some shady shit that one time she met up with Gunz. Other than that, she led a pretty quiet life.

That night, however, Gray was on another level. He knew his cousin would flip if he saw the freaky shit she had on. Gray's entire body was on display for all the thirsty niggas in the club to see. Priest didn't want to make the phone call to Cam, but he had no choice. Gray was on the dancefloor wildin'. She and her friends had formed a semi-circle as they danced their hearts out. Everyone was amping them up. All of that was innocent fun. Everything was cool, until some nigga with skin the color of D'Usse walked behind her and started grinding on her ass. Priest thought Gray would push the guy off her, but she didn't. Homegirl started backing it up on him even more. After Gray blocked

Cam, he'd told Priest to inform him immediately if anything crazy popped off. Cam was trying to give her some space to cool off before he swooped down on her. He had to play his cards right. Gray was a known runner. He couldn't risk her taking off on him, especially when he didn't know what all was said between her and LaLa. Retrieving his phone, Priest made the call that would start World War III.

"What up cuzzo?" Cam answered on the first ring.

He'd went through five blunts, he was so on edge. Quan, Stacy and Diggy tried to keep him calm, but it was damn near impossible. Cam's whole marriage was hanging in the balance. He'd called LaLa several times to see what she'd said to Gray, but the bitch wouldn't answer her phone. He knew some crazy shit went down cause there was vomit all over his office. He thought about runnin' down on LaLa but that could wait till later. The wellbeing of his wife was far more important.

"Aye, I think you might wanna get down here bro." Priest said cautiously.

"Down where?" Cam sat up on high alert.

"Onyx. Your wife in here dry humpin' some dread-head nigga in the middle of the club."

Nothing else had to be said. Cam hung up and grabbed his Glock.

"Aww shit. This nigga bout to go postal." Stacy laughed.

"Cam! Cam!" Quan tried to block his path but was seconds too late. "My g you gotta calm down. Think before you do something you gon' regret."

"Nah, fuck that. I'ma about to kill this girl." Cam stormed out of Quan's crib.

"C'mon, we gotta follow this nigga before his dumb-ass wind up in jail." Quan grabbed his coat.

"Do I have to?" Diggy whined.

He'd much rather go home and rub his pregnant girl's belly.

"Nigga, bring yo' ass on!" Quan barked, not in the mood for his little brother's bullshit.

"Fine, but you gon' buy me a fifth of Hennessy for this shit." Diggy trudged behind him.

With her eyes closed, Gray let the music take hold of her body. The DJ had started to play *Don't Cha* by The Pussycat Dolls. Anybody that knew her knew that when the Pussycat Dolls came on, Gray was going to act up. Glancing over her shoulder, she realized the man she was dancing with was none other than Kingston. Kingston was the owner of Onyx and Gunz's homeboy. They weren't super close, but they were close enough that dancing on him was a no-no. But Gray didn't care. Fuck Gunz and fuck Cam. Neither one of their asses gave a fuck about her feelings so why should she give a fuck about theirs? Besides dancing was harmless. It wasn't like she was going to fuck the nigga. *Or should I,* she thought. Throughout the years, she'd noticed how Kingston looked at her. He'd tried to hide his lust for her as best as he could but Gray peeped game.

Running her hands through her hair, she wind her hips seductively slow. Kingston gripped her waist tighter as his dick began to expand in his jeans. Being this close to Gray was a dream come true. He would've never pushed up on her while she was still with Gunz, but now that they were over, all bets were off. Gray was fair trade. Running her tongue over her top lip, Gray winked her eye at Kema who was hyping her up. Grinning wickedly, she rocked her hips from side-to-side while patting her pussy to the beat. Bending over, she twirled her fat-ass in a circle. In the zone, she flipped her hair back-and-forth like a video vixen. All she needed was a wind machine to complete the choreography she was giving. Gray was so high, she felt like she could dance all night. She moved in her skirt like her hips were made to sway against the fabric. A sheen of sweat glistened on her caramel skin. Music was a drug that brought her higher until her mind buzzed with bliss.

Onyx was on fire that night. The gleam from Cam's chains entered the club before he did. All eyes were on him and his mans as they mobbed through the crowd. Some people looked at him in awe, others in shock. It was 36 degrees outside and he'd stormed in wearing nothing but a slew of diamond chains, a wifebeater, Tommy Hilfiger boxers, a Louis Vuitton belt, skinny jeans and Timbs. Cam looked like a real life sociopath. In his mind a coat or a shirt wasn't needed. He was so hot that his anger kept him warm.

"Hey, Cam." Some chocolate chick blocked his path. "Remember me?" She ran her long fingernail down his hard chest.

"Bitch move?" He side stepped her.

"Wait! I was the one who sucked your dick at your birthday party a few months ago."

"Okay, you want a cookie? I don't give a fuck. Your head game was trash anyway. Move bitch." Cam pushed her aside.

"It probably wasn't that bad. You can suck my dick. I'll tell you if it was trash or not." Stacy gripped his dick.

"Stacy, shut your fat-ass up." The girl sucked her teeth and stormed away.

Spotting Priest up against the wall, Cam gave his li'l cousin a pound and asked, "Where she at?" Priest pointed to the center of the dancefloor. From where Cam stood, he couldn't see anything, but a massive group of people huddled around in a circle waving their hands in the air. Pushing his way through the crowd, he stood in the front and found his wife twerking her ass all on another man's dick. *Freak (Remix)* by Victoria Monet featuring Bia was on. Gray loved the song and rapped along while bending over and wiggling her ass like a stripper.

Tell you it's yours
You like your girl on all-fours (ayy)
Put that seat on double back
If it's two doors in the Porsche (eww)
Window tint, of course
Buy me that Chanel, if you afford
I do that dance on that dick for Dior (yeah)
By the way you leave your girl, I can tell you feelin'
bored (skrrt)
I'm too scared to fall in love 'cause I been in it
before (woo)
I like how you use your mind and had me open like
a pore (sheesh)
And that dick too bomb, I ain't sharin' anymore (uh
uh)
I can trust you not to tell all your friends how it feel
Be mature, I'll make a movie wit' you if I feel secure
(yeah)
Leave my message on read and I might pull up at
your door (skrrt)
'Cause this pussy too good for a bitch to get ignored
(ayy)

Cam could see the crease of Gray's butt checks as she danced slow and sexy. If that wasn't bad enough, the nigga she was dancing on was Kingston. The same Kingston who'd fucked LaLa and gotten her pregnant. The vision of him practically fuckin' Gray from behind in front of a room full of people would be etched in his memory forever. He couldn't unsee it no matter how much he tried.

"Yoooooo you see Gray. That's my bitch! Get it girl!" Stacy clapped his hands. "Fuck it up for the big people! Yo, she keep on dancing like that, that nigga gon' bust a nut. She ever wind on yo' dick like that?" He asked Cam.

"Stacy, if you don't get your fat-ass out my fuckin' face!" Cam growled.

"Don't get mad at me 'cause you keep losin' your bitches to Kingston."

"You trippin'." Quan ran his hand down his face, paranoid. "What the fuck you say that for?"

"He can tell me to shut my fat-ass up, but I can't tell him the truth?"

"Oh, y'all niggas must think this a game. This nigga about to air this whole club out. I ain't got time for this. I'm out. I ain't being no innocent bystander. I wanna live. That nigga bullets ain't got no name on it. Peace out." Diggy threw up the deuce and left.

He didn't need a magic 8 ball to know what was about to happen. Every time Gray popped her ass and Kingston smacked it, Cam got angrier. His face was red with fury. It was about to be a homicide. Pulling out his gun, Cam's index finger curled around the trigger. No words were spoken as he stalked towards his wife, placed the barrel of the gun against her temple and cocked the hammer back.

Gray immediately stilled when she felt the cold steel pressed against her sweat induced skin. Everyone around her, except her friends, started screaming and running for cover. Pure pandemonium took place as the DJ cut the track. With venom in her eyes, she turned and looked at Cam. She knew only his deranged ass would have the nerve to cheat and put a gun up to her head.

"Get that fuckin' gun out my face." She smacked it away not giving a fuck if it was loaded or not.

"You got five seconds to get yo' ass outside." Cam warned.

"One, two, three, four, five." Gray quickly counted. "Who the hell you think you talkin' to? Coming in here giving me ultimatums like I'm gon' listen. I ain't these niggas in here. I ain't scared of you."

"Well, you should be." Cam's black eyes drilled into hers.

"Well, I ain't." Gray rolled her neck.

If she wasn't so mad, she would've stood on her tippy toes and licked the tattoo of her name on his temple. He was so fine. When he was angry he was even sexier. Cam's sex appeal was on ten. The wife beater he donned did nothing but spotlight his bulging biceps and rock-hard abs. Gray examined his face. The whites of his eyes were red, and his lids hung low with sadness. He was high. He was just as stressed out as she was. Good. Gray didn't feel bad for him at all.

"I ain't gon' kill you but I will shoot you in your fuckin' knee cap! Get your shit and let's go! And what the fuck you got on?" Cam looked her up down with disgust.

"Nothing." Stacy licked his lips.

He remembered when they first met Gray, she used to be covered up from head to toe in Lane Bryant suits and shit.

"Mind your fuckin' business, Stacy!" She spat.

"Nah turn around. I like that shit for real." He tried to get a look at her ass.

Pissed off beyond belief, Cam reared his hand back to smack him in the face with his gun but Quan being quick on his feet stopped him.

"So, you gon' pistol whip me 'cause your wife got her ass out? I see what type of nigga you is." Stacy shook his head appalled.

Fed up with everyone, Cam focused his wrath on Kingston.

"And you?" He pointed his gun at him. "What the fuck is you still standing here for? Don't you got a business to run, nigga?"

"This you?" Kingston arched his brow, surprised.

"Yeah, nigga! Any other questions?" Cam pushed his head back with the barrel of the gun.

"Oh, my bad. I ain't even know." Kingston held up his hands in mock surrender.

"Well, now you do, and you already know what type of time I'm on. I ain't got too many more words for you so you might wanna back yo' monkey-ass up."

"Damn, Cam, y'all really got the same taste. Y'all niggas might be related low-key." Stacy joked.

"Stacy." Cam pinched the bridge of his nose and closed his eyes. "I'm not gon' say it again. Shut yo' fat-ass up!"

"I'm just sayin' nigga. Shit."

"Yo, I ain't mean no disrespect. If I would've known this was you, I wouldn't have pushed up on her." Kingston explained.

He prayed the outside of him didn't show how shook he was. Cam was a crazy nigga that had no chill. The last thing he wanted was smoke with him, but he couldn't look like a punk in his own club.

"Pussy, do I look stupid to you! That's exactly what yo' punk-ass would'a done! I should've murked yo' ass four years ago, but on the strength of yo' kid, I'ma let you live."

"You still on that?"

"Nigga, it's gon' be killa for you for life! You's a grimy nigga!"

"Nah, LaLa's a grimy bitch. You can't get mad that your ho choose me."

"Daaaaaaaaaaaaaaaaaaaaaaaaaaaaaaaaaaaaaaaaaaaaaaa aaaaaaaaamn!!!!!" Stacy balled up his fist and placed it up to his mouth. "That was a good one, Kingston. Yo, fam, you gotta kill' em now. If you don't kill' em I'm judging on Piru. I'm judging you dog."

"Did she?" Cam placed the gun to his side and got in Kingston's face. "'Cause she still on my dick. Let's not forget your shorty named after me. How you call yourself a man and let a bitch name yo' son after another nigga?"

"Aye, yo, ya'll smell that?" Stacy sniffed the air.

"I smell something." Kema fanned her nose.

"I smell it too." Quan joined in.

"What y'all smell?" Tee-Tee looked around, genuinely confused then smelled underneath his arms.

"I smell. I smell . . . PUSSY!" The whole crew yelled in unison then died laughing.

Kingston's face turned beet red from embarrassment.

"I'm far from a pussy 'cause if I was a pussy I wouldn't have taken yo' bitch." He shot back.

There was only but so much shit-talking Cam could take before the inner countdown to his next explosion began. He needed to fight. A part of him yearned for it. He'd read somewhere that as grown-ups people recreated their childhood, that they sought out the same disfunction they fled from. In Cam's case, this was true. The turmoil he couldn't control as a child could be contained with violence as an adult. He was no longer weak or small. He was a fully-grown man that controlled his destiny, so he used his brute strength and power to remove anything that displeased him from his world. An alarming sound pierced his ears as he blacked out and struck Kingston with the butt of his gun. The vicious blow caused Kingston to fall and cower on the ground. He tried to cover his face, but Cam was much quicker than him. Repeatedly, he struck him over and over until blood leaked. The blood gushing from his head sparkled under the neon lights. Cam missed this.

He got off on seeing his enemies in pain, begging for mercy. He was born to cause bodily harm.

"A'ight, nigga, that's enough. You gon' kill'em." Quan laughed, pulling him back.

"Nah, fuck that!" Cam kicked Kingston in the stomach, causing blood to flow from his mouth.

All Kingston could do was wince in distress and hold his stomach. He was a battered, bloody mess. He was certain Cam had fractured his skull.

"This nigga wanna brag but that bitch is for everybody. Let's be clear." Cam gripped him by the collar of his shirt. "If I call her right now and tell her to come suck my dick, she gon' come down to *your* club, get down on *her* knees and suck me off in front of you. We talkin' about the same bitch that let me nut on yo' baby's car seat."

"And the sippy cup was in there too," Stacy added.

"She told me that was fuckin' icing." Kingston creaked.

"Nah, nigga, that was my nut, and just so you know, I don't want shit to do wit' her scandalous-ass but LaLa ain't gon' ever be able to leave me alone. We got too much history so the next time you think about pushin' up on something that's mine, I would advise you to tread carefully."

"Well, since y'all got so much history together and she's yours, go marry that bitch." Gray spat with venom.

Realizing the error of his words, Cam let Kingston go. He was so in the zone that he'd completely forgot Gray was there. Slowly, he turned around to face her but the look on her face said it all. He was in deeper shit than he already was.

"I was just talkin' shit." He tried to explain.

"No, you wasn't. You meant every word you said. I can't win." She threw up her hands in defeat. "And I refuse to fight a losing battle. Y'all niggas belong with each other. It's obvious." She turned to walk away.

"Gray!" Cam tried to get her to come back but she kept walking.

"Gray!" He started to panic.

This fight wasn't like the other fights they had. She was serious this time. Gray was walking out of his life for good. A panic like no other surged through his veins. The walls were starting to close in on him. He felt claustrophobic. Like at any minute he would pass out. Was this how it felt to be in love? He'd never truly been afraid of losing her until that very second. The notion of not having her in his life was a battle he refused to lose. Cam couldn't take anymore L's.

"I know you hear me talkin' to you!"

With nothing else to say, Gray continued to make her way through the crowd.

"GRAY!" He sent two shots in the air.

The entire club broke out into mass hysteria. Partygoers started running for their lives. Tables were being pushed over and used as shields. Glass champagne flutes crashed to the floor. The chaos Cam had started didn't stop Gray from leaving tho. Along with everyone else she made her way outside. Cam wasn't letting her go that easy. Hot on his tail were all of their friends.

"Gray, bring yo' ass back here!" He pushed people out of the way to get to her.

"Stop talkin' to me like I'm a fuckin' child!"

"Well, stop actin' like one! I'm not in the mood for this shit. It's late, I'm tired and I wanna go to bed! We can talk about this shit in the morning!"

"It's always about you." She mocked.

"Star!"

"Don't call me that." She walked faster.

The sound of her heels clicking against the pavement was like Cam's countdown to death.

"Baby!" He jogged to catch up to her.

"Leave me alone, Cam."

"Nah, I'm not lettin' you run away!" He grabbed her by her arm.

"Maybe you should!" She spun around and slapped him with her free hand.

The smack was as loud as a clap and stung his face. It had been an open-handed smack that left a red handprint on the side of his face. Shocked, Cam drew his head back and narrowed his eyes at her. He was more hurt than anything that she'd resorted to putting her hands on him. If it were any other woman, he would've knocked her into the middle of next week, but this was Gray. He could never raise a hand to her. He'd eat that shit. She could slap him a billion times and he'd gladly take each lick, because, maybe, he'd driven her to this point. Maybe she was tired of using her words to get through to him. Maybe the slap was what he needed to see how much he'd hurt her. Gray could see the anger and pain in his eyes but this time she didn't care. This time he wouldn't bully her into staying. This time she was putting herself first.

"Let's face it, Cam." She threw her arms up exasperated. "I'm not the one you want to be wit'. I'm just a fuckin' seat filler for a bitch that had a baby on you."

Cam stood shocked. Her accusation was like a swift kick to his nut sack.

"That bitch don't mean nothing to me."

"You love her 'cause you damn sure don't love me."

"You don't believe that bullshit." He said once again taken aback by her statement.

"Oh, I don't?" Gray cocked her head to the side. "Then why were you at her house the other night?"

"That's what you mad about? I went over there to get a few hours of sleep."

"I thought you was at Diggy's house?"

Caught in his lie, Cam remained silent. Gray rolled her eyes, repulsed. Her entire life she'd been searching for that familial bond she'd never had growing up. She'd tried with Gunz and failed. Then she'd tried again with Cam. She thought they were building a family that was unbreakable, but he'd stripped her of that dream once again.

"Huh? What happened? Yeah, that's what the fuck I thought. Lyin' bitch! I'm so through wit' yo' ass." She used her index finger and mushed him in the forehead.

"Let me explain. I only lied 'cause I knew if I told you the truth you wouldn't believe me. On my mama, I just slept on her couch."

"That's the lie you came up wit'? Do I mean that little to you?"

"I'm tellin' the fuckin' truth." He scowled. "Fuck LaLa! I don't give a fuck about her. You want me to call and tell her? 'Cause I'll call her right now."

"You fucked her didn't you?" Gray cut straight to the point.

"On my mama nothin' happen." Cam placed his hands on each of her arms.

"Nothin' happened but you came home at two in the afternoon. Okay. You must really think I'm stupid."

"I'm sorry bro. I fucked up."

"I ain't your fuckin' bro." She broke away from his hold. "I swear to god I'm so sick of you lyin' muthafuckas. I'm leaving all you niggas behind in the New Year." Gray paced back-and-forth.

The frosty temperature should've had her freezing, but she was so mad she couldn't feel a thing until it began to rain. A crack of thunder stretched across the night sky. Rain poured from the heavens. Gray closed her eyes and prayed to god that the rain would wash her misery away.

"I wanna divorce." She spoke wearily.

"No." Cam's heart constricted.

"We're no good for each other. You know it and I know it."

"I may not be good for you, but you or nobody else has the right to say what's good for me. You think that I don't know that all this shit is my fault? I fucked up! I get it now! Just don't leave!" He begged.

Cam searched her ocean eyes for any sign of hope that she might take him back. Just a tiny flicker would do. Like a child, he held out his hand, fingers extended for her to intertwine hers with his. Gray could choose forgiveness or hate. It took no time for her to decide. Gray chose hate.

"We made a mistake. We should've never got married but we did. We got caught up in our feelings—"

"We got caught up? What the fuck is that supposed to mean?" Cam blinked the freezing raindrops away.

"We both knew this wasn't going to last. Neither one of us wanted to face it but it's here now." Gray's teeth chattered.

TEN!

The countdown had started. 2018 was only seconds away. People at the neighboring clubs were having the time of their lives while she stood on the side of the street feeling like hers was ending.

"A'ight, here it is." Cam pulled her into his embrace.

Gray's body tensed at his touch. Cam's heart sank.

"Let's acknowledge it now. We did get married fast. We don't really know each other but so what. You know how I feel about you—"

"I don't know shit!" Gray tried to fight him off to no avail.

Cam's grip was too strong.

NINE!

"You don't tell me shit! You don't tell me nothin'! I had to find out that you have PTSD from fuckin' LaLa!"

Cam's eyes grew wide as the rain beat down onto his face.

"Yeah, nigga. She told me everything. I know about the salon, your liquor stores, property and your position in the Gonzalez cartel. How fucked up is it that I had to learn all of that from your ex. I'm your wife, Cam. You know how dumb you made me look?"

"You sayin' I don't open up to you but you still sneakin' and meetin' with your ex and you had flowers that nigga sent you in our crib. How the hell you think I'm supposed to trust you and you ain't been keepin' it a hunnid wit' me?"

"No . . . see that's not fair. You don't get to blame all of this on me. You won't even say you love me. You don't think I haven't noticed that when I say it, you don't say it back."

EIGHT!

Cam swallowed hard. Despite the frigid weather and rain, he could feel sweat drench his skin. Raindrops and despair caused his eyes to throb. Holding Gray close, his fingers curled into a fist. His nails dug into the palm of his hand. Gray was right. He'd never uttered the words she so desperately wanted to hear. He thought she hadn't noticed or cared but obviously she did. He owed her those three magic words, but could he say them out loud? Up until that moment, he loved Gray but wasn't in love with her. Cam had made a pact with himself that he wouldn't tell her until he was madly, deeply, truly in love. He'd felt the flutter of being in love when he gazed upon her angelic face, kissed her lips, watched her mother Aoki and Press or when he held her in his arms at night. He felt it but ignored all the signs. It wasn't till he was on the brink of losing her that he realized he'd already fallen. He'd fallen hard.

SEVEN!

This was it. He needed to tell her how he really felt. This was the moment he needed to be vulnerable, and in his mind weak, but how could a man who had been forced to be strong his whole life expose his deepest emotions without the risk of being hurt? Cam tried to steady his rapidly beating heart but couldn't. He felt dead. The only reason he knew he was still alive was because he could feel oxygen flooding in and out of his lungs. Fear strained his guts, churning his stomach in tense spasms. Fear overwhelmed his body, making it extremely exhausted. *You can do it,* he mentally coached his self. This was the woman he loved. He should be able to tell her. Cam envisioned himself saying, "I love you. You hear me? I love you. I'll say it again. I love you. I'll say it a billion times. I love you-l love you-I love you-I love you-I love you. I knew it the second you walked into the principal's office. Remember what I told you? It's you and me forever." But instead of saying all of that he responded, "You know how I feel about you. Why I gotta say it out loud for you to believe it? I show you every fuckin' day how I feel."

SIX!

Kema, Stacy, Quan and Tee-Tee all shook their heads disappointed. Cam knew he'd fucked up again as soon as the words left his mouth. He knew he needed to prove his love to Gray, but his male pride wouldn't let him risk being hurt by another woman. LaLa had practically destroyed him with her deceit. If Gray ever played with his heart, she'd do more than destroy him. She'd kill him.

Gray stumbled back, nearly tripping over her feet. Her entire body was soaked with rain. She'd surely be sick with the flu the next day. None of it mattered. Her entire world had been blown to smithereens. She would've rather Cam spit in her face then respond the way he did. Here she was thinking they were the real thing. She'd connected to a part of his soul that others never got the chance to feel. She saw parts of him that he never wanted revealed. In those moments, he was beautiful and raw. He was realer than the blood flowing through her veins. She felt him like the beating of her own heart.

"She said you didn't love me. I didn't believe her at first but now I do." Gray said as tears flooded her eyes.

FIVE!

"C'mon, Gray, you know I have feelings for you."

"I need more. Having feelings for me isn't enough."

"Why do I have to explain how I feel about you? What is me sayin' it gonna prove to you?"

"It's gonna prove that you're in this with me. That you love me." She stressed. "I have spent too much of my life chasing after emotionally immature, unavailable, wishy-washy men. I don't have time for it anymore. I know who I am and what I want. If you don't feel the same way I feel about you then I'm done. I can't keep pretending that everything is okay."

"Can we talk about this later?"

"No. You just said you have feelings for me. Now you can't tell me what they are?"

"I need time, Gray. Damn!" He shouted, annoyed.

"Alright." Gray folded her arms. "You need time. You have five seconds to tell me you love me or it's over."

"Five seconds? Man gone." Cam waved her off like it was a joke.

"Five."

"C'mon you know how I feel."

"Four."

"A'ight chill." He tried to stop her.

"Three."

"This shit is stupid!"

"Two."

"I'm not gon' be pressured into—"

"Say it! Say you love me!" She demanded on the verge of breaking down.

"Gray I . . ." Cam stopped midsentence.

The words were on the tip of his tongue. They tugged at his heart, dying to be released but he couldn't say it. Anytime he'd ever openly loved someone they'd left, and he'd ended up on the receiving end of pain. Cam knew the ugly truth about love. It was unforgiving and filled with false hope. Love didn't keep his mother alive, his father from cheating, his squad members from dying or his first love from breaking his heart. It wouldn't stop Gray from seeing him for the wounded, emotionally retarded nigga he was and leaving him. The reality of their situation verified his theory. He couldn't do it. The bond he and Gray had forged instantly was ripped to shreds as he hid from her love once more. She'd done all she could do. She'd yelled, pleaded and let her face become wet with untold tears, but he still wouldn't return her love.

"Here I am just a girl, standing in front of a boy asking him to love me and you can't even do that."

Gray gazed into his sorrow filled eyes struggling to breathe against ribs of concrete. Cam had always been self-conscious about crying but his eyes gave away to the enormity of his grief. With each tear that slid down his cheeks, his breathing hitched. Gray watched on in agony. She didn't know Cam was capable of crying. Men like him didn't cry. He was the ultimate alpha male. He was always so strong and denominate, but as he stood before her crying, there was rawness to it, like the pain he felt was an open wound. His cries were muted at first as he tried to hide his grief. Cam glared at Gray. He was the poster child for loss and devastation. His face said it all. He was a man who had suffered tremendously and refused to do it again. Just when Gray thought she'd gotten through to him and he'd trust her with his heart, the tears stopped, and his emotions were walled off behind a mask of coping. Cold hearted, emotionless Cam had returned. Sadly, he didn't know any other way to be. He was never going to open up to her. This was all he had to give. Choking on her tears, Gray slid her wedding ring off her finger and gently placed it inside the palm of his shaky hand.

"It's over." She closed his fingers over the ring and walked away defeated.

FOUR!

"Gray, don't leave." Cam's voice cracked.

His throat burned with regret. She couldn't leave him. He couldn't stomach it. She wasn't even out of his presence and his world was already crumbling. Unwilling to turn back, Gray kept moving forward.

"I'm sorry."

THREE!

"You can't leave me." He ran and scooped her up from behind into his wet arms.

Gray wanted to cuss and scream for him to let her go as he bear hugged her, but nothing came out. The cry she'd been holding in all day suddenly sprang forth. Her body quaked with raw sobs as she shook like a leaf. Nothing about her cry was normal. It was visceral and animalistic. This was the kind of sobbing a person did when they were drained of all hope. Gray had nothing left to give. At any moment, it felt like she was going to take her last breath and die. Her tears mingled with the rain as her ghastly wails echoed in the midnight air. The pain that flowed from her was as palpable as the cold winter hail. To come so close to real love and to lose it so quickly was something no medication could heal. There was no gravesite she could mourn at. There was no coffin big enough to bury her heart. Pieces of her heart lay scattered on the pavement as her soul fled back to God. Her heart was broken. What remained was merely a mass of angry muscle.

TWO!

"I'm sorry." Cam whispered.

It was apparent he'd lost her for good. This would be the last time he'd get to hold her. His marriage was dying right before him and there was nothing he could do to stop it. How had they gotten here so fast? He was supposed to be building her up. He was supposed to be her savior, but like all the other men in her life, he'd feed her a bowl of lies and misused any faith she had in him.

"Get the fuck off me!"

"No." He held her tighter as she kicked and screamed. "Baby, I'm sorry. Just please don't leave. I need you. Come home with me."

"No! I'm done!" She clawed at his hands, drawing blood.

People on the street were watching them. Some were even recording them on their phones.

"Please, Gray. I ain't shit without you. We can figure this out. I can fix it. Just come home."

"Cam, let her go." Quan tried to pull him off her.

"This my fuckin' wife, man!"

"I know but you gotta let her go. The police comin'. Somebody called the police."

"Cam, please!" Kema begged.

Seeing the distress on Gray's face caused her to cry too. This was worse than when Cam found her beaten with a swollen eye and scrapes all over her body. He'd ruined what little faith she had left in love and men. Salty tears stung Cam's chestnut eyes. He bit into his lower lip harder than he ever had. Blood filled his mouth, but he didn't care. Reality started to kick in. Gray was leaving him, and he couldn't stop her from doing it. For the fourth time in his life he was helpless. He wanted to keep Gray next to him forever, but he couldn't keep her hostage. He had to suffer the consequences of his actions, no matter how much it would hurt. Coming to his senses, he slowly released her from his grasp. The sirens were getting nearer. Gray's feet hit the pavement. Without hesitation, she ran into Kema's awaiting arms and wailed. Cam watched as she helped her to the car. Gray could barely stand up and it was all his fault. He'd broken her. He'd reduced her to nothing but a hollow vessel. He'd ruined them. He'd ruined his one shot at pure love and now he was doomed to be alone in this cold, cruel world forever.

ONE!

"You the reason good women got it hard."- Meek Mill, "Almost Slipped"

#16

January 2nd, 2018 LaLa sat in all her glory basking in her triumphant defeat of Gray Rose Parthens. She couldn't have dreamt of a better way to enter into the new year. She'd heard all about Gray and Cam's showdown at Onyx. Video of them arguing and fighting outside the club was all over Facebook and Instagram. A Cheshire grin crossed her face when she saw the part when Gray gave him back her wedding ring. Their marriage was over, and she couldn't be happier. Getting rid of Gray was easier than she thought it would be. She thought it would, at least, take her fucking Cam to get rid of her. LaLa didn't even have to dig into her bag of tricks. Cam destroyed his own marriage by seeking her out.

Life couldn't be better. Everything was falling into place. Tresses was filled with customers. Every stylist had someone in their chair and others waiting to be serviced. LaLa sat back in her seat sipping on a glass of chilled champagne. The bubbles from the golden liquor tickled her contoured nose. To commiserate the joyous occasion, she wore black in honor of the death of Cam and Gray. A black wide brimmed hat covered her long 40-inch weave that reached down to her knees. A black Gucci sweater, frayed booty shorts and a pair of $10,000 Saint Laurent, feather-trimmed, suede, over-the-knee-boots completed her mourning attire.

"I told y'all he don't love that Beluga whale." She gloated with glee.

"You sure did." Belizean Mami agreed.

"If y'all could've seen the look on her face when I told her he spent the night wit' me. I swear that bitch lost fifty pounds." LaLa covered her mouth as she cackled.

"I don't feel sorry for the ho at all." Tia rubbed her belly. "That's what she get."

"I do. That's fucked up. Y'all gotta put y'all self in her position. That's that girl husband." Shamari stuck up for Gray.

"But he's my man." LaLa tapped her finger against her chest. "I can't help it if he still loves me. Watch, by March, they'll be divorced, and he'll be right back with me."

"Well, if he you love you so much why he marry her in the first place?" LaLa's mama chimed in.

Unlike all the women her daughter had working for her and their clients, LaLa couldn't fool her. She knew her daughter was full of shit. Cam didn't bit more want her than she wanted a S Curl.

"Didn't I say he was going through a big girl faze?" LaLa sneered.

Her mother got on her nerves. She was always trying to embarrass her in front of everybody.

"Yeah, sure that's what it is." Her mama giggled while flipping through a magazine.

"It is! You know what they say. You never get over your first love. Why you think he keep runnin' back to me?"

"Cause your dumb-ass keep lettin' him."

Everybody said she was stupid for chasing after a man that said he didn't want her, but when you'd been loved by a man like Cam, there was no easy way to let go.

"Mama, hush!" LaLa stomped her foot. "Ain't you almost done?"

"Nope. My hair ain't dry yet, and even if it was, I still ain't going nowhere."

"So, what happened when he came over?" Belizean Mami changed the subject.

"What you think happened?" LaLa sat back and crossed her legs.

"Ooooh girl you ain't shit. Was it good?"

"Ain't it always?"

"Shit, I don't know. You tell me. I been tryin' to fuck that nigga for years."

"Bitch, I will cut you with my shears."

"You know I'm just playin'." Belizean Mami lied.

LaLa would have a fit if she knew she'd already fucked Cam.

"Well, bitch, I ain't laughin'." LaLa rolled her eyes. "Anyway, like I was sayin'. Let's just say we slept until the next afternoon."

"And who was watching your son?" Her mom asked. "I bet you ain't even feed him breakfast."

"He know how to fix him a bowl of cereal and be quiet."

"That don't make no damn sense. Give that baby some bacon and eggs in the morning."

"He don't like that. He like sugar!"

"He don't like no damn sugar. You just lazy. You and Tia. I raised y'all better than that."

"Don't put me in this, Granny." Tia pouted.

"You put yourself in it and you know exactly what I'm talkin' about." Her grandmother glared at her.

"Like I said, Cam ain't never going nowhere. Him and Fatty Patty gon' get a divorce. And when he get over this big girl fetish, he gon' come crawlin' back to me like he always do. You can bet your life on that."

The words weren't even good out of LaLa's mouth before Cam swung the salon door open so hard the glass shattered into a million pieces. All the women screamed in horror, except LaLa. She knew what Cam was there for. He'd come to kill her. Dropping her glass of champagne to the floor, she took off running towards the back. She had to get to her office and lock herself inside before Cam got to her. The devil was in his eyes as he stalked after her. No matter how fast she ran, there was no escaping his wrath. Cam didn't even have to waste his time running. LaLa couldn't run that fast, especially not in five-inch heels.

Cam was out for blood. LaLa and Gunz were his prey. He'd promised Gray that he wouldn't strike back but he'd lied. He'd been biding his time before he made his move. Now that he and Grey were through, he could wreak havoc without any remorse. Gunz was going to pay for putting a hit on his life. He was a fool if he thought he'd get away with such treachery but Gunz wasn't dumb. He knew Cam was coming for him, so he went into hiding. He hadn't saw the girls in weeks.

Cam had his people scouring the city in search of him. He'd put a hundred-thousand-dollar bounty on his head. The first man to bring him to Cam would receive the funds. Until he could get his hands on him, Cam had other ways of ruining his life. Ridding a man of everything that made him who he was, was the best revenge. Sometimes, it could be even better than death. Cam had every single restaurant Gunz owned burned to the ground. He'd even torched Tia's brand-new home. While she sat chirping like a bird, making fun of Gray, her house was being burned to the ground. Gunz would surely come out of hiding when he learned his source of income was no more. It wasn't like he could get his position back in the Gonzalez cartel. Cam now occupied his spot. Now it was LaLa's turn to pay. It only took him a few wide steps to catch up to her. Grabbing her by the back of her hair, he yanked her towards his chest and spun her around. Needing to see the look of fear on her face, he knocked her hat off her head.

"That dumb-ass hat. Bitch, you ain't in formation."

"Cam, please don't kill me." She cried.

"Fuck you say to my wife?" He wrapped his hand around her throat and squeezed.

"What are you talkin' about? I ain't say nothin to her fat-ass." Tears dripped down her face.

Furious, Cam tossed her like a rag doll. LaLa's body went sliding across the marble floor until she landed against one of the stylist chairs with a thud. The impact was so hard that the chair fell on top of her fatigued body, knocking her in the side of the face. A huge lump formed on her forehead. Using what little strength she had, LaLa pushed the chair off her and tried to stand up but couldn't make use of her legs. Holding her head, she looked over at Cam. Methodically, he walked towards her slowly. The deranged look in his eyes reminded her of one of the White Walkers off Game of Thrones. LaLa literally feared for her life. Scooting backwards on her butt, she tried to put as much distance between she and Cam as possible.

"Cam, that's enough!" Her mother yelled.

"Stay out of this, Lucy."

"Now she may be wrong but that's my damn child. I ain't gon' let you put your hands on her."

"And what the fuck you gon' do?" Cam got her in face.

Anger oozed out of his pores.

"Just because yo' ho-ass a born-again Christian don't mean shit. You can quote bible verses till the cows come home. It's still not gon' erase the fact that this shiesty-bitch learned everything she know from you."

Mama Lucy gulped down the baseball size lump in her throat and hushed.

"Yeah, that's what the fuck I thought." Focusing his attention back on LaLa, Cam edged towards her.

"That's the last time you gon' disrespect my wife."

"Cam, please. Whatever she did, she ain't mean it." Tia pleaded, holding her stomach.

The baby was kicking like crazy because of her distress.

"Shut yo' wide pussy-ass up before that baby fall out." Cam warned while never taking his eyes off of LaLa. "Didn't I tell you it was over and that I ain't want yo' retarded-ass?"

"You came lookin' for me like you always do! I ain't call you and tell you to come over and sleep on my couch!" LaLa used her hands and feet to scoot back.

"I thought you said y'all fucked?" Belizean Mami interjected.

Cam halted his stride.

"You tellin' these ho's we fucked? Did you tell my wife that?"

"It don't matter what we did. You still came to my house. Did you or did you not?" LaLa shot back.

"You know why I came to your house and it ain't have nothin' to do with fuckin' you. If I was gon' fuck anybody, it would be my wife. Her pussy way better than yours." He pointed at her. "Yours." He pointed at Belizean Mami. "And yours." He pointed to the shampoo girl.

"What the fuck you pointing at them for?" LaLa's heart began to palpitate.

"Since y'all so busy discussing my business, did these ho's tell you that I fucked them too?"

"What?" LaLa struggled to breathe.

"Yeah, and a couple other people in this muthafucka, including Mama Lucy."

"Mama, you fucked him?" She looked at her mother in despair.

"We didn't fuck but I tried. It was years ago. Calm down." Mama Lucy dismissed her anguish with a flick of the wrist. "That's why I told you to leave that nigga alone. He done fucked your whole staff."

"How could you do that to me?" LaLa looked at Cam as tears blinded her vision.

"There you go playin' the victim. Bitch, you had a whole baby on me wit' another nigga. Then tried to pretend like that muthafucka was mine. Are you dumb? You was just a convenient fuck. Even if I wasn't married, I still wasn't gettin' back wit' you. You been canceled."

"Blah-blah-blah-blah-blah." LaLa rose to her feet ready for war.

Fuck being scared of Cam. He didn't deserve her fear. What he deserved was to be put in his place.

"You keep sayin' you don't want me, but your actions show different nigga! So, you can keep playin' house wit' that overweight ho until you blue in the face. You and I know that ain't where you wanna be."

Cam curled his upper lip as he looked upon LaLa with disgust. She made his insides curdle.

"You bout the dumbest bitch in Missouri. How many times do I have to tell you, bitch? I DON'T WANT YOU! You ain't even got no walls! That pussy dry and decrepit! Everything you got is because of me! This is my shop! When I met you, you ain't have shit but some fucked up teeth, flat-ass titties and a big-ass forehead!"

LaLa self-consciously placed her hand up to her head. The knot on her forehead was growing bigger by the minute, making her even more insecure.

"You ain't good for shit but suckin' dick and pressin' edges. You ain't got no formal education. You a high school dropout that barely passed the GED and you only did that cause I said I would get your teeth fixed. You a bum. Don't nobody want you and the fact that you keep chasing behind me like a mutt, even though I keep sayin' I don't want you, is fuckin' pathetic. You should be embarrassed. What kind of example are you setting for your son? And then you had the nerve to name the li'l nigga after me, knowin' I don't fuck wit' you. I ain't his pops. I don't give a fuck if you or him live or die. And since you wanna be so fuckin' slick bitch, you cut off. Any business we had together is done. Ain't no Tresses 2, 3, 4, or 5. I hope you been saving yo' money, cause if not, you gon' be suckin' a whole lotta dick, bitch."

What happened to us, LaLa wondered as her body shook violently. At one point, she was the love of his life. He would've never spoken to her the way he just did. He'd said she was his soulmate, and as the years progressed on, she believed him. Then one day she blinked, it was over, and he was with someone else. She couldn't take it. She would rather die than see him with another bitch. She'd gone from being the chick other women envied to being filled with bitterness she couldn't control. If it wouldn't kill her, she'd gladly see him buried under dirt deceased. She wouldn't shed a goddamn tear. Not one. She'd spit on his grave and go on with life as if he didn't exist. The girl he met that day coming out of 7/11 was now consumed with hatred she never knew could take root. But it was there and here they were. She was yesterday's news and Gray was the new queen of the castle.

"You dirty-ass, nigga. You gon' bring my son into this?" She charged towards him only for her mother to hold her back. "Take responsibility for your actions, nigga! You always wanna place the blame on me! It's always everybody else fault why your life is so fucked up! Don't blame me 'cause yo' weird-ass sick in the head! How you call yo 'self a killa and yo' bitch ass can't even sleep at night? Mr. I wake up in a cold sweat crying and shit."

LaLa knew she was treading on troubled water, but she didn't care. The shock and dismay on Cam's face meant nothing. He'd embarrassed her in front of everybody. She wasn't going to take that shit laying down.

"Yeah, nigga! I said it! Yo' weak-ass couldn't even save yo' battle buddies. Not one! You lousy bastard! You mother would be ashamed of you. I know I would be, if I raised a pussy like you. Nigga can't even leave out the house when the sun is out. You can't even keep it real wit' your family about your Pops and let them know what's really going on. Your whole life is a lie, nigga. Including that marriage to that FAT, PEACH COBBLAR EATING-ASS HO! I hope she die from obesity or sleep apnea! And, I'm glad my son ain't yours. You ain't no man. You a pussy! I ain't do shit but tell that bitch the truth! If you wanna be mad at somebody be mad at yourself!"

A thick silence stretched across the salon. No one said a thing. They were afraid to breathe. LaLa had put all of Cam's business out in the street. Some heavy shit had been said that a simple I'm sorry wouldn't be able to fix. Cam wasn't going to go back-and-forth with no bitch. She'd drew a line in the sand with the shit she'd just emitted. She'd taken his deepest darkest secrets and used them against him. This was why he didn't want Gray to know all of his business. People often used your secrets and insecurities against you to hurt you. LaLa had just proved it. He'd never forgive her. In fact, she was now his biggest enemy. Giving her his back, he turned and walked out of the salon without uttering a response.

"Yeah! Leave like you always do! Pussy! You's a bitch! I fuckin' hate you!" She screamed and cried.

Her mom and Tia tried to quiet her down, but she was inconsolable. LaLa was carrying on like a spoiled child having a tantrum. Tears marked her face as snot dripped from her nose.

"LaLa, stop! He's gone." Tia coaxed.

"You gotta pull yourself together, baby." Mama Lucy wiped her face.

"Nooooo this muthafucka think he run my life! I don't need him! Fuck him!" LaLa stomped her feet.

"I know but remember where you are." Tia referred to all the customers in the shop.

Everyone was watching.

"If that bitch want him, she can have him! I gotta life!" Her body trembled. "I gotta life! Get the fuck off of me!" She pushed her mother away forcefully.

"All you bitches is fake! Fuck all y'all ho's! None of you fuckin' bums gotta life! I gotta business! I don't need that nigga! This my shop! I own this muthafucka! I don't need that nigga to make moves! I don't need y'all ho's! All of y'all bitches are dead to me!" She pointed at Belizean Mami, the shampoo girl and her mother as the sound of glass shattering filled the air.

Cam had gone outside and retrieved a brick. LaLa wanted to talk cash shit like she was that bitch then he had to remind her that he was that nigga. He'd done everything for this girl. He'd upgraded her life tremendously. Without him, she wouldn't have none of the shit she had, and just because he didn't want her, she was going to make his life a living hell? No fuck that. No chick was going to have that much control over his life. He'd tried being nice. He'd told her over and over that they were through, but she didn't wanna listen. Stepping to Gray and telling all his business was the last straw. And yeah, he was wrong for seeking her out when he was in need. It was a habit he was determined to break, especially after she'd put him out on front street.

She tried to hurt him and somewhat had succeeded. Cam's biggest fear was people knowing about his anxiety. He had a reputation to protect. He couldn't be looked at as weak, but now that it was out there, he kinda felt liberated. A weight was lifted off his shoulders. He felt free. Now it was time to turn up. See, LaLa thought she'd won, but in reality, she'd lost enormously. Without Cam, she had nothing. Just like she knew his business, he knew hers. He knew she spent money as fast as she made it. Lala was in severe debt. Instead of focusing on her credit and saving, she used her income on clothes, jewels and trips. Everything was a look for her. She stayed stuntin' on social media. Without the help of him or another nigga, she didn't have the money to start another salon. She really wouldn't have the money to fix the shit he was about to destroy.

Using all the pent-up rage he possessed, he used the brick and smashed the salon window. Now there was no separation from the indoors and outdoors. Everything was clear in the open. The women in the salon scattered faster than the shards of glass from the window. The breaking glass appeared to fall with the grace of snow. It could be heard shattering down the street. Without a barrier to shield the women from the cold, several pigeons flew inside. Some of the ladies dropped down to the ground as the birds swooped over their heads.

"CAAAAM!" Tia yelled as he walked back inside the shop and picked up the brick. "WHAT IS YOU DOING?"

"This bitch wanna play me. I'm show you what a weak-ass nigga look like." He stepped over the broken glass and walked back outside.

"Uh ah." Mama Lucy shook her head. "I'm callin' the police."

The phone rang twice before a dispatcher picked up.

"911. What's your emergency?"

"We gotta crazy nigga on the loose."

"Mama, hang up! You making it worse! Tia call Quan and tell him to come get him!" LaLa ran behind Cam.

"Cam, stop! I'm sorry!"

"You gon' learn today, bitch." He assured, drawing his hand back like he was a pitcher for the Cardinals.

Pleased with his aim, Cam threw the brick at the driver side window of her brand-new Jag. With a loud bang the glass shattered and the window broke. Nowhere near done, he reached his hand through the broken window, unlocked the door and grabbed the brick.

"STOP, CAM!" LaLa begged as the women inside pulled out their camera phones and started filming.

"Girl, wait till everybody see this." One of the clients said.

"WORLDSTAR!" A young girl added.

"I bet I won't be no more bitch-ass niggas." Cam slammed the brick into the windshield.

It didn't break fully. The glass formed a design like a spider web. Picking up the brick, he worked his way around to the passenger side door as Quan pulled up and parked in the middle of the street with his hazard lights on.

"Nigga, is you dumb?" He rushed over to Cam.

"Yep."

"Get yo' ass in the car."

"Nope." Cam broke the passenger side window.

"Yo, nigga! Stop!" Quan barked, pulling him back.

"I ain't stoppin' shit. Her raggedy-ass mama done already called the police. I'm going to jail anyway." Cam shrugged, breaking the backseat window too.

"Y'all need to hurry up! He breaking all the windows!" Mama Lucy told the dispatcher.

"We have a squad car on the way ma'am."

"Cam, chill!" Quan pushed him up against the car and pressed his forearm into his neck. "I ain't gon' let you go out like this! Not behind this conniving-ass bitch! Man fuck her!"

"Because of her, I lost Gray!" Cam roared.

He'd only been without Gray a day and he was already losing his shit. The heartache he felt was like a bear gnawing at his chest. His misery threatened to devour him and eat him whole until only scraps were left. But he refused to be diminished down to nothing. He was going to build himself back up, but right now, he didn't know how. So, he did his best to ignore the pain until he couldn't anymore.

"Nah fam, you lost Gray cause you ain't keep it a buck. You fucked up. Didn't nobody tell you to take yo' dumb-ass over that bitch house. You did that. You was so fuckin' busy out here runnin' from yourself that you lost your girl. You know what your problem is?" Quan scolded him like he was his son. "See, nigga, you grew up, but you wasn't raised. You out here blaming everybody else for your problems. Only li'l boys do that shit. You a fuckin' man or are you your pops?"

"I ain't shit like that nigga." Cam scowled.

"You sure? Cause from where I'm standing that's what it look like. Instead of acknowledging the truth, you keep actin' like the shit don't exist. You got PTSD. So, what. Deal with that shit, nigga. You ain't gon' get better till you do. You gotta gang of people around you that's willing to help but you won't let 'em. You married now nigga. Let your wife be your help mate. You can't run to this funky bitch no more. Gray is supposed to be yo' peace. See, the problem is the wife you chose is better than the man that you are. You married a woman two sizes too big. You have to grow into Gray. She's a coat and you still can't fit her. She's bigger than you. She's had to cover you while you grow up. You gotta grow into her, man. She's a covering not a lid. LaLa is a lid. If you would've married her she would've stopped your dreams, but Gray is a covering. She's pushing you to your destiny."

Cam let Quan's words sink in.

"You got a good girl, man. She a firecracker I know . . . but that girl love you, dawg, and the way you did her was fucked up. Learn from my mistakes. It took me eleven years to find another Mo."

Cam inhaled deep and exhaled slowly. Clenching his jaw, he closed his eyes. Quan was right. He was handling his shit all wrong. There was no excuse for his behavior. LaLa was the devil. She could be burned at the stake for a lot of things, but this wasn't one of them.

"You know I can't stand that big head ho." Quan glanced over at LaLa. "But this ain't her fault. It's yours. Take responsibility for your shit and go make it right wit' yo' wife."

There was no escape route for the pain Cam was trying to endure. He hadn't been this sad since his mother died. Gray had become everything his mother once was. Gray took care of his needs before he knew they even needed to be met. He'd taken for granted seeing her smiling face when he walked through the door, the home cooked meals she made, her drawing his bath, the long talks they had in the morning while she lay on top of him. He missed her heavenly scent, the way her freckled nose crinkled when she pouted and the breathless moans she released while he deep stroked her middle. Even though people were watching, he couldn't conceal his need to cry. Biting the corner of his upper lip, Cam hung his head and tried to breathe. A weight of sorrow pressed into him like dirt over a grave. His mind clouded with pain as his heart numbed with pent up emotions. Quan and Cam had been through hell and back, but he'd never seen him like this. He felt the tears before they even hit Cam's eyes. Only a woman could do this to man.

"I miss her man. I need my wife back." Cam croaked, massaging his temples.

"I know you do." Quan brought him in for a hug.

He knew firsthand the sorrow his friend was going through. He'd been there before. He wouldn't wish it on anyone.

"Sorry that I've been living in my head. Holdin' onto words I ain't said yet."- H.E.R, "Can't Help Me"

#17

       With a freshly lit blunt in his hand, Cam placed it up to his lip and inhaled the smoke. His system responded quickly to the OG Kush. He needed to stay high to deal with the shit Gray was putting him through. This was how it had been all week. He'd smoke until his lungs damn near collapsed in order to feel better. But nothing including weed could get Gray out his head. She had completely shut him out and he'd been stressing like crazy. Cam needed her like he needed air to breath and she'd only grown more distant. It was his fault why they were in this position. She had every right to end what they were trying to build. He'd let her down and played on her intelligence. Gray didn't deserve that. She deserved nothing but complete honesty. He was determined to show her he could be different. Cam honestly wanted to change. Quan had spoken nothing but the god's honest truth when he said he couldn't continue on the way he had. He needed to be better for himself, for Gray, the girls and their marriage. They deserved the best parts of him and nothing less.

       The week apart from Gray had been tortures. He was tired of drinkin', smokin' and poppin' pills to get right. He needed her. He hated resting alone. He was tired of drinking his misery away, hoping to drown out the truth. Gray was the only cure for his loneliness. Cam had never missed LaLa this much. To put it simply, Gray had put a spell on him. He couldn't function without her. It was crazy how much he needed her now that she was gone. What was even crazier was that he had no intentions of ever doing her wrong but somehow he had. Now, he felt like an even bigger piece of shit. The self-loathing he harbored on a daily basis intensified. Once again, he'd lost someone he loved. Once more, he was the cause. Round and round in a circle he went. Cam pointed the finger, scarred hearts, gave way less than he received, pushed people away and wondered why he always ended up alone.

The reason why was because he was breathing but he wasn't living. Cam was silently screaming out for help. The rush of dark liquor didn't numb his pain. Hiding how he felt so he wouldn't break down no longer worked. Not sleeping at night so he wouldn't see demons, or Gray's face only stressed him more. He had to get his baby back.

If his homeboys saw him they'd be shocked. He'd morphed into a lovesick puppy. If you would've told Cam he'd end up here four months ago, he would've laughed. When he met Gray, he'd connected to her heart cause his heart had been broken too. Falling in love and getting married was never supposed to be a part of the equation. Cam was no good. His love was dressed in destruction and his love was more painful than hate. But somehow Gray had become his biggest weakness.

She'd stirred up emotions in him that he never knew he could possess. The ache in the center of chest came and went but it always returned, especially in the still of the night. Cam would give up all his riches to have Gray back, to keep her close, to laugh and talk like they used to. For during those moments, they were good. They had a chance of lasting. Everywhere he went, he saw her. She'd planted herself deep in the corner his heart. So even though she was gone, her aura still remained, making the pain worse. She'd put a move on his heart. And yes, Cam could try to get over her and learn ways to cope. Time deadened all pain. It allowed the brain to transfer and reinvest energy elsewhere. But there was no getting over a woman like Gray. She would be his forever.

Thankfully, he had his pretty girl Press on his side. Gray might've not answered his calls, but Press did. He'd called her an hour before and she'd told him they'd be going to the park with the dogs to play. It was an unusually warm day for it to be January. Saint Louis was weird like that. One day it would be freezing cold and the next it could be 60 degrees. That Tuesday it was 62 and partly sunny. It was the perfect day for Cam to pull up on Gray. Dipped low in his red 1969 Ford Mustang, he cut the engine as he stepped out into the spring like air. *Outta My System* by Bow Wow featuring T Pain and Johnta Austin bumped loud from his speakers.

> *My brain ain't stopping thinking*
> *Who she with, or where she going; is she club hoppin'?*
> *I never had this kind of problem in my life*
> *This is my first time dealing with this kind of fight*
> *It's every night, and every flight, and every time you in my sight*

It didn't take him long to spot his family. Aoki and Heidi's son ran around joyously playing frisbee with Kilo and Gram. Her long hair flowed behind her as she ran freely. It was the first time he'd seen her truly be content. Most times there was a sadness that was etched over her face. That afternoon she didn't seem so gloomy. Her little sister and his heart, Press, swung back-and-forth, going higher and higher on a swing. Behind her was Gray. Being without him seemed to not have fazed her at all. She looked better than ever. A new year had brought on a new change of hair. She'd dyed her long tresses a pretty shade of rich brown. A long swoop of hair swept over her right eye and fell into an abundance of soft, brushed out curls. Perfectly crafted brows, black winged liner, wispy lashes, highlighted cheeks and glossed lips decorated her heart shaped face. Since it wasn't cold enough for a coat, but still a slight chill in the air, she wore a Dijon colored, long cardigan sweater, the dog tag chain he'd bought her, lace spaghetti strap bodysuit, skintight denim jeans and black knee boots with gold buckles around the ankles.

Cam's dick felt like it was in a chokehold; he was so turned on by her appearance. Gray was stunning. There wasn't a chick on the planet that could fuck with her. He'd wife'd up the prettiest girl in the world. She didn't look like she'd experienced any sleepless nights. There wasn't a bag in sight on her gorgeous face. No sign of fatigue. Cam didn't know how to feel about that. He'd been sick without her. Damn near on his death bed. How had she made him love her so? He couldn't see himself moving forward if she wasn't there. Being apart from her a week proved it.

"Papa!"

Press jumped off the swing and came charging towards him at full speed. Gray's heart fell to her knees as she connected eyes with Cam. He was the last person she wanted to see. She'd just begun learning how to cope without him. Blocking him completely from her life had helped. He hadn't been allowed at the house and she'd blocked his calls. There had been no communication what-so-ever. The cards and flowers he'd sent were thrown away. Jewels from Tiffany's, bags and shoes from Bergdorf's returned. The only thing she kept was the delicious desserts from one of her favorite bakers, Every Bite I Take. She didn't want any of it. She wanted him. Sure, the nights were tough. Everybody wanted someone to hold them when they were alone. Mornings were extremely painful. It was normally the time he came home. They'd lay in bed, her on top of his chest as he caressed her back and talk. It was their time to check in with one another. Afterward, he'd flip her over and make love to every crevice, curve, dip, peak and valley of her form. Cam wouldn't stop until tears seeped from her eyes and landed on the sheets. She missed the euphoria he brought into her life, but no amount of spine-tingling dick would allow her to put up with his shit. She was done letting the men in her life dictate her happiness. Gray had cried enough tears to build an ocean. She refused to mourn another death of a relationship. She'd done nothing wrong. Cam was the one who'd fucked up. She'd loved him with everything she had to give. If anyone was going to grieve it would be him. Judging by the somber expression on his face, he'd been suffering plenty. The inner bitch in Gray jumped up and down. *That's what he get,* she thought. No Gray wasn't at 100%. She was barely pushing fifty. Sometimes, she struggled to inhale and exhale. The good thing was she wasn't curled up in the fetal position begging God to take her pain away. She was dressed and out of the house, getting some fresh air. She'd be damned if she let him stop her progress, no matter how fine he was.

Cam was no dummy. He'd pulled up on her with the intention of making the seat of her panties wet. He hadn't failed. Warm juices flowed from her center as her nipples throbbed against the lace of her top. Cam's curly box and beard had been groomed and lined to perfection with a razor. He even had his barber cut a part into the side of his head. A diamond stud shined from his ear while a gold Jesus piece chain swung from right to left around his neck. He even wore the Bulgari watch she got him for Christmas. Because of the weather, he donned a red Supreme letterman jacket, a tee shirt with Nasty Nas splashed on the front, distressed jeans and red and black Bred 1's. Yeah, the nigga was painstakingly fine but that didn't take away the bitterness she felt when she looked his way.

Press jumped into Cam's arms with the eagerness of a child on Christmas day. He'd become an integral part of her little world. With her real father being M.I.A. Cam had stepped up in his absence and played the role of father to a T. Even with him not being allowed in the house, he still called and checked up on her every day. He called her before and after school then once more before bed. He wanted Press to know that, no matter what went down between he and her mother, that he would always be there for her and Aoki too. He loved both girls, but he had better access to Press' heart. Aoki was still very closed off and angry for reasons he hadn't discovered yet. Whenever she decided she wanted to open up to him, he'd be there. Until then he'd love on his Pressy Poo. Her small arms wrapped around his neck as she used all her might to hug him tight. Her curly coils brushed against his face as he closed his eyes and relished the feel of her in his embrace. He'd missed her more than he'd realized. This was love in its purest form. Much like her mother, she didn't want anything from him except his attention and adoration.

"I did good, didn't I?" Excitement danced in her eyes.

"You did, Pretty Girl."

Press was so happy that she'd kept the secret that he was coming to see them from her mom. She usually told Gray everything. She was too little to know exactly what had gone down between them, but she did know that their family dynamic had changed, and she didn't like it one bit. The nightmares she'd gotten rid of, with the help of Teddy and Cam, were back in full force. Only Cam could make it better. It was time for him to come back home whether Gray wanted him to or not.

Crossing the grassy plain, Cam made his way to Gray. He was playing a dangerous game of Russian Roulette by using Press to get to her but what other choice had she given him? He couldn't go another day or night without her, without their family. The closer he got, the more his nostrils engulfed the delicate scent of her perfume. As he approached, Gray turned her back and groaned. Heidi, her best friend, arched her brow and tried her best not to laugh. Gray was a trip. She knew damn well she was happy to see him. Nervous as hell, he stopped behind Gray and stood. His intoxicating cologne had her stomach doing summersaults, but Gray continued to play it cool. She was determined not to fold. When no one spoke, Cam reached out his hand to Heidi and said, "How you doing?"

"I'm doing good. How you doing, Cam?" She shook his hand to Gray's dismay.

If she wasn't speaking to him then neither was Heidi or anyone else. It was ho's before bro's, chicks before dicks or had she forgot?

"Fuckin' miserable. Missing my wife but it look like she still ain't fuckin' wit' me."

"Aoki, come on! We gettin' ready go!" Gray yelled, picking up her purse.

Aoki stopped running and looked over at her mom. She wasn't ready to go. As soon as she spotted Cam, she understood why their plans had suddenly changed. Everyone else might've missed him but she was personally happy he was gone. With him out of the picture, her mom and dad had the opportunity to get back together. Aoki would give up her phone, iPad and any other electronic device she owned to make that happen. Sensing their owner, Kilo and Gram ran to Cam and started patting his legs with their front paws. With hopeful eyes, they wagged their tails. They too missed Cam. He returned the love by massaging their coat of hair.

"I thought we got rid of you." Aoki folded her arms with a sour look on her face.

"Nah, that was our other dog." Gray looked at Cam and smirked.

Drawing his head back, Cam chuckled then said, "Sick her."

On command, the once sweet dogs turned into vicious attack dogs and growled savagely at Gray. Their sharp canine teeth were uncovered, and their ears were pressed close backwards on their heads. With the intent to kill, they started edging in her direction. Gray couldn't believe her eyes. They'd turned on her that quickly, but little did Cam know she'd built her on rapport with the canines.

"Jungji." She ordered them to stop in Korean.

Without missing a beat, the dogs stopped dead in their tracks.

"Anjda." She told them to sit.

Being obedient, both Rottweilers sat back on their hind legs. Cam looked at Gray like she was crazy. *This girl think she Daenerys Targaryen and shit,* he grinned amused. Just like he'd charmed his way into Press' heart, she'd done the same with his dogs. He couldn't have been prouder.

"Good boy." She scratched lovingly behind their ears. "C'mon girls."

"Hold up." Cam reached for her hand. "Let me talk to you."

"We have nothing to discuss."

"You heard her." Aoki quipped.

"Mind yo' business li'l watermelon head girl." Cam snipped.

"My head ain't big jack-ass and why you keep callin' my mama from all them different numbers like a stalker?"

"Cause she won't answer and I'ma keep callin' her from all those numbers? Anything else, you fuckin' degenerate?"

"No but if I think of something, I'll ask."

"Aoki cut out all that cursing. Y'all ready?" Gray interrupted.

"Yes. No." Aoki and Press said at the same time.

"Gray, can I talk to you for a minute?" Cam practically begged.

He hated that sucker shit, but he had no other choice.

"Hell no."

Wrinkles formed on his forehead. Gray was tryin' it and him.

"Remember what we talked about Papa. You have to say please." Press stroked the side of his face.

Promptly, the wrinkles on his forehead disappeared. Press had that effect on him. Her sweet, endearing nature could calm any beast. Inhaling deep, Cam let out a long exhale and released his anger.

"Please."

"Nope." Gray switched past him with glee.

She was enjoying every second of Cam's groveling. She knew it was killing him.

"C'mon y'all its time for dinner."

"Gray, please let me just talk to you. I swear to god I ain't gon' be on no bullshit."

Midstride she hesitated, which let him know the act she was putting on was just a front. She wasn't as good without him as she portrayed.

"Ya'll go head and talk. I'ma take the kids and the dogs." Heidi took Press from Cam's arms. "Who wants McDonald's?"

"Me!" All the kids yelled.

"You don't have to do that. I can take 'em." Gray pleaded with her eyes.

She couldn't be alone with Cam. She'd fold.

"Girl go." Heidi urged.

I knew I should've drove my own car.

"Bye, mommy." Press waved goodbye. "Papa, are you gon' be home to tuck me and Teddy in tonight?"

"Yeah." Cam looked over at Gray who was fuming.

"Yay!"

Gray just knew that Aoki was going to put up a fight to keep her and Cam apart but even she'd turned on her. *Can't trust nobody nowadays,* she thought as he opened the passenger side door. The Mustang had a new car smell. Out of all Cam's cars, she loved his old schools the best. Cam got inside and took the car out of park.

"I don't appreciate you using my daughter to get to me." Gray snapped, staring out the window.

"Don't you know? All is fair in love and war."

"Oh, you expanding your vocabulary. Now you know what love is?"

"Because of you I'm finding out." Cam replied truthfully.

The impact of his confession weighed on Gray's chest. He was melting her resistance already. *Damn him.*

"Here." He reached over the backseat and handed her a bouquet of yellow roses.

The flowers were gorgeous, and the smell was glorious. Gray extended her hand and glided the pads of her fingers across the silky petals. They were cool and smooth to the touch. Cam stared at the side of her face. He could see the look of wonder in her eyes. The gift had affected her.

"I'm sorry." He voiced apologetically.

Gray lifted her head and glared at him.

"I been hearing sorry from niggas my whole life. That shit don't mean nothing to mean no more." She aggressively smacked the flowers against his chest.

The bouquet burst apart like a bomb of colored fragrance. Cam thought he had her, but he was wrong. It would take more than some roses to get in her good graces. Disappointed by her actions, he scooped up the petals and discarded them out the window. Silently, he placed what was left of the roses on Gray's lap and pulled off. After a few minutes of silence, she finally asked, "Where we going?"

"Somewhere I ain't been in a long time." Cam turned up the volume on the radio.

Her by Phora was playing. He'd stumbled across the track on accident one night while on Tidal and became addicted. It was like the young nigga was expressing words right from his soul.

All I see is you babe, you, yeah
All I see is you babe, you, yeah

Yeah
Lately all this pressure getting to me
I feel like I'm losing touch wit' you
Scared to lose you, I'm scared of breaking my trust wit' you
But I know you still try for me
I know that you'll ride for me
Whether I'm in a Bentley or on the bus wit' you
Just try to understand you everything I prayed for
Came for your smile but your heart is what I stay for
And even though we fall apart sometimes
We shouldn't be so afraid to show our heart sometimes
I mean, usually I ain't good with emotions
Lately, I feel like I'm losing focus
Lately, I feel like our love is broken
And I'm doing all I can just to fix it, I hope you notice

But no matter where we at in our lives, just know I'll wait for you
My biggest fear is drifting away from you
Just know I never plan on letting you go
So right here is where I'm letting you know
All I see is you

Gray sat with her arms crossed, trying her best not to feel anything but with each lyric that became damn near impossible. Cam was a man of few words. It was a well-known fact that he didn't know how to articulate his emotions. He only knew violence and rage. Anything in-between was foreign territory. What he couldn't say, the rapper was saying for him. The song was a love letter from his heart to Gray. With a stoic expression on her face, she listened intently to the heart wrenching song. Cam was killing her, and she hadn't even been in his presence ten minutes.

Look, you tellin' me I'm changin' for the worse
And I just don't know how to act now
Hate it when we argue 'cause I don't know how to back down
Starin' at me, lost like you tryna read my expression
But I love you and that's real, it's just hard for me to express it
But listen, I'm tired of fightin', I'd rather plan out some goals wit' you
I'd rather grow old wit' you and share my soul wit' you
And move away from the city and build a home wit' you
Do anything I could do just to be alone wit' you
You know I'm all about you, I write these songs about you
And if I could, I'd take the sun, make it revolve around you
But I guess it doesn't work that way
Sometimes we give all we have and we get hurt that way

But no matter where we at in our lives, just know I wait for you
My biggest fear is drifting away from you
Just know I never plan on letting you go

So right here is where I'm letting you know
All I see is you

So, he does love me, Gray twisted her mouth to the side. An eternal struggle waged in the pit of her stomach as she willed herself not cry. Was he trying to kill her? Hadn't he broken her down enough. Anything more would lead to death. Gray was barely holding on. He'd turned her into a glass figurine, perfect to the eye, fragile to the touch. He'd used his lies as weapons and ground her into dust. There was nothing left. She couldn't be broken anymore. He'd already done what she thought was his worst. Nearly a half an hour went by before they arrived at their destination. Gray frowned when she realized they were at the cemetery. Cam grabbed the other bouquet of flowers he'd bought from the backseat and got out.

"C'mon." He reached for her hand after opening her door.

Gray reluctantly placed her hand in his. From the outside looking in, she and Cam looked like a united front as they made their way across the lawn. The temperature had dropped some. Gray pulled her cardigan over her breasts for warmth. Most people were afraid of cemeteries. They found it spooky to walk amongst bones of their loved ones. Gray wasn't shook at all. Under the afternoon, cloudy sky, the air fragrant with freshly cut grass, she felt a sense of calm. Fingers intertwined with Cam's, she took in the atmosphere until they stopped at the gravestone that belonged to his mother.

"Your mother's name was Grace?"

"Yeah."

"How ironic. Grace . . . Gray."

"Hmm." Cam nodded.

He'd never tripped off that he'd married a woman whose name was similar to his mother's. Cam's grip on Gray's hand tightened as he stared down at his mother's name, birthday and death date. A picture of her face stared back at him. For the first time he couldn't help but recognize the harsh irony of the gravestone. There it was mounted in all its timeless splendor, solid, and sturdy. While it would stand the test of time, his mother had already perished and decayed. It was funny how something so everlasting could represent something so temporary. While the headstone endured her flesh returned to the earth. Grievers like Cam visited the concrete slab like they could stop destiny and make permanent what wasn't meant to exist. Gravesites were nothing more than a place to come to when people couldn't stand being apart from their loved one anymore. Cam hadn't been to his mother's grave in years. He only came when he felt like his life was falling apart. Much like now. Somehow, that block of stone always seemed to give him a new gust of energy to continue on. Until God reunited them together, he would visit sporadically like every other soul who had lost a piece of themselves in the death of someone they loved. Gently, he lay the flowers in front of the gravestone and copped a squat. Gray followed suit and sat Indian style.

"When I was little, my mother was my world. I had never seen someone so pretty until I met you. She was perfect. She loved us. There wasn't nothing she wouldn't do for her family. She was my biggest fan. She took me to all my basketball games and practices. I used to show out on the court just cause I knew she'd be in the stands cheering. Afterwards, we'd go and get ice cream. She wouldn't take my brothers or Mo. It would just be the two of us. She always made each of us feel special." Cam picked up a blue wildflower and twirled it in-between his long fingers.

Gray kept quiet. She barely wanted to breath in fear he'd retreat. Her eyes were wide with anticipation. This was it. This was the moment she'd been asking for. He was finally opening up to her. They would finally be on the same playing field.

"My mother was the first woman I ever loved. I always swore I would grow up and marry a woman just like her and I did that . . . wit' you. But just like I let you down and lied, I did the same thing to her."

"How?" Gray said confused.

"I was nine when my father went from being my hero to my worse fuckin' nightmare. He would tell my mom that we was spending father/son time together but really he would take me over his side bitch house. I wanted to tell her what was going on, but I knew if I did, my family would fall apart. I ain't wanna be the reason my mother and father wasn't going to be together no more. I ain't want that shit on my conscious but what was fucked up is I had to have the secret of him cheatin' on my conscious. I ain't wanna see my mama hurt. It would kill her if she knew, so I went along wit' the shit. She'd ask what we did, and I'd say whatever lie my Pop told me to say."

"Cam that's terrible." Gray said in disbelief.

She couldn't believe his father would put him in that kind of position. He'd unknowingly and uncaringly shaped Cam's perception of love and marriage. He'd taught him that men led double lives, that they lied to their wives, that they compromised their child's trust and that it was okay for a man to cheat.

"I hated lyin' to my mother. Every time he used me as an alibi to spend time with his bitch, I got sick. I wanted to beat my daddy's ass. My mama did everything for that nigga. He was damn near her sixth child. I'll never forget the day she died. Her and my Pop were supposed to go visit my people out of town but last minute he lied and told my mom that he had to work. I wanted to tell her he was lyin'. I wanted to tell her he was going to see A—" Cam cut his self-off before he could say her name.

"But I didn't. I kept quiet. My mother went alone, and she died alone. He was supposed to be on that plane with her when it with down."

"Oh my god." Gray clutched his hand into hers.

"She was all by herself. If I would've told her she wouldn't have gone or maybe she would have. I don't know," he shrugged.

"How old were you when she died?"

"Thirteen. She was my first love and I lost her. I felt guilty. I felt like I betrayed her. I was so angry with myself . . . and with my Pop. You know this nigga had the nerve to be boo-hoo crying at the funeral. I ain't cry once. I couldn't. I was so mad I felt sick. I ain't give a fuck about shit. I really stopped caring when, at the wake, I looked out the window and saw my fuck-ass daddy outside hugged-up wit' that scandalous-ass bitch. Can you believe that shit? The nigga actually tried to sneak off wit' that cunt. My mama hadn't even been in the ground an hour and he was already sayin' fuck her."

"That's fucked up." Gray shook her head.

"I lost my shit. I went outside and I confronted them. I told my Pop that if he didn't stop seeing her I was gon' tell everybody. The last thing that nigga wanted was for the world to see him for who he really was. He knew it would kill Mo. She idolized my mother, so he swore to me he was gon' stop. I believed him. You know everybody thought my Pop closed everyone out because he was so distraught over my mama's death, but for real, he was mad 'cause he couldn't see that bitch anymore. That flaw-ass nigga was really upset but guess what? He lied. That nigga kept on fuckin' her. He just kept the shit away from me. I found out the truth tho."

"How?"

"One day, I came home from school and checked the mail 'cause I was getting college acceptance letters around that time. I'm flippin' through the shit and come across a fuckin' letter from the Missouri Department of Child Support Services."

"Nooooo." Gray held her breath.

"That nigga got that bitch pregnant and she filed for support."

"Did you say something?"

"Hell yeah." Cam screwed up his face. "I asked the nigga what was up. He ain't deny it. I mean he couldn't. His name, her name and the li'l nigga name was on the paperwork."

"Oh my god. They had a son?"
"Yep."

"You ever meet him?"

"Yeah, I know who that nigga is." Cam stared off into the distance.

"Wooooow. Does Mo know?"

"Nah. Don't nobody know except me, my Pop, the chick, LaLa and now you."

Gray let his words sink in and then promptly asked, "Wait, so your brother doesn't even know?"

"Nope."

"Hell nah." Gray said astonished.

"Man, you don't even know. This shit go so deep that it could fuck up everything. Like it's bad bro."

"I'm sorry to hear that, Cam. I really truly am."

"I was done after that. I couldn't stay around with that secret weighing on my chest. I had so much anger and resentment in me, man. I wanted to fuck something up. I wanted to bash that nigga's head in. Any nigga that looked at me sideways was getting bodied. I was so pissed that I wanted to kill somebody without gettin' locked up, so I said fuck college and enlisted in the army instead. I went there to escape all the bullshit back home but shit only got worse. I was a sniper for the US Army. Me and my squad members were sent out on a mission. Long story short, we got ambushed, they got killed and I survived." Cam stared out into space.

"I was this close to dyin', Gray." He held his thumb and index finger together. "To be honest, I low key wanted to. I ain't wanna live after that. I wanted to be back with my mama but here I am. Them dudes were my brothers. They had become my second family. We went through it all together, and then, suddenly, just like that, they were gone. I raised my right hand to serve my country and in one day I lost everything I loved. Just in one day. Eight fuckin' hours. After serving my country for five years that was how it ended. I gotta live the rest of my life knowing that I couldn't save them. My job was to serve and protect. That was my job and I failed . . . just like I had failed my mother."

"So that's where your PTSD comes from?" Gray said barely above a whisper as she pieced everything together.

"Yeah. That day fucked me up. I can't get it out of my head. No matter what I do, whenever I close my eyes they're there on the ground covered in blood, shot the fuck up. Can you imagine laughin' and talkin' wit' somebody and in the next thirty seconds they got a bullet between their eyes? That shit outta pocket bro. I can't even leave my house on a sunny day cause the blare from the sun reminds me of when that punk-ass sand nigga had that rifle pointed at my head."

"Do you see anybody about it? Do you get treatment?"

"No. I mean, I talk to Quan about it sometimes and you know LaLa used to help me." He confessed uncomfortably.

Even mentioning her name could piss Gray off and deter all the progress he'd made.

"That's the reason I went to her crib that night. I know you don't believe me, but I swear I didn't touch her. I really went over there to sleep. To keep it a hunnid, I don't come home at night cause I'm afraid to sleep around you and the girls. I have night terrors too that sometimes can be violent. I ain't gon' lie, I also went over there 'cause I was pissed off at you. You hurt me so I wanted to hurt you. The plan was to get a few hours of sleep and then come straight home. But I had a night terror and ended up takin' one of my pills. That shit had me knocked out. That's why I came home so late."

"You on medication?" Gray said, taken aback.

Everything he said became non-existent when he mentioned medication.

"Yeah, I ain't on no crazy shit it's just Xanax. Calm yo' judgmental-ass down. That's why I ain't wanna tell yo' ass."

"No, I'm just sayin'." She giggled. "I already know you're crazy. I just had to make sure you ain't no psychopath. So, tell me. How do you cope with this? Do you go to PTSD groups with other veterans?"

"Nah, I ain't no group therapy kind of nigga."

"Well, you better become that type of nigga if you wanna stay with me." She arched her brow.

"Nah, Gray. Uh ah. I ain't for talkin' about feelings and shit. Shit, I can barely talk to you."

"That's your problem now. That's why we're here. Are you not realizing that everything that happened in your past is affecting you currently?"

"I mean . . . yeah." He shrugged.

"No, you don't." Her temperature started to rise. "Why don't you wanna get help? Everybody needs help at some point in their life. Yo' ass ain't exempt. I had to get help after my mama passed. Shit, fuckin' wit' you I'ma need it again."

"I don't need help. Therapy is wack. I don't feel any emotions besides rage. The rest of the time I'm numb to this shit."

Anger smoldered underneath Gray's indifferent expression. She couldn't believe that he was adamant about not getting help. There was no point of talking. There was no point in her being there. Once again, he'd wasted her time.

"Take me home." She unfolded her legs.

"Why?" Cam panicked.

"Cause you basically tellin' me you don't have any plans on gettin' better and fixing your personal issues that are affecting *our* relationship. I don't need to put up with this shit." She pushed him in the chest. "I understand your situation. I appreciate you opening up finally and tellin' me all of this but none of that shit matters if you're not gonna change. I am tired of babysittin' grown-ass men and playin' mama to you niggas. I got my own kids to raise and I will be damned if I try to raise another grown-ass man and teach you how to be a man. It's not my fault that your father failed you. You have to want to be better for yourself. And I refuse to be with any man that can't even say he loves me. Then on top of that you slangin' crack! Uh ah, I'm not dealin' with that shit! Take me home!" She placed her hand on the ground to hoist herself up.

"Hold up-hold up-hold up." He took her by the hand. "Wait-wait-wait-wait-wait. Everybody calm down. *Calm* down. This shit done went fuckin' left, real quick."

"No, I'm going home." She tried to yank her hand away.

"Gray, if you don't sit yo' big-ass down and hear me out." He pulled her towards him.

Once she was back seated, he took both of her hands in his and gazed deep into her pretty blue eyes.

"You're a fuckin' veteran. How did you get to sellin' dope anyway? The shit is fuckin' stupid." She spat, heated.

"I dabbled back in high school 'cause I ain't want to ask my Pop for shit. When I got home from the war, my PTSD was so bad that nobody wanted to hire me. I wasn't gon' wait for no fuckin' handout so I got it how I lived.

Look, I got a lot of stuff to work on. I get it, but despite popular opinion, I wasn't always this fucked up. Any girlfriend I had in the past, I did right by them. I ain't wanna be like my Pop. And when I got with that dumb bitch LaLa, I thought I was gon' spend the rest of my life with her but you know how that turned out. I put everything I had into that relationship, and more, and she still shitted on me. I ain't sayin' it's right but growing up and seeing somebody do that to someone you love and then turn around and have someone you love do it to you . . . that's a different type of hurt. I wouldn't even wish that shit on your baby father."

"Okay and you said all of that to say what?" Gray looked at him like he was dumb.

"WHAT I'M SAYIN' IS!" Cam rolled his eyes he was so mad. "It's not that I don't have those feelings for you. Everything you want me to say I already feel it but me sayin' it scares the shit outta me. I just broke it down to you. Everybody I have *ever* loved has left me. I ain't runnin' that risk with you."

"Why? If you feel it, why can't you just say it?" She crawled into his lap and circled her arms around his neck.

Cam pulled her close and sniffed her skin. Her scent enthralled him. That quickly, he felt more alive than he had all week. Gray was the antidote for everything that ailed him.

"Tell me. Why can't you say it?"

"Cause, man, I can't take the risk of me putting myself out there and being vulnerable just to take another L. I can't lose you, Gray. Real shit. If I lose you, I'm shootin' up daycares, movie theaters, schools, churches. I don't give a fuck. It's whatever."

"Stop. Don't say that." She laughed feeling ashamed. "You're not gonna lose me. I never had any intentions on going anywhere in the first place. I was in this for the long haul, but you be pushin' me away."

"I know and I'ma take responsibility for all that. These past couple of weeks being away from you put everything in perspective. I really need you in my life. You got a nigga out here stressin'. Shit, you leaving me is like peanut butter without no jelly. The shit don't work, and I don't wanna eat it. I need you Star, for real. Let a nigga come home. I'll even eat that Korean shit. If you want me to."

"I don't know, Cam. This shit is a disaster." She huffed.

Cam held her tighter and buried his face in her bosom.

"Just bare wit' me. I'm tryin'. It's not like I'm not gon' put forth no effort. I just need a minute. I never needed anybody in my life the way I need you. I ain't never have these kind of feelings for ole girl. This shit is blowin' my mind. I need a minute to adjust. I went from not wanting to be in a relationship to being married and a step pop to some Asian kids, and one of 'em just might be more gangsta than me. I went from having nothin' to having everything I ever wanted with you and the girls. I'm afraid that if I say those words out loud I'ma jinx it."

Gray pushed him back so she could see his face.

"Well, you gon' have to do something. I gotta see your actions. Ain't no coming home until you get it together and tell me you love me."

"How can I share what I don't wanna admit? I feel weak, and for a nigga like me, weakness ain't an option."

"And I can't be wit' a man that's not willing to fully commit!"

"That's really how you feel?" Cam scowled, not liking what she was saying.

"Yeah, I can't have my daughters around no dysfunctional shit no more. I need a man that's not afraid to love us the way we deserve."

"But I do."

"Show it!" She mushed him in the head.

"I am, just give me some time, Star. Let me come home so I can show you. How am I supposed to fall asleep without your head being on my chest?"

"The same way you fell asleep over that bitch LaLa's house."

"Now, you ain't even have to go there. You do too fuckin' much." Cam pushed her off his lap. "We was having a good-ass conversation and here you go with the fuck shit."

"Oh, well. It's the truth. You either gon' take these digs and fight for your marriage or we can get in that car and you can drop me off and we can never speak again. What's it gon' be?" She challenged.

There was no way Cam was spending another night without Gray.

"I'ma take these digs, man." He massaged the back of his neck, feeling like a pussy.

"That's what I thought." Gray smirked, feeling high.

"You know the last time I came here was to say goodbye to my mother before I went off to the army. I thought that being alone in the dark was where I was supposed to be. Then you came along with all this light . . . and I just knew I had to be near you." Cam brushed her hair from her face.

"I feel the same way too." She quacked from his touch.

"I'm a dangerous man tho, Star."

"I know."

"Do you? Are you willing to take the risk of being in my life?"

"No." She said flatly. "I'm willing to love you but I'm not willing to die for you. Leave that drug shit alone and get help or we get a divorce."

Gray was asking him to give up everything that made him who he was. He'd made millions off selling dope. Could he really just walk away and go legit? Yes. For her he could do anything.

"I got you."

"You gon' stop?" Gray's heart skipped a beat; she was so excited.

"Yeah, man."

"You promise?"

"Once I lock down this convenient store I'm tryin' to use as my drop off spot, I'll be done. Just give me till March 12th and I'm out."

"You better be, or I'm done." She swore.

"I know, man. I'm not gon' fuck up."

"Also, this beef between you and Gunz has to stop. It's gettin' out of hand."

"A'ight." Cam rubbed her back lovingly.

The ache in his heart had ceased. He had his girl back. He could breathe without feeling like he was going to keel over and die. Gray rested her forehead against his and closed her eyes. She was taking a big risk by taking him back. She'd been in this position before where she had to choose between being alone or forgiving a man who'd misused her trust. Her mind was telling her to be strong and to continue on life without him. It was obvious he wasn't ready for marriage. Cam needed to work on his self. He was battling demons that even the biggest dragon couldn't slay. Hell, Gray had shit of her own she needed to figure out, but she couldn't let go. Her heart was already connected to his. The desire to save him from himself motivated her to stay.

Cam traced her upper lip with his thumb. Without warning, his lips pressed against hers. Gray instantly fell right back down the rabbit hole. Cam's kisses were filled with passion, aggression, love and affection. Any resistance she had vanished. His hands roamed her body, leaving sparks in their wake.

"I'm yours and you're mine. That's it." Cam rotated between sucking her top and bottom lip.

The world fell away with each stroke of his tongue. Each lick was soft, slow and comforting. Cam's thumb caressed her cheek as their breaths blended. Gray ran her fingers through his curls and pulled him close, so their chest touched. There was no way she was letting this go. Every time Cam gazed into her eyes, it was like an ounce of breath was taken from her lungs. When they kissed the world stopped. Each time they made love it felt like he was untying all the knots in her stomach. Her universe began and ended with him. Loving him was like a story she never wanted to end. All her life she'd yearned for a love like this and now that she had it, she couldn't bear to lose it.

"If I can stay in her hair forever, that'd be fine by me."- The Carters, "Summer"

#18

The opportunity of a lifetime had landed in Gray's lap. For months, she'd been trying to figure out what her next career path would be. She'd yearned to start working again but nothing had really intrigued or motivated her. Then out of nowhere on a random Monday morning, she got the call that would change the course of her life. The mega brand, Fashion Nova, reached out to her to be the face of their new Girl Boss campaign. The company loved that she was a self-made entrepreneur that took charge of her life. The goal was to make fashion more sustainable for the everyday woman. They'd chosen Gray to spearhead the U.S. campaign because of her striking good looks, massive social media following and because she was a self-made millionaire.

Gray was stunned by the offer. At first, she didn't know what to think. She'd work her ass off and gone to school for journalism not to be a model. Gray knew she was a beautiful woman, but she preferred to use her brain and not her body to garner attention. After ruminating over it for days and talking it over with Cam, she decided to take the offer. It was a onetime gig that would be a fun experience and wouldn't lead to anything or so she thought. She didn't have anything to lose. Plus, the $250,000 contract they offered didn't hurt. The shoot would take place in Indonesia. She'd never been to that part of the country or Korea for the matter. Her mother was too poor to take them back. As a part of deal, Gray negotiated that she be able to bring two guests, which would be Cam and Kema of course. Quan wasn't having being without for her almost a week, so he decided to come as well. That then led to Stacy and Heidi booking a flight too. Now it had become not only a work trip but a group vacay. Tee-Tee wanted to come but stayed behind to watch the kids.

After a twenty-hour flight From St. Louis to Java, Indonesia Gray and crew were finally there and settled into their hotel rooms. Fashion Nova had put them up at the Amanjiwo Resort. As soon as Gray stepped foot outside the van, she was amazed. The word amazed wasn't even the best way to describe it. She felt like someone had took a spark of wonder and poured on gasoline. The smile on her face didn't reflect what she felt on the inside. A joy like no other bloomed in her chest. Even though she was there on business, this was what she and Cam needed. It was their first vacation together and the closest thing to a honeymoon they'd experienced. Somehow, being in Indonesia made her feel closer to god. She was surrounded by greenery, rolling hills, statues and rice paddy views. The sweltering heat didn't even bother her. Everything was so mystical, serene and beautiful including the resort.

Inspired by the 9th-century Buddhist sanctuary of Borobudur, Amanjiwo's Suites featured four-pillar, king-sized beds on raised terrazzo platforms, spacious garden terraces, some with private swimming pools and lounging pavilions. Views include terraced farmland and the Menoreh Hills. She and Cam had been set up in the resorts Garden Pool Suite. It was 2,615 square feet and featured a bathroom with a sunken outdoor bathtub, personal bar, private pool, and daybed for outdoor lounging. Once they were settled into their room, she and Cam took a long nap then got dressed so they could join their friends for dinner.

Even at night it was scorching hot, so Gray opted to wear as less clothes as possible. Cam didn't even mind that she wore a red bralette that tied in the front and a matching red skirt with ruffles along the hem. On her feet were a sickening pair of red Giuseppe Zanotti single sole heels that tied up the leg. Gray refused to have her hair touching her neck, so she wore it up in a messy top knot. Around her neck were the dog tags and C chain he'd given her. Gold shimmer lotion gleamed from her honeysuckle skin. Gray looked so good he wanted to bite her. There was something so disarmingly sensual about her curvaceous physique. Cam's eyes trekked from her gorgeous face to her long neck and then to her mouthwatering breasts. Without support of a bra, they didn't sit as high and were less close together, but each were so flawlessly molded to her form. If Cam kept admiring them there was no doubt that she'd be naked and on the bed taking back shots with her booty high in the air.

"Give me a kiss." He demanded, pulling her into him.

Gray did as she was told and pecked his lips.

"Fuck all that cute shit. Kiss me like you mean it." He smacked her hard on the ass.

Doing as she was told, Gray pushed her lips into his firmly then inserted her tongue. Soon they started swallowing each other, making the kiss more intense. This went on for minutes until Cam's head started to swim and he pushed her back.

"I'm fuckin' the shit outta you later." He pledged.

"Lookin' forward to it." Gray smiled flirtatiously.

She and Cam had been fuckin' like crazy since they reconciled. She was beyond proud of him. He'd been doing great since their talk and had been doing everything he'd promised. It really meant a lot to her that he was keeping his word. Most men would feed a woman a bunch of lies in order to get back into her good graces. The fact that Cam had told her the truth made her heart swoon. She prayed he kept up the good work 'cause he was looking fine as fuck. Cam was dressed in Gucci from head to toe. The Gucci tee shirt, fitted joggers, socks and sneakers was fly as fuck. As always he was iced out. Several small chains filled with diamonds rested on his solid chest. On his wrist were two diamond bracelets and his Bulgari watch. Gray would most certainly be sucking his dick that night. She had to put her mouth to use some way. It wasn't like she'd be eating much during dinner. She wanted to look as fit as possible for the shoot the next day. She'd be damned if she got on camera with a food baby at the bottom of her stomach. She was already a curvy girl. She didn't need to look any bigger.

Hand-in-hand, she and Cam headed to the dinner program. The moon was full, and the air was clean and fresh. Gray wasn't big on being outdoors because she was afraid of bugs, but she loved the atmosphere. Cam was enjoying his self too. Being in Indonesia reminded him of his time in the service. He wasn't so sure about Gray and this modeling shit, but he was going to roll wit' it. Fashion Nova had prepared a night of wonder for them and the other models on set. There would be performances throughout each course. The setup was breathtaking. A long table lit by candles and dressed with flowers was placed in front of the Olympic size pool. The chef had prepared a glorious meal of surf and turf. Gray's mouth watered at the food, but she couldn't have any. While everyone ate the high calorie meal, she had a salad and salmon. Halfway through dinner her manager, Selicia, arrived.

"Sorry I'm late." She kissed Gray on her cheek. "My connecting flight got delayed."

"No problem, boo. I'm just glad you could make it on such short notice. Let me introduce you to everyone. This is my husband Cam that I was tellin' you about."

"Ohhhh, so you the one that's burning down buildings and pistol whippin' niggas in the club. You remind me of my brothers and cousins back home."

"Where you from?"

"Philly nigga."

"Well, what's good broad street bully?" Cam gave her a handshake and a pound.

"Selicia, these are my friends Heidi, Kema, Quan and Stacy. Guys, this is my manager Selicia."

"Hey everybody." She waved, taking her seat at the table.

Selicia wasn't even good in her seat before Stacy was on her. He'd been eye-fuckin' her since she walked down the steps. In his 37 years on earth, he'd never seen a badder bitch. Selicia was fine as fuck. She had smooth brown skin, slanted coffee colored eyes and full lips. When she smiled, he swore he saw the sun. Her face was stunning. Baby girl had more body than a li'l bit. Like Gray, she too was plus size. Her breasts weren't as big as Gray's, but they were still a mouthful. The pale pink, off the shoulder, wrap dress she rocked accentuated her waist and round hips. Stacy was determined to have her.

"Where yo' fine ass come from?" He asked, placing his elbows on the table.

Selicia scrunched up her face, taken aback. She'd been around plenty of disrespectful niggas, but she had a feeling this fine-ass, 6-foot 6 fool was about to take the cake.

"My mom's coochie. Da fuck? Gray, who the hell is this clown?"

"Your future husband." Stacy replied.

"Girl, that's Cam's friend Stacy. Ignore him." Gray waved him off. "Stacy, leave her alone. She ain't the one nigga."

Anybody that knew Selicia knew that she didn't play. She was known to cuss and beat the fuck outta people when pushed too far. Homegirl had a reckless mouth and no chill. She could either be your best friend or your worst fuckin' nightmare.

"I like 'em feisty. I ain't scurred." Stacy bit his bottom lip.

"It's *scared* nigga not *scurred*. What the fuck is a *scurred*?" Selicia corrected him.

"Oh, you gotta li'l Meek Mill in you. Let me find out you fresh outta jail."

"Oh my god. Get him away from me before I tase his ass." She groaned.

"Ain't nothin' wrong wit' a li'l electricity. It might make my dick stay hard longer."

"Your dick will never come near me, pervert."

"You sure?" Stacy gave her his sexiest face.

Selicia pretended like he wasn't affecting her, but he was. Despite his brash behavior there was no denying that Stacy was cute.

"I ain't never been so sure in my muthafuckin' life." She quipped instead.

"Why not? I like 'em thick."

"And I don't. I don't fuck wit' fat niggas."

"Why not? You fat too."

Selicia's small eyes bulged as she clutched her chest and gasped. Everyone at the table sat stunned as well.

"No, this muthafucka didn't." She threw down her purse. "Bitch, I ain't fat! I'm thick!"

"Nah, nigga, you fat but you fine as fuck tho. I'll eat it and I don't even be eatin' bitches pussies like that."

"That's the only thing yo' fat-ass don't eat."

"Yo, this is a match made in heaven." Quan cracked up laughing.

"Ya'll niggas meant to be together." Cam agreed.

"No, the hell we ain't. If they would've let me on the plane wit' my gun, I would'a been shot this nigga." Selicia clarified.

"The greatest love stories begin and end with destruction. Shit, look at Cam and Gray. If they can make it, I know we can."

"Fuck you, Stacy!" Cam and Gray said at the same time.

"See, this what happens when muthafucka's be in denial. Me and you ain't gon' be like that tho. Ain't that right sweetheart?"

"We ain't gon' be like shit. Nigga, I don't want you!"

"That's what your mouth say." He lusted after her more.

"No, that's what my taser say." She pulled out her taser, having had enough.

"Damn, you got a taser for real? Yo' she the one." Stacy fell deeper in love.

"Yeah, that's you. All the way." Cam nodded his head.

"Didn't I just say I don't fuck wit' fat niggas? Two fat people can't be together. It's a sin. That shit should be against the law. It's unnatural. I don't want yo' stomach pressed against mine all sweaty and shit. And I for damn sure ain't suckin' yo' titties."

"I ain't got no titties. This man meat." Stacy poked out his muscular chest.

"That's lunch meat," Cam joned, bugging up.

"Fuck you, nigga. I'm on that Keto shit right now. And I done lost ten pounds."

"NIGGA WHERE?" Everyone said in harmony.

"In my dick." Stacy gripped it hard.

"That's just trifling. That's nasty as hell." Selicia tuned up her face.

"You like it. Say you don't. Come kiss it."

"Uh ah. I have had enough. I'm going back to my room before I kill this nigga. Ya'll have a goodnight. Gray, I'll see you in the morning."

"Selicia, I am so sorry." She apologized.

"Yo, let me walk you back to your room. Maybe we can have a nightcap." Stacy stood up.

"Only cap you gettin' is a cap in yo' ass if you don't leave me the fuck alone." Selicia sashayed away.

Stacy admired the sway of her hips and the way her booty cheeks bounced as she walked.

"And that ass fat. Yep, *I'M FUCKIN' YOU TONIGHT*!" He sang a lyric from R. Kelly's song.

"Now, nigga, you know better. R Kelly is fuckin' canceled." Kema grimaced.

"Period." Heidi added.

The rest of the dinner went smoothly. After listening to the president of the company talk about the brand and the campaign, everyone watched Indonesian children perform a traditional dance. Gray's heart swooned at the little boys in their native garb. She'd wanted nothing more than to have a boy but Gunz had taken that away from her. The universe must have felt her pain cause an elderly woman approached her. She introduced herself as a spiritualist.

"Hello." Gray shook her hand.

Instead of letting go, the woman held on.

"The creator wanted me to tell you that you have trouble up ahead. Your days will become very dark but there will be light."

Gray looked over at Cam. He gazed back at her with apprehension in his eyes. What the lady was saying couldn't be true. Their darkest days had to be over. She couldn't take anymore gloom.

"I sense a dryness in your womb."

Gray felt gutted. The old woman had stabbed her in the stomach and twisted the blade until her skin turned a color of ash grey.

"No worries, my child. It can be fixed. You will bear more children. I see four in your future." The spiritualist spoke confidently.

Tears welled in Gray's eyes, because at that moment, she knew the old woman was full of shit. Her problem couldn't be fixed. Her tubes had been cut and burned. She was ruined for life. She'd never be able to give her husband a child of his own. It was a subject they pretty much avoided, but this spiritualist had forced them to face the facts. It would just be them, Aoki and Press. Cam would never have a mini me that looked just like him. Being the loving attentive man he was, Cam massaged her shoulder and kissed the side of her face. He hated when Gray cried. She was so strong that when she did break down it messed with his psyche.

"No disrespect, old lady, but get the fuck on. You betta be glad I don't shoot old people 'cause right about now I would light yo' old ass up." Cam held his weeping wife in his arms.

Gray buried her face in his chest and cried silently. She'd just gotten her marriage back on track, now she was faced with the reality that she might not be able to keep Cam forever. Eventually, her not being able to bear children would be a problem.

"Stop cryin' ma. That old bitch trippin'."

"I know." She wiped her face and sat up.

She couldn't let the Fashion Nova executives see her distraught. She had to remain professional.

"I look okay?" She gulped down the rest of her tears.

"You look better than okay. You're beautiful. Ain't a bitch out here that look better, and I done seen some bad bitches since we got here."

"Shut up you asshole." Gray burst out laughing.

"For real, don't let what that crazy bitch said upset you. Whether we have kids or not, I'm good. It ain't like we ain't already got four kids anyway."

"Four?" Her brows dipped.

"Yeah Kilo, Gram, Aoki and Press." Cam said seriously.

"You are fuckin' insane." Gray leaned forward and lovingly kissed his lips.

"Only when it comes to you." He rose to his feet and tapped a butter knife against his glass. "Excuse me everyone. Uh sorry to interrupt dinner. I just wanna take a minute to congratulate my wife on this momentous occasion in her career."

"Momentous?" Stacy screwed up his face. "This nigga up here using big words like he can read. Spell it."

"F-A-T A-S-S." Cam scowled.

"Fa'tas? What the hell that mean?" Stacy looked around confused.

"Anyway, back to what I was sayin'. Even though she ain't gotta work, I want her do whatever that's gon' make her happy. And if modeling some thirty-dollar clothes made in China is gonna do that then so be it."

"Cam." Gray touched his hand mortified.

"What? Shit it's the truth. Look, being around you these past couple of months has shown me that there are good people in the world. The world needs more people like you. I find myself tryin' to be a better person and a better man because of you. Hell, I ain't caught a body in I don't know how long—"

"Wrap it dawg. You going left." Kema urged.

"Nah, that's real shit. He makin' progress. Nigga doing good out here. I'm proud of you bro." Quan raised his fist in the air.

"The fuck. I'm tryin'. Bear wit' me Kema, damn. You know I ain't good wit' words and shit. Look, Star, basically what I'm tryin' to say is I'm proud of you. They couldn't have picked anybody better for the job. You gon' murder that shit tomorrow. But before that happen, I got a li'l surprise for you."

On cue, the hotel staff appeared holding Eco White Wish Lanterns. One by one they handed them along with a Sharpie to everyone at the table.

"If you don't know what these are, they're them li'l gay lanterns muthafucka's be using to makes wishes and shit. Even though my wish already came true." He looked down at Gray. "I figured we all could create new ones together. No homo."

"Baby, that is so sweet." Gray leaped into his arms.

"I figured you would like it. C'mon, let's do this shit so we can go back to the room and fuck. My dick hard than a muthafucka."

Gray didn't even care that he was being crass. He could do whatever he pleased. It meant the world to her that he'd gone out of the way to do something so special for her.

"What is your wish gonna be?" Gray hugged him from the side.

"I told you I already got my wish."

"What is your new one gonna be?"

Cam paused to think for a minute.

"That no matter what happens, we always find our way back to each other."

Gray's heart dropped. She could see the look of fear in Cam's eyes. He was genuinely afraid that one day he was gonna lose her forever. He wasn't the best nigga and he knew it. He'd been doing good but how long would it be before he fucked up again? Every night before bed, Cam prayed to god to keep him on the straight and narrow. For each day that passed, his love for Gray grew more and more. There wasn't a thing he wouldn't do to keep her happy and safe. She'd never have to beg for his affection. From day one she'd had it.

———

From the jet lag and the boiling hot heat, the sleep Cam tried to avoid overtook his body. Out of fear of what would happen, he tried to keep his eyes open. The plan was to get a few hours of rest while Gray was at her photo shoot, but after busting a fat ass nut in her womb, it was lights out. Tiredness swallowed him whole. At first everything was fine. Cam slept comfortably next to his wife while lying on his back. The further he got into the rapid eye movement stage of sleep, better known as REM, his reoccurring nightmare began. Soon, his breathing increased. Rapidly, he took gasps of breath while trying to reach for his pocketknife. The masked Taliban solider was getting near. At any second Cam would be dead. He had to do something. Digging his feet into the dirt he edged back. Gray rose from her slumber and found him in a state of panic while sleep. Moaning for help, he kicked and thrashed his feet. Half delirious and afraid, she tried to end the torture he was end by waking him up. Gray had made a big mistake. As soon as she touched his skin, Cam jumped up and wrapped his hand around her neck. She tried prying his hand away, but his grip was too strong. Cam tightened his hold around her throat, cutting off her air supply. Gray pleaded with him to stop but no words came out. She was too busy struggling to air. Clawing at his hand, she believed she was going to die. Cam's eyes were open, but he wasn't there. Just that quick, their near perfect night was about to end in tragedy. Then abruptly, it was as if a light switch clicked on in his brain, Cam came back to himself. Seeing the sight of him strangling Gray and her face turning blue caused him to leap back in fear. Gray held her throat and took deep gulps of air. This was what Cam had been trying to avoid. How had he done this to her? Gray lay slumped over the side of the bed, coughing roughly. He'd never forgive himself for this. He was a monster.

"Baby, I'm sorry." He uttered in complete shock.

Once she'd calmed down, Gray turned over and said, "Take one of your pills."

Cam looked at her surprised. He expected her to yell, cuss or be deathly afraid of him now. He should've known better. Once again, Gray came through in the clutch. Once more, she'd saved him from himself. Gray couldn't blame him for something she knew he didn't have any control over. She knew he wasn't himself in the moment. She'd be anything less than a wife and a good human being if she made him feel bad. She loved Cam. She was going to doing everything in her power to help him concur his demons.

———

The plan was for Cam to wake up when Gray got ready for her photo shoot and go with her then catch a few Z's. All of that changed after he took his medication. He ended up sleeping half the day away. By the time he woke up it was noon. He hadn't slept more than a few hours since his last night terror. Per Gray's request, he'd been attending therapy. Not with a group but with a private therapist. At first, he didn't want to participate, but after the third session, he began to tell his story. Talking about all his issues really was therapeutic. He wasn't in no way healed but the process to healing had begun. Showered and dressed, he grabbed a bottled water and headed out to the rice fields where the photo shoot was taking place. Remnants of his medication made him feel like he was in auto pilot. He hated how groggy his meds made him. That coupled with the hot muggy heat put him in a sour mood. Even the gorgeous scenery didn't perk him up.

A whole crew of people were on set. There were the Fashion Nova execs, photographer, art director, stylist, makeup artist, hairstylist, nail tech, gofers, Selicia and more. Amongst the slew of people, Gray stood out the most but for all the wrong reasons. They had her hair flowing in soft beachy waves. She rocked a strong brow, lashes and extra-glossy nude lip-gloss. Body butter covered her skin from head to toe. All of that was fine. That he could live with. The gag was she had on a leopard print, triangle cut bikini that barely covered her nipples and showed off the tattoo of his name on her pussy. With the backdrop of the rice fields and Gray's devilish body on full display, the ad campaign was sure to be a hit. Yeah, that was cute, but Cam wasn't trying to have the whole world see what was his. He had already knocked several niggas' heads off because of her. Was he going to have to kill every nigga on the planet now?

"What kind of freaky shit is this? Baby, they got you in a porno?" He barked stepping right into frame.

"No, Cam, and move! You messing up my shot!" She pushed him back.

"I ain't going no fuckin' where!" He mean-mugged her.

"Move! You can't be over here!"

"The fuck I can't. This some Porn Hub shit. Cut the fuckin' camera off!" He snatched the camera from the photographer. "Y'all got me fucked up!"

"Stop, Cam! You're embarrassing me." Gray whined.

"I assure you, sir. Everything is on the up and up." The president of Fashion Nova assured.

"The only thing that's gon' be up is my foot going up yo' ass! Why the fuck y'all got her out here naked?" He got up in the man's face.

Cam was about to go postal and fuck everyone up. The president of the company jumped back afraid for his life.

"If you get me fired, I swear fo god." Gray warned, ready to snap.

"Cam, she has on a bathing suit. Calm yo' retarded ass down," Selicia groaned, not in the mood.

She didn't know Cam from a can of paint, but she didn't have time for this shit. If his crazy-ass fucked up this opportunity for them, she was going to take the razorblade out of her mouth and cut 'em with it. She didn't play when it came to her money.

"Bathing suit these nuts! Her whole ass is out!" Cam roared. "She supposed to be a fuckin' girl boss but ya'll got her in fuckin' dental floss."

"Sir, the collection consists of dresses, suits and swimwear. We're shooting the swimwear portion first."

"Do I look like I give a fuck! I don't want my wife's ass out!"

"Well, for the next two hours that ass belongs to Fashion Nova, so I suggest you back yo' lanky-ass up. You goddamn giraffe. They paying her a quarter mill for this. You betta shut up and let us secure the bag." Selicia shot back.

"I'ma let you know something, Philly Freeway." Cam pointed his fingers in her face like a gun. "You betta make sure her titties and shit is covered before this shit hit the net or yo' ass gon' be 6F?"

"Murphy Lee, back yo' ass up. Ain't nobody scared of you. Talkin' bout some damn 6F. I don't even know what the fuck that shit mean."

"You gon' know if I see a nipple coming down my timeline."

"Yeah-yeah whatever. Get the hell on. We got work to do! Sorry for the interruption everyone! Let's get back to work!" She clapped her hands.

Cam looked over at Gray. Her eyes pleaded with him to stop. After the hell he'd put her through the night before, calming down was the least he could. This was her moment. He didn't want to spoil it.

"We're gonna have to cover this up some more. It's starting to show through." The on-set makeup artist spoke loud enough for Cam to hear.

Wondering what the hell she was talkin about, he eyed Gray closely. Red circular marks decorated her neck from the night before. Cam wanted to throw up. He'd done that to her and now the word around set would be that he abused his wife.

"How did that happen?" The girl whispered.

Embarrassed, Gray linked eyes with Cam and said, "I fell."

"Mmm hmm. Sure, you did." The makeup artist shot Cam a dirty look.

Gray placed her hand under the girls chin and made her look in her direction. She would be damned if this woman labeled her husband an abuser. She didn't know shit about her and Cam or their marriage.

"Mind your fuckin' business. Whatever you think you know, you don't. You're here to do a job or do I need to tell them you're making me uncomfortable so they can bring in a new makeup artist?"

"No ma'am." The girl shook her head profusely.

"That's what I thought. Now, do your job before you don't have one."

As time went on and Cam settled into the director's chair he'd stolen and watched the rest of the shoot in silence. He still didn't like none of the shit Gray had on. They went from putting her in a napkin they called a leopard print bikini to a yellow swimsuit to lastly a black sports bra and thong. By the time the shoot was over, she'd stripped down to nothing but the thong that had Girl Boss written on the crotch. Cam's blood pressure spiked. It was about to be a mass murder in Indonesia. Quietly, he stood up and pulled his burner out.

"Ya'll got five fuckin' seconds to clear this bitch out or bodies is hittin' the floor." He warned with a sinister look in his eye.

The staff saw the gun hanging by his side and went into panic mood. Nothing else had to be said. Camera equipment, clothes, shoes, makeup, everything was packed up. People were scattering like roaches.

"Really?" Selicia cocked her head to the side pissed.

You could practically see the steam shooting out of her ears.

"Now, I gotta go talk to these white people and calm they scary-asses down because you wanna act fool. Gray, I want extra!" She snatched up her belongings. "Because of your lunatic husband, I gotta go grin up in these fuckin' Republicans' faces and pretend like I want this goddamn wall built!"

"Selicia, I am so sorry. Please tell them not to fire me." Gray begged as she put her top on.

She was truly embarrassed.

"They ain't gon' fire you. They gon' call the cops on his ass!"

"I don't give a fuck what they do. I see the muthafuckin' fashion shoot is over. Won't be no mo photos today." Cam shot indignantly.

"See, this why I don't fuck wit' you Midwest niggas now. Ever since Nelly was out here playin' wit' Ashanti's heart and had her rockin' sideburns, I knew ya'll wasn't shit. You betta be glad I couldn't get my gun on that plane."

"Yeah okay, Peedi Crack. Just make sure my wife don't get fired. If she do that's yo' ass."

"If she do you gon' pay me my fuckin' percentage and more. Had me flyin' all the way out here to no man's land for this bullshit. I should kick both of ya'll asses. Bye Gray! Let me go make sure this check still gon' clear." Selicia stormed off, leaving them alone.

Before Cam knew it, Gray started hitting him in the chest repeatedly.

"I can't believe you did that." She punched him hard in the arm. "You can't go around threating people every time you get mad. They already think you kicking my ass. I really had fun today and you might've ruined it. That shit ain't cool."

Seeing how upset she was, Cam quickly began to regret his actions. He never wanted to intentionally hurt Gray. She was his world. His number one job was to make her happy.

"My bad. I fucked up."

"You always fuckin' up. You can't handle yourself like that. Grow up! Do you see me threatening bitches every time you do something stupid? What if you would've hurt somebody? It's kids stayin' here."

"You act like I pulled the trigger."

"That's not the point jackass!" She hit him again.

"Okay, okay. You right. I gotta chill. My bad." Cam restrained her arms and wrapped her up in his embrace. "I ain't mean to ruin your shit. I just wanna keep you all to myself. I'm not comfortable knowing niggas gon' see you wit' yo' ass and titties out. If I was takin' pictures wit' my dick out, you would have a fuckin' heart attack."

"You damn right I would. That dick is all mine. You ain't crazy."

Cam moved her hair out of the way and kissed the right side of her neck. As his soft lips landed on her skin, the tension in Gray's body vanished. Whenever she was near Cam like this, all rational thoughts ceased.

"I'm sorry again about your neck. That shit is fuckin' wit' my head yo. I never wanted you to see me like that."

"It's okay. You weren't yourself."

"Nah, puttin' my hand on you under any circumstance is not cool."

"Well, what do you suggest we do? You can't avoid sleep for the rest of your life."

"I've been doing good at it so far."

"Barely." Gray joked.

"So, you really like this shit?"

"Yeah, I do and you betta hope I don't get fired."

"So, if they ask you to do it again you would?" He rocked her side-to-side.

"I didn't plan on it at first but now that I've done it, yeah. I've always been on the other side of the camera. I was the one with the final approval. Being the subject was weird at first, but as the day went on, I found myself loving it. You heard the photographer. They loved me. He said I was a natural. Who knows, maybe this could be my next career step."

"Yeah . . . maybe." He pretended like everything was okay and continued to hold her close.

Cam wasn't so sure how he'd feel about Gray going back to work full-time. Since he'd known her, she'd been available to him whenever he called. He'd gotten used to her being at home, waiting on his every need. Since he was a boy, Cam had always wanted a stay-at-home wife. His mother had executed the role perfectly and so had Gray. The whole dynamic of their marriage would change if she went back to work. He and Gray couldn't take anymore shake ups. They were barely holding on by a thread.

"All these chicks poppin' pussy I'm just poppin' bands."- Juicy J featuring 2 Chainz & Li'l Wayne, "Bandz A Make Her Dance"

#19

Oh, this is ladies night, Gray shimmied in her seat feeling her cunt. It had been ages since she and her girls got together for drinks and kicked it. After the amazing time they had in Indonesia, they had to continue the turn-up. Gray hated her time in Indonesia had to end. She'd truly had the time of her life. For four days, she did nothing but work and make love. When the shoot was over, the gang decided to stay an extra day and went to the ends of the earth at Devil's Tears Bay, walked through the Rainforest Canopy and visited the beach where the girls swung on swings over the ocean. The trip not only renewed her faith in her abilities to make a coin but in her marriage as well. After a few weeks of living separately, Cam was back home. He'd gone above and beyond to prove that he was going to do right by her this time. Sure, he messed up from time-to-time. This was Cam for god's sake. Miracles weren't made in a day. Instead of focusing on the negative, Gray focused on the positive. The good thing was he still was going to therapy. Outside of when they were in Indonesia, he still didn't sleep much to Gray's dismay. He was, however, coming home at night. Cam would lay in bed with Gray snuggled in his arms and watch television while she slept peacefully. She would take that any day over how things were. The pressure of thinking he was out cheating no longer weighed on her chest. She and Cam were solid. Life was grand.

Gray, Kema, Selicia and Heidi were on their sophisticated shit. Clubs weren't really their thing anymore. Kema still went out every other week. She and Quan stayed poppin' bottles in the VIP section. She loved the nightlife. Gray had been over the scene for years. She would much rather be home with her kids and husband. However, on nights like this she loved putting on a dope-ass outfit and enjoying a glass of wine with her friends. Bright Tap House & Wine Bar was the place to be that night. Located in downtown, St. Louis the bar housed over 55 beers on tap and 100 plus in bottles, in addition to over 100 plus wines. The goal was to provide a classy yet comfortable atmosphere where patrons could kick back and impress.

It was Gray's first time being there, but the place lived up to the hype. It was a Saturday night so every seat in the bar was filled. Gray and her girls sat drinking wine and talking shit like always. Each woman was dressed to the nines. Gray wore her hair in a high ponytail with loose curls. Lashes and a black matte lip made up her face. The mood for the night was laidback and cute. Cam's black and gold Versace print shirt was unbuttoned down to her stomach and tucked inside a pair of dark wash jeans. Strategically placed rips were at each knee and the hem of the jeans were cut above the ankle and frayed. Gold necklaces, a Versace baroque buckle leather belt, stack of Cartier Love bracelets and black, pointed toe, Manolo Blahnik pumps finished off her look.

"I'm so sick of this nigga callin' me." Selicia rolled her eyes to the sky.

"Who?" Heidi asked.

"Stacy."

"Wait a minute." Kema cracked up laughing. "You gave him your number? I thought you said you didn't like him?"

"I don't."

"Well, how he get your number then?" Gray rolled her neck like a li'l girl.

"None of yo' nosey-ass business."

"You fucked Stacy." Gray exclaimed so loud the people next to them stopped their conversation to look.

"Say it louder, why don't you? For your information, no I didn't. You know I'ma virgin."

"I forgot you keepin' that puss on lockdown." Kema frowned disappointed.

"You damn right. I ain't got time to be stressin' over these niggas like ya'll do."

"SHADE!" Heidi grinned.

"Nah, that ain't shade. I'm already crazy without sex so with sex I'm bound to commit a couple homicides."

I hate you so much right now! I hate you so much right now!

Gray drew her head back. She hadn't heard from Gunz in weeks. Ever since New Year's day when she and Cam confronted him, he'd gone into hiding. Gray never thought she'd see the day where Gavin 'Gunz' Marciano was scared of anyone. Cam truly had him shook. Gunz had finally meet someone who was bigger and badder than him. Wondering why he was texting her so late, she opened the text message and read it.

Gunz: So, this the nigga u married?

Confused by his statement, Gray clicked on the video that was attached. Her mouth instantly dropped when she saw Cam at the strip club throwing stacks of money at strippers. Gray wasn't the insecure type when it came to exotic dancers. She bigged up any woman that was confident enough to take off her clothes for money. However, there was a limitation to everything. What she didn't like was ho's grinding on her husband's dick while he smacked them on the ass. She knew how long, thick and hard that dick could get. The crock in it only made her want it more. There was no telling how he was making the strippers feel. At any minute, one of them was going to want to fuck and then the ho would have to die.

Gray: So, u can text me about my nigga, but u can't text me about ur kids. FUCK U!!!

"Lousy-ass nigga." She shook her head on ten.

"What's wrong?" Kema saw the look of rage on her friend's face.

"Look." Gray handed her the phone.

Kema watched the video. She didn't see anything wrong until she spotted Quan off to the side slappin' dollar bills on bitches' pussies.

"Oh, hell nah!" She shot from her seat and headed towards the door.

"Where she going?" Heidi rose to her feet.

"To kill Quan and I'm going wit' her." Gray covered the tab and got up.

"What happened?" Selicia followed suit.

"Her nigga and my nasty-ass husband at the strip club showin' out."

"Oh shit. This gon' be good." She scurried behind Gray.

———

Gray handed the doorman a twenty-dollar bill, got her hand stamped and stepped inside the dark club. She'd never been to a strip club before, so she didn't know what to expect. She knew there would be chicks dancing on a pole and men throwing money, but she had no idea how much debauchery went down. Neon lights lit the dark room. From wall-to-wall there were people. She thought it would just be niggas, but it was like a club in there. It was just as many women as men. *Shake That Monkey* by Too Short featuring Lil Jon and The Eastside Boyz bumped through the speakers. The whole strip club went crazy. Something inside the strippers was activated and they all started to act up. On the stage one girl hung upside down in nothing but a thong and stripper heels. Another chick was dry humping the floor with her bare pussy while doing the split. At least ten girls surrounded her twerkin' their asses to the beat. All Gray saw were asses shaking up and down and right to left in clothes that barely covered anything. The floor was covered in dollar bills. Gray estimated there had to be, at least, forty g's scattered around. The strippers danced and stepped over the money like it was nothing.

Even trying to get through the crowd was crazy. With each step she took niggas were tryin' to holla at her. After the fifth time telling a dude she was married she instantly grew irritated and started elbowing niggas out of the way. It quickly became clear that the strip club was not her thing. Gray stood out like a sore thumb. Even though she cussed like a sailor, she was way too sophisticated for a place that smelled like fried chicken and weed. She had to find her man, snatch his ass up and get out of there before she caught the shingles or something worse.

> *Bounce that ass up and down to the floor*
> *Shake that shit till you can't no more*
> *Twerk that monkey, lemme see you get low*
> *Freak that nigga till your shit get sore*

The longer the song went on the crazier the crowd and strippers became. Gray turned around to see if her friends were still behind her and found Heidi holding her nose, Selicia threatening to punch niggas in the face and Kema bent over shaking her ass.

"Bitch, stay focused!" She popped her on the arm.

"Girl, this my shit!" Kema did the stripper bop while sticking out her tongue.

"This is some bullshit." Gray said, irritated.

It was too much niggerdom going on at once.

"Shame . . . shame . . . shame!" Selicia flicked holy water on the strippers as they gyrated.

"C'mon ya'll! Gray about to flip out." Heidi rubbed her friend's back.

"She is so damn dramatic." Kema huffed, mad that she had to stop dancing.

It seemed like it took forever for them to get to the roped off VIP section where Cam and the guys were. When they finally walked up the steps, any feeling of being irritated went away. Anger took over as Gray watched her man turn up. It was just like the night she ran into him at his birthday party. There he was standing in all his glory. Cam was the life of the party. He'd left the house after her, so she hadn't seen him get dressed. Cam was turning her on to the fullest. Low over his eyes was a Rebel Eight denim cap. A toothpick dangled from between his pink lips. Three diamond Cuban link chains shined bright against the black fitted tee he wore under a denim jacket. The jacket was filled with different patches and buttons. The jacket was sick. She'd never seen anything like it. PRPS jeans that showcased the print of his massive dick hugged his legs. On his feet were a pair of fresh-ass Dsquared2 boots.

Every female there was eye-fuckin' the shit out of her nigga and it made Gray sick. Now she knew how Cam felt when men gawked at her. She hated the lustful look in the women's eyes. Cam or one of his pot'nahs was getting chosen. It was too much big dick energy in one room. Not only were Cam, Quan, Stacy and Diggy there, but Drake, the Migos and Future stood right along with them poppin' bands. Cam stood out the most tho. Like always, he had to be extra and line up four strippers. Each girl held onto the railing and poked their asses in the air. Doing a jailhouse pose, he looked in-between one of the stripper's legs as she shook her butt cheeks in his face. Taking a rubber band off a stack of ones, he threw half of it onto her ass. Gray was outdone. *So, this how this nigga act when I'm not around,* she thought.

If that wasn't bad enough only one of the girls had clothes on. The other three were butt-booty-naked. When the DJ dropped Blac Youngsta's *Booty,* they did whatever they could to get the money out of Cam and his friends' hands. Two of the naked strippers got on all fours and hit each other with their ass cheeks until they made a clapping sound. Then one of them laid on her back while the other one lay before her and rested her head in-between her legs. Using her stomach muscles, the girl placed her legs over her head and rolled over backwards until her pussy was in the other girl's face. Cam walked up and spread her cheeks apart until everyone could see her asshole and the lips of her vagina. Out of nowhere, Stacy slapped a stack of bills on her pussy. At that point, Gray had seen enough. She was going to jail. Ducking under the velvet rope, she ran up and smacked Cam in the back of his head.

"You Kareem Abdul Jabbar lookin' muthafucka! Have you lost your goddamn mind?"

Caught off guard by the hit, Cam spun around to see who'd been crazy enough to lay hands on him. Once he realized it was Gray he stuttered and said, "Wha-uh. Oh shit. Hey-hey babe. What you doing here?"

"Don't worry about that. What the fuck are *you* doing here? That's the question." She placed her hands on her hips.

"We just chillin'." He replied like a kid on the verge of getting an ass whoopin'.

"Chillin'? These bitches tryin' to fuck for a buck. You ain't single!"

"Yo' who is that? Shawty bad as fuck." Drake licked his lips, eyeing Gray hungrily. "You know I like 'em BBW."

"*Hey Drake.*" Gray blushed, wiggling her fingers hello.

"Nigga, that's my wife. Don't make me break your face in here. Advert yo' eyes elsewhere before you end up like Wheelchair Jimmy for real." Cam took the toothpick out of his mouth ready to kill.

"My bad, homey, but shit you got a bad one."

"Keep tryin' me, Drake. I ain't Chris Brown and she for damn sure ain't Rihanna. I don't play about mines. Keep fuckin' wit' me and you won't leave out this muthafucka alive."

"Chill nu mi yute. All respeck me bredrin. Mi neva kno sey dat was your goody." Drake spoke Jamaican patois.

"Shut the fuck up. Fuckin' fake-ass West Indian. Nigga, you Canadian." Cam checked him.

"You know what? This is some nasty shit." Selicia walked up in Stacy's face. "I can't believe you in here slappin' bitches on the pussy."

"Oh shit!" He jumped. "What's up boo? I been lookin' for you."

"Lookin' for me where? Not up in this muthafucka."

"Come here cutie. I was just about to walk to Philly to get you." He tried to give her a hug.

"You bet not touch me with them chlamydia infested fingers." She pushed him with all her might.

"What's wrong wit' you? Why you always so tense? I got some ones. Bust it open for a nigga."

"Nigga, do you see me." She squinted her eyes and rolled her neck. "This is Chanel. Do I look like I need them funky-ass ones?"

"Nah, but you look like you need some dick tho."

"Go jump in a lake." She hit him with the middle finger.

"You are married!" Gray's anger rose to a new level. "We don't do this type of shit no more. Got me out here lookin' stupid. Muthafucka's textin' me, sending me videos and shit. Once again, here I am lookin' dumb as hell cause Cam don't know how to control his self."

"Who texted you?" Cam died to know.

Gray wanted to piss him off and say that Gunz did it, but she knew that would only make matters worse. The beef between them had just started to die down. She didn't want to spark it back up again.

"None of your goddamn business." She replied instead.

"A'ight." Cam sucked his teeth.

"Pick it up!" Gray stepped into his personal space.

"Pick what up?"

"The money nigga. You ain't about to be giving these bitches money that could be spent on me. Pick . . . it . . . up!"

"Pick it up. Pick it up. Pick it up." Quavo adlibbed, while bouncing his shoulders to the makeshift beat in his head.

"Shut the fuck up Quav! I'm about sick of you fuckin' rappers always adlibbin' some shit! Mind your business!"

"I'm sayin' nigga that might be the next hit right there." Offset added.

"Fuck all of that!" Gray waved her arm. "Pick up the fuckin' money before I kick you in the back of that peanut head."

Cam unconsciously pulled off his hat and ran his hand over the top of his head. A roar of laughter erupted in Quan's chest. Gray was punkin' the shit outta Cam.

"What the fuck you laughing at?" Kema stepped up. "You too nigga! Think this a game."

"Why I gotta pick it up? I ain't even do nothin'." Quan stomped his foot like a child. "Damn, nigga. You always gettin' me in trouble. I stay in some shit because of you." He started scooping up the money he'd thrown.

"I ain't gon' tell you again." Gray warned, getting even closer.

"C'mon, Gray. I can't do that."

"You got five seconds to pick it up or I'ma drag one of these ho's."

"I'm sorry y'all." Cam bent down.

"Uh ah! Put that back!" One of the naked strippers got off the floor. "Ya'll know the rules! I don't give a fuck what she say!"

"Who the fuck you talkin' to you?" Gray pushed Cam out of the way. "You ain't gettin' this money."

"Watch me." The girl challenged.

"Watch you?" Kema immediately started taking off her earrings. "See, I ain't beat a bitch ass in a minute. I might be a li'l rusty, but it'll come back to me. It's like riding a bike." She cracked her knuckles.

"Baby please, no." Quan bear-hugged her from behind.

"Nah, nah, nah 'cause who she talkin' to? You heard what she said! Wit' yo' stank pussy ass!" Selicia squared up.

"I swear to god I love her. On everything this my soulmate." Stacy gushed.

"Babe, chill. Just let 'em have it. We don't need it. C'mon we regulars here. I can't be no fuckin' Indian giver." Quan pleaded with Kema.

"You heard what the fuck I said. It's your fault I'm even in here arguing wit' this bitch. Up in here actin' like you single. Smackin' they nasty-ass pussies like you ain't got a girl at home. We just got done playin' stripper last night. I took you to my champagne room and everything."

"My friend pussy ain't nasty bitch!" The clothed stripper spat.

"Everybody chill! Everybody just calm down!" Cam shouted. "Now look, we ain't in here on no bullshit, ma. Why don't ya'll have a seat. I'ma order some bottles and another hookah for you and your girls."

"Hookah?" Selicia repeated. "Shit, you should've said that five minutes ago. I'm sorry Gray but you can be mad by yourself. I'ma about to kick it." She took a seat next to Heidi who was already on her third glass.

She and Diggy had been drinking the whole time the argument went down.

"You ain't shit." Gray mouthed disappointed.

"Get yo' ass over here Catwoman. You always tryin' to fight somebody wit' yo' cute ass." Quan planted a hard kiss to Kema's lips.

Just like that, everything was good between them. Gray was the only girl left standing. Cam looked at his wife. She was so fuckin' cute when she was mad. Her little freckled nose crinkled like an accordion.

"So, you just gon' stand there lookin' dumb? You know you wanna throw these ones wit' me."

"No, I don't." She folded her arms and poked out her bottom lip.

"You don't wanna throw this money wit' me? You don't wanna sit on my lap?" He tugged on the belt loop of her jeans and pulled her close.

"You make me sick." She continued to pout as he rubbed her booty.

The way her ass was sittin' up had his dick as hard as a steel pipe. Now that he'd stopped the strippers from losing their life, Cam and Gray sat on the couch, her in-between his legs. Her ass sat right on his dick as he handed her a stack of ones that totaled 10 g's. Gray hated to waste money, but she couldn't be a stick-in-the-mud all the time. Sometimes, she had to let loose. Gray had no choice but to turn-up when the sound of a classic guitar riff started to play. Instinctively, her hips started to dutty wine. Instantly, she morphed back to the early 2000's when she was young, carefree and didn't give a fuck about anything. Smoking on a blunt, Cam sat back and enjoyed the view of his wife giving him a lapdance to Juvenile and Soulja Slim's *Slow Motion*. Gray leaned forward while winding her ass in a circle and sang along to the song.

Uh I like it like that she working that back I don't know how to act
Slow motion for me, slow motion for me, slow motion for me, move in slow motion for me

Drake, The Migos and Future dipped shortly after that but the party continued on for Cam and the rest of his crew in the VIP section. Numerous bottles of Ace of Spades, Ciroc and Hennessy were devoured. The turn up was real. He went from nearly getting his head knocked off by Gray to throwing stacks of ones with her. Gray was a little stiff at first but after she got a little Ace in her system the rest of the night was a movie. She and her homegirls smacked a few asses and gave their men lap dances. Cam couldn't have asked for a better night. Needing to piss, he kissed Gray on the cheek and told her he was headed to the restroom. The pressure to pee almost had him doing the pee-pee dance. Inside the men's bathroom, he leaned his head back and drained his bladder full of Hennessy. A sense of relief washed over him as he relieved himself in the urinal. Once he was done, Cam zipped up his jeans and washed his hands. While glancing at himself in the mirror, he made a conscious decision to drink water for the rest of the night. If he drank anything else, he'd be sloppy drunk. He couldn't be out with his girl fucked up.

Heading back to his section, he slowly made his way through the club. The place was even more packed than it was when he got there. It was so crowded that it had begun to get hot. That didn't stop the dancers from going hard in the paint when the DJ started to play *Make It Rain* by Fat Joe & Lil Wayne. Ones were flying in the air as booties began to shake extra hard. Each step Cam took people kept stopping him to say what's up or show some love. In a good mood, he chopped it up with a few people. Everyone, including Cam was so caught up in the sexual hedonism that no one noticed that all the doors were being locked, except one. The security cameras had already been blacked out so no evidence of what was about to occur could be traced. The DJ, bouncers, security guards, bottle girls and some of the dancers pulled black ski masks over their faces with the letters MCM written on them in white. Semi-automatics, Glocks and pistols were drawn with the intent to kill. Without warning, gunshots cracked into the air loud like thunder. At first, everyone thought it was a sound effect until a storm of metal rain cascaded over the crowd targeted at Cam. Panic broke out, causing everyone to duck and run. Partygoers tried to push the exit doors open, only to realize they'd been barricaded in. Shear panic erupted. It was like the Orlando Nightclub Shooting all over again. Forced inside, some people hid in the bathroom, the dancers in the back hid in the dressing room while the bartenders hid under the glass bar.

Cam quickly leaped behind a leather couch. Traumatic screams pierced his ears as he went into military mode. Holding his breath, he surveyed his surroundings and drew his gun. A sheen of sweat trailed down his spine. Flashbacks of Afghanistan bombarded his mind. Cam shook his head profusely, determined to rid himself of the anxiety ridden thoughts. Now was not the time for his PTSD to rear its ugly head. He had to protect the people he loved and the patrons in the club. There was no way he and Gray weren't leaving out of there alive. Turning the safety off on his gun, he aimed and shot, hitting two masked men in the head.

Gunshots covered the club thick like winter rain. Bullets cut through the space oblivious to a particular target. Each one ripped into flesh whether it be woman or man. The shooters didn't give a damn who they killed. Their mission was to take down Cam and anyone moving. As Cam took care of business on the lower level, up on the balcony in the VIP section Quan covered him and blasted off hitting anybody with an MCM mask on. Never far behind, Stacy handled his business by bodying several niggas too. Gun less, Diggy stood back helpless. The one time he left the house without a strap a mass shooting would break out. The shootout was further confirmation that he was over the club scene and all the street shit that came along with it. Gray and the girls nosedived to the floor, covering their heads. Huddled together, fear overwhelmed their bodies. Each second seemed like an eternity as the blood bath ensued. Gray squeezed her eyes shut as visions of Aoki and Press' little faces danced in her brain. This was why she stayed in the house. She couldn't die like this. She had to live for her kids. Her girls would not end up motherless like her.

One by one, bodies hit the ground. Blood gushed from their lifeless forms onto the money filled floor. Cam couldn't believe his eyes. Every corner of the room was stained by the gore of red flowing blood. It was a massacre. Cam had expected Gunz to retaliate but not like this. He'd been taught that women and children were off limits in war. Gunz obviously had different views. The nigga was soulless. He didn't give a fuck about anyone. Cam, Quan and Stacy tried their hardest to fight back as best as possible, but their pistols were no match for the choppas letting off rounds. Things were looking grim. Cam had taken out a few more of the masked assailants. With his sniper background his aim was impeccable, but he'd shot off 10 of the 14 rounds in his clip. The members of the Marciano Crime Mob had way more ammunition than he and his people.

Things then went from shitty to pretty fucked up when one of the masked strippers caught Stacy in the shoulder. Stacy was so high off adrenaline that he didn't even know he was shot until warm liquid began to pour from the bullet wound. Stacy stopped shooting for a brief second to examine the wound. That brief second was all it took for him to lose his life. Like in the movies, one by one his body was riddled with bullets. He was hit in the chest, twice in the stomach and once in the leg. The bullets tore through his flesh with dangerous precision, easily tearing his soft human tissue. On impact his arteries split in two. Each bullet was like a searing hot poker to his epidermis. Diggy watched as Stacy's large frame fell backwards hitting the ground. Slick and thick blood coated the floor underneath him. Needing to help his friend, Diggy swiftly crawled on his elbows and knees to get to him. Using the red rag from his pocket, he applied pressure to the stomach wounds hoping that would help. Things weren't looking so good though. Blood seeped from Stacy's mouth and nose as his body went into shock.

Seeing his dear friend laid out on the floor covered in blood sent Cam into a tailspin. He wasn't going to stop until every member of Gunz's crew was deceased. He and Quan ferociously avenged their boy by emptying what was left in their clips and killing as many targets as possible. By the time they were done, seven more members of MCM were killed but there were still more left. They were outnumbered. Cam and Quan were gonna die. He wasn't gonna live to see another day. This was it for him. His day to join his mother in heaven had come. Cam said a silent prayer to god asking for mercy as the one door that hadn't been locked was opened. God was showing him mercy. Someone had called for help, but Cam was wrong. Help wasn't on the way yet. The person walking through the door was his worst enemy.

Dressed in all black and a bulletproof vest, Gunz strolled leisurely through the door by the VIP section. Unlike his henchman, he didn't wear a mask. He wanted Cam to see his face. He'd told him that the next time he came for him he'd do it his self and he meant it. Gunz was going to make Cam hurt in ways he never thought imaginable. He'd taken too much away from him not to make him pay. Gunz might've been out of the life but his name still rang bells so when Cam burned down his restaurants and Tia's home, Gunz rounded up some of his old crew. Unlike Cam, Gunz didn't run off emotion. He stayed in the cut, plotted and planned to destroy. It was the best form of revenge. Gray lay quivering on the floor, scared out of her mind. Gunz hated to see her that way but she'd done it to herself. There was no love lost between the two. She'd chosen sides and apparently she'd chosen wrong. Gray had no idea that he'd used Cam's outing at the strip club to lore her there. Like a dummy, she took the bait. Taking the bait now was going to end with him taking her life. The sound of soft whimpers and heavy breathing filled the space as all fire seized. Gunz stepped over her friends trembling bodies and yanked Gray up by the back of her hair.

"Ahhhhhhhh!" She wailed as tears streamed from her frantic eyes.

It felt like her hair follicle's were being ripped out one by one.

Hearing his wife's blood curdling scream, Cam rose to his feet. Quan spun around and watched as Gunz wrapped his left arm around Gray's neck and held a sharp knife to her throat. He was only inches away from Gunz. If he had more bullets he would've shot him, but he was all out of ammo. Diggy continued to tend to Stacy's wounds while pleading with him to hang on.

"CAM!" Gray cried for help.

Her mind couldn't calculate what was happening. She didn't know why she was being targeted until Cam said, "Gunz let her go."

This war was between them, not Gray. A guttural cry escaped her lips when she realized what was going on. The man she'd once loved, adored, gave ten years of her life and two kids to was about to kill her. How had she not seen how much of a monster he was sooner? Cam stood out in the open not giving a fuck if one of the masked men or women aimed their gun and shot him in cold blood. He'd gladly die if it would keep Gray safe. Hell, without her he had nothing to live for. The devious look in Gunz's eyes told him otherwise. Gray would not make it past that night. His intent was to kill. He wanted Cam to see how it felt to have everything he loved snatched away from him without warning. Never did he think he was going to get away with taking his girl, beating him, almost slitting his throat, burning down his businesses and property. With a devilish grin on his face, Gunz made Gray look over her shoulder at him. She didn't want to, but Gray did as she was told. Fear and hate were etched into the specks of her irises as she glared into his demonic eyes. The cold steel of the blade penetrated the skin of her neck, threatening to slice it all the way open. If she made any sudden movement her life would be over.

"Tell 'em goodbye." Gunz said lowly.

"No-no-no-no-no-no-no-no." Gray begged as she counted down the seconds till she saw black.

Was he really about to take her away from their kids? *POW!* Gray's entire body flinched. The gunshot reached everyone's ears before they realized his intent was never to slice Gray's throat but to use her as a distraction as he shot Diggy. Red fluid drained from the back of his head. Quan's heart sank as he watched his little brother lose control of his body and go limp. A second later, his lifeless body lay slumped over Stacy's blooded one. Gunz released Gray from his grasp and pushed her to the ground. He'd lost his best friend Bishop years ago. The lost turned him cold. Now Cam would know that feeling. Keeping his gun aimed, he walked backwards out the door. The other masked hitta's followed suit. The doors were unlocked as they ran to the awaiting get-a-way cars. Quan inched towards his brother's body as the sound of sirens neared. He was almost afraid to get near him. The closer he got, the realer the situation would become. Cam jogged up the steps. Emptiness filled his heart as he gazed at the carnage before him. Salty tears flowed from his eyes, numbing his brain. Sheer devastation engulfed him entirely causing his legs to buckle. Cam fell down to his knees. How could he still be breathing when there was no more life in him? This was worse than death and Gunz knew it. He'd left him alive to mourn the death of his two best friends. A dark void swept over Cam. A never-ending void consumed every crevice of his soul until he was left feeling nothing.

"When they killed my nigga Snoop, I seen my young nigga in the casket. He ain't even have no blood in him."- Meek Mill, "We Ball"

#20

Cam hated funerals. He made it his business not to attend them. He never knew how to act in the situation. There was no way to comfort someone who'd lost a loved one. If it wasn't for the love and respect he had for Quan and his family, he wouldn't have even come. Every pew of the church was filled for Diggy's home-going service. Donning all black, he and Gray made their way down the aisle to the front of the church. Funeral etiquette forced him to pay his respect to Ms. Nicky, Quan, Li'l Quan, Diggy's girl Tara and their kids DJ and Taylani. It was the last thing he wanted to do. Dealing with death and seeing the people he loved grieve was a slow death in itself. It was hard for him to face Ms. Nicky, knowing that it was his fault her youngest son was dead. No one else had blamed him. Cam blamed his self. Life since the shooting had slowed tremendously. It felt like he was living in cruise control. Every day was a blur. He still hadn't fully grasped what had happened that fateful night. Thirty-five people, including Diggy were killed. Fifty-eight were severely wounded, including Stacy. It was touch and go at first. He'd died on the table and was brought back to life using resuscitation. After major surgery, he was placed in ICU. Because he was shot in the stomach, he'd have to use a colostomy bag for six months until his intestines healed. Doctors and nurses were watching him around the clock.

Sorrow tore through Cam's insides as he hugged Ms. Nicky, Quan and Tara. Grief rushed through Quan with each expelled breath. He'd lost a piece of himself with the death of his brother. A feeling of emptiness took over his soul, threatening to kill him completely. A heavy feeling of nothing rested on his shoulders each day he waked and there was nothing he could do to get over it. A permanent hole was in his heart. Nothing or no one would be able to fill it. Tara sat next to him holding onto her kids for dear life. A waterfall of tears made her foundation look like a watercolor painting. She and Diggy had just hit their groove. He'd applied for school, was staying home more and she'd learned from Quan that he'd even been looking at rings. They were finally about to get their happily ever after but now she was forced to sit through her worst nightmare.

Cam tried to figure out the right words to say to ease their pain, but nothing came to mind. It should've been him lying in the coffin, not Diggy. Diggy was the last person on earth that deserved to die. He was a good person. He was a great father. He didn't bother anyone. He was trying to change his life. He had so much to live for. It was truly messed up that the new baby he had on the way would never know her father.

By the time they made it to the burial, Cam was over it. He was mentally and physically drained. The church service had gone on forever. Everybody and they mama had a story to share or a song to sing. Cam couldn't bear to hear another funny, poignant memory or gospel hymn. His heart was under enough stress. He was sure Quan felt the same, if not worse. Cam felt horrible for his friend, no his brother. Quan was his brother. Only thing that separated them was blood. It didn't feel good seeing him in so much pain. This was the first major loss he'd had. Quan would feel this for years—hell, probably decades. There was nothing like losing a close family member. Cam knew all too well.

Gray tried her best to comfort him as they all said their final goodbyes, but it was of no use. Cam was inconsolable. Steady tears poured quietly down his stoic face. His insides felt like jelly. To know that this would be the last time he saw Diggy brought on a new onslaught of tears. His eyes never once left the casket. Fresh flowers rested on top as his lifeless body was slowly lowered into the ground. Ms. Nicky and Tara's wails of despair could be heard from miles away. They both cried as if their brains were being gutted from the inside out. Ms. Nicky sobbed as if the ferociousness of her cries might bring Diggy back from the dead. Her baby boy was gone, and no prayer, wish or hope was going to return him to her. She'd never get to see his warm smile or the bright gleam in his eyes again.

Cam would remember the sound of her cries for the rest of his days. No parent expected to bury their child. It was supposed to be the other way around. She was so distraught that she tried to jump in the plot with him. Quan and Cam tried to hold her back and calm her down, but nothing worked. The thick, heavy tears they both harbored weakened them to the core. Gray stood back not knowing what to do. She too was in a fog. She still hadn't fully grasped that Gunz had put a knife to her throat and killed Diggy in cold blood. Gray no longer felt safe anywhere. Things had gotten way out of hand. Since August, her life had been a whirlwind of drama. If one more thing happened, she was sure to snap.

———

Instead of staying at the wake, Cam and Quan decided to visit Stacy in the hospital. Neither one of them wanted to stick around. They both needed fresh air and Stacy's daughter was dying to see her daddy. Gray didn't want Cam to leave but he had to. If he didn't, he was sure to drink his self into an oblivion. For her, he'd tried laying off the booze. Diggy's murder had him wanting to take a bottle of Henny to the head every hour. Cam honestly would never be right. Even avenging his death wouldn't make him feel better, but if it was the last thing he did, he was going to destroy Gunz Marciano.

"Big Stace! You up nigga?" Cam said strolling into his room.

"What's up ya'll?" He opened his eyes and used the remote to lift up his bed.

Quan was happy to see his pot'nah improving but he would give anything to be walking into his brother's room instead. The irritating sound of the IV pole with a digital monitoring system echoed throughout the space. A few of Stacy's personal belongings like his phone, tablet and sleepwear rested on a table by the bed. There wasn't anything special about the room. Like most hospital rooms there was a window, cold tiled floor, mechanical stiff bed, phone and a call button. About five different tubes were hooked up to Stacy's body. A breathing machine aided with his oxygen. Quan had never seen the big guy look so frail. He'd lost at least ten pounds since his surgery.

"Daddy!" Kyla, Stacy's 8-year-old daughter leaped from Cam's arms.

Everyone who came in contact with her instantly fell in love. She was the cutest little girl anyone had ever seen. She was a cute girl version of her dad. Kyla was Stacy's everything. He was a single father who took raising his daughter very seriously.

"I miss you." She hopped up and down enthusiastically.

"I miss you too, baby girl." He said weakly.

"When you coming home?"

"Soon. Daddy gotta heal up first. You been being good for grandma?"

"Yeah, she won't let me watch nothin' but the Word channel. She said the Disney channel is a sin. What Timon & Pumbaa do?"

"Nothin' baby girl. I'll talk to her." He chuckled. "You cool?" He surveyed Quan.

His boy was out here bad. Anger and sadness resonated from his pores.

"Nah." He shook his head somberly. "I ain't gon' be cool till that nigga 6F and that's my word."

"I feel you."

Knock, Knock

Everyone's eyes focused on the door. Selicia awkwardly smiled and entered the room. Although she and Stacy fought like cats and dogs, she wouldn't wish what happened to him on her worst enemy. The shootout was horrendous and put everything into perspective. Life was too short. One day you could be here and the next day you could be gone. She was thankful to god that Stacy had pulled through. The least she could do was check on him. A glimmer of happiness shone in Stacy's eyes as she came near. Selicia was a beautiful woman. The black fitted, knee-length dress she wore only enhanced her sex appeal. Stacy didn't know what was happening between them. Selicia ran hot and cold. Her coming to see him was a genuine shock to his system. He hadn't expected her to visit.

"Hey everybody." She waved.

"What's up, Selicia?" Cam and Quan spoke up.

"What's up, boo? You was worried about me?" Stacy licked his lips.

"Even shot the fuck up you can't help but be ignorant." She laughed.

"A couple of war wounds ain't gon' change a nigga."

"I see." She put down the vase of flowers she'd purchased for him.

"Daddy, who is that?" Kyla eyed Selicia with wonder.

She wasn't used to women coming around her daddy. Stacy made it his business to keep the women he fucked wit' away from his daughter.

"Daddy?" Selicia turned up her face. "Who in the hell was crazy enough to procreate with you?"

"Kyla, meet your new mama Selicia." He ignored her sarcasm and dished out a batch of his own.

"Baby, ignore yo' daddy. He high off painkillers. I am not your new mama."

"Not yet."

"But it is a pleasure to meet you." Selicia smiled, extending her hand.

Kyla happily gave it a shake.

"Who you been fuckin'? You lookin' thick as fuck." Stacy used what little strength he had and smacked her butt.

"I knew I should've stayed at the repast and minded my damn business, but nah everybody was tellin' me to come see you. Against my better judgement, I said let me be nice for once and take this man a plate. I knew I should've listened to my first mind."

"Quit frontin'. You know you wanted to see me."

"Sure, I did." She quipped, knowing damn well she really did.

"Thanks for the flowers. What else you bring me?" He eyed the bag in her hand.

"These fire ass ribs Cam's auntie made."

"Thanks boo. I knew you loved me."

"Keep it up. I'ma pull one of these tubes out."

Cam laughed at their silliness. It was the first time he'd found anything funny in days. The war between him and Gunz was just getting started. Then it dawned on him. Maybe the spiritualist was correct. Dark days were ahead.

"My mama used to pray that she'd see me in Yale. It's fucked up she gotta see me in jail."- Meek Mill, "Trauma"

#21

The aroma of creamy garlic butter chicken and potatoes wafted through the house, making everyone's stomach growl as Gray cooked Sunday dinner. She hadn't even been back in town five hours and she was already slaving over a hot stove. All she wanted to do is take a long, hot bath and pass out but she couldn't. Making sure her family had a home-cooked meal came first. It was the least she could. They hadn't seen her in days. The press tour for the 'Girl Boss' campaign had her flying all over the world doing interviews. The media and customers loved the collection. It sold out in under an hour. Gray couldn't believe her fortune. She'd gone from feeling like a failure to being back on top. Who knew she'd be back in the public eye for modeling? She couldn't believe the curveball life had thrown her. It was very unexpected but greatly appreciated. Because of the success of the collection, other brands like Christian Sirano, Boo Hoo, ASOS and Pretty Little Things were now eyeing her.

Pausing for a second, she stopped and yawned. Her king-size bed was calling her name. The garlic butter chicken and potatoes had thirty more minutes to go in the oven. By the time it was done the sautéed asparagus would be finished. Gray grabbed the olive oil and poured a tablespoon full into the skillet. Once the pan was hot she'd add garlic, red pepper flakes and a little salt along with the asparagus. As she patted the asparagus dry, she swore she heard the sound of Press and Cam singing. Leaving the kitchen, she creeped into the living room and found the two of them dancing to a song from Press' favorite movie The Greatest Showman. There wasn't a day that went by where she didn't watch it. Other kids her age loved Moana or

Frozen but Press loved a movie based off the story of P.T. Barnum's creation of the Barnum & Bailey Circus.

Gray and Cam had been forced to watch it with her no less than twenty times. Cam acted like he hated watching the musical starring Hugh Jackman, Zac Efron and Zendaya but judging by the way he twirled Press around the living room that was a lie. He was just as into it as she was. Dressed in a king crown and royal cape, he sang just as loud as the character Jenny Lind and Press. Press wore her princess costume as she and Cam sang *Never Enough* to the top of their lungs. Cam knew every word as if he wrote them. Gray had to capture the moment. Running back to the kitchen, she grabbed her phone and turned on the camera. No one would ever believe that Killa Cam was singing a fucking showtune.

> *All the shine of a thousand spotlights*
> *All the stars we steal from the night sky*
> *Will never be enough*
> *Never be enough*
> *Towers of gold are still too little*
> *These hands could hold the world but it'll*
> *Never be enough*

Gray couldn't believe her eyes. Press really had Cam ballroom dancing around the living room. He barely liked to two-step in the club. The most you could get out of him was a head bob and a shoulder lean. Covering her mouth, she tried to stifle a laugh but failed tremendously. Laughter erupted from her belly and floated across the room and into Cam's ears. Immediately, he halted dancing and looked over at her then focused on the camera.

"I'ma beat yo' ass! You bet not be recording me!" He rushed over in her direction.

Gray wasted no time taking off running. It took no time for Cam to catch up to her. Using his longs arms, he scooped her up into the air bridal style.

"Delete it." He tickled her stomach.

"No! It's too good!"

"Delete it or I swear to god yo' ass gon' wind up missing." Cam tickled her some more.

"Okay—okay I won't post it but I'm not deleting it." Gray pushed his hand away.

Her stomach was starting to cramp from so much laughter.

"Quan, Diggy and Stacy gon' die when they see this." She dissolved into a puddle of laughter then quickly realized the error of her words.

Gray immediately stopped laughing. Cam did too. Life for both of them was just starting to get back on track. It was moments like this that reminded him of the pain he was trying to ignore.

"My bad. I'm sorry, Cam." She apologized, feeling like shit.

"It's cool. I don't give a fuck. Show 'em. Can't none of them beat my ass no way." He put her down and pretended like he hadn't taken a blow to the chest.

"You know I'm here if you need to talk." Gray assured.

"I know." Cam eyed her lovingly and placed a trail of kisses on her face.

He missed his wife. He found the bed they slept in cold and lonely without her. He didn't want to rain on her parade but her being a career girl again wasn't really vibin' right in his spirit, especially after Diggy's death. He needed his wife near to ensure she was safe and to keep him sane. He wasn't used to the women he dated being away from him for long periods of time. Cam was a selfish nigga. No one wanted to give away the thing that meant the most to them. Gray being out in the world alone made her more susceptible to meeting another men or better yet him cheating. He'd been doing a good job at being faithful. Other women attracted him, but instead of getting his dick wet with random bitches, he went home to his wife. The problem was lately he had no wife to go home to. Gray kept his head on straight. When she wasn't around, Cam was more than likely to give into his urges. Prayerfully, the surprise he had coming up for Valentine's Day would encourage her to stay home more.

"Thank you for holding a nigga down. I wouldn't have made it through this shit without you." He said sincerely.

"You're welcome and thank you for loving my girls the way you do. Well . . . Press," she grinned.

"That's my baby and I care about Aoki too." He replied as his phone rang.

He and Gray looked down at the screen. They had spoken Aoki up. It was her on the line. Both of their foreheads wrinkled. Aoki never called Cam.

"I got it. Finish cookin'. I'm hungry than a muthafucka." He pushed her back towards the stove.

Gray put the asparagus into the piping hot skillet and started to sauté it.

"Yeah." Cam answered the phone.

"May I speak to Cameron Partherns please?" A female asked.

"Who the fuck is this?"

Ho's he'd fucked with in the past didn't call him by his government name.

"My name is Duckie. I'm a manager at the Forever 21 in the Saint Louis Galleria mall. I'm calling because your daughter Aoki has been caught shoplifting. I need you to come down to the store and pick her up or I'll be forced to get the police involved. Cam closed his eyes and flared his nostrils. He could hear Aoki in the background crying hysterically while begging him not to tell her mom.

"I'll be there in a minute." He hung up.

"Is everything okay?" Gray turned away from the stove and faced him.

Cam should've told her the truth, but they'd been through enough recently. He didn't want to upset the peace they'd just started to get back.

"Yeah, she just ready to come home. I'm gettin' ready to go pick her up."

"And she called you and not me?" Gray said skeptically.

"Yeah, nigga. Is that a problem?"

"No. I'm actually very happy. It shows she's starting to accept you being around."

"I'll be back." Cam took off his crown and cape.

"Hurry. The food is almost done." Gray kissed his cheek.

~ 412 ~

"Papa, can I go?" Press asked as he picked up his keys.

"Not this time, Pretty Girl. I'll be right back." Cam gave her a forehead kiss.

"Aww man. I'ma call my boyfriend then." She skipped and picked up her phone.

"What I tell you? You ain't got no fuckin' boyfriend."

"King is my man." Press placed her hand on her imaginary hip.

"No, he ain't."

"Yes, he is."

"Okay, I'm beatin' you and King's ass."

"You ain't gon' touch him. That's gon' be my husband."

"That's my nephew. I can touch him if I want. No pedo."

"Bye, Papa." Press sassed, sitting down on the couch.

"We gon' finish this conversation when I get back." Cam walked out the door.

The usual twenty-minute ride to the Galleria only took him fifteen. He was livid. After picking Gray up from the airport, Aoki had begged to be dropped off at the mall with her friends. It was something Gray allowed her to do from time-to-time, so she said yes. Aoki had a reckless mouth, but for the most part, she was a good kid. Outside of the fight with the twins, she rarely got in trouble for anything major. Gray did have to stay on her about her mouth and piss poor attitude. Aoki was never happy. She walked around with a stank expression on her face most of the time. Cam chalked it up to her being a moody child. He'd been one too, but now that she'd been caught stealing, he realized there was something deeper going on. Getting off the escalator, Cam stepped into the extra girly store and prayed he didn't break out in hives. He could smell the polyester and cotton blend from the door. He wanted to kick Aoki's ass for stealing out of the cheap-ass store. He had given her a hundred dollars before she got out of the car. She didn't have a reason to shoplift.

"Excuse me, I'm lookin' for the manager." He asked one of the sales reps.

"She's right in the back. Just knock on the door." The girl pointed.

Cam nodded and made his way over to the partly closed door. Not bothering to knock, he walked into the office. Duckie looked up from her paperwork and found the most handsome man she'd ever seen standing in her doorway. Cam's tall, ripped physique took up half the room. His presence was hypnotizing. The tattoos covering his neck and hands made her nipples sprout like rosebuds in May. She was more than certain there were more under his jacket and shirt.

Cam noticed the cinnamon colored beauty salivating over him but paid her ass no attention. He was used to ho's being on his dick. Aoki sitting slumped down in her seat was what had his attention. The dried-up tears on her cheeks tugged at his heart. He didn't even know the li'l devil had it in her to cry. Like him, she masked her pain with anger and bravado.

"Really dawg?" He barked, making her jump.

"Umm . . . are you Cameron?" Duckie stood and held out her hand.

"Yeah but call Cam." He left her hand hanging.

"It's very nice to meet you, Cam. I wish it was under different circumstances." She dropped her hand down to her side.

"Yeah, me too. Bring yo' li'l thieving ass on." He scowled at Aoki. "What the fuck was you thinkin' stealin' outta Forever 21? This cheap ass shit. Everything in this muthafucka is $17. What were you tryin' to steal? I need to see what the hell was so important that you risked going to jail for."

"It was this." Duckie held up a $6.80 silver necklace with a heart and key hanging from it.

"You got to be fuckin' shittin' me." Cam glared at Aoki with contempt. "I ought to break yo' fuckin' neck. What type of dumb shit is this?" He snatched the necklace from Duckie. "That shit is ugly."

"Little girls her age are always trying to steal things out of here. I think she only did it to fit in with her friends 'cause I overheard them encouraging her to do it."

"Where they li'l raggedy asses at?" Cam looked around.

"They took off runnin' and left her?"

"Them dusty bitches left you?" He fumed, looking at Aoki.

"Yeah." She sniffled distraught.

"That's what yo' dumb-ass get. So, what's gon' happen now?" He turned his attention back to the manager.

"In order for us not to press charges, I'm gonna need you to sign this release form stating that she will never come into our store again. If she does, she will be handcuffed immediately."

"And if I don't?"

"Then we have no choice but to press charges." Duckie regrettably glanced over at Aoki.

"A'ight then lock her ass up. I'm about to go get me some FroYo." Cam turned to leave.

"Cam wait! No! You can't leave!" Aoki burst out into tears again.

"Nah man, I don't fuck wit' thieves. You need to go to jail."

"I won't ever do it again! I promise! They gon' get my booty if I go to jail!"

"You wasn't think about yo' li'l ass booty when you was stealin!"

"I know, I'm sorry! Please!" She sobbed uncontrollably.

"Shut yo' whining-ass up. I ain't gon' let you go to jail. Give me the fuckin' release form." He snatched the paper from Duckie's hand.

"We're gonna need to take a photo of her too so our security can know if she ever comes into the store again."

"Gone and take your li'l mugshot." Cam forced Aoki to stand up. "Yo' ass wanna be Tommie from Love and Hip Hop so bad. Fake-ass thug. You the dumbest criminal on the planet."

Aoki's lower lip quivered as Duckie snapped the picture. In all ten years she'd been on earth, she'd never felt so low. When her mother found out what she'd done, she was gonna be so disappointed. Aoki couldn't take Gray being upset with her.

"I'm so sorry this was how we had to meet, but if you need anything, feel free to call me." Duckie placed her card in the pocket of his jacket.

"I won't." Cam took Aoki's hand so they could leave.

"Don't be so sure. You never know."

———

Inside the car, Aoki placed on her seatbelt solemnly. The ass whoopin' she was going to get when she got home was going to sting for weeks. It was sad because she didn't even fear Gunz's wrath. Over a month had passed since she last saw him. Aoki missed her father desperately. It was weird not seeing him every day. The sound of Cam's phone buzzing in the cup holder almost caused her to jump out of her skin. It was her mother calling. Her life was officially over.

"What's up, babe?"

"Ya'll on the way back? The food is done."

"I just got in the car. We headed home now."

"How long will that take?"

"I'll be home before you can say I love you." Cam flirted, loving the sound of her sweet voice over the phone.

"Hurry yo' fine ass up then. We miss you."

"We?"

"Yeah me and Miss Kitty." Her cheeks burned red.

After the mishap in the kitchen, she needed to do something to lift her man's spirits. Sex always made Cam feel better.

"Aww yeah. That's how you feel? Tell her I'm on my way then."

"Bye boy." She giggled, hanging up.

Cam ended the call and placed the phone back in the cup holder.

"You gon' tell my mom?" Aoki spoke barley above a whisper.

"Why shouldn't I? You bold enough to steal then you bold enough to suffer the consequences." He leaned against the driver side door and ice-grilled her.

"You better be glad it was a black woman that caught you. You a little black girl. You think 'cause you got wavy hair and chinky eyes that these white folks won't string yo' ass up?"

Not having a reply, Aoki sat silent. She'd always lived a privileged life. She'd never been faced with the disadvantages of being black.

"Why did you do it?"

"I didn't really want to." She said meekly.

"Then why did you?"

"I don't know." She shrugged. "My friends kept tellin' me to take it, so I did."

"I thought you were smarter than that. I didn't know you was a follow the leader type muthafucka."

"I'm not!" Aoki yelled back, irritated.

"I can't fuckin' tell. You probably had more money in yo' pocket than all them baby bitches and you up here stealin'. Now I gotta watch my shit when I'm around you. I'm tellin' you now, my shit come up missin' I ain't askin' no questions. Yo' ass takin' one to the dome."

"I'm not a thief!" Aoki grimaced, ready to fight.

"Then what the fuck are you?! What the fuck is wrong wit' you?!"

"I'm sad, alright! I'm sad!" Her lips trembled as her shoulders heaved with emotion.

Cam wanted to look away. He hated when girls cried but he couldn't stop staring. Aoki was showing genuine emotion for once. She was hurting deeply, and everyone had failed to see that she was drowning. For months, she'd been screaming out for help, but no one was listening. Right there, in that time and space, Cam concluded that he and Aoki were more alike than he'd care to admit. She was a mirror image of him. If he didn't know any better, he would've sworn she was his biological daughter.

"What you sad about?" He blew hot air into his hands and turned on the heat.

From the looks of things, they would be sitting there a while. Aoki swallowed hard. Talking to Cam was the last thing she wanted to do. He irritated her soul, but Aoki was tired of hiding the truth. She needed to tell someone her secret before something worse than stealing happened.

"I know about my dad."

"Know what?" Cam said perplexed.

The only thing that came to mind was that she'd found out that he'd killed Diggy.

"I know that he's not my real dad," Aoki finally confessed.

Cam's eyes grew wide as he sat shell shocked. That was the last thing he'd expected her to say.

"How you find out?" He asked after a moment of silence.

"I googled my mom's name and came across a newspaper article from when my real father tried to kill her."

"Damn." Cam let out a heavy sigh.

"Is that why my daddy hasn't been coming around?"

"What you mean?

"Now that you're here, he doesn't have to pretend to be my daddy anymore." Aoki's voice croaked.

Cam wasn't a soft man, by any means necessary, but these girls were turning him into one big giant pussy. He'd cried more in the last three months than he had his whole life. This time he refused to let his feelings get the best of him. He'd cried enough at the funeral. He'd just punch the next person that looked at him funny or shoot a squirrel.

"I don't fuck wit' your Pop at all but I can say that he loves you." Cam lied.

Any father that could go weeks without seeing or speaking to his kids couldn't possibly love their children. Gunz was a fuckin' pussy.

"He's just working a lot."

"I'm not a little kid. Don't lie to me." Aoki narrowed her eyes at him.

"Who you bossin' up on?"

"You. You know damn well he ain't workin'. You burned down all his restaurants."

"How you know that?"

"I got my ear to the streets."

Cam couldn't help but chuckle.

"This li'l girl too grown for me." He spoke underneath his breath.

"You need to have your eyes on them school books. Fuck what the streets talkin' about."

"I see you ain't denyin' it." Aoki folded her arms across her chest just like her mother.

"You ain't gotta deny something you know you ain't do. Now check it. It's fucked up you had to find out about your paternity the way you did. From what your mom told me, she wanted to wait until she felt you were old enough to tell you."

"So is it true that my real father raped her and that's how she had me."

Cam ran his hand down his face. This was not a conversation he wanted to have with someone else's child. He felt out of place.

"I think you should talk to your mom about that."

"No!" Aoki freaked out. "I'm not ready for her to know that I know."

"You're gonna have to talk to her about it eventually."

"Just not yet, okay?" She pleaded.

"I don't know. I can't keep this from your mom."

"Please! You can't tell her I know or about me stealing. I'm dead if she finds out."

"You askin' a lot shorty."

"I know. I swear I'll tell her everything myself. Just give me some time."

Telling her no was the right thing to do. Cam needed to go home and tell his wife everything that had gone down but they'd just started the healing process of getting over Diggy's murder. They didn't need any more turmoil in their home. Plus, the desperate look in Aoki's slanted blue eyes wasn't helping. It made him go against his better judgement. After months, they were finally making progress. He didn't want to betray her trust. If he did, they'd go back to being mortal enemies. Like Gray, he wanted nothing more than for all of them to be one big happy family. Having Aoki on the outskirts didn't feel right.

"A'ight look, I'ma let you tell her but yo' ass is on punishment. Ain't gon' be no watching TV and that phone is mine." He held out his hand.

Aoki gave it to him without putting up a fight. She understood that she deserved her punishment. It would be far worse if her mom found out the truth.

"And I bet not catch you playin' the game."

"You won't. I swear. I'm gon' be on my best behavior." She swore.

"Yo' ass better be or I'm snitchin' the first chance I get." He started up the engine.

Aoki sat back in her seat, feeling like a weight had been lifted off her tiny shoulders. Cam had really come through for her. They weren't bff's but she had a new-found respect for him that she didn't have before. Maybe he wasn't so bad after all. Maybe with time, she could be close to him too.

"Thanks Cam."

"You welcome but don't be doing no more dumb shit. If something's on your mind, come talk to me, a'ight?"

"A'ight." Her heart smiled on the inside.

"All a nigga know is how to fuck a good thing up.
Run from the pain, sip lean, smoke tree up. "- J.
Cole, "Kevin's Heart"

#22

"You sure I can't change your mind?" Cam took Gray's hand in his.

They both were headed to the airport but going in different directions. She was going to New York for Fashion Week and he was heading to Los Angeles for All-Star Weekend.

"Cam, we've talked about this." Gray pulled her hand away, annoyed.

They'd gone over this a million times before they even left the house. He knew she couldn't come along with him. The fact that he kept on trying to persuade her was irritating as hell. Cam acted like she was supposed to be at his beck and call 24 hours of the day. There was more to her than being his wife, a mother, cook, maid and somebody for him to fuck on. She'd been his superwoman since Diggy's death. Anything he asked of her, she did and more. She understood he was still hurt. She was too but life had to go on. They couldn't stay stuck in such a dark place. It wasn't healthy for either of them.

"I'm sayin' tho. You know what this weekend is and you still not gon' come?"

It was really fuckin' him up that she knew it was the anniversary of his mother's death, and instead of being by his side and making sure he was okay, she'd rather go to fuckin' Fashion Week. In Cam's mind that was some insensitive, selfish-ass shit. Gray had practically begged him to be transparent, and the moment he was, she acted like his feelings weren't shit. Every year when his mother's death day came around, he grew depressed. Memories of his past were edged to the forefront of his brain. All of the loss and regret he harbored toyed with his mind. His whole family took the time of year hard. Everybody emotionally shut down. The death of Diggy wasn't helping the situation. It added to his misery. Cam needed Gray more than ever. He was on edge and his temper was at an all-time high. There was no telling what he might do if he was tested.

"Cam, you know if I could go I would but I gotta work. I'm under contract. If I don't go, they can sue me. I can't afford to not show up, especially after the way the photoshoot ended. Selicia has set up a press junket with different bloggers and journalists about my transition from being editor-in-chief to a plus size model. People are saying I'm the next Ashley Graham. I'm this close to signing all four deals that were presented to me. I can't stop my momentum now."

"So, what you tellin' me is that shit is more important than what the fuck I got going on?" He quipped, pissed.

"See, now you puttin' words in my mouth but if that's how you feel." Gray let him draw his own conclusion.

She was trying her best not to fight with him. The driver they'd hired to escort them to the airport could hear everything.

"The fuck you mean if that's how I feel? Like I'm some bitch or some shit."

"First of all, did I say that?" She snapped her head in his direction. "Second of all, you gettin' bent out of shape over something I can't control. You actin' like I just said fuck you."

"That's exactly what you sayin'. My homeboy just died. My mama's death date is tomor and you can't come chill wit' me? It's already bad enough I've been home by myself lately. You don't think that's a problem?"

"No 'cause when I'm home alone it's fine. You could care less."

"You're my wife. Your supposed to have yo' ass at home. I'm a man. I can do whatever the fuck I want."

Gray held her stomach and bugged up laughing. Cam had officially lost his damn mind.

"You know what?" She chuckled. "Not today Satan. Everything was going good. I'm not about to argue wit' you. I refuse."

It took everything in Cam not to punch a hole through the window. Gray ignoring his feelings not only hurt but made him feel like she simply didn't care. She knew he wasn't the kind of man to out right say I need you. Him asking her over and over to come with him should've let her know there was a reason behind his request. And yeah, he should've just came out and told her what he was feeling. He should've said she'd hurt him by denying his feelings, but Cam wouldn't be Cam if he didn't do the complete opposite. He did what most people do when in pain, he lashed out.

"It's a lot of shit you ain't been doing." He shot.

"And what the fuck is that supposed to mean?"

"Just what the fuck I said. You ain't been taking care of home like you used to. You lettin' this fame and shit go to yo' head instead of focusing on your family."

"What the hell are you talkin' about?" Gray's heartrate spiked; she was so offended.

"You ain't been to none of Aoki cheerleading practices. Every time you leave Press be having nightmares and shit. And the one time I ask you to come make sure I'm good, you tell me nah. That's fucked up Gray and you know it. Especially after everything I've told you. But you the same muthafucka that wanna bitch and moan about the shit I don't do. Ain't that the pot callin' the kettle black." He huffed, sparkin' up a blunt.

Cam needed an herbal remedy to prevent himself from blacking out on Gray. He should've listened to his first mind when she was offered the modeling gig and said no. If he had, they wouldn't be having this fight.

Here they go again with the back-and-forth bullshit. From the day they met, Gray and Cam had been doing nothing but fighting. It was growing tiresome and Gray was sick of it. It took everything in her not to spazz out. Never in a million years did she think Cam would talk about her parenting. He'd always said how good of a mother she was. Now, in the blink of an eye, she was a shitty mama who neglected her kids and placed her husband on the back burner? Fuck that. She'd put a nigga first before in the past and in the present. She wasn't doing it anymore. If Gray hadn't learned anything it was to put her needs first. Men had been doing it since the beginning of time. She no longer gave a fuck about pleasing Cam or the driver overhearing their argument. Cam had her all the way fucked up.

"Okay, but what about me? I'm supposed to be there for everybody else and neglect myself? I waited on you hand and foot for four months! I lost my business. Do you know what that did to me? You have no idea how that shit feel! I finally found a career that makes me whole and now I'm a bad person? So basically, fuck what I want? Fuck my dreams, fuck my goals, fuck everything I want in my life! I'm just here to suck your dick, cook you meals and be Mary fuckin' Poppin's to my fuckin' kids!'" She waved her hand furiously.

"Everybody in this bitch can be happy and do what they want but Gray? Nigga, I'm college educated. I have a fuckin' master's degree! You think I'm supposed to sit on my ass all day? That ain't in the cards for me. I ain't depending on no nigga to take care of me. You want a bitch that sell Flat Tummy Tea and waist trainers aka LaLa. I'm not that girl, so if that's what you lookin' for, I don't know what to tell you. Right idea, wrong bitch." She grabbed her purse and slammed it down onto her lap.

They were only minutes from the airport. As soon as they pulled up to the curb, she was hoppin' out. Cam could kiss her ass with his chauvinistic attitude. She understood that his friend had just died but that didn't give him any right to be asshole. Flicking his nose, Cam massaged his beard then sucked his teeth. Gray claimed not to want to fight, but with the shit she'd spewed, it was apparent she wanted war.

"Muthafuckas got master's degrees but posing nude in thongs and advertising twenty-dollar jumpsuits." He inhaled the smoke deep into his lungs and slowly exhaled it out. "Fuck outta here. You need to get yo' tuition back."

"I can pose nude or in a jumpsuit. At least I'm making money legally and I ain't killin' the black community in the process. How you gon' protect your country and destroy it at the same time?" She shot.

An eerie silence filled the SUV. Gray practically could hear the thump in her chest from her heartbeat. She'd gone too far. If she could, she'd run but fuck that. He'd come for her throat and she'd slit his.

"You wasn't complaining about my drug money when it paid your mortgage, bought you cars, the jewels around your neck and the shit you packed in that Louis luggage. Matter of fact, the more I think about it, you ain't been complaining in years. Wasn't it illegal money that started up that wack-ass magazine company you couldn't even keep afloat?"

Words left Gray. She desperately searched Cam's eyes to see if he meant what he'd said. She prayed to god he didn't. Glaring at one another, they both wondered how they'd ended up here. Neither one of them ever expected this argument to go the way it had. So much foul shit had been said that would leave stains on their souls. No amount of I'm sorry's would erase the damage that had been done. That was fine. After Gray got her shit off her chest, she was done.

"This ain't got nothin' to do with my magazine." She unzipped her purse. "This is about you actin' like a fuckin' child every time you can't get your way. At the end of the day, you need to learn how to cope with your feelings without depending on a bitch to take care of you." She pulled out her Miu Miu shades. "I'm not LaLa and I have no intentions on being her. I am your wife, not your babysitter or your therapist either. I have my own shit to worry about. I don't have time to hold your fuckin' hand all day. It's not my job to make you feel like a man. I can't make you be something you're not. And let's be real. You can't be that fuckin' sad over your mother and Diggy when you takin' yo' ass to All -Star Weekend so you can stunt for a bunch of niggas that don't give a fuck about you."

Gray zipped her bag back up as they arrived at the drop-off area at the airport. The driver placed the car in park and unlocked her door.

"So, I'ma tell you like this." She looked him up and down. "You go down there and deal with whatever fake feelings you wanna pretend like you have and I'ma go to New York and do me." She placed the shades over her eyes and gave the driver her hand.

"Have a safe flight."

———

Six-time NBA all-star James Harden's party at Poppy in West Hollywood was lit as fuck. The Who's Who of the industry was there. Lebron and Savannah, Kyrie Irving, Mary J. Blige, Jessica Alba, Leonardo DiCaprio, The Game and more were in attendance. Poppy wasn't your typical nightclub. It had a bohemian vibe to it. Gorgeous chandeliers hung from the ceiling. Velvet couches and leather chairs were used to sit. Behind the DJ booth was a bookshelf filled with books and knick knacks. Abstract art lined the wood panel walls. The place was flooded with bottles being passed around. Cam, Priest and Quan stood posted with Wiz Khalifa, Post Malone, Cardi B and a few of the Kardashians. Stacy wanted to come but he was still at home recuperating. It would be a minute before he could kick it again.

Pretty girls with stick-figure bodies like models tried to capture Cam's attention from the dance floor down below. The amber glow from the lights kissed his golden hue. Residential smoke from the trees being burned hung in the air like ghost. Weed smoke flowed down Cam's throat. His lips formed the letter O as he exhaled and created rings which lingered in the air. Usually, weed and liquor was his poison of choice. That night he needed something much stronger to ease the tension in his chest. The cup of lean got him lifted. The potent drink was like Novocain for his brain. He needed something to take away the remains of

Gray's name. If only he could have amnesia for the day. For Cam was the newest member of the broken hearts club.

Everyone else was kickin' it, having a ball but he hadn't really said a word at all. He was too far in his head to speak. His fight with Gray was stuck in his head on repeat. He didn't want to take it there with her, but she'd pushed him too far. He couldn't let her continue to test his manhood and get away with it. Gray had gotten beside herself. He'd let her get her shit off at the strip club but enough was enough. The woman he'd married would've never left him to the wolves. She would've been right by his side but no. There he stood alone, hoping that the answers to his problem lie at the bottom of the Styrofoam cup. The more he sipped the longer the night went on and the more faded he became. Few words were exchanged between him and his homeboys. The words that were spoken were few and far between. Everybody was in a funk. Partying just wasn't the same without Stacy and Diggy there.

Visions of mother's sweet beautiful smile from the last day he saw her face flashed before his eyes. Questions of whether or not Gray made it to safely New York danced in his head. They hadn't spoken since she departed the car the day before. Cam thought about calling to check up on her, but instead, he took another sip from his cup. The devil was in him and Cam was willing to let him in. He was two sheets from the wind and didn't give a damn about anything. Gray told him to do him so that was exactly what he was going to do. He'd tried being the good guy. He'd done everything she asked of him and where had it gotten him? Nowhere. Gray was a big huge model now. That was what she was focused on. Cam had obviously become an afterthought. She hadn't even bothered to call. What more evidence did he need? They hadn't even been having sex like they used to. She was always too tired or too busy.

They weren't even a year in, and shit was already going downhill. It was like their sex life declined and the arguing increased. Cam felt lost. He didn't even know if Gray still looked at him the same way she used to or if she still held him in the same light. She used to adore him and hang onto his every word.

Then the mesmerizing scent of her Dior JOY perfume knocked him back to the present. Cam searched the area for her. She was near. She had come to him. The anticipation of seeing her angelic face soared through his body. It tingled through him like electrical sparks. Cam felt her hand on his shoulder before he saw her face. Turning around, a sly grin graced the corner of his lips then formed into a scowl when he realized it wasn't his wife. LaLa stood before him in all her hood rich attire. She wasn't alone. Her raggedy friends Alexzandria and Lynn were right behind her. All three of them wore Dior down to the socks. Cam hadn't seen her since he bust all her windows after New Year's Day. He would've preferred to keep it that way. LaLa looked deep into his eyes. They were blood shot red and glossed over. Cam could barely keep his eyes open he was so high.

"You okay?" She asked genuinely concerned.

She'd reached out to him a few times after Diggy's funeral, but he hadn't responded. That quickly, Cam went from loathing the sight of LaLa to being thankful for seeing a familiar face. Those two words changed everything.

"I'm straight."

"You don't have to lie to me. I know you're not." She caressed the side of his face.

"I should'a known ya'll stank asses was gon' be here." Quan smacked her hand down.

"You know damn well they ain't gon' pass up a chance to get pregnant by a ball player." Cam added.

"Fuck you and fuck you too." LaLa hit them both with the middle finger.

"Hiiiii Priest." Alexzandria slid next to him.

"Back yo' big head ass up." He gripped her weave and pushed her back to where she came from.

"Oww nigga. That hurt." She massaged the back of her head.

"I know today is hard for you. You ain't gotta down play your feelings. We've been down this road before." LaLa kept her focus on Cam.

He would never tell her, but she was right. When things were good between them, she was always a shoulder for him to lean on during troubled times. Every year on his mother's death day, she went the extra mile to make sure he was good. Whether it be buying him a pound of Kush, sexing him into a coma or laying by his side and being quiet. The main thing was she cared, and she showed it with her actions. It was way more than what Gray had done.

"What you drinkin'?" She sniffed his cup.

"Some shit that'll put you on yo' back." He took another swallow.

"Let me be the judge of that." She took the cup from his tattooed hand.

Cam didn't even bother to stop her. He was too far gone to care. He missed his friend and he missed his wife. Wrapping her freshly manicured hand around the cup, LaLa raised the cup to her pink painted lips while never breaking eye contact with Cam. The cool drink made her recoil like a little girl. Yet she enjoyed the way it made her feel. Cam eyed her mouth. Her lips curled around the rim of the cup, leaving traces of her lipstick. She used to leave the same print when she sucked his dick.

"You playin' with fire." Quan said loud enough for only him to hear.

"I ain't even did shit."

"Yet."

Cam shot him a look of annoyance and replied, "I'm about to take a piss."

Holding up the front of his jeans by the buckle of his belt, he drunkenly made his way to the restroom.

"Watch my purse. I'll be back." LaLa sat the cup down.

"Where yo' ho ass think you going?" Quan aggressively seized her wrist.

"To pee. Do you mind?" She pulled her arm away.

"Actually, I do."

"Well, frankly, I don't give a damn." She switched through the club.

Quan knew she was full of shit. She wasn't going to pee. She was going to find Cam. And Quan was right. LaLa did just that. She followed him into the men's restroom and entered his stall. She didn't even bother locking the main door. Any of the other men inside could hear. She didn't care. Nothing was going to deter her from getting what she wanted. Even after he'd disrespected her, cussed her out, called her out of her name, fucked all her friends, destroyed her shop and car she still wanted him. She'd always want him. Before Cam could close and lock the door, she slipped inside the stall with him.

"What you doing?"

"Shhhhhhh. Let me make it all better." She tried to kiss his lips, but Cam dodged her attempt.

"C'mon, Cam. You know you want this." She pressed her breasts against his chest and unzipped his jeans.

Cam's steel rod was at full attention. It had been hard since he saw her. Visualizing that she was Gray, he aggressively reached under her skirt and ripped off her thong. If LaLa thought this was going to be some passion filled sexual encounter, she thought wrong. There would be no pleasantries, kisses or words spoken. This would be nothing but a cold, hard, fuck. Lusting for the dick, she leaped into his muscular arms and slid down his thick pole. The first stroke of his cock put an arch in her spine. She'd forgotten how good he felt inside of her. Cam's dick filled her up. She could hardly breathe. His teeth nipped at her neck as he pumped feverishly. Palming her ass, he drilled into her pussy. LaLa's moans of mercy echoed throughout the restroom. She could feel him in her stomach. Closing her eyes, she surrendered to his carnal pounding. Cam had never fucked her this savagely before. He fucked her like he hated her. And Cam did. She wasn't Gray. It was her who he should've been fucking but she wasn't there. She was off in New York doing her. The thought pissed him off even more, so he picked up the pace. Cam was fucking LaLa so hard that her breathing had stopped. Eye-to-eye, they used each other for their sexual needs. Slapping her ass, he drove his cock in and out.

"Ooooh yes fuck me." LaLa begged, savoring each stroke.

Who knew when she'd get a sample again. Cam's dick was drowning in her pussy. Juices rained down on his dick. On the verge of cumming, he pulled out.

"What you doing?" LaLa panted.

"Swallow the evidence." He ran his hand up and down his throbbing cock.

Without hesitation, she got on the dirty restroom floor and took him in her mouth. Cam watched hungrily as she sucked his dick like a girl with daddy issues. LaLa pulled out all her old tricks. She sucked, slurped and gagged until Cam spilled his seeds down her throat. Like a horny little slut, she swallowed every drop until his dick went soft in her mouth. Cam leaned his head back and gathered his emotions before fixing himself and walking out.

"Where you going?" She rose to her feet.

Cam looked in the mirror at his self. What he saw he didn't like. The man staring back at him was a cheater. Unwilling to face the reality of what he'd done, he quickly washed his hands and left LaLa behind with no explanation. Stumbling out of the restroom, he ran into the last person he wanted to see. Quan stood there eyeing him with disdain like he was the moral police. Disappointed in his behavior, he shook his head. It didn't take a rocket scientist to know he'd fucked LaLa. The look of guilt was written all over Cam's face.

"Fuck you shakin' yo head at me for? You supposed to be my Pop now or somethin'?"

"If I was ya' father, you wouldn't be actin' like this."

"Man watch out." Cam tried to step around him, but Quan blocked his path.

"Nah, nigga. You think can't nobody say nothin' to you about the dumb shit you be doing but you gon' hear me." Quan pushed him back by the restroom's door. "What the fuck were you thinkin'? Why you go and fuck that girl?"

"Cause I wanted to. You see my wife anywhere around here? No. I asked her to come be wit' me and you know what she said? No. She would rather be in New York watching bulimic bitches strut down a runway than be with her husband so fuck her! It ain't always just me that's fuckin' up. Gray be fuckin' up too."

"So, since she told your overgrown ass no for the first time you go and fuck the spawn of Satan? What kind of logical sense does that make? Like make this make sense for me bro."

"It ain't gotta make sense. It's what the fuck I felt like doing. She wanna do her so I'ma do me." Cam barked indignantly.

"You know what, dawg? You a fuckin' lost cause." Quan said ashamed to be his friend.
"You got one more fuckin' shipment and you're out! I done locked down the convenient store off Jefferson and everything! We ready to go! March 12th my nigga and that's it! You get to wipe your hands clean of all this shit! I thought the goal was to put all this cartel shit and the ho's to the side and be a family man or has all that changed cause you mad?"

"You talkin' all that shit but you ain't talkin' about her not being here! She knew I needed her, and she still said fuck me!" Spit flew out of Cam's mouth.

Quan wiped the spittle from his face. If Cam wasn't a drunken mess, and his best friend, he would've took off on his ass, but he didn't. He'd been Cam before so he knew how his story would end. Alone.

"Yo' you selfish as fuck. Everything is about you. My li'l brother just died. You think I wanna be standing here having this conversation wit' you? You a grown ass man. Act like it." He gripped Cam by the collar of his shirt and shook him.

"Listen, this my last time tellin' you this. Get your shit together. You ain't gon' find another woman like Gray. That girl has endured more pain birthing you than she has her own kids. She has sacrificed the last six months uncovering the painful areas of your manhood and covering the areas that could have exposed you. She deserves everything you can give her. You understand what I'm saying? Instead of fuckin' bitches in the bathroom, you should be figuring out ways to honor her. You got a good woman dawg. She gave you what you couldn't give yourself, which is a chance to heal while still seeing the god in you."

Because he was a cocky, ego driven muthafucka, Cam would never admit that Quan's words had gotten to him. They were like kicks to the stomach with a steel-toe boot. What he'd done with LaLa was downright awful. There was no way to justify it. He'd betrayed his wife for a few minutes of pleasure. The guilt sat on his chest and inside his head. It was like gasoline to his guts.

"You saw what I went through wit' your sister. You know how fucked up I was when I saw her wit' Boss and the twins for the first time? I was sick. I could barely get my ass outta bed. I felt like a bitch. That shit had me laid up in the fetal position, straight up. That was supposed to be us, but because of my dumb-ass decisions, I ruined anything we could ever be. Keep it up and you gon' end up just like me. I'm tellin' you, ain't nothin' worse than seeing the woman you love, love somebody else."

"You done, TD Jakes?" Cam shot sarcastically.

He was over the lecture. He didn't want to be reminded of the sin he'd committed. The realization of his dirty deed was already weighing heavily on his conscious.

"Whatever dickhead. I got my own shit to worry about." Quan gave him one more look of disapproval and walked back to their section.

Once the coast was clear, LaLa came out of the restroom and took Cam by the arm before he could get away.

"You wanna come back to my room and finish?" She ran her hand up his firm bicep.

"Nah, I'll get up wit' you later." He left her there without saying another word.

"But Cam, wait! I ain't even cum yet!" She yelled after him.

Cam kept going. He had to get out of there. Life was a blur as he made his way back to the hotel via Uber. He didn't even bother to tell his friends that he was leaving. He had to get the stench of LaLa off of him. Like a whore, he felt dirty. Maybe after a steaming hot shower and a goodnight's sleep he'd feel better. Maybe he'd wake up and realize that the last two days had been nothing but a bad dream. Staggering to stand up straight, he tried using his hotel key. Everything around him was spinning in a circle. He was dizzy as fuck. It took him several tries before the key worked. For a second, he thought he was going to have to sleep in the hallway. Drunk as a skunk, he haphazardly stumbled into his suite and found Gray laying on her side sound asleep. Like in the comic book when Thanos snapped his finger and bodies disintegrated into dust, any cold syrup or weed in his system was soaked up by panic. Fright consumed every cell in his body. Cam pressed his back against the wall and slid to the floor. Fear of the end of his marriage covered him like a pillow over his mouth and nose. He was suffocating. He hadn't felt this helpless since he lost Diggy. Cam needed help but there was no way out of this mess. He'd have to lay in it and wait till the guilt consumed him or his deceit was revealed. Just when he thought Gray had given up on him, just when he thought she didn't care anymore, she went above and beyond to prove her love. A million thoughts ran through his mind as he gazed at her sleeping face. Like how beautiful she looked. How long had she been there? What if he would've went back to LaLa's room? What would happen if she smelled her scent on him? There were too many variables and all of them led to his demise. He'd known it before but now it was crystal clear. He didn't deserve Gray. He wasn't mature enough to handle her love. The first time she scratched his heart, he betrayed her trust.

"Baby." Her eyes fluttered open.

"Yeah, Star . . . I'm here." He got up and sat on the edge of the bed. "You came." He ran his fingers through her silky curls.

Gray's hair was sprawled over his pillow just how he liked it.

"It's you and me forever, remember?" She kissed the outside of his hand then held it close to her heart.

Silent tears begged to grace his cheeks. Cam could barely see. The sight of her face was starting to blur.

"I tried waiting up for you."

After attending two shows, Gray booked the first flight to L.A. It wasn't sitting right in her spirit being that far away from Cam and them not getting along. She'd vowed to be there for her husband through good and bad. What kind of wife would she be if she didn't show up in his time of need? She didn't want to repeat the mistakes she'd made with Gunz. Hearing Cam say the same thing Gunz had said about her putting her job before her family tore her up on the inside. If she was going to grow as a woman, and as a mate, she had to take the necessary steps to change.

"You know I love you right?"

Gray sat up straight and scooted back like a chick in a horror film.

"What did you just say?" Her heartrate increased.

Internally, Cam knew it was the wrong time to say I love you. He'd just fucked LaLa in a bathroom stall but seeing Gray there laying in his bed put everything in perspective. Quan was right. He would never find a woman better than Gray. She was an angel sent from heaven. He had never known what love looked like until he saw her laying in his bed. She was perfectly imperfect. Every time he looked at her he became lost in her beauty. Any mistakes he'd ever made disappeared. All negative energy was rinsed away. Her ocean blue eyes saw right through him. Gray saw him for exactly who he was, but she didn't focus on his selfishness, rage nor that he was self-centered. She looked past each flaw and saw him for the man he was inside. Just like her, he was perfectly imperfect too.

"I love you. You're an incredible mother and an incredible wife. I was just in my feelings. I had no right to put my bullshit off on you. You're the best thing that has ever happened to me. I love you, Gray for real."

~ 442 ~

Gray leaped into his arms. All the invisible wounds he'd punctured during their fight were sealed with love. The black cloud that had been hovering over her head was replaced with sunny skies. She always knew Cam loved her. He showed her every day with his actions. To hear him finally say it took their relationship to a whole new level. Now they were invincible. They could survive anything together.

"I got plans to cut you off. I know that you won't like it."- Meek Mill, "Almost Slipped"

#23

     It was the sixth time that Los Angeles had hosted the All-Star Game. Every seat in the Staples Center was filled. Gray and Cam entered the arena holding hands as photogs snapped pictures like they were Jay-Z and Beyoncé. Everyone wanted to know who the glamourous couple was. Each of them looked like a million bucks. He wore a white tee-shirt, grey hoodie, dark jeans, Timbs and a lynx floor-length, fur coat. Barton Perreira aviator shades shielded his eyes from the flashing lights. Cam was happy he'd decided to wear them inside the building. The last thing he needed was his PTSD flaring up. His C Chain encrusted in diamonds and several gold diamond rings were the only jewels he donned. Cam was giving off daddy vibes. Gray knew she was going to have to beat bitches off with a stick the whole night. Cam had flown in a hairstylist and makeup artist last minute as a thank you for her coming through for him. Tokyo Stylez and Priscillaono had done a phenomenal job putting her look together. Tokyo dyed her brown tresses black and flat ironed it bone straight. Priscilla focused on her gorgeous eyes by giving her a black cat eye and long wispy lashes. Since she was the global makeup artist for Fenty Beauty, she decorated Gray's lips with Stunna Lip Paint. The color was a fire engine red. Matching her husband, she rocked a Lynx floor-length fur but hers had a hood. As they walked to their seats, the hood was draped over her hair. The coat was the perfect silhouette to the white fitted long sleeve top, white biker shorts and Fendi logo mid-top sock sneakers.

     Gray overheard someone say that's the girl from the Fashion Nova ad and smiled. People recognizing her had become a recurring thing. She really didn't know how to take all the attention. She was used to being behind the scenes. Strangers knowing who she was kind of freaked her out. Once they got to their courtside seats, they sat next to Chris Rock and supermodel Karlie Kloss who also was from St. Louis. It was crazy because Cam had spent over 25 g's a piece for the seats. Gray would've never blew so much money to watch a basketball game up close, but basketball was Cam's first love. If he wouldn't have gave up on the sport after his mom died, he'd probably be on the court playing. By halftime the hangover he'd been nursing all day had become unbearable. His head was pounding. He could barely concentrate on the game and the team he was rooting for was winning. Cam was also having a hard time being around Gray. Every time he looked into her eyes he felt like shit. The guilt of cheating was already eating him alive. His baby was so happy, and he couldn't even bask in her joy without feeling like a flaw-ass nigga.

Gray giddily enjoyed her soda and popcorn. She was still floating on cloud 9 after Cam said I love you. Cutting her trip short and joining him had been the best decision she'd ever made. Unbeknownst to her or Cam, LaLa sat ten rows back damn near on suicide watch. She'd watched as he and Gray strutted into the venue like they were Kim and Kanye. She couldn't believe he had the gall to prance his show pony around like he hadn't fucked her less than 24 hours before. His dick had damn near punctured her lungs. She wondered after he zipped up his jeans, did he return to his room and do the same thing to Gray. Knowing Cam, he probably did. She didn't put anything past him at this point. Cam was only out for self and what felt good in the moment. Marriage hadn't changed him not one bit. She kind of felt bad for Gray. She sat next to him, grinning like a fool, not knowing she'd married a liar and a cheat. Knowing all of that, LaLa would still trade places with her any day. Good fortune came along with being with Cam. Money, clout, prestige, envy . . . fear. She wanted it all and LaLa wasn't going to stop until she had it.

"I'm finna go find me some aspirin. I'll be back." Cam placed a small kiss on the side of Gray's lips.

"You want me to go wit' you?"

"Nah, stay and enjoy yourself. The halftime show is about to begin."

Gray nodded her head, hating to see him go. More than ever, she felt deeply connected to her husband. They'd reached a new plateau in their relationship. There was no place to go but up from here. Seeing Cam on the move, LaLa rose from her seat.

"There she go following in behind that lousy-ass nigga again." Lynn sighed, rolling her eyes. "You ain't tired yet?"

"Jealousy will get you nowhere." LaLa shot back.

"Yeah, I'm jealous of a nigga that nutted down your throat then left you to go be with his wife." Lynn chuckled, amused.

"Whatever, bitch. You could've stayed yo' hatin' ass at home. If it wasn't for me, yo' broke-ass wouldn't even be here so keep your opinions to yourself before you be on the first train back home." LaLa clapped back.

"Train? Bitch, we got flew'd out."

"You sure did but I got the power to put you on the midnight train to Georgia." LaLa spat, walking down the steps.

"I can't stand that big yellow bitch." Lynn fumed with fury.

She couldn't wait till LaLa got what was coming to her. Due to the enormous crowd, it took LaLa a while to catch up to Cam. He stood in line patiently waiting to make it to the front.

"So, what happened to you last night?" She rolled up on him.

Cam hung his head back and groaned. His head felt like 100 little people were stomping around in combat boots. The last thing he wanted to do was talk to LaLa.

"What you talkin' about?" He kept his eyes ahead.

If Gray caught them talking he didn't want her to think anything foul was going down on his part. He'd already done her dirty the night before. He didn't want to add more drama to his overfilled plate.

"Why you ain't wanna come back to my room?" She tried to push up on him.

"Why would I?" Cam stopped her from getting close.

"What you mean why would I?" She froze in place. "You know what happened."

"And? That was then and this is now. The fuck."

"Hold up. So you sayin' that meant nothin' to you? Why even fuck me if you knew you had no intentions on even messin' wit' me like that?"

"I been told you I didn't fuck wit' you." Cam finally faced her. "You the one that followed me in the bathroom. That ain't my fault you be on my dick and you can't take no for an answer."

LaLa didn't know why but she was mortified by his words. Sure, he'd told her time and time again that he didn't want her, but this was the first time she believed him. After seven years, she finally took the rose-colored glasses off and saw him for exactly who he was.

"Woooow. Okay. You know what? You a selfish muthafucka."

"Go head with that, man." Cam brushed her off.

"No, you are. You don't give a fuck about me. You don't even give a fuck about your so-called wife. The only person you care about is yourself."

"No, bitch, I don't give a fuck about you." Cam got in her face. "You don't know shit about us. I love the fuck out my wife. The moment I stuck my dick in you I realized I would rather end my life than lose her."

LaLa hated him. She wanted to claw at his face with her nails. How could someone who claimed to once love her talk to her and treat her so bad? No, she hadn't been an angel, but he'd led her on and gave her false hope for the last three years. Didn't he have to pay for his fuckboy behavior? Why was she the only one who had to hurt?

"Like Boyz II Men, we at the end of the road, baby girl."

"Although we've come to the end of the road. Still I can't let go." Quan sang while casually strolling by.

Fuming LaLa placed her shoulders back and held her head up high. This time she wouldn't crumble and make a fool out of herself.

"You know what? You're right? This is the end. Cause what I'm not gon' do is keep dealin' wit' you and yo' bullshit. You not gon' keep leading me on. You not gon' keep treating me like I'm crazy and disrespecting me. I ain't your wife. You can put her big-ass through that bullshit. 'Cause mark my words, yo' ass ain't gon' never change."

LaLa noticed rage brewing in his eyes. She'd hit a nerve. Loving that he was the one in the hot seat, she continued to play on his insecurities.

"You betta hope she don't fuck around and have a baby on you by another nigga. Lord knows, yo' ass deserve it. You a trifling, selfish, arrogant, self-centered, bastard. Ain't shit good gon' come to you, so enjoy your li'l fake-ass marriage while it last. 'Cause just like me, she gon' come to her senses and leave yo' ass too." She snarled, before whipping her long weave in his face and storming off.

———

Tapping her foot, LaLa stood impatiently waiting for Gunz to pick her up from the airport. She hated the airport, especially Lambert Airport in St. Louis. It was so outdated and lame. Unlike other airports, it didn't have any luxury stores or current restaurants. After her confrontation with Cam, she hopped on the first flight and left her friends in L.A. They could figure out their own way home as far as she was concerned. She was over All-Star Weekend and she was most certainly over Cam. She loathed him now. It would be a cold day in hell before she ever fucked with him again. The nigga could be dying right in front of her and she wouldn't lift a finger to help.

Gunz blew his horn to get LaLa's attention. She was so mad, she was in her own world. Getting out, he helped her with her luggage then got back in. Tia would've came to pick her up herself, but she'd just had the baby. Gavin Marciano Jr. was finally here. Gunz was over the moon to have a son. LaLa plopped down in the passenger seat and slammed the door.

"What the fuck is you slammin' my damn door for?"

"I'm so tired of these niggas, I swear." She pouted like a child.

"Who done fucked you over now?" Gunz pulled off.

"That wack-ass nigga Cam."

"I told you to stop dealin' with that nigga."

"Oh, trust me, I am now. That nigga gotta world of trouble coming to him. He got life fucked up if he think he gon' fuck me over and get away wit' it." She seethed with anger.

"So, what you sayin'? I been ready to finish this nigga off, but you kept bullshittin'. You finally put yo' big girl panties on?" Gunz glanced over in her direction.

"Yeah and I know exactly how I'm gon' do it. Listen to what I overheard."

"There will never come a day you'll ever hear me say that I want and need to be without you."- Brain McKnight, "Never Felt This Way"

#24

"Can I take this stupid-ass blindfold off now?" Cam groaned, becoming irritated.

"No, you can't. You big baby."

"Huuuuuuuh." He huffed.

Cam had too many enemies to be riding around the city blindfolded. Niggas straight wanted to hit him up like he was Tupac. Gray was gon' fuck around and get him murked.

"We almost there. Just chill."

"Yeah, Papa, chill." Press reiterated from the backseat.

"I thought you was on my side, Pretty Girl?"

"I am but you have to patient. Bad bitches don't whine remember?"

Aoki and Gray cracked up laughing.

"I ain't no fuckin' bad bitch! I'ma real-ass nigga and don't you forget."

Cam was even more irritated now. His baby girl was calling him a bad bitch and they'd been riding for what seemed like forever. He understood that it was Valentine's Day, but did he have to sit through a bumpy car ride in order to receive his gift? Gray could've easily told him what it was, and he still would've been happy.

"Okay! We're here!" She parked the car.

Excitement rang in her voice. She couldn't wait to show Cam what she got for him. She'd been working on it for the last few weeks. Getting out of the car, she went over to the passenger side door and helped him out. Cam felt like an invalent as she escorted him to wherever they were going. The girls trailed behind them making sure not to accidently reveal the surprise. Gray unlocked the door and held the door open as Aoki helped Cam inside the building.

"Gray, if I fall I'ma beat yo' ass."

"Boy, hush and c'mon."

Cautiously, he tapped his foot on the floor to ensure there were no steps or dips ahead of him.

"Just walk straight ahead. There's nothing for you to fall or trip on." She assured.

Cam did as he was told.

"Okay, stop." Gray instructed, smiling a mile wide.

Her cheeks burned red from happiness. She prayed her gift had the impact on him she'd hoped for.

"You ready?" She stood behind him and jumped up and down.

"If you don't bring yo' ass on." Cam couldn't help but grin.

"Okay, Mr. Grumpy Pants. This is from me and the girls." She pulled the blindfold from over his head.

Cam blinked his eyes a few times to adjust his vision. Looking around, he tried to figure out where they were. He didn't recognize the place. Gray noticed the look of bewilderment on his face and explained herself.

"Welcome to the Grace Parthens Community Center."

"You like it, Papa?" Press asked eagerly.

Words tried to form in Cam's brain, but none were good enough. Slightly, he staggered back. He was truly shell shocked. His mind couldn't register that Gray had really got a community center dedicated in his mother's name. It was by far the best gift he'd ever received. No one had ever thought to do something so special for him. He thought when he talked to her about his mother that she didn't really understand how dear she was to him. She never really initiated conversations on the topic. Hell, she rarely ever talked about her own mother. To know that she'd gone to such great lengths to preserve his mom's memory meant the world to him. He'd never be able to repay her for being so thoughtful. Cam walked further into the establishment in awe. Gray had truly gone all out. The community center was state of the art. There was a full gym, rock-climbing wall, children's garden, dance room, computer room and a basketball court. She'd even dedicated the auditorium in memory of Diggy. When spring hit, construction on an outdoor pool would begin. Kids would have a place to go after school and on the weekends that would be safe and educational. If Cam hadn't already married her, he for sure would now.

"You like it?" She asked hesitantly.

Gray was starting to get scared. Cam hadn't said a word. She hoped she hadn't overstepped her boundaries. She never wanted to offend him or the memory of his mother and Diggy. Cam tried to keep his dignity but broke down and cried like a baby.

"Aww c'mere." She enveloped him into her hold.

At first Cam was rigid but eventually he melted into her warm body. His limp arms dangled at his side like a ragdoll. Gray held him close as his tears wet the nape of her neck. Guilt from being unfaithful spread through Cam's body like cancer. He wanted to tell her what he'd done. The words were on the tip of his tongue, but he couldn't say it. Cam couldn't bear to be without her. Admitting that he'd cheated would ensure the end of their marriage. He couldn't lose Gray. He wouldn't be able to survive it.

"Yo, you tryin' to kill a nigga." He wiped his face. "How did you pay for all of this?"

"I used my Fashion Nova check."

Cam swore someone had reached inside his chest and squeezed his heart. Knowing this piece of information made him feel like an even bigger asshole.

"Word? You used your money on me?"

"Your mom was the light of your life. She gave you so much joy. There are a lot of children who have never felt that kind of love. With this place they can get all the love and enrichment that a child needs. It was nothing for me to spend my money on something that would not only be a gift to you but others as well."

"Why were you cryin' Papa?" Press tugged on the leg of his jeans. "You don't like it?"

"I love it." He picked her up.

"You betta. That money could've been put towards my college tuition." Aoki smirked.

"Thank you Li'l Boosie Bad-Ass." He pulled her in for a hug.

Aoki hugged him back. She was genuinely happy that he liked the place. She for damn sure would be there every day after school when it officially opened.

"Well, shit. I don't know if I can top this but c'mon." Cam led them out.

Taking one last look before leaving, he sent a kiss up to heaven. Grace and Diggy had to be smiling down on them. Back in the car, Gray drove across town to the address Cam gave her. The roles had reversed. She now had no idea where they were going. After a twenty-minute drive, they pulled up into the driveway of a majestic Georgian home. The mansion sat on two-thirds of an acre with seven bedrooms and fourteen baths. On the main level was a sweeping formal and informal living room, a large formal dining room and a vast kitchen with a terrace-side breakfast room. On the lower level was a roomy theater, wine cellar, tasting room, game room and gym. A glorious broad terrace overlooked the lawn and the fountain-splashed swimmer's pool and spa. High-end amenities included five fireplaces, a sauna, elevator, smart home technology system and a five-plus car garage for all their cars.

"Who stay here?" She asked, mesmerized by the stunning home.

"We do." He handed her the keys.

"Nooooooo. Shut up. For real?" Gray said stunned.

"C'mon." Cam grinned, proud of his self.

Gray and the girls raced out of the car and ran up the steps of the home. Frantically, she unlocked the door and walked in to find the front of the house covered in bouquets of red roses. Flowers and candles lined the steps and floor. He even had them in glass bowls on top of Lucite boxes. The display of love was beautiful.

"Cam." She hugged him so tight he could barely breathe. "You bought us a house?"

"Yeah, this place is both of ours. Your name is on the deed too. We need to start this marriage off right. No more separation."

"I agree. Thank you." She planted a sweet kiss to his awaiting lips.

"This cute and all but where is our gift?" Aoki said sassily.

"I thought we was cool now? You still gon' keep bossin' up on a nigga?"

"Quit being so sensitive. You know you the homey."

"Yea a'ight." Cam handed her and Press their gifts.

Press and Aoki smiled gleefully. The boxes were from Tiffany's. There was no way Cam could go wrong getting them a gift from there. Inside Press box was a gold necklace with a small key pendant attached. In Aoki's was the same silver necklace she'd tried stealing from Forever 21. Except this one was made out of real sterling silver and cost $175. Aoki tearfully gazed up at Cam. Crouching down, he came down to their height. Cam wanted to look them square in the eye when he spoke so they would know what he was saying was real.

"I know I'm not your real dad, but I look at both of you as my real daughters. You and your mother mean the world. There ain't nothin' I won't do for you, so I want you to wear these necklaces, knowing that no matter what, you'll always have a piece of my heart."

"Thank you, Papa." Press kissed his cheek.

Aoki didn't say a word. Overcome with emotion, she hugged Cam with all her might. The gift meant more to her than he would ever know. It proved that he saw past her sarcasm and tough exterior. He saw her for who she really was, which was a little girl yearning for an unbreakable fatherly bond. Gray didn't know what was going on between Cam and Aoki. All of a sudden, they'd started to become buddy-buddy. She didn't know why or how it happened, but whatever the reason was, she wasn't going to complain. This was all she'd ever wanted. Her family was whole now.

"A'ight ya'll go play. I got us a whole game room."

"Yay!" The girls sprinted to go find it.

"C'mon. I got something else for you." Cam took Gray by the hand and led her upstairs.

In one of the seven bedrooms was a black coffee table with over fifty long stem roses surrounding a bag from Cartier. At least 300 more long stem roses were strategically placed around the room in bundles. Gold inflatable balloons that spelled out the words I love you with heart balloons attached finished off the extravagant display of affection.

"Oh my god, Cam. It's beautiful."

Gray had never seen anything like it. Her breath was truly taken away.

"Here. Open it." He handed her the Cartier bag. Inside was her last and final gift.

Gray giddily pulled out three small velvet ring boxes. Inside each was a ring. Cam had gotten her a new wedding set. She now had a gold Cartier Love ring, a

Maillon Panthere paved row ring and an 8 carat round cut diamond ring. The set was gorgeous. Gray was spellbound. Cam slipped each ring onto her ring finger then kissed the outside of her hand. He would give anything to always make her feel like this. The look of pure joy on her face made his perforated heart whole. Cam made it up in his mind that he was taking the secret of fucking LaLa to the grave. Gray could never find out. One drug filled night would not ruin the love they shared. He'd waited his whole life for her. She was his dream girl sent from above.

Staring into her eyes, he pressed her back against the wall. Nothing was said as he breathed in the aerial lightness to the rose scent of her perfume. Needing to feel her body pressed against his he circled his arm around her waist and pulled her close. Gray closed her eyes and felt his fingers glide through her hair. Cam loved the silky tendrils. Slowly his hand moved down her cheek to her lips. Gray's eyes popped open as he planted a kiss to her soft lips. The second their mouths connected she was lost. A tsunami of emotions swarmed her. Together their lips moved like two trained dancers. The natural rhythm of their tongues took her to a place of no return. This was love personified. Gray cupped his face lovingly and kissed him back with all her might. Cam loved the way her lips felt against his. With a hungry, animalistic look in his eye he lifted her off her feet. If he didn't get inside her soon his dick would break. Gray's legs circled his back. Cam's hand found her breasts and rubbed her nipples. Peeling her top down he pulled her titties out and sucked them with fervor making them hard. The second he saw her perfect tits he turned into a teenage boy. Desire burned in his loin. Gray's warm breast and nipples pressed against his tongue was driving him crazy. The soft cushiness of her flesh was devoured with licks and kisses.

Cam's dick thumped against the zipper of his jean, dying to get out. Fervently, he relieved himself. Gray dug her hand into his scalp as he ripped off her thong. Cam swiped his finger up her juicy slit and used her wetness as lubricant for his throbbing cock. Guiding the tip of his dick inside her entrance, he felt her moisture and groaned. He couldn't believe that after months of fucking Gray was still so tight.

"Mmm baby fuck me." She bit her bottom lip.

Gray tried to keep her moans to a minimum. She didn't want the girls to hear her sexual cries, but Cam felt so good it was hard to keep quiet. With each thrust of his dick she could feel how hard he was. Pushing through her tightness he went deeper into her drenched pussy. The harder he pumped the louder Gray begged for more. Her nails clawed into his neck and hair as he stretched her wide. Cam's hard dick rubbed against her clit. He was so deep she could breath for him. Gray sucked his bottom lip then slipped him her tongue. Gazing into each other eyes he continued to rock into her slowly. He and Gray had developed a cadence and tempo that was unkept. Their love was an asylum of pleasure and pain. In a state of madness, he held her tight. This was home. She was home. He'd go crazy without her. Loving every second of their unexpected tryst Gray ground her pussy into his cock. The size and girth of his cock filled every inch of her hole. It was so big she could hardly breathe. Cam squeezed her ass and grinded against her with matching desperation causing her pussy to weep. She rained down on him recklessly. He could feel it coming. An explosive orgasm was approaching.

"I love you." The words escaped as a sexy whisper.

Gray started moaning like crazy. Shock waves of pleasure were erupting left and right in her pussy. Her blue eyes and mouth were ajar as her breasts shook.

"I love you, you hear me?" He pounded harder.

"Yes." Gray breathlessly moaned

"I fuckin' love you. Forever. I'ma love you forever." Cam swore as an inferno of heat took hold of their body and took them under.

"I guess your body ain't the only thing flexible. You bend the truth."- Russ, "Ain't Nobody Takin' My Baby"

#25

The mall was unusually packed for it to be a Monday afternoon. Gray was experiencing sensory overload. Every time she hit the mall, she found herself going from store to store wanting to buy everything in sight. Saint Louis Galleria was one of the last good malls in St. Louis. While malls like Jamestown and Northwest Plaza were closed down, The Galleria held strong. Nothing except the music selection and styles of clothes had changed since she was a teenage girl. The temperature, lighting, aroma and polished floors all remained the same. Instead of heading home to feed a hungry Cam, Gray continued draining her bank account by buying shit she really didn't need. She and Aoki were having a grand ole time. They'd spent a few racks in Urban Outfitters, H&M, Aldo and Akira. The plan was to stop in Champs and The Gap on the way out, but first Gray headed towards Forever 21. There was a jumpsuit she saw online she wanted. Gray and Aoki had been walking hand-in-hand the entire time they shopped. As soon as she stepped foot near the entrance of the store, Aoki let her hand go and froze in place.

"What you doing? C'mon girl. We gotta hurry up and get home so I can cook. Press and Cam are waiting on us."

Salty tears dripped slowly like falling snow down Aoki's cheeks. Gray looked back at her confused. Aoki's silent weeping was worse than any tantrum she had ever threw. Her blue eyes flooded with sorrow her young soul should never possess. Aoki twiddled her thumbs while trying to speak but no words came out. Gray walked over to her child and examined her face. Something had terrified her, and Gray had absolutely no idea what it was.

"What is it, baby? You can tell me. Whatever it is, I won't get mad."

"Yes, you will. You gon' whoop me."

"I promise, I won't." Gray lied.

Depending on what she said, an ass whoppin' was most certainly coming.

"You promise?"

"Pinky swear." Gray held out her pinky finger.

Aoki wasn't sure if she could trust her. Her mom had tricked her before by pretending to be cool, calm and collected when shit was going down. The last thing she wanted was to tell her the truth and end up being in trouble. Reluctantly, she twisted her pinky finger around Gray's. Once the deal was sealed, she took a deep breath.

"I can't go in that store no more." She wept as her chest heaved up and down.

"Why not?" Gray held her breath and waited for her response.

"Because . . . I'ma go jail and they gon' get my booty!" Aoki wailed, falling into her mother's arms.

———

"So, you knew my daughter got caught stealin' and you ain't think to tell to me?" Gray stormed into the house and slammed the door behind her and Aoki.

Cam paused the game and looked over his shoulder at her. Her words had come at him like a freight train. He had no time to prepare a rebuttal. Him and Press had been chilling playing Fortnite. He hadn't expected her to come home on some rah-rah shit. He thought she'd fry him some chicken, they'd eat, put the kids to bed and spend the rest of the night exploring each other's bodies with their tongues. The look of rage on her face showed that none of that would be going down. Cam was officially in the doghouse. Depending on how the conversation went down, there was no telling when he'd get out.

"Oh, now you can't hear? What the fuck was you thinkin?"

"Aye, yo' go in your room, real quick." Cam spoke to Press.

Being obedient, she scooted off the couch and ran to her room. Press might've only been six, but she knew some shit was about to pop-off. She would much rather play with her dolls than listen to her mom and pop argue.

"Really?" Cam ice-grilled Aoki as she walked past him sniffling.

"I'm sorry. I had no choice."

"Get yo' ass in that damn room!" Gray ordered on ten.

Fearing her mother would swat her behind, Aoki took off running to her room. When the coast was clear, Gray started right back up again.

"You didn't think I needed to know that?"

"We can talk but chill out wit' all that yellin'. Talk to me like a fuckin' adult." Cam threw down the controller.

"I can yell if I want to! You the one who lied to me!"

"Now you puttin' ten on ten. I ain't lie to you about shit."

"Omitting the truth is lyin'! You big dummy!" She smacked him upside the back of his head.

"Don't put your hands on me no more." Cam warned, giving her the eye. "Look, I told Aoki I would give her the chance to tell you."

"Oh, Aoki the parent now? Let me know so I can stop feeding her, clothing her and paying that high-ass tuition for her school!"

"Cut all that fuckin' yellin' out!" Cam didn't have the energy to argue and fight with her anymore.

For once, he wanted to have a civilized conversation.

"No! You had no right!" Gray's bottom lip trembled. "I should've known what she did! We're supposed to be a team! You can't just leave me out in the cold! You should've told me Cam, but nooooooo! Once again, here I am left in the dark like always! Everybody knows the truth but me!"

"Yo, I get that you're upset. You have every right to be. I can't even argue back wit' you 'cause I know I'm wrong. I'm sorry, I didn't tell you. I just felt bad for shorty. She gotta lot shit wit' her and I ain't wanna be the one to add more stress." Cam spoke from the bottom of his heart.

If Gray would've seen the look of despair in Aoki's eyes that day, she would've made the same decision too.

"Stress?" She looked at him like he was dumb. "What the hell does a ten-year-old have to stress about? She ain't payin' no fuckin' bills around here!"

"The shit is bad, Gray. She knows." He stressed.

Gray drew back her head and screwed up her face.

"Knows what?"

Cam hung his head low. Once he let the words slip from his mouth, everything would change. He and Gray would never be the same. She'd probably hate him. Like his father, he'd go from being her biggest hero to her worst enemy.

"She knows ole boy ain't her dad."

The color in Gray's face went from a warm caramel shade to paler than a sheet of paper. A wave of nausea hit that was so intense it almost knocked her off her feet. Projectile vomit spewed from her mouth almost choking her. Chunks of food from lunch that resembled pink potato soup propelled into the air and splattered to the floor. The stench was horrendous. Gray heaved again and some more until there was nothing left in her stomach but dread.

"Baby." Cam carefully came near her.

"No." She stepped back, shaking her head.

Hot tears dripped from her eyes. Gray never pitied herself when it came to being a rape victim. She'd put it behind her. At least she pretended to. She drowned out the memories with overworking and being a great mother to her kids. She never wanted being raped to define her. She most certainly didn't want it to define her daughter either. Neither one of them deserved to be branded with the title of rape; she a rape victim and Aoki the product of rape. They were much more than that, but Truth's dirty deed would follow them for their rest of their days. No matter how much they tried to escape it.

"This can't be happening. You're lyin'. She can't know."

"She found out on the internet." Cam tried to hold her.

"How long has she known?" Gray side stepped him again.

"That I don't know."

"You know everything the fuck else! You know more about my child than I do!" She yelled, unable to control her anger. "What kind of fuck shit are you on, Cam? Why the hell wouldn't you tell me that? Matter of fact, how long have you known?"

Cam rolled his neck around in a circle and groaned. His answer would be another nail in the coffin.

"She told me the same day she got caught stealin'."

All Gray could do was chuckle.

"So now you got my own kids keepin' secrets from me. Just cause you lie and keep shit close to your chest don't mean you gon' have my kids doing the same thing."

"Hold the fuck up."

"No, you hold the fuck up!" She got in his face.

Gray didn't even care that she'd stepped in her own vomit.

"Aoki and Press are my kids! Ain't shit you can say to me! The minute she told you that shit, you should've come to me! Even if you ain't tell me about her stealin', you should've told me that! That shit not only affects her, but it affects me as well! I have walked around for ten years wearing a scarlet letter on my chest behind what her father did to me! I gotta live knowing that nigga raped me while I was passed out! I gotta live with the memory of him tryin' to kill me as I ran around my living room screaming for help! I expected my first child to be birthed from love not by sexual assault. I wanted to tell her! It should'a came from me! I don't want her walkin' around here thinkin' something is wrong with her."

"She good. She know ain't nothin' wrong wit' her."

Whap!

Gray's hand cracked across his face, snapping it back with force. Cam's head turned to the side. Black dots blurred his vision. He didn't play that shit when it came to female's putting their hands on him. Gray had crossed the line several times now. If he were any less of a man, he'd give her a dose of her own medicine, but she was upset and low-key he deserved the smack.

"And who the fuck are you to be the judge of that, Iyanla Vanzant! Last I checked you ain't got no goddamn kids! You think 'cause you play a couple video games and twirl around in a king costume that makes you a dad? No, nigga, it's more to it than that! And judging by the way you handled this situation you ain't fit to be nobody's daddy!"

If Gray had wanted to hurt him she'd succeeded. It was like a shot from an AK-47 had been blasted into his heart.

"Are you fuckin' serious, dawg?" He muttered out his response. "I was the one that went to Aoki last two cheerleading competitions 'cause yo' ass couldn't go. She wasn't even fuckin' wit' me then and I still showed up because I wanted to go out of my way to build a relationship with *your* daughter! I'm the one that's up in the middle of the night putting Press back to sleep when she's having nightmares. I'm the one that helps her with her letters and numbers after school. Meanwhile, your fuckin' baby daddy ain't been nowhere in sight. She think he been M.I.A. cause I'm around and he ain't gotta be her dad no more but really that nigga too pussy to face me like a man. Let's not forget the only reason I'm at war with this nigga is because of you. Even though I don't fuck wit' that nigga and it's still on sight when I see his pussy-ass, I still went out of my way to tell her he loves her." Cam cornered Gray against the wall.

His temper rose to a new level of anger he didn't even know he could achieve.

"So yeah, I made a mistake by not tellin' you. I can admit that but what you not gon' do is stand here in my face and downplay me as a father. I love the shit out of them girls, and if you even doubt that for a second, then what the fuck are we doing?"

Gray gulped down the rest of her tears. To spite him she refused to answer. At this point, she didn't know what she and Cam were doing. Their so-called marriage was all fucked up. Seeing that she wasn't going to answer and that she declined to reassure his place in her life, Cam became fed up.

"Yo I'm out. I ain't got time for you and yo' dysfunctional shit." He grabbed his keys and dipped.

Emotionally distraught, Gray made the long trek to Aoki's room. Cam and his attitude didn't mean shit to her. The only person she was concerned for was her child. Aoki sat on the bed with her knees up to her chest holding onto her pillow. A galaxy of emotions swarmed her face. Gray was angry and felt bad for her at the same time. She didn't know if she should shake her or hug her. Gray was clueless. This was a conversation she'd been preparing for Aoki's whole life and she still wasn't ready.

"Aoki I—"

"Mom, I know I'm in trouble, but can I just take my punishment and leave it at that? I don't wanna talk about this with you. I just want my dad." She held onto the pillow for dear life.

It was if the wind had been knocked out of Gray. She'd been the one bending over backwards trying to be everything and more for the girls while Gunz played war games with Cam. He'd barely picked up the phone for the girls. Yet, Aoki wanted him in her time of need. Defeated, she simply closed the door. Gray could've put up a fight, but her tank was on E. Aoki and Cam had drained her.

———

Drinking had never really been Gray's thing. She was never good at it. The taste of alcohol was bitter and burned her stomach. That night, she needed something more than Jesus to keep her afloat. After her failed attempt at talking to Aoki, she cleaned up her mess and took a long hot shower. Now that she was fresh and clean, she sat on the couch and stared at the amber liquid in her glass. She was on her fourth cup of Hennessy. Hennessy was Cam's favorite drink and the only hard liquor they had in the house. Gray poked at the glass-like ice cubes with the tip of her fingernail. She'd passed tipsy and was full on drunk. So drunk that she watched intently as the ice cubes clinked against each other. Needing another sip, she picked up the tumbler and placed it to her dry lips. Her stomach was in knots. The day's events weighed heavily in her guts. Gray let the Hennessy burn her tongue and throat, hoping it would ease her nausea. Slouched, she lay back and closed her eyes. Her head was spinning. She'd drank way too much. Regret would come in the morning, along with more vomit. Sleep was the only thing that would take her misery away. It didn't take her long to go under. Unbeknownst to

Gray, while she lay passed out, Aoki had text her father 911 saying she needed him to come over asap.

Ding, Dong! Ding, Dong! Ding, Dong!

Hoping not to wake her mother, Aoki ran to the door and opened it. Thankfully for her, Gray didn't move an inch. It would take more than a doorbell to wake her up.

"Daddy." She shrieked, leaping into his arms.

Seeing her dad was like discovering money from the tooth fairy for the first time. Gunz held his first born close. To ensure he stayed alive, he'd stayed away but when Aoki texted him and said she needed him asap, nothing in the world was going to keep him away. He'd let his family down in the past. He wasn't going to do it again.

"I missed you baby girl." He kissed her forehead sweetly.

"I missed you too daddy." Aoki held on for dear life.

She never wanted to let him go. Gunz was her whole entire world. No man on the planet could compete with him in her eyes. Sure, she was growing to like Cam. He'd turned out to not be the douchebag she thought he was. But Gunz was her daddy. He was the man she idolized and adored. He was her first love. Having him there, live in the flesh proved that the bond they'd forged since birth was real. She had no reason to doubt his love for her. If she ever needed him, Gunz would be there. He knew he was taking a big risk by coming to Gray and Cam's house, but he didn't give a fuck. He'd proved the damage he could inflict when pushed. Nothing was going to stop him from checking on his baby girl.

"You alright?"

"No." She shook her head.

"What happened?" Gunz pulled out his gun.

For all he knew, Cam could've done something to his child or used her as bait to lore him there.

"I know you're not my real dad."

Gunz's arm fell to his side. That was the last thing he thought he'd hear.

"Is that why you don't love me anymore? Is that why you haven't been around?" Aoki cried.

Gunz let her words sink in. For the first time he felt like he'd failed his kids. Aoki should've known, without a shadow of a doubt, that no matter what he was always going to love her and be her daddy.

"Where ya' mama and her lame-ass nigga at?"

"Mama right there sleep." Aoki pointed. "And Cam gone."

"A'ight." Gunz put her down. "I ain't gon' be able to stay long but we need to talk."

Aoki closed the door and led her father back to her room. Gunz noticed Gray on the couch knocked out as he walked by. He wondered how she would react if she knew he was in her house. Gunz entered Aoki's room and looked around. It was the first time he'd seen his little girl's room in person. He'd seen glimpses of it on Facetime but that was about it. Not having the access he used to with his kids was killing him. He missed coming home and seeing their smiling faces as soon as he walked through the door. He'd taken a lot of things for granted when he had them all under one roof.

For a twenty minutes, they sat in her room catching up. Gunz explained to her that despite him not being her biological father, she would always be his baby girl. He also pinky promised that he'd make more of an effort to spend time with her and Press. When her eyes started to droop, he put her to bed. Before heading to the front of the house, he stopped in Press' room and kissed her goodnight as well. Gunz hadn't felt this good in a long time. Life with Tia wasn't what he thought it would be. All she did was spend his money and post all their business on the Gram. If it wasn't for their son, he would've been left her lazy-ass alone. Being around Gray and the girls reminded him of how good life used to be. Gunz would give up all his riches to have his family back. But things were all fucked up. The line had been drawn in the sand. Gray and Cam had taken him over to the dark side again. After the club massacre there was no way in hell she would ever come back to him.

As Gunz approached the door, his mind told him to leave. He'd successfully visited his daughter without Gray or Cam knowing. The delight in knowing he'd infiltrated their home without them knowing should've been enough but Gunz always had to take it a step further. He approached the couch and looked down at Gray. On her back, she lay as still as a brick. The only way he knew she was alive was because of the slight rise and fall of her chest. She reminded him of an angel. Gunz eased his way around the couch to get a better look at her. There was no telling when the next time he'd get to be this close. Gently, he sat on the edge of the couch and smoothed her hair away from her face. Her round face was slightly lighter than honey. When open, her sapphire eyes sparkled with bliss and when sad they were dim and dark like the bottom of the sea. How he missed those blue eyes. Throwing caution to the wind, he leaned forward and lightly kissed her pouty lips. Gray stirred in her sleep but didn't open her eyes.

"Cam." She instinctively circled her arms around his neck.

Gray was barely lucid. Gunz didn't utter a word as he kissed her again, this time deeper and more passionately. Yes, what he was doing was wrong. He was violating her space and her marriage but Gunz didn't care. In his mind she'd always be his.

"Mmm." Gray moaned French kissing him back.

The sweet taste of mint on his tongue danced on her taste buds. Both of them were so into the kiss that neither of them heard the front door open. After blowing off some steam by playing pool with his boys, Cam headed home. He figured by the time he returned, Gray would've calmed down and they could talk sensibly. Never in a million years did he expect to walk in the house and see Gunz not only in his home but making out with his wife. His worst fear had come true. Like LaLa, he'd finally pushed her into the arms of another man. Since they'd gotten together, he always had suspicions that she still had feelings for Gunz. Seeing them making out on their couch confirmed it. It also confirmed she was a snake. Echoes of the gun blasting rang in his ear. Visions of Diggy's brain matte gushing out of the back of his head ran rapid in his brain. Thoughts of him dead on the floor made him see red. Why would Gray have the man that killed his best friend in their home? Did she hate him that much? Had he pushed her that far? Rational, level-headed Cam went out of the window. Within a blink of an eye, Killa Cam entered the building and he blacked out. Grabbing Gunz by the back of his coat, he slammed him head first onto the ground. His head bounced off the floor with a loud thud. He tried getting his bearings, but Cam was in beast mode. He'd been waiting months for this. Gunz had tried to take his life, killed his best friend and disrespected his home. It was high time he meet his maker.

Hovering over him, Cam rained down blows as if he wanted his head to become one with the oak floor. Punch after punch, he pounded his fist into every area of his face. Cam intended on breaking every bone until his head was deflated like a basketball. He didn't give a fuck about his bruised knuckles or the blood all over his hand. Gunz Marciano was dying tonight. Kilo and Gram barked loudly ready to attack. The entire house was in a state of uproar.

"Cam!" Gray screamed, horrified by what she saw.

She didn't know what was going on. One minute she thought she was kissing her husband and the next he was beating her baby daddy to a pulp. She didn't even know how Gunz had gotten in their house. Cam ignored her pleas and kept sticking Gunz with jabs to the face. If Gray had any sense, she would've shut up because as soon as he was done with Gunz, Cam was coming for her next.

"Papa stop!" Press stood in her nightgown and wailed like a baby.

All of the commotion had woken her up. This time not even Press' cries would save Gunz. Taking out his pocketknife, Cam flicked it open and ferociously jammed it into Gunz's left eye.

"Ahhhhhhhhhhhhhhh!"

Gunz flopped around like a fish out of water from the excruciating pain. His retina detached, causing his vision in that eye to turn black. Cam held onto him and twisted the knife further until he heard a crunching sound. Blood and spinal fluid leaked out and trailed down his cheek.

"Get off my daddy!" Aoki tried to push Cam off of Gunz.

Cam was seconds away from killing Gunz, but once again, the girls saved him. Even though he hated him, and their mama, Cam wouldn't be able to live knowing he'd killed their father while they watched on. Out of breath, he rose to his full height, jerked the knife from Gunz's eye, harked up a glob of spit and spat on him. Gunz was so weak and disoriented that he couldn't even wipe the saliva off. Gray looked down at Gunz. The sight was grotesque. His right eye was engorged, the left one was attached to Cam's knife and bloody spit dribbled from his slack jaw.

"You're fuckin' dead to me." Cam pointed his finger at Gray.

Her heart dropped down to the pit of her stomach. Putting everything together, she realized that the man she had been kissing was not her husband. It was Gunz.

"Cam, wait! It's not—"

"SHUT THE FUCK UP!" He barked so loud the chandelier shook. "On my mama I'm done fuckin' wit' you." He gave her the look of death and slammed the door behind him.

"No use wondering why your changing heart has wandered."- Alessia Cara, "Out Of Love"

#26

Almost a month had gone by since Gray last seen or heard from Cam. She'd called him numerous times, but after a while, he blocked her calls. Gray was love sick. It took everything in her to even get out of bed. If it wasn't for her kids and her job, she would've gladly withered away. When Cam left, he took a big chunk of her with him. She'd gotten so used to coming home to him each day that not having him around made her feel like a mudslide had smothered her. All of this was one big misunderstanding. From the outside looking in, she knew it looked crazy. If she was Cam, she would've believed she'd cheated too but she hadn't. Gunz had taken advantage of her drunken state. She would've never kissed him if she was coherent. She hated Gunz for doing this to her. It kind of scared her to think how far he would've gone if Cam hadn't walked in. Would he have raped her like Truth did? Gray didn't even want to think that far. The notion was bad enough. The ass whoopin' he'd got from Cam would make him think twice about taking advantage of a woman. Gray never wanted to see his face again. She was disgusted by his behavior. She made sure the girls understood that he was not welcome at their house. She'd drop the girls off at his mother's house and he could pick them up from there.

Resting back in her chair, Gray closed her eyes and tried to relax. She was at Aunt Vickie's house getting her hair braided. Aunt Vickie's house was the go-to spot for everything. You could get a plate, your hair braided, buy fake check stubs and file your taxes. It was funny cause the first time Cam brought her there she was deathly afraid of the hood area. Over time, she grew to love the close-knit neighborhood. A gorgeous coco skinned girl with short platinum blonde natural hair by the name of Mel braided her hair. It was the first time she was doing Gray's hair. Gray had booked her appointment for eight feed-in braids that would go up into a ponytail. She'd been there for a little bit over an hour. Thankfully, Mel was almost done because Gray's butt was starting to hurt. She had almost fallen asleep when she heard the sound of two loud voices. Opening her eyes, she found LaLa's homegirls Lynn and Alexzandria at the door picking up an order. Alexzandria spotted Gray and rolled her eyes. Gray glared back at her, daring her to do something. It would take nothing for her to hop out of the chair and break her fuckin' face. Alexzandria didn't want no smoke though. She hadn't forgotten the damage Gray had done to LaLa's nose. Instead, she decided to be messy.

"Girl, I can't believe that bitch left us in fuckin' L.A." She started up the conversation knowing Lynn would get mad all over again.

She'd wanted to beat LaLa's ass when she learned she'd left them stranded. When LaLa checked out of the room, the girls were left with nowhere to sleep. Their luggage had been placed behind the front desk when they returned from the game. Lynn was livid. The next time she saw her ex best friend it was on sight.

"Fuck that bitch. That's why Gray gon' beat her ass again when she find out she fucked Cam in the bathroom." Lynn spat not even knowing Gray was sitting right there. "Nasty bitch. You know you a lowdown ho when you fuckin' in public restrooms."

She lyin', Gray tried to tell herself. She had to be, but deep down, she knew she wasn't.

"Cam's ass ain't shit. How you gon' have both yo' ho's at the game at the same time? Gray was just sittin' there the whole game cheesing and shit like her and Cam were the shit. I'm lookin' like girl! Yo' nigga just fucked his ex the night before in the men's restroom!" Lynn bugged up laughing.

Gray's stomach tightened with despair. Any minute she was going to throw up, but she couldn't. Gray refused to embarrass herself in front of everyone. She was already the brunt of everyone's joke. To prevent herself from vomiting, she swallowed back the bile, but her throat kept clenching in response. No matter what she did, the warm sensation kept rising. She could taste it in the back of her mouth. Cam had done this to her. He'd made her look like a fool. He'd betrayed her and the sanctity of their marriage. Gray couldn't even be surprised. The signs had been there all along. Cam and LaLa were stuck together like glue. Where one went the other was sure to follow. The question was had their argument been that bad that he had to step out on her? Now she wondered when he said I love you did he even mean it, or did he just feel guilty for cheating? There was no way she was ever going to know until she confronted him. But before she did that, she was going to see the one person who would give her the advice she so desperately needed.

―――――

"I'm so sorry, Gray." Mo rubbed the back of her hand. "My brother is a fuckin' dickhead."

"He said he would never cheat on me, especially not with her." Gray sobbed.

Her eyes burned with heavy, thick, tears. The tears and vomit she held back at Aunt Vickie's house came flooding out of her system as soon as she walked in Mo's crib. If she wasn't crying, she was throwing up. It was so bad she couldn't even leave the bathroom. She and Mo sat on the marble floor next to the toilet. Mo held back her hair and wiped her face as the tears seeped from her caerulean eyes.

"Listen, I'ma tell you like this. My brother loves you, but he is not gonna change until he wants to. I know he thinks he is, but Cam is not ready for marriage."

"That sad part is I know that. I loved him so much that I tried to look past it." Gray whimpered.

"And that was your first mistake. Never ignore the warning signs. Now, don't get me wrong. Ya'll connection run deeper than whatever he had with that trout-mouth bitch or any other girl he's dealt with. That I know that for a fact but Cam gotta grow up. He gotta lot of shit he needs to deal with, and you can't be his savior. And plus, you ain't got time to play mama to him no way. That baby in your stomach gon' put an end to all of that."

"What? Girl, you must be smokin'." Gray cackled. "I am not no damn pregnant. Have you forgot my tubes are tied?"

"Well, they did a shitty job. Girl, I got 37 kids. I can smell when a bitch is pregnant."

"You buggin'." Gray flicked her wrist, dismissively.

"Okay." Mo reached under the sink and pulled out a pregnancy test. "Prove me wrong."

"There's not a thing I could say. Not a song I could sing, for your mind to change."- Alessia Cara, "Out Of Love"

#27

      Gray felt like a visitor as she rang the doorbell to the home that was supposed to be hers. Holding the strap of her purse on her shoulder, she tilted her head towards the sky. A million bright stars dotted the night horizon. *Lord, please don't let us fight,* she wished upon a star. Cam jogged down the steps wondering who could possibly be at the door. No one knew where he stayed. Looking out the window he saw that it was Gray. The rage he'd been suppressing for weeks boiled to the surface. How dare she have the nerve to show up on his doorstep. When he said it was over, he meant it. Furiously, he unlocked the door. Gray took her eyes off the sky and gazed up at her husband. He towered over her with a mean scowl on his face. Cam wore nothing but a frown, hopping shorts, Nike socks and matching slides. His tattoos, lean muscles, rock hard abs and dick print were on full display. His third leg rested low against his thigh. If they were on better terms she would've reached out and touched it. Knowing better, she took her mind out the gutter and focused on the fact that he hadn't said a word. He just stood there looking at her like she was a piece of shit. Gray didn't know what to do. The silence threatened to engulf her. The tension was thick and chilly. If one of them didn't say something soon she was sure to vomit or pass out.

      "So, you not gon' let me in?"

      Cam folded his arms across his broad chest and glared at her. Getting smart was the last thing Gray needed to be doing. Shuffling from one foot to the other, she tried to figure out her next move. Cam wasn't making this easy on her. The silence was starting to feel like poison. The void of sound made things abundantly clear. The love they used to share was no more.

"Look man, I came here to tell you that what you think you saw is not what it was. I would never cheat on you, especially not with Gunz. You gotta know I would never do no shit like that to you."

"I don't know shit." Cam finally replied. "I know what my eyes showed me."

"You gon' believe your eyes or me?"

Pissed off by her response Cam barked, "What the fuck do you want, Gray? I ain't got time for your fuck shit. I'm busy."

"Too busy for me?" She cocked her head to the side.

"Say what the fuck you gotta say or leave!"

Every fiber of her being wanted to go off but now was not the time to be defensive. If she wanted to have a civilize conversation, she was going to have to drop her ego and keep it real.

"I'm sorry you had to see what you saw but I didn't call him over there. Aoki did and that nigga kissed me. The only reason I kissed him back is because I was drunk, and I thought he was you."

"You supposed to love me so much, but you don't know the difference between me and that nigga? Fuck outta here. You fucked up. Just admit it. Own your shit like you like to tell me."

Here he had been sick behind cheating on her and for what? She was on some other shit too. She didn't give a fuck about him or their marriage. If she did, she would've never had her fuck-ass baby daddy in their house. Cam had gone through hell and back to prove his love to Gray and this was how she repaid him, by kissing the same nigga that had blacked her eyes, kidnapped her kids, put a hit on his life and killed his best friend?

"I am. I mean there's no way for me to go back and undo it. If I could, I wouldn't have drank so much but I was so fucked up after you told me about Aoki that I couldn't handle it sober. You know how that feels to want to drown out the pain. There was so much shit going on that I went into system overload. It's just been one thing after another. It's like I can't get a fuckin' break, and to be honest, I can't keep up anymore. And with everything that's going on, I need you more now than ever. Aoki been actin' out. She got suspended for fighting again—"

"So, what you tellin' me for? Ain't you the one that said I wasn't fit to be a father figure for your kids?" Cam used her words against her.

Gray sucked in her bottom lip. She hadn't meant to go there, but in the moment, she was hot. Everybody knows that in the heat of the moment people say things they don't necessarily mean.

"You know that's not what I meant."

"I don't know shit but what I do know is you got me fucked up!" Cam stepped down onto the porch and got in her face.

Gray stepped back, praying she didn't fall.

"You always tryin' to act like I'm the villain but yo' ass ain't shit! You just as grimy as fuckin' LaLa. Now I see why Gunz cheated on you all them times. You fuckin' Keyser Söze out this bitch! I don't know who the fuck you are!"

Anger boiled deep in Cam's system as hot lava. It churned famished for destruction. The pressure of his rage would force him to say some shit he didn't mean but Gray was taking him there. She had balls enough to cheat but couldn't even admit it. What kind of fool did she take him for? *I should just walk away,* she thought. Things were getting out of hand. This was exactly what she didn't want but she also didn't want to leave without coming to some kind of resolution. Even though he was the one who had actually cheated, too much was at stake to just completely call it quits. Low-key, she kind of blamed herself for him stepping out. Maybe if she hadn't been working so much he wouldn't have sought Lala out. A million what if's plagued her. All she knew for sure was that this was her last try. She and Cam had gone through hell and back to make this marriage work. They had to figure out something. If for no other reason than for Press, Aoki and the baby she was carrying.

"You do know who I am. Despite how fucked up we are, we're connected to each other forever. Lord knows I don't wanna be here fighting with you, but the girls need you. We need you." She placed her hand on her stomach.

Cam's eyes landed where she'd placed her hand.

"What the fuck? You bloated?"

"I'm pregnant."

Gray was in total denial when Mo suggested that she was pregnant. She thought the girl had lost her mind. She'd still been having vaginal bleeding. It wasn't until she got home and continued to throw up that she started to become concerned. Five pregnancy tests later, her suspicions were confirmed. A visit to her OB/GYN further confirmed that she was indeed pregnant. Gray was dumbfounded. She didn't think she would ever conceive a child with her tubes being tied. She learned from her doctor that tubal ligation did not 100% guarantee contraception. Gray's fallopian tubes had apparently grown back together. That's how she'd gotten pregnant. She was three and a half months. They'd created their miracle baby over Thanksgiving. Gray hadn't had any symptoms besides fatigue. She chalked that up to all the drama and traveling. Holding her lower stomach, Gray searched Cam's face for any kind of reaction but got none. Silence hung in the air like the suspended time between when a glass fell and shattered to the floor. Naively, she expected a smile to break out on his face and for him to scoop her up in the air. None of those things happened. Instead, he shot her a look of disgust. His reaction seeped into her blood system and paralyzed her brain. Gray's pupils dilated as nausea took over. Cam's face was one of disdain. He didn't even pretend to care about her feelings or to fill the awkward silence with a fake gush of joy. If Gray didn't get it before, she got it now. He didn't give a fuck about her anymore.

"You pregnant?" He paused then chuckled. "Really, Gray? You always on that dumb shit. You really expect for me to believe that shit? Now you the virgin fuckin' Mary."

"I'm not lyin'. I went to the doctor and everything. She confirmed it. I'm just as shocked as you are."

"I can't believe you would stoop this low to get me back. You gon' pull a LaLa on me. For real, Gray?"

Cam was outdone. He never thought Gray would stoop so low.

"Why the hell would I lie to you about something like that? I'm really pregnant."

"You ain't pregnant, and even if you are, the baby ain't mine. It's Gunz's."

The first jab stung a bit, but she didn't fold. Gray took the hit like a seasoned prize fighter and stood firm.

"I keep tellin' you I didn't fuck him, and you know it!"

"And I keep tellin' you, I don't know shit besides you're a lyin', conniving ass bitch! You try to act all innocent but you ain't shit. You just like the rest of these ho's. LaLa was right about you. Yo' ass is a snake. I should've just fucked you and kept it moving. What the fuck was I thinkin' giving you my last name? If that nigga didn't marry you after ten years, I should've saw that as a red flag. Now you got the nerve to tell me you pregnant, and let me guess, I'm supposed to be your third baby daddy? You supposed to be Erykah Badu? Man go head." Cam waved her off and stepped back in the doorway.

Gray clutched her abdomen and tried not to keel over. This time he'd hit her with a gut punch to the stomach. This one hurt bad. She'd feel the remnants of the blow for weeks, maybe even years. Drips of water flowed one after another from her sorrow filled eyes with no sign of stopping.

"If you are pregnant, which you're not, get a fuckin' abortion. Fall down the steps, put a hanger up your coochie. 'Cause I don't want shit to do wit' you or that fake-ass baby you done conjured up. You fuckin' Gunz was the only time you was gon' get over on me. Shit, now that I'm thinkin' about it, you probably been fuckin' him the whole time."

The thought made Cam hate her even more. This was the moment where Gray could hit him back with the information she knew about him and LaLa, but Gray didn't have the strength to fight dirty. Besides, blasting him didn't even matter. They were over. She'd come there strictly to clear her name and tell him she was pregnant. Any feelings she had left for him vanished with each venomous word that came out of his mouth.

"You like gettin' abused." He continued his assault. "You want a nigga to treat you bad. Maybe if I would've treated you like shit you would've acted right. But a bitch like you ain't got no self-respect."

Cam delivered one body shot after another. Gray could no longer withstand the blows. The left hook to her liver had her up against the ropes. With her gloves up, she tried her best to defend herself, but with each hit, she grew weaker and weaker.

"Let me tell you how this shit gon' work. Don't come here no more. Don't call my phone. Whatever shit I got at your house keep it, burn it, give it to Gunz or one of your three baby daddies for all I care. Stay the fuck away from me. Don't ask my sister about me. Don't ask Kema or Quan. And you bet not take yo' ass over my Aunt Vickie's house no more! Keep my fuckin' name out your mouth! If you see me in public, don't part your fuckin' lips to say shit to me! I don't fuck wit' you! I don't give a fuck about you! I wouldn't piss in your mouth if you was dyin' of thirst! This shit is a wrap bitch. This marriage is null and void! We gettin' a fuckin' divorce!"

"Babe, are you alright?"

Cam's anger subsided as he heard the sweet sound of his company's voice. Gray's heartrate slowed as she furrowed her brows. Her worst nightmare was coming true. Cam had moved on with another girl. Was it really that easy for him to discard their marriage, her, their love? Stepping to the side, she looked past him to see who the girl was.

"Why you in here yellin'?" Duckie walked in behind him wearing nothing but one of his tee shirts.

Like a character in a cartoon, Gray's mouth fell to the floor. Her eyes had to be playing tricks on her or either she was hallucinating. Cam couldn't be dating one of Gunz's side bitches. Life couldn't be that cruel. Did god hate her that much? It seemed like they had been slap boxing since birth.

"Devin?"

Stunned as well to see her arch nemesis standing there, Devin looked her up and down and said, "Gray?"

It took everything in Gray to keep standing erect. She swore she'd been gutted with a butcher's knife.

"I thought yo' name was Duckie?" Cam asked confused.

"It is but my nickname is Duckie."

"How the fuck you know my wi—I mean, how you know . . . her?"

"We got a lot of history together. Ain't that right, Gray?" Devin draped her arm around Cam to signify ownership.

Whatever their relationship was, it was now officially over. Devin would fight tooth and nail before she gave up on Cam. Gray cried as if someone had died. She cried as if the ferocity of her tears might put the pieces of her broken marriage back together. Emotional pain flowed from every pore of her body. Cam knew he should put her out of her misery and walk away but he couldn't. No matter how much he denied it, he still loved Gray. Watching as her lips trembled and her shoulders heaved was like seeing his mother being buried into the ground. Gray's long lashes brimmed with tears. Her hands clenched close to her chest in a frantic battle against heartache. If it wasn't already bad that he was fuckin' another chick, knowing that he was fuckin' Devin of all people in her house took the cake. Any fight that she had left was gone. She couldn't float in an ocean that had already been drained. Each tear that she shed at his feet was in vain. She was no longer the woman he respected and adored. She'd switched places with LaLa and become public enemy #1.

"You almost done here. I'm ready for round two." Devin smirked, devilishly.

Cam gave Gray one last look.

"Yeah, this conversation is over. Get the fuck off my doorstep."

And just like that the fight was over and she'd been knocked out. The slam of the door to her face solidified she was down for the count. Gray wished she had another round in her, but she couldn't defend herself properly. She'd sustained serious injuries to her heart and soul. The uppercut to the jaw had knocked her flat on her ass. She wished someone was there to help her up, but this battle had to be fought alone. She had no choice but to lick her wounds and go home. Despite the loss, she'd fought a good fight but now she was done. She'd come to the point where she had nothing left to give. Gray was emotionally constipated. Cam had done his worst. Nothing could hurt her anymore. After that night, she was going to make sure of it.

"It's 4AM and I'm back up poppin' with the crew."- Travis Scott feat Drake, "Sicko Mode"

#28

Sleep never came easy to Cam. Nights where he stared absently at the ceiling was natural to him. Most nights he asked God to forgive him for all his sins or plotted revenge on his enemies. Duckie, or better yet Devin, lay next to him on her stomach with her naked ass propped in the air. She made sure he had easy access to her pussy at all times of the night. Cam had wore her ass out. For hours, he drilled into her like a maniac. All the anger he wanted to take out on Gray, she got for three hours straight. She was wore out, but Duckie being the freak she was, seemed to always be down for more, but Cam was off that. She'd came multiple time, but he wasn't able to bust one nut. The convo between him and Gray replayed like a song stuck in his head on repeat. She'd come there to tell him she was pregnant. Cam didn't believe her at first. He kinda still didn't now. Gray no longer being able to bear children was one of the sore spots of their marriage. Now all of sudden, after he'd broken up with her she was pregnant. What a convenient coincidence. Cam honestly didn't know what to think. That's why he found it hard to even lay in peace. He couldn't rest easy knowing she might be pregnant with his seed. Having a kid had always been a dream of his. Gray knew this. She wouldn't play on that emotion for sympathy or for a place back in his heart or would she? Cam didn't put shit past her at that point. After seeing her with Gunz, his entire opinion of her had changed. Gray was scandalous as fuck. It had become clear that there were no good females in the world. The only way he would know for sure if she was telling the truth was if he made her pee on a stick his self. Even then, if she was indeed pregnant, that still left the question if the baby was his or not.

He'd come in and found her and Gunz kissing. Who's to say they hadn't already smashed before then. Finding out if she was really pregnant was the first step in all of this madness. He'd figure out the rest after that. But first, he had to go take care of business. It was March 12th. The day of his last big shipment. Thirty kilos of cocaine had been transported from South America to a local convenient store hidden inside fresh pineapples. At least that's what it would look like from the naked eye. When the box of fruit was opened from the outside, it would look like a regular shipment of pineapples. But when the shell was removed, you'd see the inside had been hollowed out and filled with cocaine compacted into cylinders. The cocaine cylinders, which carried between 800 and 1,000 grams each, were coated in a yellow waxy substance. The wax coating helped to conceal any odor the chemical product might contain. The store owner had no idea that drugs were inside the containers. He simply accepted payment for the drop-offs and minded his own business.

Since Cam had taken over as Lieutenant, he'd had several successful shipments brought in. He and his crew had been flying under the radar. That day would be no different. He'd ensure that all the kilos were accounted for then go holla at Gray. He might not fuck with her like he used to but the way he'd spoken to her the night before didn't sit well in his spirit. Cam kept seeing the look of complete devastation on her face. He'd never be able to get the vision out of his head. He'd decimated her. In the moment it felt good to make her hurt. Maybe then she'd know how she'd made him feel. Witnessing her kiss, the very man that killed Diggy was the equivalent of finding out his mother had passed away. It was the death of their relationship or maybe their marriage had ended the moment he stuck his dick in LaLa. Either way, marriage wasn't suitable for either one of them. They'd both failed each other. Him more than her, but in the game of love and war, there were no winners.

Cam hurried and got dressed. His day would be shit, until he talked to Gray. He had to hurry up and handle his business so he could get to her and they could figure this shit out. Fully clothed, he made his way out of the bathroom and looked at Duckie. It was 4:00 a.m. and she was wide awake. On her side, she lay naked with desire in her eyes. He still hadn't gotten over the fact that she was one of the many girls Gunz had cheated on Gray with. St. Louis was small as fuck. If he would've known that bit of information before hitting her up, he would've never taken it there with her. He wasn't that spiteful of a nigga, but the deed had already been. He couldn't take it back. He'd been bustin' Duckie down for weeks.

"Where you going dressed in all black like an omen?"

"I gotta go take care of some business." He grabbed his phone and keys.

"You want me to wait on you to come back?" She purred, rubbing the space where he once laid.

"You can do that." Cam licked his bottom lip.

His dick was starting to brick up, but he didn't have time to dick her down again. He had to go. Gray's face kept dancing in his head. Fuckin' Duckie could wait. And yes, he was going to continue to mess with her. Whether Gray was pregnant with his baby or not, divorce was still on the table. He and Gray were toxic or maybe it was just him that was the bad seed. Regardless, they needed to leave each other alone. Neither of their sins could ever be forgiven so it was over.

"It's food in the fridge. I'll be back." Cam left out without giving her the kiss she so badly wanted.

He and Duckie weren't like that. Right now, she was just something warm for him to lay next to at night. Cam jogged leisurely down the steps. He was only inches away from the door when it was forcefully kicked in. Without warning, several federal agents came barreling through the door with weapons drawn on him.

"Get on the ground!" One of the agents yelled.

Knowing it was best that he comply, Cam slowly made his way to the floor. He quickly learned that an indictment had been issued with allegations of an international cocaine ring that he and other members of the Gonzalez Cartel allegedly distributed throughout Missouri, Illinois, Michigan and Ohio. According to the indictment, they'd confiscated 30 kilos of cocaine found at a convenient store through a confidential informant.

Cam knew for a fact none of his boys had snitched. Hell, they were probably being ran down on too. Only one person had the motive to drop a dime on him . . . Gray. It took everything in him not to start spazzing out. Yeah, they were in a bad place. He'd violated her, and in front of Duckie of all people, but was taking away his freedom the only way to get back at him? No way had Gray done this to him. There had to be someone else who hated him just as much but who? Cam had so many enemies he could hardly keep count. None of his enemies knew the exact date or location of his final shipment. It wasn't by accident that he'd cussed Gray out and then the next day his house was being raided by the Feds. Cam needed answers and fast.

After being handcuffed and read his rights, he and a now clothed Duckie sat against the wall as federal and local law enforcement agents spent hours raiding his home in search of narcotics they wouldn't find. Cam wasn't dumb. He would never have drugs in his home. Linking him to the cocaine they'd found would be damn near impossible. Cam had made sure that if anything went down the drugs couldn't be traced back to him or his crew. The cops did, however, find two pounds of marijuana and three unregistered handguns. Because he was a convicted felon, Cam was prohibited from legally purchasing a gun. Now that they'd found something they could pin on him, he was escorted in a squad car to the DEA building. Since she was innocent, Duckie was released.

Inside the interrogation room, Cam was handcuffed to the table. The cold, steel dug into his wrist. At this point, most criminals folded but not Cam. He'd been here before. No matter what they threw at him, he wasn't saying a word. The agents tried to scare him into confessing the drugs were his, but Cam was no fool. No response was the best response. The Federal agent eventually grew tired of his nonchalant attitude and arrogance and gave up. After that, everything happened so fast. Cam's lawyer arrived and he was arraigned. Locked in handcuffs, he stood before the judge as he ran down his charges. Cam thought he was going to be hit with a barrage of criminal acts. The way the FEDS had been talking, he was going to be put underneath the jail. To his surprise, he was only charged with felony possession of a firearm. The prosecutor tried to stick him with a 924 C which was misconduct involving a federal drug trafficking offense, but his lawyer immediately had that thrown out.

"In the case of Cameron Parthens Jr., you are being charged with felony possession of a firearm. How do you plead?" The judge asked.

"Not guilty."

Cam took the charge with a grin on his face. A possession of a firearm charge was far better than a drug charge. Whoever had snitched on him had fucked up. He'd be out of jail in no time, and as soon as he was released, Cam was coming for blood.

"Your honor." The prosecutor interjected. "The defendant is a powerful man. He's a flight risk and is still a part of an ongoing investigation of being associated with the Gonzalez Cartel. He's also a known gang member. I ask that his bond be denied."

"I agree. Bond denied." The judge threw down his gavel.

"The fuck!" Cam growled as he was escorted out of the courtroom.

"I'ma gonna get you out of this." His lawyer assured.

Cam was livid. He just knew he'd bail. His lawyer was good, but he wasn't that good. The fact still remained he was on probation. By law, he would have to serve time. He, along with several other prisoners, were transported to St. Louis County Jail. After changing his clothes and being placed in a brown jumpsuit, Cam finally got to make a phone call. Questions needed to be answered and only Gray could answer them. Standing at the payphone, he dialed her number. Cam held the phone up to his ear, waiting to hear her voice. He had to hear her voice. It was the only way he'd be able to calm his suspicions, but Gray didn't answer. The sound of the operator clicked in.

I'm sorry, you have reached a number that has been disconnected or no longer in service. Please hang up and try your call again.

Dread sat in the pit of his stomach, tying it up into a knot. Dismay set into his face like rigor mortis, causing his jaw to clench tight. Fear creeped up his spine like a poisonous spider leaving a path of silk in its wake. Frozen in space, his feet were stuck to the ground as if they had been submerged in concrete. All Cam could do is pray things began to make sense because he was about to blow. Quickly, he called Quan.

"What's the word?" He answered on the first ring.

"Gun charge."

"Fuck. They got Priest too."

Cam dropped his head. That was the last thing he wanted to hear.

"You talk to Gray?" Quan questioned.

"Nah, I called her, and the line was disconnected. I was about to ask you if Kema spoke to her."

"She called her too and got the same thing, so we went by the crib to make sure she was straight but she ain't answer the door. Her car was in the driveway though so Kema used her key to go inside. She was freaking out and shit, thinkin' something had happened to her, but when we got in . . . no one was there. All of her shit was there, but the majority of her and the girls' clothes were gone. The dogs were gone too."

All of Cam's suspicions were confirmed. Gray had betrayed him in the worst way possible. Cam morphed into one giant ball of fury. Without warning, his breathing turned from steady to a labored gasp. He sucked in air like it had abruptly become thick and too hard to lure in. Cam immediately became deaf to Quan calling out his name. His rage was irreparable. Using the receiver as a weapon, he smashed it into the payphone repeatedly, prompting the guards to tackle him into the ground. By the time they got him on the floor, the payphone was dangling from the wall. Cam roared like a lion as a heavy knee was placed into his back. Because of Gray this was how his life would be. He'd be shackled and imprisoned away with no doors or windows. Every day would be hell. There was no place to run or hide. He'd be surrounded by guards and four white walls. Cam could already feel his lungs start to cave in.

He would hate Gray forever for this. Revenge ate away at his soul. It festered like a poisoned wound. Gray would pay for this. Her day was coming. An untimely death was in her future. Until he could get his hands on her, Cam would bear a grudge until the day of his release. As soon as those prison doors opened, there would be no mercy. He was going straight sicko mode.

To be continued in Sicko Mode.

Afterword

Please don't hate me! I simply am giving you all the story that Cam and Gray wanted me to tell. I have fallen madly in love with these two crazy kids. When I wrote First Wives Club, I had no idea that we would get here but Gray and Cam's story just kept growing and growing. These two have drove me crazy. It has been a labor of love writing their story. There is so much angst and confusion mixed up in their undeniable love. In Sick Mode we will see where life takes these two. Hopefully, everyone lives to see another day.

I wanna give a huge shout out and thank you to the people that helped me with this book. My buddy Ryan, thank you for giving me all the information I needed on Cam's stint in the army. Thank you for doing all that you do protecting our country. Keep working hard and looking fine while doing it. Also thank you to Alexzandria, Sheridan and Tasia. These three ladies are long time readers, now turned Ginny pigs and friends. Anytime I needed you girls you were there, and I greatly appreciated it. Brenda, my long-time agent, second mother, editor and mentor I love you.

Last but certainly not least, thank you Cherita aka Cam and Selicia. You have been a tremendous help and blessing to me throughout this journey of telling Gray and Cam's story. If it wasn't for you, I don't think I would've fallen in love with them so much. Your enthusiasm and genuine care for their characters and this story is unperilled. Love you li'l sis!!!! Now we gotta create magic all over again with Sicko Mode. You ready C? Let's go get 'em!!!!!

XOXO Keisha

About The Author

Keisha Ervin is the critically-acclaimed, best-selling author of numerous novels, including: **The Untold Stories by Chyna Black, Cashmere Mafia, Material Girl 3: Secrets & Betrayals, Paper Heart, Pure Heroine, Emotionally Unavailable, Heartless, Radio Silence, Smells Like Teen Spirit Vol 1: Heiress, Mina's Joint 2: The Perfect Illusion, Cranes in the Sky, Postcards from the Edge, Such A Fuckin' Lady** and **First Wives Club Vol.1 Melanin Magic**.

For news on Keisha's upcoming work, keep in touch by following her on any of the social media accounts listed:

INSTAGRAM >> @keishaervin

SNAPCHAT >> kyrese99

TWITTER >> www.twitter.com/keishaervin

FACEBOOK >> www.facebook.com/keisha.ervin

Please, subscribe to my YouTube channel, to watch all my hilarious reviews on your favorite reality shows and drama series!!! YOUTUBE >> www.youtube.com/ColorMePynk

Printed in the USA
CPSIA information can be obtained
at www.ICGtesting.com
BVHW031743020823
668138BV00013B/109